C155358422

The Harbour

FRANCESCA BRILL started her professional life as an actress, training at RADA and working in theatre, film and television before becoming a screenwriter and film maker. She has lived and worked in France, Italy, India and America and currently lives in London. *The Harbour* is her first book.

www.francescabrill.com

FRANCESCA BRILL

BLOOMSBURY
LONDON • NEW DELHI • NEW YORK • SYDNEY

First published in Great Britain 2012
This paperback edition published 2013

Bloomsbury Publishing, London, New Delhi, New York and Sydney

50 Bedford Square, London WC1B 3DP

A CIP catalogue record for this book is available from the British Library

ISBN 978 1 4088 3151 9
10 9 8 7 6 5 4 3 2 1

Typeset by Hewer Text UK Ltd, Edinburgh
Printed and bound in Great Britain by CPI Group (UK) Ltd, Croydon CR0 4YY

www.bloomsbury.com/francescabrill

For Bobby, Rebecca and Romy

‘I saw his heart in his face.’

William Shakespeare, *The Winter’s Tale*, Act 1, Scene 2

Part One

Chapter One

Hong Kong – June 1940

There was a distant rumble and the close-cut grass trembled under her feet. Then the horses were in front of her. The shock of the noise and speed was astonishing every time. There was a thrill to it – what if one of those sweating, immoderately muscled creatures strayed by just a few feet? It would be upon her right there, where she stood next to the flimsy wooden railings. Stevie caught sight of her own wrist. So fragile, those little bones. So easy to break.

And then the last hooves threw up the final pieces of mud and were gone. A few blades of trampled grass fell through the air. She had lost and she didn't like it. The ironically named Happy Valley racetrack was a despicable place, really. There was no excuse. It wasn't as if she didn't have enough vices already, though on the scale of her current degeneracy a spot of small-time gambling hardly counted.

She ripped her ticket into pieces and threw it on the ground to join the other torn dreams. The confetti of disappointment.

'I thought you were giving it up.' Declan McKenna, the unruly Irish journalist whom Stevie had first met at some cocktail thing at the Astor House Hotel in Shanghai, pushed through the crowd, smiling in delight at finding her. He was built for survival in the turf-gathering swamps of Western Ireland, his stocky torso and huge hands not well suited to sitting behind a desk and typing. She hadn't known he was in Hong Kong, but Declan's travels never surprised her.

'Oh I have. I'm here for strictly professional reasons.'

'You're buying a horse?'

'I'm fearlessly reporting back to my loyal readers at home from the most dangerous place in Hong Kong.'

He laughed, his generous mouth widening even further. The swagger of a slickly made-up Chinese girl caught his eye as she wove through the press of mostly Chinese men, and Stevie smiled to herself at the ease with which he had been distracted. She knew that as the only non-Oriental woman down here away from the stands she was conspicuous. Her short dark hair did not particularly distinguish her but the breeziness of her cotton dress, and her lack of lipstick, gloves and a hat did. The Europeans and Americans as a rule stuck to the safety of the stands, where their wallets were less vulnerable to the pickpockets, if not to the bookies. There was little love lost between the disparate communities here on this strange anomaly of an island, but winning and losing was, as ever, a truly efficient leveller. Declan returned his attention to her, the laugh still in his eyes, which seemed permanently on the verge of an insolent wink. Stevie was reminded that he had come a long way from home, too.

She leaned towards him, frowning. 'I want to understand one thing, though. What makes them run, these horses?'

Declan shrugged, amused by her, but wary also.

Her voice was light, her American accent tempered by the years abroad. 'Want to know my bet? It's for the hell of it. That's why they run.'

'You got that from the horse's mouth, did you?'

Shaking her head in acknowledgement of how feeble the joke was, she said, 'I know that's why I would. Run, I mean.' And smiling she turned away.

He stopped her. 'Need a lift back into Central? I wangled a car on expenses.'

'No. I'm all right.'

'More than all right, I'd say.'

She accepted the compliment with no comment but broadened her smile.

Emboldened he tried again. 'Can't even tempt you to a whisky soda at the Peninsula?'

'No, sir, not tonight.'

'That boyfriend of yours keeping you in lockdown?'

She laughed. 'He knows better than to try.'

There was a slight movement in the crush of people around them and Declan caught sight of a slender, high-cheekboned Chinese man in a very fine linen suit heading towards them. He sighed and gestured in his direction. 'Talk of the devil.'

Stevie turned and to her great surprise she saw Declan was right. Jishang never normally came to the racetrack. He hated the ubiquitous hawkers and the spitting, shouting, pungent hordes. His gambling habit was confined to private rooms in discreet casinos.

She smiled as he drew near. 'Have you decided to see how the other ninety-nine per cent live?'

'I've brought a jacket and a hat. They're in the car.'

'That's very thoughtful of you but why on earth such concern for my outfit?'

'There's no time to waste. You'll just have to do as you are.'

Jishang put a long-fingered hand on her arm and began to propel her away from the track. She pulled back.

'Can you just wait a moment?' She indicated Declan, who had watched this encounter with raised eyebrows. 'You remember my colleague Declan McKenna? From the *Irish Times*.'

Jishang put out his hand and they shook in greeting. 'Yes, of course. Please excuse me, Mr McKenna, but Miss Steiber and I have urgent business.'

'Pleasure to see you again, Mr Wu.' Declan tipped his hat and winked at Stevie as she turned away.

Stevie allowed herself to be pulled across the springy grass towards the Happy Valley gates but she could not resist walking with a slightly exaggerated swing to her hips, knowing that Declan was watching her, svelte and splendid.

'What is going on, Jishang? This is crazy.'

Jishang did not break pace as he said, 'We have a meeting with Madame Kung.'

She stopped dead, her ears ringing. 'What did you say?' Her arm nearly came out of its socket as Jishang kept on walking.

'You heard me.'

'My God, you are so annoying.' She was being dragged along again and had to skip to try and keep up. 'A meeting? When? Are you sure? Who told you?'

'Yes, a meeting. Now. I'm quite sure and what was the last question?'

'Now?'

'Ah yes, I remember. Mr Leung telephoned me an hour ago, which is how long it's taken me to find you.'

'Mr Leung?'

'You sound like a child, all these questions. Yes, Mr Leung,

Madame Kung's private secretary, the man you have been pestering for months.'

They were at the gates and Stevie could see their rented car glinting black in the sun, the driver leaning casually against it engrossed in a newspaper.

'Oh my. Right now, huh? Thanks for bringing my hat and jacket. The navy blue?'

The driver caught Jishang's eye and folded his paper hurriedly, throwing it through the open window on to the front passenger seat with one hand and opening the back door for them with the other.

'Yes, the navy blue. Of course.'

Stevie held back. 'I'm not ready. I can't go.'

'You can and you must. This is your chance. There will not be another opportunity.' Knowing he was right, she accepted his outstretched hand and stepped into the car. This was it after all. The encounter she had been waiting for.

The day could not have been more beautiful. It was hot of course, but not yet in that fierce summer state where it sticks, heavy and bitter, in the back of your throat. As the car climbed further up the steep Peak road the air was becoming noticeably lighter.

Stevie leaned her head out of the open window. The breath was taken out of her by the speed and she laughed at the pleasure of it. Way below the expensively maintained terraces a sapphire sea pounded – nature controlled by money, but only to a degree.

The car slowed as it approached a pair of fabulously ornate iron gates, curlicues casting a harsh shadow on the pale gravel beyond. Stevie sat back into the leather and leaned momentarily into Jishang, dissolute but graceful, next to her. He glanced at her.

'Your hair,' he said.

Stevie brushed her hand over her wind-tangled bob.

'Really? Who cares?'

'I do. And so will she.'

Stevie reluctantly made a serious attempt to smooth her curls. She felt nervous, disturbed by the rushed nature of the meeting; it did not seem propitious. Nothing about it felt right. She turned a defiant stare to the magnificent gardens passing slowly outside the window.

She could almost have reached out and touched the lush purple hydrangeas, over-heavy and compliant, that bordered the drive. Even she – determinedly world-weary – could not suppress a low whistle at the sight of the white-pillared palace that emerged at the end of the cool green corridor of shrubbery.

Jishang allowed himself a half-smile. 'What did you expect?'

'A hovel, obviously,' she said, nudging him in the ribs with a sharp elbow.

As the car came to a halt, the door was opened by a man in unlikely white and gold livery. The dusty scent of the flowers mixed with the faint dark human smell of the manservant invaded the sticky leather interior of the car. Jishang's thin fingers caught her wrist as she began to step out.

'Be good.'

The pressure on her skin was fierce. Even after she was out of the car and the gravel was crunching under her unglamorous round-toed pumps, she could feel the shadow of his grip. He let her take a few steps towards the house before getting out himself, unfolding his limbs like a sea anemone.

As she sank deep into the rose chintz sofa, Stevie wondered at the dryness clutching at her throat. She glanced towards Jishang, hoping for reassurance, but he had picked up a rare and shiny new copy of *Time* magazine from the glass coffee table. His fingers rested lightly on the slippery paper. On the cover, a black and white Franklin Delano Roosevelt stood behind CBS microphones. He was glancing to one side; away from or towards a challenge? Jishang flicked through the pristine pages. Stevie glimpsed the headline that he lingered over – 'War In China, Chungking Bombings'. She looked away, not wanting to think about the dying and the dead and tried to find saliva in her mouth. Doubt and fear were her unwelcome but ever-present chaperones. Her battles with them had inspired all the defining gestures of her youth. They had led her far from places of safety. Doubt that she could do anything at all, chased by the fear that she would certainly fail, had dogged her steps as she danced through the hotel lobbies of Shanghai along with the other flotsam of the world. They would be exactly what her father had cursed her with as she left for the last time. They would be 'the death of her'.

Struggling against the gravitational pull of the over-stuffed cushions, Stevie attempted to sit up straight, as a sleek, apparently ageless woman approached in a bird-like skip across the marble hallway.

'Who is this Stephanie Steiber?'

Madame Kung, her hair piled high and stiff, was fifty and formidable. She made no attempt to lower her voice despite the fact that Stevie and Jishang were clearly within earshot. Her tone was slightly contemptuous and certainly dismissive. Her private secretary, Mr Leung, buttoned to his neck and almost grovelling, answered as he scurried to keep up with but not overtake her.

'A journalist, Madame. Your cousin Wu Jishang has brought her. She's already spoken to your sisters – about the book?' He dropped his voice. 'She has telephoned about a hundred times and this morning you agreed to a meeting.'

Stevie's grasp of Mandarin was rudimentary but she got the gist. It was true, she had approached Madame Kung many times since she had arrived in Hong Kong only to be rebuffed.

Madame Kung was the eldest of the three famous Soong sisters and oddly the one who had been hardest to pin down. Madame Chiang Kai-shek had brokered the deal a year earlier. Stevie had interviewed her for a little piece about political wives she was hoping to sell as part of a series. Light-hearted of course, a woman's piece. How do you cope with your husband's absences and what does he like to eat when he gets home from saving the world? That sort of thing. Through Jishang Stevie had been introduced to her at a function in Shanghai and had managed to persuade her that such a piece would be harmless and maybe even helpful. After all, the great American public had a deeply prejudiced attitude to China, which sprang from ignorance. If they could find something to relate to in the article, their understanding would be enhanced, and maybe even their sympathy engaged.

As the wife of the leader of the Chinese Nationalist government, Madame Chiang, or May-Ling as she allowed Stevie to address her, was one of the world's most consummate diplomats. Her charm, beauty and perfect American accent had enchanted everybody on the world stage and she had formed a particular friendship with the Roosevelts. Stevie had immensely enjoyed their meeting and had been thrilled when Madame Chiang reacted encouragingly to her bold proposal to write a book about all three sisters. Who could not be fascinated by the amazing story of the three little girls who had gone on to marry three of the most important figures in China? Stevie had chosen not to underline the fact that they had not exactly been born in a barn. Theirs was still an amazing story. And she had scooped it. She, Stevie Steiber, the peripatetic reporter of humorous social observation, had been allowed the opportunity to write a serious and important document tracing the power struggles of modern China from the inside.

So she had spent time with the Chiang Kai-sheks as the government struggled to find an adequate response to the overwhelming aggression of the expansionist Japanese and their merciless assault on China. And then she had been granted a series of interviews with Ching-Ling, the middle sister, who as the widow of Sun Yat-sen, the founder of the first Chinese republic, had become an adamant supporter of the Communist cause. As such she was the sworn enemy of Chiang Kai-shek, her brother-in-law, and had in fact only recently come back to China from her years of self-imposed exile in Soviet Moscow in order to help broker an awkward alliance between the two factions so that a unified China could concentrate finally on defending itself from Japan. The fractures in most families, including her own, were considerably less extreme. Stevie had only to think about her tear-stained and fraught relationship with her mother to see a clear example. Consequently she had been extremely moved by the depth of the affection that still existed between the sisters.

Now here she was, newly arrived in Hong Kong, with the express purpose of meeting the third Soong sister.

Madame Kung, or Ai-Ling as she was known to her family, had not married directly into politics but into commerce. Her husband was generally considerd to be the richest man in China and known to be the shadowy banker to the besieged Nationalists. The fact that both her sisters had vouched for

Stevie seemed not to be enough for Madame Kung. Neither was the fact that Jishang, a distant cousin much removed but still acknowledged in the Chinese fashion, had brought Stevie to Hong Kong to see her in person. She was far from persuaded that the book was a good idea. She of all the sisters had no public agenda and certainly there was no obvious advantage to be gained in being more exposed to the outside world. In fact, quite the contrary.

Madame Kung glanced around the room. If she had been really looking she would have taken in the great luxury of the decor, the houseboy hovering in the opposite doorway, and through the windows two husky men who could only be bodyguards lounging in the shade of a tree. But she was not looking. She was surveying. She found all to her satisfaction and now she acknowledged Stevie and Jishang with a tiny inclination of her perfectly poised head.

Nothing about her fragile, doll-like appearance translated into her personality or her presence. For all the trepidation she inspired in Stevie, Madame Kung may as well have been King Kong himself.

Jishang had unravelled his long legs gracefully and was standing to attention. Stevie was on her feet just in time. Madame Kung extended her immaculate little hand. Jishang pressed it to his lips.

'Madame, thank you so much for giving us your time.'

Hearing him speak Mandarin always thrilled Stevie. She had a flash of the first time she had heard his low voice and how she had turned towards him. It seemed a lifetime ago but it was only a year. One hell of a year.

Madame Kung's voice was girlish and affectionate and her American accent, slightly Southern in lilt, was absolutely perfect.

'You're a bad man, Wu Jishang, don't think I haven't heard.'

And then her attention was on Stevie, the flirtation over. Under her scrutiny, Stevie fervently wished she had been able to change her dress. It was inappropriately simple and one of the pockets was slightly torn. She was glad of the jacket Jishang had brought because a button was missing where the puffed short sleeve of the dress closed on her upper arm. Also the fabric was sticking in all the wrong places and she was visibly damp right down her back. Madame Kung's appraisal said, 'That skirt length was all the rage last year but, really, who is your dressmaker, she should be shot.' What she actually said was quite a lot worse.

'You seem impatient.'

Stevie, wrong-footed, glanced at Jishang for encouragement but he was no help. His crisp shirt cuffs were apparently in great need of his attention. Madame Kung continued, a steamroller in high heels.

'You need to be patient if you're going to write the truth.'

Stevie's voice was thin and tentative. 'I've been living with Chinese people long enough to –'

Madame Kung interrupted, eyebrows raised. 'So I hear.'

Her eyes flicked to Jishang and her meaning was brazen and clear. Jishang continued to be absorbed in his shirt cuffs. Stevie could not help herself. A perverse laugh forced itself past her parched lips. Immediately she knew it was all over. She had blown it. She had been waiting months for this meeting, pacing the floor of her tiny apartment in Shanghai until finally losing her cool and flying into this crummy colony on the small chance that she and Jishang could make it happen. And now she'd gone and blown it with a stupid, sardonic laugh.

But to her surprise Madame Kung did not turn on her heel and disappear in a puff of displeasure. Instead, she seemed to be appraising her all over again. Her voice was as tender as a lullaby as she turned back to Jishang.

'Wu Jishang, be a good boy and run along,' she said. 'Find something else to do.'

Ten minutes later, Stevie was perched on the edge of the sofa, leaning forward, the fabric irritating the back of her knees. Opposite her, Madame Kung was listening with the kind of attentiveness that must have seduced Mr Kung himself. While she talked, Stevie had to fight against the distraction of the older woman's soft hand, which elegantly waved a feather fan.

'I came to China for a fortnight. That was three years ago.'

There was no glimmer of a smile from her audience. Stevie understood that her usual breezy tone just might not be the right one. She braced herself and plunged into the frightening territory of sincerity.

'Stop me if I'm telling you things you already know. I'm a freelance reporter based in Shanghai. I write pieces for the American press, newspapers and weeklies and then there's *Direct Debate*, the magazine Wu Jishang and I run . . .'

'I hear it's subversive.'

'No, absolutely not.' Those exquisitely raised eyebrows again. 'I mean, I admire political action, the passion of it, but personally I'm more interested in people than ideas.'

'Why should I co-operate with you if indeed you have no political agenda? How can it be to my benefit to be gossiped about?'

'I don't write gossip, Madame. I'm a journalist. I'll write a testament to you and your sisters. An unprejudiced testament that will give a fair portrait of your remarkable family for history to read and understand.'

'My sisters are not strangers to the public stage. It seems my youngest sister spends most of her life in front of a microphone on a lawn or waving on steps or perched on armchairs at a convenient angle for the photographers. I see the pictures and her head is always inclined in an attentive listening posture.' Madame Kung narrowed her eyes. 'It must be most uncomfortable.'

'Perhaps talking to me was a welcome break.'

'Or perhaps like the rest of the world, you have been seduced by her intensity and passion.'

'Actually, what really impressed me was her constant search for exactly the right word.' Stevie paused. 'That and her amazing wardrobe.'

Madame Kung laughed. Her tiny, even teeth glowed white.

'You couldn't possibly say the same for Ching-Ling.'

'You're right. Madame Sun Yat-sen impressed me in quite a different way.'

'And what way would that be?'

'There's something about her shyness and her low voice. You know, you have to lean quite close to hear what she is saying.'

'All those simple dresses and that under-furnished house – I suppose you would say it reflects her serious-mindedness and dignity, would you?'

'I would. She manages to be both fragile and sturdy at the same time.'

'You think so?' Stevie felt a trap. She held Madame Kung's gaze and said nothing. The fan speeded up as Madame Kung sighed. 'Oh, I couldn't stand it, myself. All those fervent scholars and radical young men hanging around, waiting to hear her quiet pronouncements.'

'We got along pretty well.'

Stevie saw that Madame Kung was looking at her, stern and forbidding. She knew that she was being tested – but would she pass? Without Madame Kung agreeing to talk to her further, the book idea was useless. The project pointless. She was overcome with a feeling of hopelessness. It was only because of Jishang's stupid faith in her that they were stagnating in Hong Kong. It didn't matter that the other two sisters had already, miraculously, agreed to the book, Stevie was suddenly sure that Madame Kung, the eldest and most stubborn of the fabulous Soong sisters, would not. How much longer were they going to have to play out this charade? Her mother's voice echoed in her mind. 'You're no great shakes, Stephanie, not when all's said and done.'

Madame Kung's expression wavered; her gaze glided away from Stevie and out of the window towards the extravagantly irrigated green of the lawn. Stevie could feel all she had worked for slipping away from her.

She leaned further towards Madame Kung, her voice suddenly thick with passion and urgency.

'Madame, I really want to write this book.'

Madame Kung's eyes drifted back to her.

'Look, actually, I need to write it. I need to show I can. I want to be taken seriously, I want to be more than just –' the weight of sincerity felt heavy on her tongue.

'More than just?'

'More than just a columnist. I'm a good writer, I'll do your story justice.'

The fragrant stateswoman scrutinised Stevie's uncharacteristically vulnerable expression. The fronds of her feather fan stirred in the breeze.

'And don't be too concerned about the magazine.' Stevie smiled apologetically. 'Honestly. Nobody reads it anyway.'

Chapter Two

The thin paper, slightly damp like everything else, stuck to his fingertips. The rangy Englishman, languid in shirtsleeves, laughed out loud as he read. He rocked back even further in his chair, counterbalanced by his legs resting on the neat desk top in front of him.

A flustered, red-faced young man pushed the door open. 'Bollocks to this heat.'

Harry spoke without looking up from the magazine. 'You're in the presence of a senior officer.'

The younger man, Sergeant Ken Ramsay, saluted sarcastically. Harry still didn't look up. 'We're late, sir.' No response. Ken tried again. 'Lunch, sir. With Mr Takeda, Japanese Board of Trade.'

Harry, still deep in the magazine, laughed his generous laugh. He glanced in Ken's direction, tapping the article he was reading. 'You should read this. It'll lighten the burden of your ignorance.' And he chucked the magazine at him.

Ken, too late, fumbled for it. The unbound sheets of *Direct Debate*, covered in tightly printed text in English and on alternate pages in Chinese, fluttered to the floor.

Harry snorted, not too unkindly. 'Not in the First Eleven, I take it?'

Ken, cursed with an easy blush, bent down to gather the papers.

Harry continued. 'That Steiber's always worth reading. Funny too.'

'It's not a he, you know, sir, it's a she, a Yank journalist.' Ken reached for the stragglers. 'The S stands for Sally or Sophie or something.'

'You don't say?'

'I do, actually.' Ken was clearly very pleased to be able to offer this information. It wasn't often he had the opportunity to tell Harry something he didn't already know. On his secondment to Intelligence the year before he'd been sanguine about the many jokes from his fellow soldiers referencing his lack of qualifications for the job, but once he had got to know Harry he thought his mates might just have been right. Major Field had a way of being one step ahead without apparently making any effort to be so. The day-to-day work was far from glamorous, consisting mainly of reading transcripts of as many of the hundreds of printed pamphlets that came in and out of the Colony as humanly possible. They had to respond to the day's news from the mainland and brief the top brass on anything considered significant. They had recently been involved in the discussion about whether the censor should allow the children of Hong Kong to see the animated film of *Snow White and The Seven Dwarfs* in case it was some kind of dangerous political metaphor.

Ken's finest hour had been in his first month. Major Field and he had been involved in a case that was both civil and military. A chap had arrived from England to be Director of Air-Raid Precautions; a sop to those who were already sabotaging economic morale by predicting a Japanese invasion. He was an airman sent as an expert on civil defence. Unfortunately, he became rather too friendly with a certain Mimi who was secretary to the civilian supplier of concrete blocks for the construction of the air-raid shelters. It turned out that not only had he been persuaded to spend government money on buying concrete at a hugely inflated price but the blocks were also severely sub-standard and would not have endured a hammer blow let alone a bomb. Consequently, the shelters were useless. Ken had assisted Harry in pursuit of missing documents which incriminated the airman and he had tracked down Mimi, who had conveniently vanished as soon as the game was up.

They were generally charged with checking up on the finances of fellow officers in case one of them suddenly became inexplicably flush, but overall the cloak and dagger stuff was disappointingly mundane and not nearly as exciting nor clandestine as Ken had hoped. They arranged for various suspect characters to be followed, they read transcripts of telephone calls, they monitored the arrival and departure lists to keep an eye on the comings and goings, but Major Field somehow always seemed to know more than anyone else, and certainly more than his sergeant.

Ken attempted to add a suave note to his tone, but it was marred somewhat by the bending over and the fading blush. 'She's a leftie, got a Chinese boyfriend and everything. Came in from Shanghai, the pair of them, no doubt looking for trouble. Might even be a real threat. Worth keeping an eye on, I'd say.'

Ken caught the laugh in Harry's eyes and sighed. 'Ah, one of yours already. Of course.' He was deeply disappointed and the shadow of the blush threatened again.

'Unfortunately, yes. God save me from dangerously misguided American women, especially ones who are good at their jobs.'

Harry dropped his feet to the floor and pulled his lean frame up to sitting. Glancing again at Ken's disappointed face, he couldn't resist another dig. 'Which is more than can be said for some around here.'

The ribbing landed, shame flashing across poor Ken's plump cheeks, and Harry, a little sorry now, consoled himself with the fact that Ken made it too easy.

'It just so happens that the Chinese boyfriend is a rather interesting chap too. I did mention him in the last briefing but no doubt you had more thrilling things on your mind at the time.' He did up the top buttons on his shirt, slid his jacket off the back of the chair and slung it over his shoulder. 'He's a puzzle. Seems to be connected to just about every faction in the country but I can't quite work out where his loyalties lie. He's a writer too. Brilliant in my humble opinion. I'm looking forward to meeting him.'

He headed for the door.

'Come on then, Sergeant. Tokyo's finest awaits.'

'So?' Jishang asked as soon as they were in the car again.

Stevie shrugged. 'Your guess is as good as mine.'

'That's great.'

'It is?'

'Yes. At least she didn't say no.'

Stevie sighed. Damn the Chinese and their damn Chinese contrariness, she thought. But he was right, Madame Kung had not said no. Stevie glanced over at Jishang's fine profile. His high cheekbones like ski slopes under his pale, glowing skin and the deep black of his hair were so extremely contrasted he looked like an ink engraving.

Halfway down the perilously steep road she asked if they could stop the car. She needed to walk. Nothing in this world would have persuaded Jishang to take unnecessary exercise so she stepped down on to the melting tarmac alone. As soon as she was out in the damp hot air she felt a little better. She waited a moment as the car disappeared around the bend, its brakes protesting the gradient. The view from up there was spectacular. Stevie felt she had joined the swooping birds looping the loop in the heavy air over the buzz of earth-bound humanity. The huge, hilariously self-important mansions of the Peak, built in every style known to man, and some that were not, stood their ground among the fragrant shrubbery of the pine-scented mountainside. The sheer cliffs and the pockets of exotic overhanging flowers and stunted trees were still as curious to her as they must have been to the land-starved and exhausted drug-smuggling British sailors who first occupied the harbour in their floating worlds. So very far from home. The scenery around her was a sweet-smelling clarification of exactly why they had smothered this exotic island with comfortingly poignant names: Victoria Park, Port Stanley, Gloucester Road, Queen's Road and, most inappropriately, Aberdeen.

Directly below the mansions were the sturdy apartment buildings where the civil servants and the secretaries and the optimistically middle-class Chinese families lived. She could just about make out the building in which she and Jishang were renting a few rooms, just beyond the curve of the bay, half-hidden by a sharp cliff. Below it climbed the dank alleys of Central, where the real business of the colony was conducted at high speed and in several languages. This intense activity contrasted with the empty expanse of Victoria Square with its stolid unconvincing statues and its grand overweening Palladian buildings, thrown up to impress any passing visitor with the permanency of the British Empire and the gravity of its intent. Despite the best intentions of the empire-builders, however, it still seemed to Stevie that Hong Kong amounted to nothing more than a parasite irritating the furthest reaches of the underbelly of the giant China.

The beauty of the harbour, though, was astonishing. The turquoise water, criss-crossed by numerous sampans and ships and dotted with emerald-green islands, was one of the most remarkable things she had ever seen. The overbearing humidity was the only element that she imagined would not be present in paradise. The small paths that wound through the orchid-strewn bushes were a deep pleasure. Stevie stopped to undo the buttons on the front of her dress. The air was so hot it hardly registered on her bare skin and, with a glance around to make sure she was really alone, Stevie undid the whole of the bodice. The silk of her slip stuck damply to her chest. She looked down and noticed to her surprise that there was a distinct line where the sun-darkened skin of her upper chest met the pale rest of her. A butterfly whispered past her hand like a moving flower, a short-lived brushstroke. For a moment she abandoned her cynicism towards this colonial backwater and let go of her singular passion for bawdy and gaudy Shanghai. This, right here, was the best of Hong Kong. It was about as far as she could have travelled from the small town of her birth in upstate New York.

Her early life in the big old house in Utica seemed to belong to someone else. It hadn't exactly been an unhappy childhood – just a dull one. Stevie had wanted to be different from the very beginning. It was she who had insisted on shortening her name. Her mother had been bemused and then gratifyingly annoyed. 'It's a boy's name. Why would you do that?' and she had steadfastly gone on addressing her as Stephanie. Stevie didn't actually want to be a boy but it seemed so clear that the boys had all the fun. The boys didn't have to tread carefully and endlessly brush their hair and play with paper dolls. They were allowed to run and shout and swim. They were free in the world in a different way. It was the freedom she had really longed for, rather than the boyishness. Her sisters seemed to accept their lot with the barest of shrugs. Her father, distant in his domain in the bank building on Genesee Street under the arching elms, found her amusing and encouraged her tomboy ambitions partly, it was now clear to her, to agitate the calm waters of his marriage. Soon enough, Mrs Steiber accepted defeat, stepped back and shared her passion for amateur theatricals and art galleries with the other two girls, leaving Stevie at relative liberty to roam. And Mr Steiber, when not managing the small Utica branch of the bank, took Stevie to the races and taught her how to paddle a canoe. By the age of fourteen Stevie had so thoroughly embraced her inner boy that the onset of her period had traumatised her for weeks.

She continued the descent, deep in thought, but her restlessness returned as soon as she remembered her intense disappointment at Madame Kung's apparent indifference to her approach. The anticipation of a possible meeting with her had built up to such a pitch that Stevie had thought she might go mad with it. And when the moment had finally come she had messed it up. She was sure the whole project was over. She felt ridiculous as well as a failure. The most infuriating thing was that she knew she had only herself to blame for the whole misconceived exercise. She came to a standstill. Here she was, fired up and feeling like a fool, half-naked on a mountainside at the very edge of the known world. She pulled the bodice of her dress round her again and did up the slippery little buttons. Oh, it was all too upsetting.

Then she had a thought and suddenly she was very clear about where she was going next. This fresh clarity of purpose mingled thrillingly with a familiar cocktail of anticipation and shame as she set off again down the mountain.

They sat on the veranda of the Hong Kong Club as the late afternoon sun began its descent. Harry stretched out his legs, the very picture of a relaxed Englishman downing his first serious drink of the day. But his posture belied the alertness of his gaze. The remains of a light lunch disturbed the white linen-clad table: cold chicken, slices of ham and a potato salad. Below them, heavy-bodied Wolseleys and Austins vied with rickshaws, bicycles and bony, bare-chested men, sweating as they pushed carts laden with everything from pomegranates to coal, and wheelbarrows with apples and baskets of squawking chickens suffocating in the damp heat. Up here in the club all was quiet and orderly.

He raised his glass. 'Cheers.' A satisfying clink of ice.

His companion, Yoshi Takeda, raised his glass in response. Behind them, Ken Ramsay sat at a small distance and checked his watch with ill-concealed impatience. He let his gaze wander over to the pretty little companion of a corpulent man at another table. Her long dress was revealing plenty with its split to well above her knee and that's where his eyes rested.

Harry leaned back in his chair. 'There was a great Chinese scholar who was known for his weakness for alcohol. He was visited by a friend who was surprised to find him sober. He asked him why. And the scholar said, I've decided to give up drinking until my son comes home. Oh, the friend asked, where's he gone? To the shop, came the answer, to buy more wine.'

Takeda's laugh was loud and warm. A few heads turned. There was nothing surreptitious about this meeting. Nearby, Ken yawned.

Takeda leaned towards Harry. 'Are you sure he wasn't Japanese?'

Harry picked at a slice of ham. 'I notice there was an extra shipment of steel cable this month.'

Takeda frowned. 'I don't know anything about that.'

'No? Maybe you should take a look. Otherwise the customs chaps might get wind of it and take it into their heads to make enquiries.'

'I understand.'

'Maybe you could remind them this isn't a free port. Worth it in the long run, don't you think?' Harry made to stand up. 'Have a word with someone on your side. Let them know we're watching. Don't want them to get the idea they could sneak anything past us.'

Takeda stood too, fleshy from a sedentary life and somewhat shorter than Harry. They shook hands warmly.

'Next lunch is on me.'

As Ken followed Harry back into the bar he couldn't resist saying, 'Do we really have to rub up the Japs quite so publicly, sir?'

Harry laughed and patted him on the shoulder. 'Where would you have us meet – at midnight in a brothel, I suppose, wearing disguises and speaking in code?'

'I don't know, sir, doesn't seem right to me. He's a shifty bugger, isn't he? What's he going to say right out there in the open?'

Harry's tone changed, the light-hearted banter replaced by something darker. 'Take it from me, Sergeant, Mr Takeda is the least shifty bugger you're ever likely to meet.'

And Ken felt the heat of a blush spread across his face and chest yet again.

* * *

The harbour in the fading purple light of dusk drew Stevie on. At first sight, compared to Shanghai's sophisticated and cosmopolitan shoreline, it seemed almost quaint. Sure, there were buildings crammed along the water's edge and there was also the city of boats that reclaimed the water by at least half a mile and which must have swollen Hong Kong's landmass by some small percentage. But the huge commercial port of Shanghai with its seventeen-storey tower blocks and staggering twenty-four-hour commotion was in a state of constant swagger and self-importance. No one who tried to make their way through the broiling crowds and heard the cacophony of languages could doubt its importance on the world's stage. By comparison this small island colony felt like a backwater.

But Stevie could not deny that the harbour was picturesque as the last of the sunshine spread its fingers across the water. The scabby, small junks, tied to each other to form a floating village, were gilded in the dying light. Their wooden hulls creaked and groaned as they scraped against one another. Shrill voices skimmed the water. Among them one distinguished itself – angrier than the others. Stevie recognised it as Yang's as she made her way towards him. The anticipation almost tripped her up. She stumbled over a loosely coiled rope and had to steady herself against the harbour wall. The excitement never abated. More cautiously now, she walked over the splintering decks of the other boats and, as she stepped on to Yang's familiar junk, she was as thin-skinned and flushed as if she were racing to meet a lover. Stocky and middle-aged in loose trousers and a filthy vest, Yang hurled a last insult at his neighbour followed by a well-aimed spit, and turned back towards the cabin, barely acknowledging Stevie, although his unease at the Caucasian woman's presence was profound.

Yang brushed aside the curtain that hung limply over the low entrance. Stevie followed. Sickly sweet smoke filled the cabin. In stark contrast to the golden light outside, the interior of the boat was as gloomy and musty as a cave, a squalid, narrow place with low day beds lining the length of the boat. Heavy brocade curtains, originally dark red but now rusted into murky brown, separated the day beds at uneven intervals. In the windowless gloom, bodies lay against the boat's sides on bitter-smelling cushions.

As he walked through his little empire, Yang paid no attention to the waxen faces of men, all Chinese, slumped, deep in drugged sleep. Some were dribbling and twitching, others moaning. Before them on the low wooden tables, black opium bubbled in pipes, the legacy of British free marketeering down the centuries.

Stevie found an empty couch and, settling on its sour cushions, she leaned over the table, concentrated. Her fingers deftly rolled the black, sticky opium into a ball and dug it into the pipe. She inhaled long and deep. The rush of euphoria came fast, wonderful, thrilling, consuming. She felt herself returning to the secret sanctuary which, all those months ago, she had first approached with trepidation and curiosity and then, miraculously, found to be better than home. Better than anything. Her veins ran with pleasure and she shivered before her eyes flickered shut. She slumped back, letting go of the pipe. Letting go of it all.

Later, through the lovely haze, she heard a blurry voice. It seemed to come from far away, perhaps through an ocean. 'Look at you. A white girl with that mark. It's disgusting.'

It was Jishang. She had no idea how long he'd been lying opposite her. He reached for her hand and she felt his touch as if through velvet. He turned her hand palm up, looking at the black, oily smudge on her left forefinger. He rubbed at it harshly. It didn't go.

She marshalled all her strength and pulled her hand away. 'Leave me alone, can't you. You can hardly talk.'

'I know what I'm doing.'

'And I don't?'

'No. You absolutely don't.'

'Then why did you start me off?'

'You wanted to try.'

'That's your answer to it all, isn't it.' She was suddenly tired of him. Tired of his know-it-all voice, his impeccable control. 'Everything is somebody else's fault. It's none of it anything to do with you.'

Stevie leaned forward again and, lifting the pipe to her lips, defiantly drew the thick smoke into her lungs. But something was wrong. The burn was too intense and she tried to find fresh air to cool it. Suddenly she convulsed. Molten steel poured along her airways. Her whole body felt as though it was disappearing into a void. There was wave after violent wave of retching and ugly, awkward movements as she flung out her arms and legs, thrashing against the cushions. She was drowning and could not save herself.

Jishang roused himself to sit up. He shouted, his voice harsh. 'No doctors.'

He swayed, unable to shake the drug's torpor himself. Stevie retched again from deep inside. What she heard above the flailing of her own tortured limbs was the sound of wings. A flock of maybe twenty small birds whirred and beat around her face. She struggled to claw them off, then fell back on to the floor.

It was Yang who pulled Stevie to her feet.

'Get out of here, both of you. I don't want anybody dying here.'

Jishang carried and dragged Stevie's half-conscious body through the pools of red light cast by the paper lanterns, their unsteadiness exaggerated by the constant rocking of the boats, the stench of vomit clinging to her clothes.

As Jishang adjusted Stevie's dead weight around his shoulders, a quiet, watching man sank deeper into the shadows.

Chapter Three

Cold morning light filtered through the blinds. Their clothes scattered where they had been dropped, Stevie and Jishang lay awkwardly in a tangle of sheets. She moaned in the remains of her opium sleep and pushed him away.

A scuffling and a tapping sound came from behind the wall facing the bed. And suddenly a bird burst through the wallpaper. Its wings beat wildly as it careered through the room, searching desperately for a way out.

Stevie, her pulse racing, opened her eyes and sat bolt upright. There was no bird. She shivered and drew the sheets tight around her.

It wasn't meant to be like this. She remembered images from the night before: the putrid sweet smell, identified as the remains of the sick that stained her clothes; Yang's face, contorted with rage; Jishang's harsh grasp as he pulled her along the near-empty streets, up and up the hill.

At first the whole opium thing had been a gas. Priding herself on never saying never, Stevie felt almost obliged to try anything. The steeper the challenge, the harder she was prepared to pursue it. Who in the end was she proving herself to? She couldn't say, but as she felt the stale taste of the night in her mouth she acknowledged that it really was no fun any more. Perhaps she'd stop. Jishang seemed to have a preternatural capacity for hedonism, he was able somehow to slip through its dangers without mishap. Stronger men had fallen by the wayside but he powered on, smooth as silk, through a life of incredible excess. It amused him to apply the same survival skills to politics now. He engaged in the dark, hidden corners of subversive politics with the same dry smile and sly ease as he occupied the opium dens and the brothels of Shanghai. She turned to look at him. Still and clear as a statue, Jishang's face in repose was as beautiful as it was brazen. Maybe it was the danger itself, the profound thrill of transgression, that motivated him.

The spoilt elder son of an old-time, Chinese aristocrat, Jishang had been born to a life of grace and feudal rites. This modern world made an anomaly of him. Not that he cared. The magazine, started on a whim, had become the only uncensored voice in Shanghai, a city of many voices. Printed in two languages, it represented as clearly as possible the cacophony of opinions that rose and fell in the streets and back alleys. It refused to take a political line and was therefore equally loathed by all parties, and this was its perilous path. Jishang didn't seem to care for anything – but he stood firm; deeply and darkly. He would not be told what to do. Not by a political party, not by the occupying Japanese forces or their collaborators, nor by the extreme Communist faction. She snorted to herself – he was an aristocratic rebel who just happened to fall on the side of right because of a deep-set stubbornness. Yes, stubbornness was his overwhelming quality. And it made him irresistible. You felt he must be right.

Stevie sighed, remembering the first meetings. The seduction. The kick of being invited into the heart of the China that none of her expatriate friends had access to. The secret courtyards. The mimosa-scented paths, the dark wood screens behind which they explored each other's foreign and thrilling bodies. And always the musky smell of him.

Throughout her travels she had always left the last episode behind with very little regret. After all, there was the next party, the next article or horse race, the next man. But Shanghai had seemed different to her. The intensity of the city had been consuming. She hadn't quite ever got to grips with the heaving, shifting movement of it. Also, Shanghai was where she had become aware of her power.

Stevie had hidden herself in trousers and loose shirts and practical clothes since her adolescence. Modelling herself on her close contemporary Katharine Hepburn, she had chosen to draw attention to her boyishness and her pragmatic qualities, the more to stand out. Girls and their preening and their obsession with boys had made her contemptuous. She was clear from the beginning that her ambitions lay beyond a husband, a house and a car. In college she had been happy, proud even, to be an anomaly. A girl in the geology department. Her interest was not in catching one of the men but in beating them. And as she grew through her twenties she found that if she kept her head down and made better calculations than the men, she could be accepted as one of them. Enough anyway to get the opportunity to travel as she had.

But everything had changed in Shanghai. The undercurrent to life in the city was brazenly sexual. It was inescapable and in the end she had not wanted to escape it.

The international quarter was a world unto itself. It would have been perfectly possible to have made a life there without ever even stepping into the Chinese parts of the city. And plenty of people did just that. Naturally there were servants and tailors and merchants of every description from the native population, but they mostly made the journey into the wide tree-lined streets. On a cool day one might have been in any occidental commuter town. The green banality and silence were deadening.

Stevie had been drawn out into the shouting, spitting, reeking streets of the port. She had befriended Irena, a beautiful, statuesque girl from Lithuania who lived in a decadently draped apartment just off the Bund. Daylight never penetrated it. She had a particular penchant for leopard skin. It turned out that she was the mistress of one of the Swiss League of Nations representatives, a skinny, angular man with delicate ribbons of fair hair brushed over his balding pate. Irena had studied to be a medical doctor and also liked to discuss Russian history in terms of the great novels. She pushed those books at people with the enthusiasm and guile of a drug-dealer. Stevie had lain back on the animal-print cushions in Irena's lair and fallen asleep many times, a huge, heavy, badly translated book in her hands.

Irena had looked at her in horror when she arrived to chaperone her to the first dance.

'No. No. No. No. No.' She had actually stamped her foot in its shiny cream leather.

'I guess it's no, then.'

Stevie had thought she'd done rather well. Her skirt was neat, her shirt was clean and her hair was relatively well brushed. Irena had practically ripped the clothes off her and insisted that she put on a dress which she herself chose from the explosion of little dresses she had stuffed into the wardrobe. It was Stevie's Cinderella moment. The pale-green satin followed the geography of her. It was cool on her skin. She felt absolutely naked. But even she could see in the age-spotted mirror on the back of the door that she had been transformed. She looked like – well, she looked like a girl. A very pretty girl. Her curves were fine and her limbs lithe. It was like being someone else. A distant cousin she'd never met, perhaps. She drew the line, though, at the strappy shoes Irena thrust at her.

That first evening she drew men and attention and compliments like a debutante, which in a way she was. And she liked it. She found the greatest pleasure in this new game. Almost dizzy with it, she became a lepidopterist of compliments. At first, any ordinary or garden variety thrilled her. Soon she became more discerning. The rare and esoteric quickly held more value. She collected the attention, revelling in her new-found power. She played the game well and soon the most subtle of its rules were in her armoury. She had become that most dangerous of creatures – a beautiful and clever woman.

Through Irena she had been invited to those events where the more adventurous members of the international community tentatively chatted to carefully chosen Chinese men. It was at one such party – to celebrate the opening of a department store – that she had first lain eyes on Jishang. He was glorious and different in his traditional clothes, a marked contrast to all the other men, who looked stiff and uncomfortable in heavy woollen suits and ties. He was tall and languid and moved through the party like water. His invitation to her to visit his mountain retreat was, naturally, irresistible. In some ways they were very alike, each aware of opportunity, each hungry for experience, each well defended from any dangerous depth of feeling. But in others the chasm between them was unbridgeable.

Her visit to Jishang's mountain place had been chaste enough. The house was almost European in its structure. Two storeys of handsome wood with a wrap-around veranda, it stood in a clearing by a lake near the summit of the mountain. They argued about the definition of mountain. Stevie was more inclined to consider it a hill. A tall hill but a hill nonetheless. She told him he'd comprehend mountains when he saw the Rockies or the Grand Canyon and the thought of Jishang, tall and graceful, his traditional robe billowing as he peered over the edge into the distant chasm below, was so incongruous it made her laugh. They were sitting on the veranda watching the sun disappear behind the rounded peaks of the range. The thing that most struck her was how incredibly like a Chinese painting of a mountain the Chinese mountains were. They really were round and almost out of focus with their soft, greyish-green coating of fur, like dragons sleeping. It wasn't difficult to see where the legends came from.

The crickets scraped, the fireflies winked, the phonograph played Glenn Miller's 'In the Mood'. She was acutely aware of his expressive hands as they gesticulated and then lay still on the thighs of his extended legs.

'You know, I came alive when I discovered English literature. I was filled with possiblities. It's hard to describe how alive it made me feel. All the old certainties of my education were overthrown by these books. Quite literally, a new world beckoned.'

'Shakespeare?'

'Yes, of course, Shakespeare. But also Tennyson, George Bernard Shaw.'

'Really? Shaw seems so old-fashioned. So like an old man, I suppose.'

'He is an old man. I met him, you know. He came to Shanghai.'

'How was his beard?'

'In good health. It kindly brought the rest of him along too.'

They laughed and she leaned forward. 'I'm jealous.'

'Of my meeting his beard?'

'I'm jealous of your discovering English books. For me they were things to get past, obstacles not doorways. It's only now I can begin to appreciate them for what they are. I guess I was impatient.'

He nodded, smiling and animated. 'Doorways, yes, exactly that.'

The heady perfume of jasmine came, carried on the breeze, and this pleasure in each other was the very definition of romance. Maybe they both rebelled because of it, but some time later they said goodnight without touching. Jishang made a small bow and one of the silent servants led the way to her room. Her clothes had been put away in the black varnished and inlaid wardrobe, her night clothes laid out on the bed. An exquisite bowl of blood-red peonies stood on the bedside table. Jishang was a man whose taste and sense of the moment were pitch-perfect. Stevie opened the window to the night. It was completely dark. The trees around the lake sighed in the light wind.

As she lay on the silk sheets, slippery and unpredictable, in that wooden house in the mountains of China, she wondered at the vastness of choice and experience. And more than ever she had wanted it all.

It was he who had challenged her to write something serious. And it was he who had made the Byzantine connections that led them to Hong Kong and to Madame Kung and to the possibility that she might get the journalistic coup of the decade.

The idea had emerged one steamy, frenetic Shanghai night. Or not strictly speaking night. More precisely it had come to them at that moment when night is becoming morning. There's something about daybreak which inspires new thoughts and lacks the rationale that puts the brakes on the most outrageous ideas. And this had been an outrageous idea.

They had been slumming it in the Del Monte with its dance hall, wide veranda, large garden and Russian girls, most of whom had by that time of the night found company and retired professionally to the discreet rooms upstairs. Stevie was wearing her favourite dress – sleeveless pale-blue satin and a self-consciously tight waist. Jishang's grey linen suit had been custom-made like all his others and he looked like the prince he perhaps was. The club was serving breakfast and they sat in the wicker chairs on the veranda with plates of scrambled eggs on the rickety table in front of them and watched the stars fade into the yellow dawn. Jishang had attracted some furtive looks even here, more curious than antagonistic, and they were so used to drawing attention that they barely registered the sideways glances.

They had started the night at teatime, as so often, at the Cathay Hotel on the Bund. Taking tea in the ballroom on the top floor with its view of the immense, filthy, river. They watched the sampans and merchant ships vie with each other for space in the estuary which was the end point of the mighty Yangtze, dangerously close to each other in their river dance. And then, as usual, tea had been followed by a cocktail, why not? Then they had strolled through the crowds of aristocrats and crooks, ignoring the shrill calls of the rickshaw men, and went in search of entertainment. God, how Stevie loved that city. It seemed to her carnal and suicidal, vital, strident and turbulent, the beginning and the end. They talked as they walked, she and her lover Jishang, past the vividly painted, fluttering banners outside the shops, their red characters competing with the night's glittering lights. The whole city illuminated as if it were day.

They passed the dark recesses of the sailors' bars in Blood Alley where little girls would service men behind dirty curtains for the price of a beer and Stevie tried to persuade Jishang to drop in at the Palais Café, but he had some business to do so she idled instead at a small table in a dark Chinese tea house in Hongkew while Jishang spoke in a low voice with three young men in traditional Chinese gowns at another table nearby. She had given up trying to get to the bottom of Jishang's 'business'. He was so irritatingly opaque when pressed that she had taken to gleaning what she could without his help. Jishang was a great gatherer of information. He seemed to be at the hub of various political and social worlds – and it was these which provided him with the material for the magazine. She didn't in any way resent it. Rather, she embraced these quiet moments and felt in her aloneness that she was truly a part of the city of light. The night had then fallen into the habitual haze of drinks and dancing and an amorphous crowd of people they knew and many they didn't, forming and dispersing as the hours passed. And then in the end they were in the dawn and in that dawn Jishang's challenge didn't seem daunting at all. It even made sense.

'Why are you wasting your time writing about cricket matches and cabaret acts?'

'Because that's what they pay me to do. That's what the great American public like to hear about.'

He snorted in contempt. 'You should at least write something serious about the women.'

It was her turn to snort. 'What about the women?'

'My mother grew up in a different universe. She couldn't have imagined this world.' He indicated the empty veranda but she knew what he meant. 'She couldn't have imagined a world in which Madame Chiang Kai-shek is more visible than her husband.' He took a sip of the lukewarm tea. 'Her feet were bound when she was six years old. She hasn't taken a step that wasn't painful since then.'

Stevie already knew this. They'd had plenty of conversations about the barbarity of that particular tradition but reference to it was guaranteed to rouse her general sense of injustice.

'Madame Chiang Kai-shek is hardly a typical little Chinese girl from nowhere.'

'So? She and her sisters have all made a huge impression. They're visible in a very new way. Internationally.'

'They're certainly visible. But it's because they married powerful men. That's not exactly a huge new leap in the empowerment of women.'

'You know, they're my cousins.'

She hadn't known. 'The whole of China is your cousin.'

There was a small silence as she felt the full impact of his challenge. She knew what he was thinking while he smiled his secret smile and took a mouthful of congealing scrambled egg.

He leaned across the table towards her. 'You don't want that, do you?' And he took her plate before she could answer.

Chapter Four

It was anarchy in the narrow street. Rickshaws and bicycles vied with the pedestrians and the occasional bold car tried its luck, adding its horn to the riot of noise. Even at this time of the morning there was no room to manoeuvre. Harry loved it. He slid through the chaos, his uniform of no interest to the people he passed.

Eventually he was forced to stop by a bottleneck of people and, taking advantage, he groped in his pocket for the piece of paper with the address scrawled on it. Checking it, he glanced around him. There was no sign of any numbers on the tall buildings. Above him were cliffs of brick, overhung with brightly coloured washing and the occasional wireless aerial. He smiled his big, empire-soothing smile, full of confidence and authority, at the rickshaw-driver next to him, who was also at a standstill. He showed him the piece of paper. The rickshaw man pointed his chin to the building directly beside them and then moved on. The blockage had cleared.

Harry stood for a moment, an island in the sea of movement, looking at the decaying building. Battered red and gold ideograph banners were draped listlessly from it. Inside, he climbed the stairs two at a time. He stood back against the wall as a neat girl clattered down, tip-tapping in her high heels.

On the third-floor landing he pressed the bell by the door before he had composed himself. Then he noticed that it was slightly ajar. He waited another moment, then pressed the bell again. Nothing. Shrugging, he pushed the door open and took a tentative step inside.

'Wu Jishang?'

His voice seemed incredibly loud. He had stepped directly into the living room of the apartment but it took him a moment to adjust to the gloom. The blinds were firmly drawn, casting shadows across the clutter. He saw crammed bookshelves, multi-coloured cushions strewn on low divans, piles of papers, a dress hanging over the back of a chair.

Suddenly there was an inhuman scream.

Propelled by a rush of adrenalin, Harry ran across the room in the direction of the cry. He was brought to a premature stand-still by a heavy flying object. Harry sprawled on the tiled floor while the monkey that had launched itself at him squatted next to him, chattering its large teeth. A damp stain spread across Harry's immaculate shirt front and he could smell the monkey pee as it pooled on the tiles.

A young and bespectacled Chinese girl squinted at him from the door to a bedroom. She looked deeply disapproving.

'Oh my God, that animal is absolutely disgusting.' Her tone was vehement.

Before he could wholeheartedly agree, another door opened and Stevie appeared in a dressing gown – tousled, hungover and angry.

'Who the hell are you?'

A little later and Harry was sitting on the low divan. His long legs were splayed awkwardly in front of him and he was wearing a most fetching floral silk dressing gown, which, apart from anything else, was definitely too small for him. Jishang, elegant in a pale linen suit, sat by the window, holding a teacup. The disapproving young Chinese girl, introduced as Lily, who at a second look was probably seventeen or eighteen and not the child she had at first seemed to be – sat quietly at the table in the back of the room and Victor the gibbon had been banished to the bedroom.

Harry persevered. 'Mr Wu, I'd very much like to hear your opinion on the state of affairs in Shanghai.' He hesitated, an informal smile. 'I hope you don't mind my looking you up like this, but when I heard you were visiting Hong Kong I felt I couldn't miss the opportunity . . .'

'Not at all, Major Field. The honour is all mine. I've read several of your essays – especially your work on the colonial relationship between the Portuguese and the Japanese. Fascinating.'

Harry demurred, just enough to be polite because he was thrilled and a little suspicious. Nobody had read his academic work, he was convinced of that. After all, why the hell would they?

'I'm only sorry to have received you in such an – unprepared way.' Behind the convenient veil of manners, Jishang was mortified. Preparation was everything and it was a rare occasion when something or someone genuinely took him by surprise. He did not like it.

Stevie pushed open the door from their bedroom. Her dress clung confidently to the contours of her body. She felt instantly unclean in the full glare of the British officer's glowing wholesomeness, hoping that there was no trace on her of the drama of the previous night. She looked away from Harry and noticed the almost transparent china cup in Jishang's hands. So delicate, like paper.

Harry pulled himself to standing. He felt incongruous in the dressing gown and disconcerted by her beauty.

She glanced back at him.

'I'm sorry about your uniform. Victor is extremely jealous but he doesn't normally launch an attack like that.'

'It's perfectly all right. Really.'

Stevie laughed. 'Just as well you're British – so polite!'

Her gaze met his and for the longest time – a split-second probably – a web-thin thread seemed to vibrate between them.

Jishang's interruption was cool and pointed. 'I've translated your Happy Valley piece. The printer wants the proofs as soon as possible.'

Stevie flushed, the heat of humiliation rising in her. Jishang knew she was ashamed of the report from the racetrack. In a country at war, stories about social betting were ridiculous. She understood his warning.

'Can't it wait?' As she spoke the humiliation was complete. She knew she sounded embarrassingly petulant.

Harry rescued her. 'You're publishing *here*? I thought *Direct Debate* was strictly a Shanghai enterprise.'

'It doesn't make any difference where we print the magazine. What matters is that it is read.' An infinitesimal pause. 'And who reads it.' With a small bow of his head Jishang delicately put the teacup down on the low table. 'You'll excuse me, I'll collect my papers and maybe you'd like to continue the conversation en route to the printer's?'

Jishang went into their bedroom. As he closed the door, Harry averted his eyes from the glimpse of their rumpled bed.

Stevie leaned against the wall. It appeared to Harry to be an impossibly languid gesture. In fact, she was afraid she might faint. Not enough sleep and the nightmares of the darkest hours had left her frail and disturbed. She shrugged. Her words said, 'Business as usual. Don't you just hate it?' Her tone said quite the opposite. There was a slight pause and then she swung a brittle smile at him.

'And what exactly do you do, Major Harry Field?'

'I'm the Japanese Language Officer for the British Army here in Hong Kong and Liaison Officer for . . .'

'Oh good, you're a spy.'

'As I was saying, I'm Liaison Officer . . .'

'Exactly. A spy.'

Utterly unused to being so shamelessly outed, he struggled for a moment. Caught on the verge of indignation, he furrowed his brow and shook his head.

Stevie watched him struggle and took pity on him. 'I won't tell anyone. Honest I won't.' She was having fun now. Disarming people was her absolutely most favourite thing to do. Harry looked right at her.

'You're very beautiful.' It came without warning. She caught her breath – amazed at his boldness and looked at him with new respect, her turn to be disarmed. It was brazen and so far from a compliment that it made her feel like laughing. His hair was a halo in the dim room. He looks like a wild angel, she thought. Jishang's voice cut through the game.

'Is this dry enough?' He was at the door with Harry's uniform shirt folded over his arm.

They both turned to him, each strangely grateful in their own way for the interruption.

* * *

During the week the humidity rose. The air lay heavy and damp and seemed to penetrate her very bones. There was no respite from it. Through the high, narrow windows of the apartment, the afternoon light settled as a kind of mellow glow over the disarray. Stevie considered the manner in which she lived to be evidence of how busy she was and how many better things she had to do. In reality it was evidence of laziness. She was comforted by the chaos and quite happy to be told it represented the state of her mind. Yes, she'd say, my mind is full and there aren't enough minutes in the day to pick up every thought or every stray piece of clothing as I go. So what? The people she lived with had to surrender or found themselves cast as housekeepers.

Lily, Jishang's cousin in some tortuous, complicated way, wasn't prepared to take on the role. She had come with the apartment. When Jishang had announced that he was arriving in Hong Kong for an indefinite stay, she had been sent by her mother to find a place for them to rent and she had driven a much harder bargain than the landlord had counted on. He had been taken by surprise by her negotiating skills, not expecting a child to be quite so canny. She was practised and thoroughly enjoyed the effect of her youthful looks on people who were quick to dismiss her. They rarely did so twice.

Lily's great gift was stealth. She had quietly gone about doing exactly as she pleased all her young life. It was she who had decided to take the diploma at the Oxford School of Secretarial Skills in Central. It didn't seem to have any connection with Oxford beyond its name, not even a European-educated teacher, but she had worked hard and passed every level without drama and now her diploma was framed and hanging on the wall in her parents' house next to the household shrine. She and her friends were industrious and ambitious. They competed over the speed with which they could mimic the clothes and hairstyles of their favourite film stars. She herself favoured Myrna Loy but there was much discussion of the relative merits of the more highly strung and therefore feminine and fragile Merle Oberon. It never occurred to any of them to model themselves on Chinese stars, except perhaps Butterfly Wu, whose elaborate Western-style wedding pictures they had all pored over in the magazines and whose dimpled smile they tried to imitate.

Lily was proud of her Western assimilation and her British citizenship and impatient with her parents' old-fashioned concerns. She was forward-looking and modern, and as her family lived in the New Territories she was happy to be in the city for a while. She was grateful to Jishang and his strange, tall American girlfriend with her big teeth and messy hair, but she felt no obligation to play housekeeper.

Typing sounds came from Stevie and Jishang's bedroom as Lily, by force of habit, lined up the cushions on the divan. The phone rang, startling her. She stood absolutely still. The typing noise didn't falter.

Victor, the disgusting monkey creature, was curled up in a corner of the other divan. Lily looked at him suspiciously. He looked back at her from under his heavy brow. The phone rang on. Shrill and jarring.

Exasperated, Lily slipped past Victor on her way to answer the phone. 'What's the bloody point of you anyway?' she hissed at him.

She picked up the sticky black receiver and listened for a moment. The voice of the woman on the other end was precise and businesslike. When she put the phone back in its cradle she shouted, 'Stevie'.

The typing stopped.

Stevie's voice came from the bedroom, irritated. 'For God's sake. What is it?'

Stevie stomped into the living room and was greeted by a rant. By now Lily was seething. It was really all too much, the unpredictable and late hours, the expectation of housekeeping and now telephone answering too. Her English was flawless despite her fury.

'Answer your own telephone and clear your own table. I don't understand what kind of people you are. Tell Jishang I can't stay another minute. I'm going back to my parents.'

'Wait, just wait a minute. You can read English as well as shout in it, right?'

Affronted, Lily sniffed. 'Of course.'

'Great.' Stevie thrust the sheets of paper that she was holding into the younger girl's hands.

'Check these for me, would you? You know, proofread them. Thanks.' She turned to go.

'By the way, you might like to know – Madame Kung agrees.'

Stevie stopped in her tracks.

'What did you say?'

'That was the telephone call. Just now. Nobody answered so I did.'

'She agrees?' A sharp intake of breath. Stevie wasn't sure she had understood. 'Oh my God, she agrees!' Stevie's world shifted. She thought she might burst with triumph. It had all been worth it. The leaving Shanghai, the hanging around in this stuffy place, the long sessions with various grim men attached to Madame Kung's entourage. But above all, the hope. The secret hope she had allowed herself to invest in being taken seriously.

Stevie flung out her arms towards an even more disgruntled Lily.

'What are we waiting for?'

She put her arm through Lily's and pulled her towards the front door. 'Let's celebrate.' She was a force of nature and Lily couldn't resist. But she had something else to say and as she was bustled out of the apartment she said it.

'You should be more careful who you flirt with.'

Stevie glanced at her, puzzled. Then, with a flush of embarrassment, she remembered.

'You don't mean that dreary British officer? That wasn't flirting. That was . . .' But she gave up. 'Where do you get a proper drink around here, anyway?'

The euphoria didn't last long. About as long as the hangover and not half as long as the anticipation. The serious business of being taken seriously kicked in. Stevie had to submit the draft interviews she had already conducted with the other two Soong sisters. She had to meet more members of Madame Kung's entourage. She had to wait for Madame Kung to come back from a shopping trip to Shanghai. What, she asked Jishang, did he think she was shopping for? Information and a few handbags, not necessarily in that order. She was waiting again. So it was out of despair that she accepted an invitation to a cocktail party from the Clarke-Russells, the Colony's self-appointed pillars of society. And it was out of mischief that she accepted on behalf of both herself and her companion, Wu Jishang.

As she walked up the drive towards the detached colonial bungalow arm in arm with Jishang, she brushed against the thin branch of a camelia bush. An overblown flower came apart and drifted through the darkness to the ground. It released its frail scent into the heavy air and Stevie drew Jishang closer. She felt the cool, exquisite silkiness of his long traditional coat. Light spilled on to the gravel and over the clipped lawn. Equally clipped voices could be heard through the open windows.

'What are the odds it'll be sherry?' she teased. Jishang barely deigned to reward her with a smile.

Over-stuffed British ex-pats sat on sofas in the chintzy drawing room. Through the French windows at the back bloomed a rose garden. The only sign that they were in the Orient and not in the Home Counties were the Chinese boys in white uniforms who passed among the chattering pink people, carrying trays of glasses.

Harry exchanged his empty glass for a full one. He, like many of the other men, was in uniform. He stood with their host, the earnest, humourless Director of Medical Services, Dr Clarke-Russell, and his wife Phyllis, who carried every year of her forty-five but to whom her still red hair was a source of great pride. She was talking in her habitual, head-girl voice. The one that made quite sure no servant argued back.

'You're quite wrong, of course. Hong Kong is as safe as houses. The Japanese have nothing to gain by pushing further into Nationalist territory. It's ridiculous to imagine they'd risk making trouble with us, after all.'

'Naturally. How could those funny little barbarians take on the might of the British Empire as represented by – well – by us?' Harry indicated the well-fed partygoers. Phyllis didn't quite catch the mocking irony but she knew enough about manners to be offended.

Just then a young, blonde woman appeared at Harry's side and took his arm, gripping it tightly. Her voice was tense.

'Oh don't get in such a tizzy, Phyllis, really. We all know Harry thinks he's being amusing when he talks like that.' She smiled but it didn't disguise her disapproval.

Turning to Harry she spoke in a little girl's wheedle.

'Darling, come and meet poor Muriel, would you. She's dying to join the tennis club. I told her you might put in a word.'

Harry glanced at the sofa and caught poor Muriel's keen gaze. She waved. He smiled weakly. Phyllis' attention was momentarily distracted by a glimpse of her eight-year-old pyjama-clad daughter peering, part anxious and part sullen, around the door frame across the room. She made her way swiftly to her.

'Margaret, what's going on? Where's Nanny?'

'She's in the kitchen.'

'What on earth is she doing there? You should both be upstairs.'

'I sent her.'

'Well, that was very naughty. Mummy and Daddy are busy.'

Margaret put a hand out and grasped a handful of her mother's shiny taffeta skirt.

'I'm hungry.'

'Didn't Nanny give you tea?'

'Yes but I'm still hungry. It was disgusting soup.'

Phyllis pulled her skirt out of Margaret's fingers. 'Well, you jolly well have to eat what's put in front of you.'

Margaret's voice was plaintive now. 'Mummy, will you read me a story?'

'Oh, for goodness' sake, Margaret, this is hardly the time. Even you can see that.' She seemed to regret her tone immediately but exasperation was never far away in her encounters with the girl. She softened her voice. 'Be a good girl and run along now. I'll read to you tomorrow, all right?'

Margaret's eyes glittered, dangerously close to tears. Phyllis patted her hand. 'You'd like that, wouldn't you?' Gratifyingly,

Margaret nodded. 'Good. We often have nice teas and things, don't we. So be a good girl and get back to bed.'

Across the room, Jishang and Stevie hovered for a moment in the doorway, the sea of uniforms and floral tea dresses rippling before them. The white-gloved hand of a Chinese waiter offered a glass of sherry to Stevie. She took it and caught Jishang's eye, her raised eyebrow an 'I told you so'. The waiter looked at Jishang with confusion and hesitated before offering a glass to him, the only non-European in the room apart from the waiters themselves. The hesitation was insult enough.

Margaret surprised Phyllis by raising the hand that was still absent-mindedly patting her own to her lips and kissing it. 'Oh,' Phyllis said unconvincingly, 'that's nice, darling,' and Margaret let go and withdrew towards the stairs. Relieved, Phyllis glanced around the room, instantly spotting the new arrivals. She charged towards them, her hand extended.

'So glad you could come, Miss Steiber. We're always happy to see new faces in dull old Hong Kong.'

Her gaze moved to Jishang and the slight flinch of surprise was visible before her manners kicked in.

'And I see you've brought someone. How nice.' Her voice betrayed her.

Stevie swigged the sweetly cloying sherry and smiled a honeyed smile. 'Perhaps you could find a waiter's uniform for my friend, it might make you feel more comfortable in his company.'

Those fellow guests in earshot exchanged anxious and thrilled glances. Surely there wasn't going to be a scene? While Phyllis reeled, a rotund, balding man stepped aggressively towards them.

'We'll have none of that kind of talk. Your sort is not welcome here.'

Phyllis held out a restraining arm. 'No, it's all right, Mr Evans. Thank you.'

Before Mr Evans could continue his blustering defence of the Colony's honour, the tall, broad figure of Harry strode towards them, his voice carrying across the room.

'Miss Steiber – Mr Wu, what an honour.' With his clean smile – his direct gaze – he was at their side. Stevie, not used to being rescued, felt an unfamiliar sense of relief. She hadn't meant to cause a scene, she just couldn't let the insult ride. Her mother was right. She would be the death of herself with her stupid sharp tongue and her bad attitude to authority. 'How marvellous to see you both.'

And with that Harry took Jishang by the elbow and guided them deep into the room. The wall of conversation built around them.

Stevie excused herself and made her way back to where Phyllis was instructing one of the waiters on how to pour the correct measure. Stevie plunged straight in. 'Listen, I'm sorry. That was intolerably rude of me.'

'Think nothing of it.'

'That's very kind of you but I'm utterly mortified. I'm a fool and not really fit for polite society.'

Phyllis, while not exactly warming to her, could hardly resist the apology.

'It's perfectly all right. I'm delighted you brought your friend.' A tiny pause. 'You can't imagine how difficult it is to meet Chinese people here.'

For a second, Stevie's eyes met Harry's over Phyllis' shoulder. And for a second Stevie was lost. He held her look and seemed to reel her in. But Phyllis drew her back. 'May I introduce you to Mrs Harry Field.'

Stevie saw a neat-featured, pale face surrounded by a cloud of baby-fine blonde, wavy hair. A pocket-sized doll with a tight smile. Stevie was reminded of the Little Bo-Peep nursery rhyme. A surprising disappointment crept over her. Of course he was married. Of course. And anyway, why should it matter at all to her? Why should it mean anything?

'Sylvia, this is Miss Steiber. She's new in town.' Stevie took the small hand that Sylvia proffered. Her skin was incredibly soft, like a child's, and the handshake was weak and unconvincing.

'I know how frightfully clever you are. My husband has tried to make me look at your magazine.'

'How awful for you.'

Sylvia laughed a nervous laugh, betraying her loathing for clever women. The girls who answered the questions at school had seemed to her like a different species. But just look, her expression seemed to say, here she was married and running a household and where were they? She glanced at her straight-backed, clean-shaven husband for reassurance and Harry moved towards her. As soon as he started talking, though, her eyes clouded over with a familiar, bitter resentment.

'Miss Steiber, perhaps you could help settle a matter we've been discussing.' He indicated Jishang and another, younger man with freckles and a uniform, Ken Ramsay.

'Don't you agree that the day of the white man is well and truly over?'

Sylvia, maintaining her social smile, turned her disappointed eyes on him and hissed.

'You're drunk.'

But Harry was not to be deterred. 'We're finished but we just won't admit it. This is exactly like the last days of Rome, only this time we're racing blindly towards the extinction of capitalism. Fiddling, all of us.'

Sylvia tilted her pretty head.

'I think it's time to go home, darling.'

The chill in Harry's voice was unmistakable.

'Yes. Good idea. Off you go.'

Sylvia, tears glinting in her eyes, spun on her delicately clad heels and walked away. Stevie was acutely aware of being alone in the crowd with Harry.

'That wasn't very nice. You probably are drunk, you know.'

'Of course I am. It's traditional here. One either gets drunk or one gets married. I seem to have done both.' She could sense the life in him. He was so close. 'Hong Kong is the end of the line for all the useless sods of the empire. Don't know what to do with a chap? Send him here.' Harry gestured contemptuously around the room at the maze of uniforms and complacent faces. 'I mean, just look at them.'

Stevie looked at them. Then back at him.

'And what makes you so different?'

'Nothing. Absolutely nothing.' Stevie's blood seemed to be pumping so fiercely around her body that she was sure he must be able to hear it.

The barrel-chested little man who had been so quick to get rid of her rolled past. He leaned towards her and whispered. 'I know your sort. You won't get away with it here. This isn't Shanghai, you know.' He turned to Harry. 'Look here, old man, the lovely Sylvia is waiting for you, we thought we could all share a cab back down together.'

'I don't think so, Evans, I have business to attend to.'

But Mr Evans was gripping Harry's arm and seemed to be ready to physically remove him from Stevie's company. And

Jishang was coming towards them with a beaming and excited Phyllis by his side. She started talking while still some distance away, unable to contain herself.

'It's so delightful to speak to someone with such an intimate knowledge of the mainland. I can't tell you what a thrill it is. Really.'

Harry held Stevie's gaze as he allowed himself to be drawn apart from her by Evans' machinations. And before long he was dutifully in that shared taxi rolling down the steep Peak road, while Stevie bore witness to the familiar sight of Jishang charming every reluctant soul within half a mile. But for once, she felt no pride in the fact that it was she who would be going home with him at the end of the night.

Chapter Five

'Why would I want to stay in this dump, anyway?'

Stevie knew she sounded childish. The shabby concourse echoed with voices and buzzed with energy. Normally she loved airports. The sense of excitement – all those places she could go. All those adventures waiting to be had, the huge richness of possibility. But today she felt none of this. A sudden dread gripped her as Jishang checked his ticket one more time. A young woman with a child holding each hand pushed past her. In the noise and disarray Stevie felt adrift and afraid.

'Take me back to Shanghai with you. Please.'

'No.' Jishang must have sensed the unusual panic in her. He softened. 'No. And you know why.'

'Remind me.'

'Because you've got unprecedented access to all three Soong sisters and you're going to write a great book about them and make the world take you seriously.'

'If you say so.' She had the sensation that Jishang was far away already though they were standing close to each other. 'Look, I know Hong Kong's not up to much but I wish you'd stay.'

She sounded petulant when what she felt was vulnerable. She had no rights over him and hadn't wanted them so where was this tone coming from? And he had already stayed longer than he had planned. He had business to attend to, important decisions to make, people waiting for him in Shanghai, and she had monopolised him in an unprecedented way. Though she had no doubt that his meetings and discussions here in Hong Kong would be put to good use in one way or another, she also knew that he had lingered for her.

Jishang took her hand and examined her thumb and forefinger. He rubbed at the dark opium stain.

'You've got to stop doing this. You have to stop. It's not so funny if you're caught using it. You know what happens?'

He drew a line with his fingernail across Stevie's throat, leaving a faint red mark. Stevie pulled her hand away.

'Tell me everything's going to be all right.'

'Prediction is a dangerous game.'

'Ancient Chinese proverb?'

He laughed. 'No.'

Suddenly Stevie leaned in to him, holding him tight, feeling the beat of his heart through the expensive double-breasted jacket. She kissed him on the lips. A lover's kiss which surprised them both. It was given in defiance of the fact that he had become more like a brother to her and she could barely remember the last time they had actually made love. People stared as they passed. Jishang gently disentangled himself.

'Work well.'

Stevie shrugged.

'I shall. There's nothing else to do in this hole after all.'

Jishang smiled and slipped into the crowd.

* * *

Stevie smoked as she typed on her baby Hermes. The smoke curled round her head. Flying fingers making words, words, words.

She snatched the paper out of the machine and pushed her chair back. She paced the room, avoiding the sharp corner of the bed, as she read. She sat down at the desk again and leaned her head on her hands. Her eyes began to close.

The door opened and, quietly, Lily surveyed the scene. Walking in her purposeful and graceful way she stepped into the room and picked up some of the stray pieces of paper from the chaos on the floor.

'What the hell do you think you're doing?' Stevie's voice was indignant.

'How can you work in this mess?'

'I know where everything is, all right? What's it to you, anyway?'

'I'm your assistant. Wu Jishang has employed me to be your assistant. So that's what I'll be.'

Stevie sat back in her chair, outraged.

'He's impossible. Does he think he owns me? That I can't look after myself?' She brought her hands down hard on the desk in front of her, making a satisfyingly loud slap. Her palms stung. 'My God. My God.' Sighing, she glanced over at the tough little figure planted firmly in the middle of the faded Persian rug.

'Can you type?'

As the days passed, Stevie understood that she was slowly infiltrating the layers of etiquette and sycophancy that cushioned Madame Kung from everyday realities. It was ever thus for the exceptionally wealthy. Knowing that someone is rich beyond one's wildest dreams is one thing. Being allowed into their lives to witness how they live is quite another. At the very beginning Stevie had felt crushed by the chasm between herself and Madame Kung, but the surprising thing was that Madame Kung was brilliant and shrewd. In a way she was the sister that Stevie had expected the least of.

She had spent the day at an old Kung compound in the New Territories on the mainland. A traditional estate, it was one of the most beautiful places she had ever seen. It would be somewhere she would revisit often in her dreams. A whole world of serenity and profound beauty was contained within the whitewashed walls and the huge fortress-like painted gates. A world serviced by a world's worth of silent staff. Each courtyard offered a different version of peace. Each veranda, a different vista; in one direction the distant hills marking the boundary of the New Territories, in another the restless waters of the bay. Each room contained simple but lush comforts. The dark wood of the interior complemented the pale light in the series of courtyards. There was light where you needed it and shade where you could listen to the rustle of the leaves above you. You could lose yourself here and forget which century you were living in.

But Madame Kung was no Sleeping Beauty.

Stevie was quiet during these visits. She watched as Madame Kung held court, listening to villagers' grievances like an old-time feudal queen. She organised the staff and rewarded relatives and strangers alike with an occasional favouring smile. When the moment came Madame Kung would summon Stevie with a nod of the head and they would sit together. Today it had been on the veranda, and she had allowed Stevie to ask questions. She answered slowly and gave her time to make notes while sipping fragile Lushan Cloud Mountain tea between pronouncements. Her English was idiomatic and the accent faultlessly American.

To Stevie's immense relief, instead of impressing on her yet again the importance of her much-publicised and certainly worthily well-intentioned Chinese Industrial Association, which created job opportunities for women in weaving, sewing and traditional crafts, she was reminiscing about her school days at Wesleyan. Arriving as a fourteen-year-old princess, Ai-Ling had found America strange and terrible and lonely, and she had understood nothing about the loud girls she had landed among: their clothes, their manners, their shrill voices, the disgusting milky drinks, the lack of respect to the adults. Madame Kung shivered delicately as she remembered. Stevie laughed – it wasn't a million miles from her own experience of American youth. She may not have come so far but it was all pretty much incomprehensible to her too at the time.

'Was there anything you did like about it?' she asked.

'I liked to dance. "Wait til the sun shines, Nellie".'

' "By the light of the silvery moon".'

' "Meet me in St Louis".'

' "Oh you beautiful doll, you great big beautiful doll".'

And now Madame Kung was on her feet. Stevie took her tiny hand in hers and they were dancing up and down the veranda, ungainly and out of step but laughing. When Stevie ran out of the words Madame Kung hummed the tune and they danced back to their chairs. Releasing her hostess's hand, Stevie stepped back and gave a little bow of thanks. Madame Kung made a small curtsey and they settled down again, panting a little. Stevie glanced up and saw amazed faces at every window around the courtyard, each of which disappeared back into the cool darkness as she watched.

'My husband is too busy to dance, you know, Miss Steiber.'

'That's a shame, Madame.'

'It is indeed.'

It was with a new kind of intimacy that the conversation resumed.

The gates to the compound swung open later than usual for the journey back to Hong Kong island. The sun was setting over the bay, small birds spun and whirled in the dying light like motes of dust. The two motorbikes swept out first, startling the silence with their roar. Close behind was the low-slung heavy car in which Stevie sat opposite Madame Kung. The smell of leather was pungent and every piece of hardware gleamed. Stevie glanced towards the shore, and was startled to see a car parked on the verge. She was even more startled to see Harry Field and the freckly younger man from the party looking right back at her. Were they following her or Madame Kung? Or both? For a moment she was frozen – a combination of fear and fury. It was one thing for them to be interested in Jishang's movements, but what business was she of theirs?

She sat forward and in a bold confrontational gesture she waved at them. Ken was taken aback.

'Did she just wave at us?'

But Harry, oddly ashamed, looked away.

Chapter Six

July 1940

. . . so, when are you coming home? I had news from my old friend Marguerite, who manages to write despite the air raids and terrible things going on in poor old England. She says she can hardly think for the horror of it. Everybody says the Germans are not behaving too badly in France but I don't suppose we'll be seeing the sights of Paris in this life. Jane and Faye tell me you haven't written to them either. You always were selfish but since there's a war on and all, you'd think you'd let us know how things are. I guess I'll have to wait till I read it in the paper. Yours ever, Mother.

The letter lay in her hands, a pale-blue tissue of recriminations. The phone rang again. Stevie ignored it and after five or so shrills, it stopped.

She let the letter go and it drifted, a leaf, to the floor. It was incredible how tight the bonds of guilt still were. It really made no difference that she was on the other side of the world from her mother – one tug and the cords were restricting her again. No distance was far enough. She debated starting a reply, even took a step towards the desk where the paper lay waiting, imagining the pleasure on her mother's face when she opened the mailbox at the edge of the grass at the front of the house and found the pale-blue news. This image was instantly replaced by the sides of her mother's mouth drooping in disapproval, her eyebrows arched higher than ever in a combination of disappointment and incomprehension. How would it be if Stevie actually wrote the truth of her life? She laughed out loud at the very thought.

The sound of footsteps running across the parquet floor interrupted her thoughts. Stevie was already on her way towards it when the door to her room was flung open. The letter skittered further over the floor in its wake. Lily, uncharacteristically flustered and clearly distressed, spoke in a rush, the words falling over each other.

'We've all got to go. Just like that. How can they do this?'

In the living room the phone started up again.

'Go where?'

'Away. We're being evacuated. All of us. Not you. I don't think it means you. It's us, the British women and children. What am I going to do? I mean, where will they send us and what about my things?'

'Where did you hear this?'

Lily sat down on the bed. 'Susie told me. I was picking up the fabric for my blouse, you know, the one I saw in *Vogue*, and I bumped into her and she was running home.'

'Where did she hear it?'

'Her boyfriend. The soldier. He said it was a secret but he'd typed out the order and thought she should know.'

The phone rang on and on. Lily, irritated, got up and went over to it. Stevie tried to stop her.

'Don't pick up. I know who it is.'

But the receiver was already in Lily's hand.

'Yes?' She glanced across at Stevie. 'No, she's still not here, Major Field. I can take another message.'

Changing her mind and surrendering her unilateral boycott of communication with him, Stevie was across the room in seconds. She grabbed the phone and kept her voice level.

'What's all this about, anyway? Where have they got to go?'

Harry's voice, rich and low, disconcerted her for a moment. 'Ah. Miss Steiber. At last.'

'Don't bat your eyelashes at me. What's all this about an evacuation?'

'Do you by any chance mean the evacuation of British women and children to keep them safe in the unlikely event of a Japanese invasion?'

'Don't make a joke of this. Yes, that's exactly what I mean. Does this imply that the British government is in a state of panic and finally acknowledging the inevitability of the Japanese not respecting a crown colony just because it's owned by the great Emperor of England and treating it and us in as heinous a manner as they have been treating the poor Chinese?' She took a breath. 'Oh and by the way, if you're spying on me I can spare you the effort. I'm just a lawful citizen going about my lawful business.'

Harry's laugh was genuine and also extremely irritating.

'Well?' she snapped.

'I don't know how you lawfully came across this classified information and I couldn't possibly comment on the kind of gossip that suggests there might be evacuation plans for the women and children to go to Australia.'

'Australia?' Stevie glanced across the room and saw Lily's eyes widen.

'As I said, I couldn't possibly comment.'

'Thank you.'

'You may be aware that I've been trying to contact you and since I've finally got through, I was wondering whether you might have a moment.'

Stevie's resolve not to see him had been fading while they spoke. Now it snapped right back into place. She couldn't have put into words exactly why, but she knew he was dangerous and, bold though she was in her life, she wasn't looking for more complications. As far as she was concerned she was only in Hong Kong for a finite period, long enough to finish the book. Then she would be straight back to Shanghai and her real life.

'Sorry. Not a single one.'

She replaced the receiver just in time to catch Lily as she swayed.

That week Madame Kung took another extended trip to Chungking to make an appearance at the Chinese Industrial Association and check in on her husband, who was serving a brief tenure as Premier in the Kuomintang government, a token nod towards Western power-sharing before handing the reins back to the all-powerful Chiang Kai-shek. Consequently, Stevie was again left to her own devices in Hong Kong. She felt cut loose. There was no Jishang to walk and talk with, and Lily's state of anxiety fed into her own. She avoided the Colony's claustrophobic social events and there were only so many hours she could actually stand to be at her desk. The pressure to make something of the book felt overwhelming. She was constantly tired. An iron-band of pain gripped her head most days and the nightmares had come back. They were the same terrors that had haunted her childhood and she could not shake the memories of shivering on the night-cold linoleum of the hallway during the journey to her parents' bedroom, only to be rebuffed and sent back to bed alone. Like a virus, they lingered in her system.

In the end, once she had made the decision, the pain lessened immediately.

She walked fast and with focus along the narrow strip of pavement by the harbour. The wooden hulls of the junks creaked and groaned as they scraped against each other, a chorus of disapproval. She had not been there since that disastrous night after her first meeting with Madame Kung and she ignored the pangs of guilt at breaking her farewell promise to Jishang. As she stepped on to the first boat she nearly lost her balance. She scrabbled from boat to boat – hell, which one was it? They all looked the same in the overcast daylight. Come on, come on, she thought, driven by the promise of the absolute release that only opium could deliver: the bliss of it, the softening of the world, the fading of boundaries between wakefulness and sleep, the lostness.

At the beginning the thrill had been tied in with the transgressive nature of her secret life with Jishang. Their mutual passion had to be played out in dark corners and on languid afternoon trips into the countryside. They were hardly the first couple to cross the racial divide but it was inevitably the foreign men with their Chinese girlfriends who paraded through the cocktail bars and dance halls of Shanghai. And she had been tentative about the romance for good reason: apart from anything else he was married. Jishang had assured her that his wife was traditional in her outlook and entirely unconcerned with his life outside the domestic arena. An assurance which she chose to take at face value. As the months passed it became clear that theirs was a connection that transcended the sexual and had become even more precious because of their shared excitement about ideas, so they stepped out into the open. The magazine had been their baby.

One day Jishang had insisted that they stop at his family home on the way to a meeting. He needed to find a particular book to illustrate a point he intended to make. Stevie had stood awkwardly on the veranda, uncomfortably aware of the sounds of family life coming from inside the pretty house. There was the metallic noise of pans being washed and Billie Holliday scratchily sang 'Strange Fruit', giving the afternoon a disturbing tinge. A compact woman in a beautiful navy-blue cheomsang high in the collar, giving her an even longer neck and straighter bearing, had come out of the house and bowed her head before shamelessly looking Stevie up and down. Stevie had instantly realised she must be Jishang's wife, of whom he spoke with great pride and respect. Feeling slightly panicky, she had shuffled her feet and muttered a greeting.

Wu Mei's voice had been suprisingly assured. 'My husband will not be long.'

'I hope we're not interrupting you too much.' Shrinking under the full unblinking gaze of Wu Mei, Stevie blathered on witlessly. 'We're on our way to a meeting with the printer. Jishang thinks he doesn't understand how to set the type to its best advantage.'

Wu Mei had raised her hands in a gesture of defeat. 'According to him, no one understands anything quite well enough. He thinks only he can do everything right. Tirseome, no?'

Stevie nodded, embarrassed and a little afraid to be having this conversation, and wondering whether Mei had any idea who she was or what her relations were with Jishang.

Wu Mei continued. 'If you wouldn't mind, could you please make sure he doesn't come back until late this evening? We're having family to stay and I don't want him getting involved in the arrangements. It will take twice as long.'

Stevie was so dumbfounded that she laughed. 'Yes. I'll do my best.'

'You know, I'm really very grateful to you.' She was interrupted by a shout from inside the house, and Mei turned to go before glancing back at Stevie and saying, 'You are skinnier than I thought.' She was swallowed back into the cool dark of the house and Stevie felt slightly humiliated though she couldn't work out why. Later, Jishang tried to explain that Mei knew Stevie was no threat to the marriage and would leave in the end, unlike a Chinese girl, who might have ambitions to be the second Mrs Wu. It was yet another opportunity for Stevie to ponder the cultural gap between them. She never completely understood the apparent pragmatism that Wu Mei had applied to her husband's extra-marital interests but she was grateful that Jishang's wife had accepted her presence in her family's life with such singular serenity.

Jishang's otherness was a source of complete wonder to her. She could spend hours exploring the creases in his skin. Everything about him seemed miraculous because it was so unfamiliar. When he assured her that his wife considered it practically a compliment to her that he had taken a European lover, she was prepared to accept it. When he paraded her into his own house and sat her in state in the main room while the servants laid out tea and Jishang presented his small children to her – none of this seemed worthy of too much questioning. It was all delightfully picturesque. She was caught in the hazy moral code of an unfamiliar culture and chose to interpret things in her own light. The drug was part of it: the sleazy dens, the opium dreamscapes, the long, long nights.

And now, alone in Hong Kong, caught up in the fringes of someone else's war, afraid that she might not be able to do justice to the opportunity the book was giving her, all she wanted was the forgiving forgetfulness of the opium pipe. Just this once, she had told herself, as she put on her jacket and left the apartment. Just this once thrummed in her head as she found the junk with the curtain over its door and pushed it aside.

Inside the boat a young woman looked up, startled. Her baby lost its grip on her breast. The nipple dripped pale milk and the baby started to wail. The noise echoed wildly in Stevie's head as she stepped back, dropping the curtain, the wrong curtain.

As she crossed on to the next boat, Yang slipped out of the cabin. He recognised her instantly.

'Not dead,' he stated, poker-faced.

'No.' She saw him twitch, look over his shoulder, he was jumpy. 'I want to buy.'

'Not possible.' And he turned to go.

Stevie, disconcerted by this dismissal, was now desperate. She followed him as he opened the curtain and ducked inside. With one glance she surveyed the gloomy cabin. What she saw made her gasp out loud. She had caught sight of the last man on earth that she'd expect to see there. His head was bent awkwardly under the low roof – what the hell was Harry Field doing there? She was flooded with shame. Both for herself and for him. How could it be that she had got him so wrong? Major Field a fellow opium-smoker? And instead of making her feel complicit and comfortable, the shame redoubled.

She dropped the curtain instantly and stepped away but Harry was on the deck before she got far. His voice held her, angry and contemptuous.

'You're even more ridiculous than people think you are.'

Stevie, craven in herself but on the offensive as ever, said, 'And you? I thought alcohol was more your thing.'

Harry came close enough to take hold of her elbow. 'Shut up, you silly, silly girl. And keep walking.' They walked.

The restaurant was all bustle and business. Through the window the neon lights glowed noisily. Families crowded around the tables, which were crammed claustrophobically into the impossibly small space. There was a scrum of plates, steam and trolleys of dim-sum.

Stevie's back was tight against the corner. Harry had somehow managed to trap her there. Why? In case she tried to run away? His chair was set close to hers at an angle to the small table. His back was to the room and he spoke in a low voice under the clatter of diners.

'You must know how dangerous it is. What were you thinking?'

'Yang sells good stuff, the right colour and not too dry or too sticky.' Harry's frown deepened. 'Don't look at me like that, I'm not an addict really, you know.'

'Actually, I don't know.' His tone was serious and concerned. 'What about you?'

'Me?'

'Don't tell me, it's all right for you, you can handle it.'

He laughed in surprise. 'Not my thing at all. Yang is a helpful chap, he has all sorts of interesting things to say, we were catching up. What's your excuse? To be honest, Miss Steiber, I'm disappointed, I had you down for an intelligent girl.'

Shame flushed her cheeks and Stevie suddenly felt the need to explain herself. She looked down at her hands and laid them out, fingers spread, on the sticky table. Keeping her head down she shrugged.

'I want to know everything, experience everything.'

'Experience isn't the same as knowing.'

Stevie looked up at him. 'And what makes you so wise?'

He held her gaze. 'Why opium?'

'It stops me drinking alcohol, which is a good thing, but it's time-consuming as a habit, I'll give you that. I really like the lying down. The lying down is nice.' She heard the flippancy in her voice and recognised it as another habit that was surprisingly hard to break. 'What were you really doing there, anyway?'

Harry didn't miss a beat. 'Research.'

'Me too!'

Harry couldn't help noticing the curls of shiny hair that fell over the sharpness of her cheekbones, softening them. 'This research, it can't possibly be to do with the estimable Madame Kung or even one of the other Soong ladies. Or have we all missed a very big piece of scandalous gossip? Don't tell me you're supplying China's wealthiest woman with drugs? Maybe it's part of a cunning plot to bring down the Kuomintang leadership. You're working for the Communists after all!'

Stevie sat back in admiration of the riff. She waited a moment after he had finished. 'All done?' Harry nodded, smiling. 'Actually, if you really want to know, it's for a piece I'm doing for –' She stopped mid-flow. 'Hey, wait a minute. You're so clever. You find out for yourself.'

'Don't worry, I shall. May I ask, though, I'm curious, how have you managed to get such access to the Soongs? They're a notoriously closed clan. Is Mr Wu in some way related to them?'

Stevie was instantly on guard again. She had no idea exactly what he was after but he was clearly looking for information and she had no intention of slipping it to him, whatever it might be. Also the mention of Jishang stung her like a slap for more reasons than she was ready to admit. She crossed her arms over the thin cotton of her dress.

'How did I get access? My natural charm, obviously.'

'Obviously.' Harry took a sip of beer straight from the bottle. 'Look, I'll get to the point. We need to know what's happening both in Chungking government circles and also in the Communist hierarchy. Details, no matter how small, would help us put a clear picture together. We do have lines of communication of course but the Kuomintang have their own very particular version of the truth. Perhaps you . . .?' Harry frowned. Stevie was laughing again. He sat back. 'You're unbelievable. You're laughing at me?'

'Well, you're hilarious. Ever heard of subtlety? And anyway, the answer is no. I'm not going to betray any confidences and I will not identify my sources.' A pause. 'And most certainly not to a Limey.'

'I might begin to wonder whose side you're on.'

'I'm on my side. Every time.'

Harry considered this for a moment. He sat forward again. 'Maybe information isn't all I want.'

Stevie's heart skipped a beat. Her voice was low so as not to betray the shaking.

'My God. You might just be as unscrupulous as I am.'

'How unscrupulous is that, exactly?'

She held his gaze. 'Anything for a story. Everything for a good story. The end always justifies the means.'

'Hmm. That doesn't explain why you're on the run.'

Stevie rolled her eyes, mock-exasperated. 'Hello, Dr Freud, who invited you?'

'We're all on the run, why else would we be here?'

Suddenly Stevie felt taut and thin-skinned, inexplicably burdened with honesty. The words came with difficulty, a confession.

'I'm not running. I'm the exception that proves the rule. But –' a pause '– if you must know, I've frightened myself. I'm afraid I can't actually write the book. Maybe I can't write it.'

His look of sympathy was too much to bear. She brightened her tone back to brittle.

'God, I can't wait to get out of here. I'd do anything to get back to Shanghai. It's heaven there.'

His gaze didn't waver. 'That's ridiculous. I mean, yes, Shanghai's marvellous and all that, but the thing about the book, I don't understand. You could write anything. I know it because I admired your work long before I admired you.'

She was acutely aware of the burning flesh between them, between their almost touching knees, almost touching hands.

Then Harry's wrist was in the grip of an old woman, so twisted in the spine that she was almost doubled over. The world crashed in on them again. The noise, the penetrating smells of cabbage and sharp sauces seemed even more overwhelming than before. Her skin was thin as rice paper. Harry had swivelled towards the old woman, whose fingers traced the lines on his palm. The bony fingers of her other hand grasped his wrist. He tried to pull away. Her voice was a gravelly whisper, caught in her twisted trunk.

Harry looked to Stevie. 'What did she say?'

She translated from the whispered Cantonese. 'She said, are you afraid?'

The old woman was still muttering as she looked at his hand. 'Much trouble. Great love. Separation. Hard life.'

She released him. He pulled a coin out of his pocket. She took it and shuffled away to accost the people at the next table.

'So?' Harry asked.

'She said great love and long life. Much joss – luck.'

'Nothing to be afraid of, then.'

Stevie shook her head. 'No.'

'What does frighten you? Apart from writing your book.'

'Nothing much. But sometimes I'm afraid of myself.' She felt his scrutiny and, alert again to the heat of his leg so close to hers, she felt an urge to get away. She stood up, uncomfortable between the table and the wall, and reached for her jacket, which was over the back of the chair. Harry also stood and helped her with the jacket. She was suddenly struck by something.

'You don't speak Chinese?'

Harry shrugged slightly, apologetically. 'Japanese and Portuguese.'

'Well, I suppose that explains why the British Army posted you to China.'

'Quite.' Harry had stood back to allow her to squeeze out from the table. Now he spoke formally, the intimacy banished. 'In fact, I wonder if you've got a moment? There's something I was going to ask. Sergeant Ramsay and I could do with your translation skills.'

Stevie hesitated, disappointment rising. Maybe this was only a professional dig for information after all. He was frustratingly hard to read and she was wrong-footed, used to being one step ahead.

'His Majesty's Government would be most grateful.'

She glanced at him, relieved to hear the playful tone again and gratified to see the amused creases next to his eyes.

'Oh, well in that case . . .' she said.

The office was on the third floor of an undistinguished administration building in the business district. They had walked there, Stevie conscious of him reining in his long strides so they could stay shoulder to shoulder. Afterwards she thought that she knew even then that they were walking towards their future and that nothing would be the same again. That afternoon they looked like a handsome pair of colleagues making their way in a fairly leisurely fashion back to work, not speaking much but pleased with each other's company.

As Harry closed the door behind them Stevie cast her eyes around the office. On his desk, among the debris of his working life, was a framed formal studio photo of Sylvia and her grim little smile.

Stevie turned abruptly away. 'I can give you half an hour. I'm going to the movies with Lily this afternoon. She wants to see the Olivier film but quite honestly the thought of him doing another buttoned-up Brit in breeches routine doesn't appeal to me much.'

Harry closed the blinds on the window. For maybe the first time in his life he wasn't thinking beyond the next moment. He couldn't remember what he was supposed to be doing or where he was. He forgot about his pale, distant wife. He was intent only on Stevie. The room darkened and Stevie almost swayed with the intensity of the atmosphere.

'There is no translation, is there?'

He turned to look at her, saying nothing. She held his gaze.

'Are you going to lie to me often?'

'No. I try to stick to the things I do well.'

'Like seduction?' Stevie could feel her own surrender. But she also felt an incredible charge of energy fuelling every nerve-ending in her body. 'Be careful. I may just call your bluff and then you'd be sorry. I've never had much of a conscience where married men are concerned.'

Now Harry was there in front of her. So close. His mouth. His eyes. She was drowning. His voice a whisper.

'How sorry do you think I'd be?'

'Very.'

And his mouth was on hers. She felt him pick her up and she was weightless. He pushed the papers off his desk to clear space for her and she was sitting on the desk. The blunt edge of the wood dug into the top of her thighs. All the time he was kissing her, urgent and abandoned. Sylvia slipped face-down on to the floor. And all was sensation. Her legs around his waist. Hungry and fast. Their faces very close, breathing each other's breath.

'Oh my God, Stevie.'

'You'll have to make up your own lie. She's your wife.'

And they were on each other again. Lost.

Chapter Seven

August 1940

On a clear day in early August, heavy with damp heat, a convoy of cars raced through the emerald-green landscape of the New Territories, the land between the island of Hong Kong and China. The paddy fields were bordered by little clay paths and the shallow water channels sparkled like broken glass. A farmer looked up from under his wide hat at the unusually large number of cars and narrowed his eyes in concern. Having ascertained that they weren't stopping, he relaxed a little. But he kept his eyes on them until they were out of sight. On the other side of the world the battle for the skies of Britain was being fought but there was no echo of those blood-drenched encounters in the wide cloudless grey of the horizon.

The cars stopped outside the walls of Kun Lung Wai, a small traditional village which had not seen so much action since the Boxer Rebellion in 1900. Stretching their limbs and desperate to cool their hot, damp skin, a motley collection of Europeans climbed wearily out of the broad-beamed black cars. The women steamed with a great sense of purpose, the few reporters who had come along for the ride exchanged amused glances.

A little while later in the central square, a large crowd for such a small town had gathered. Curious villagers and a few European women and children took stock of each other whilst keeping a polite distance. On an improvised platform, a couple of planks of wood balanced on oil drums, the statuesque Phyllis Clarke-Russell talked into a microphone. She seemed not to understand that her voice was thereby magnified and so she was shouting. Very slowly.

'As the Chairman of the Hong Kong branch of the British Ladies' Charitable Association it gives me great pleasure to present this first-aid box to you, the people of Kun Lung Wai.'

A bemused man, representing the equally bemused people of Kun Lung Wai, approached the fragile platform and, reaching up, accepted the tin box from Phyllis. There was muted applause initiated by Sylvia, who fervently admired Phyllis, as she had fervently admired the head girl at school in Surrey.

Standing to one side, Declan McKenna, at twenty-five already more cynical than he was born to be, leaned slightly towards Stevie.

'When the Ladies' Charitable Association has been evacuated to the parched fields of Australia, who'll be left to patronise the natives?'

Stevie laughed. She had last seen him a few weeks before at a military press conference. He had been there on behalf of the good people of Ireland as the foreign correspondent of the *Irish Times*; she, to report on what the foreign correspondents were wearing for a flippant little piece to be syndicated across the States. She liked his intensity and the fact that he was incapable of hiding his innate optimism. She felt protective of his Tigger-like energy and enthusiasm.

'God, Declan, doesn't Hong Kong make you nostalgic for China?'

'This is China. We're on the mainland, or hadn't you noticed?'

'You know what I mean.'

He clutched his chest in mock horror. 'You mean there is a part of China where the British Ladies' Association doesn't reach?'

Stevie nudged him and he pretended to fall so that she had to put out her hand and pull him back to standing. Her gaze drifted across the square. Under the eaves of a traditional red-painted house she caught a glimpse of Harry in deep discussion with a skinny, high-cheekboned youth wearing the loose pyjama-like shirt and trousers of the local peasants.

The sight of him shook her. Something rose in her throat. It had only been a week since he had gallantly opened the front door of his office building to see her out, but it may as well have been a year. He had thanked her for her help. She hadn't looked at him for fear of giving everything away and had lost herself as fast as possible in the crowded street. She had not answered the telephone since.

The unexpected image of him, leaning earnestly and sympathetically towards the intense young man, took her right back there. Instantly, she was in that office again. The blinds down, the air hot but not as hot as his breath on her skin. Her limbs had felt heavy and the grip of wanting him had completely taken her by surprise. She was used to being the object of desire. She was used to accepting homage and to the pleasure that men's passion gave her. But this desperation she did not recognise. Afterwards, it frightened her.

It was Harry who had heard the footsteps immediately outside the office door. It took all his strength to pull away from her, to take his hands from her body and help her down from the desk. By the time Ken opened the door they were still in disarray and Stevie could not have spoken if her life had depended on it. Ken had understood in a flash of recognition. The papers on the floor, the figures in the dim light, Major Field, his shirt loose with his hand protectively on the back of a girl. He coughed and backed off, deeply embarrassed. He closed the door and stepped back into the corridor. He had been at a loss as to what he should do next. He saw the blinds being opened and walked away as fast as he could down the corridor, as embarrassed as if he himself had been disgraced. There was nothing in his emotional vocabulary to express the shame he felt.

Somehow Stevie had left Harry, the room, the building. She had done her utmost not to think about it since. And as the minutes, hours, days had passed she persuaded herself that it had been a surprising encounter, yes, but nothing more nor less. From the distance of a whole week it seemed more like a dream. She was practised at brief affairs. It was her area of expertise and it suited her. Wilfully unmarried, she considered it a badge of honour that she hadn't been trapped in the shadow of a man. When asked, she had often quipped that she wasn't married because she hadn't yet found a good enough wife.

Stevie glanced back across the square. Harry was still there, leaning his long body against the wall of a house, listening intently to the boy, who suddenly she felt sure she'd seen somewhere before. That brush of hair, those arched eyebrows, were familiar. Then she remembered – the boy she and Lily had bumped into in the market one day. Lily had been flustered, so had he, and after Lily had introduced him as her relative he had scurried away. It was then that Stevie had learned that it was useless to try and get information out of Lily if she didn't want to give it. She had definitely not wanted to talk about the boy. Stevie had the impression she was afraid. In any case, it was family business and she had backed off.

Declan followed her gaze. 'Business or pleasure?'

Stevie shrugged. 'I know that boy, I think his name is Chen. He's Lily's cousin or brother or something.'

'Looks like one of the Communist lads to me.'

The boy slipped away between the houses. Harry looked up and, extremely unconvincingly, appeared to notice Stevie's presence as if for the first time. He strode across the dusty square towards them. Stevie held herself very still.

Harry nodded a cool hello to her and shook Declan's hand.

'Got anything for me?' Declan asked.

'Nothing the readers of *The Times* would appreciate hearing.'

'All good news, then.'

'Good for the Japanese, certainly.'

'You know what I like about being briefed by you, Major, it's your marked optimism.'

Harry laughed. 'When there's good news, Mr McKenna, you'll be the first to hear.'

He turned to Stevie and said, with breathtaking nonchalance: 'Miss Steiber, I have something to ask you.'

Declan, young but not stupid, butted in.

'Favouring the American press now, Major?'

He understood exactly what the nature of the enquiry was. And he couldn't help his momentary disappointment. Stevie was the best-looking girl in the place as well as possessing the sharpest wit.

Harry stepped away. Stevie shrugged at Declan as if to show ignorance of what this could possibly be about and followed. Declan was not fooled for a moment.

They reached the edge of the square and stood in the shade of the banyan tree. Stevie's dress stuck to her as if she had been swimming in it. A slightly fetid smell drifted from the paddy fields and her skin was itchy from the heavy heat. Under the umbrella spread of branches, his voice was urgent.

'Yes, all right, so I'm married, and you and Wu Jishang are engaged in a spectacular love affair. But you could bloody well be polite enough to return my calls.'

Stevie was acutely aware of the curious and disapproving eyes on them. This was very public. Was he going to cause a scene? She glanced nervously towards Sylvia. At some distance away she was engaged in demonstrating how to apply a bandage on to a willing village woman. The woman found the whole thing absolutely hilarious and was shrieking with laughter, as were her friends. Sylvia forged determinedly ahead with her task. Stevie couldn't restrain her anger.

'Why are you doing this? Everyone can see.'

'If you'd answered my calls like a normal person, I wouldn't have to, would I?'

'You have no right to talk to me like this.'

'No, maybe not. But you can't run away from me for ever. What did you think, that I'd just go away as if nothing had ever happened?'

'Well, you've got me now. What do you want to say?'

Harry wavered, then he shook his head. 'I don't know.'

Stevie looked at the ground. A trail of ants wove a path through the dust.

'I suppose I'd like to know what you want. I mean – who you want. Or what you want to do.' He tailed off.

'You can't possibly imagine that I want you? What in God's name would make me want a married British soldier –'

'Officer.'

She glared at him. 'A married British soldier who just happens to be a drunk?' She shoved her hands into the pockets of her dress. 'Just because we've – we've –' she faltered, 'it does not give you any rights over me.'

This was intended as her parting shot and she took a step away from him. He grabbed her by the elbow.

'All right, I've heard what you don't want. Fair enough. But one thing's clear and it's the last thing I expected from you – you're a coward.'

Stevie wrenched herself free and stormed back towards Declan, steaming with fury. How dare he? How goddamn dare he? She, a coward? She who lived her life exactly as she chose to, with no thought for custom or niceties or what other people made of her? It was nothing less than an outrage. Of course she thought, sneering, that's what comes of refusing a man who expects to be loved. He resorts to heinous insults. Pathetic. By the time she reached Declan she felt much better.

'You all right? Got any headlines for me?'

'No. He – we had some unfinished business from a while back. Anything happen while I was gone?'

Stevie gestured towards the bandage demonstration. The women of the village were still finding much to laugh at and Sylvia was struggling with an explanation of what to do with the brown glass bottle of disinfectant. She narrowly managed to wrest the bottle back when one of the women tried to take a sip.

Stevie couldn't resist a glance over her shoulder at Harry. He had withdrawn further into the shadow of the houses and was in intense conversation with two Japanese men in suits. Stevie frowned and Declan followed her gaze.

'Ah, the charming Mr Takeda and the charmless Mr Shigeo, unless I'm much mistaken.' Stevie looked at him, impressed. 'They're unofficially attached to the Japanese consulate and seem to pop up at every opportunity.' Stevie raised her eyebrows in unspoken understanding.

'And officially?'

'I gather Mr Takeda, the chubby one on the right, represents a Japanese manufacturer of spectacles.'

'Appropriately enough.'

'Quite so. And Mr Shigeo is employed by a canned fruit importer. Or so his business card claims.' Stevie looked closely at them, the heft of the one and the spareness of the other. 'They're perfectly pleasant, apparently, but personally I feel there's something wrong about socialising with them when I've seen what their colleagues are doing elsewhere.'

Stevie narrowed her eyes. 'I don't suppose they're here for a social engagement any more than we are.' Then, turning to Declan, she batted her eyelashes and trilled in an excruciating Southern accent.

'Oh fiddle-de-dee, Mr McKenna, sir, all this war talk sure spoils the party.'

And Declan returned in an even worse one, 'Why, Miss Scarlett, you minx, you.'

It was their favourite game. They had established it when standing at the back of an endless military briefing a few weeks previously and they could quite easily play it for hours.

Suddenly there were shouts between the men. The raised voices brought everybody's attention to the far side of the square. Sylvia hesitated in her demonstration, the safety pins in mid-air. The village women stopped shrieking with laughter. Stevie and Declan headed straight for the scuffle, pushing through the crowd. She could see that Chen, Lily's young man relative, was landing punches in the direction of the two Japanese men. Harry's voice could be heard over the yelling, trying to calm things down.

'Gentlemen, please, there's no need for this.'

But the atmosphere had changed from festive to sinister faster than it seemed possible. Harry was struggling to keep Chen at arm's length of the Japanese, but the crowd was threatening now and a few other Chinese men were entering into the fray. The younger, fleshier man, Mr Takeda, was faring badly. A few blows had landed and there was blood on his shirt, which had come untucked from his trousers. Mr Shigeo, older and leaner, was returning the aggression pretty efficiently and had caused some damage. Harry was doing his best in their defence but the fighting was increasingly nasty. There were screams now from the women and some of the British children were crying. Phyllis held her daughter's face firmly into her skirts, which came as a pleasant surprise to Margaret, who was more used to being pulled off her mother than hugged to her. Margaret made a half-hearted attempt to escape the folds of crisp cotton. A warning 'Margaret' reached her muffled ears and she surrendered again to the unfamiliar closeness of her mother.

Moving on instinct, Stevie pushed deeper into the brawl. She caught sight of Harry shouting for calm but couldn't hear his words over the scrum. A punch landed hard on her cheek, catching the side of her eye socket. For a moment the world was silent and then the thumping throb of pain bit in. She had been hit by the flailing hand of Mr Shigeo, whose lean sweating face loomed towards her. Her response was immediate. Her open palm swiped him back, an answering sting on her own hand. He stared at her with fury and humiliation in equal measure. In that instant Stevie felt the icy grip of fear but Shigeo was distracted by the pull of another assailant and, as he disappeared from view, Stevie felt herself being dragged backwards. Declan had one arm around her waist and with the other, he pushed a path through the baying crowd.

When they were clear he let her go.

'War wound, baby,' he whistled.

Stevie could feel warm wetness on her face.

'You've gone and done it now.'

He gently dabbed at the cut with his handkerchief, none too clean, but she wasn't looking.

'I should care? They're bastards, all of them.'

'Forget the Japanese,' Declan indicated the horrified face of Phyllis, who was bearing down on them at speed. 'Much worse – you've upset the Charitable Ladies.'

Stevie smiled and winced. 'Yep, that is scary, I'll give you that.'

Phyllis, with Margaret still clinging on to her, spoke with a very English mix of disapproval and concern. 'Are you all right, Miss Steiber? Only we have several trained first-aiders with us.'

'Thank you, I'm fine.'

Margaret released her grip on Phyllis' skirt long enough to get a good look at Stevie's face.

Phyllis was clearly affronted by Stevie's refusal of help. 'That'll be quite some bruise, I'm afraid.'

'I'll live.'

'Oh I don't doubt that. Your resilience has already been noted and is a matter of much admiration.'

Stevie didn't have time to fully appreciate the undercurrent of censure because their attention was drawn by Harry, who had jumped on to the low wall behind him. Pushing aside the peony bush that spread across the stones, he raised his voice above the shouts and screams. At first it wasn't clear what he was doing but gradually people turned to look at him and as the cacophony died down Stevie could hear that he was singing, and badly at that.

'Heaven, I'm in heaven and my heart beats so that I can hardly speak . . .'

The shaky rasp was bizarre enough to earn a few snorts of laughter.

'And I seem to find the happiness I seek, when we're out together dancing cheek to cheek.'

Gradually the baffled faces all turned to him. Stevie's mouth was open. She'd never seen anything like this before and was deeply impressed. There was a moment of silence and then the nervous laughter grew. The will to fight had dissipated and under the scattered laughs a low buzz of conversation started up. The young men of the village drew back among themselves. Taking a peremptory bow, like a boy in a school concert, Harry jumped down from the wall. Mr Takeda, clearly still very shaken, shook Harry's hand, vigorously thanking him.

Phyllis, joined by her posse of ladies, turned away from Stevie. There was a general sense of disappointment in their long-planned moment of civic glory having been so crassly stolen. They had sat on committees for weeks to organise the day and a public brawl had most certainly not featured on their meticulously typed agenda. Stevie nodded towards the bruised and shaken crowd.

'Good thing they've got that first-aid box.'

Phyllis was in no mood for banter. 'You may think you're funny but you're not, you know. You're just bad mannered.'

As the ladies swept on in the direction of the parked cars Stevie heard Sylvia say, 'Harry says she's awfully intelligent.' Only an English woman could imbue the word 'intelligent' with quite so much contempt.

Declan grinned at Stevie before heading towards the remaining pack of angry young men.

'Well, I got my headline. "War Skirmish Breaks out at Charitable Ladies Meeting". It's a winner, don't you think?'

It took Harry a few minutes to find his way to Stevie's side. He winced at the sight of the rapidly darkening bruise on her cheek.

'Are you all right?'

'I'm fine.'

To her horror she could feel the sting of tears behind her eyes. He was short-circuiting her defences. Damn him. She was instantly on the offensive.

'How can you cosy up with the Japanese like that, shaking their hands and all?'

'It just so happens we're old friends. Mr Takeda and I have a shared history.'

'But you've seen what they're doing. It's not waging war, it's demonic and merciless. In Shanghai they cut people up just for looking at them: girls, babies, they don't care. And their favourite weapon? They don't waste time with bullets and guns, oh no, rape is much more effective. It's great for morale and saves ammunition too. They just love it.'

While she spoke Harry looked more closely at the damage to her face.

'Let me look at that. It's pretty nasty.'

She shrugged him off.

'I told you, I'm fine. Look, it's simple, the way I see it, where there's murder and rape there's an enemy, not a friend – however far you go back.'

'I'll take you to a doctor.'

'No. Thank you.'

She glanced at him, catching the depth of concern in his eyes, and softened.

'Nice song, by the way. Do they teach you that at military school?'

'You're coming with me.'

Harry called over to the discreetly hovering Ken Ramsay. 'Be so kind, Sergeant, as to offer your driving services to Mrs Clarke-Russell and the committee members.'

Turning back to Stevie, he put his hand on her elbow and began guiding her towards the parked cars. Most of the associated ladies were already ensconced in their motor cars and the sound of engines igniting and throttles being pulled drowned out the shuffling of the dispersing crowd.

Stevie snorted. 'Is it only in English that you don't understand the word "no"?'

His voice was as firm as his grip. 'I'm taking you back to Hong Kong. You're a danger to the peace of mainland China.'

Stevie's smile lit up. 'Oh, all right, you sweet talker, you, if you insist.' And she let herself be steered to the waiting car, only dragging her feet for show.

They were quiet in the car. Once the doors had been closed and Harry had driven them out of the village, the sudden insulated silence of being inside the car numbed them. The leather of the seat burned through her thin cotton dress. Stevie felt oddly distant from the moment. She watched the wide green fields blur past as if in a dream. The car smelled of oil and something damp as well as the musty memory of *Je Reviens*. It was an island.

Stevie was jolted back when Harry swept the car off the main road to the left.

'Surely it would be better to stay on the road through Tuen Mon.'

'Want to drive?' He was laughing at her.

'Nobody laughs at me. It's not allowed.' This in mock indignation. 'Except when I say something very funny. Then you're obliged to laugh, preferably a lot.'

Harry put his foot on the brake and they came to a standstill. The engine crackled as it cooled down. A young girl with a baby in a sling on her back walked past along the narrow unmade road without displaying too much curiosity. But the baby gazed right at Stevie – its tiny hand curled against its cheek. Stevie and Harry did not look at each other. The silence was strange, the clicking engine, the calls of swallows as they swooped over the vivid green fields.

Harry spoke, his gaze keen on the road ahead. His voice seemed unnaturally loud.

'I just want to say that – my marriage – I –'

But Stevie interrupted.

'Oh please, let's not exchange histories. We're too grown up for that, don't you think?'

Harry looked at her for a long moment. He nodded as if to himself and turned the ignition on. The engine coughed and rose. As he shifted the car into gear he said, 'Whatever happens you're not to write about me.'

'Are you planning on being particularly interesting?'

'Absolutely not.'

Stevie laughed. 'If people don't want to be used in a writer's work they should stay away from writers.'

The car heaved itself into action. Stevie's gaze rested on a lone water buffalo trampling a path across the plains.

The street outside Stevie's apartment building was relatively quiet. The afternoon pause before the onslaught of the evening.

The car hummed as it pulled up by the kerb. They had barely spoken for the rest of the journey. Sitting next to each other on the ferry, the disturbed water of the harbour beyond the railings, their awareness of each other was so sharp that words seemed intrusive. Negotiating the streets of the city, Stevie hadn't questioned where they were going and Harry didn't suggest the doctor again.

Stevie looked up at the limp banner that hung on the building. 'Thirst Stops Here', followed by the red and white Coca-Cola logo. She put her hand on the metal door handle and was surprised by how cool it felt to the touch. A moment of clarity made her look over her shoulder at Harry. His head was bent forward, giving him the earnest look of a man much older.

'You're not going all British and gentlemanly on me, are you?'

She turned back to the door and opened it cleanly, fast. The heat of late afternoon struck her as she stepped out on to the pavement. All her senses heightened, she heard rather than saw that he was following her.

Sunlight streamed into the room. They stood at the door. The gleam of the metal bedstead. Reflections from the water in the glass on the bedside table played over the pale-green walls.

Stevie felt the heat of him.

'This thing that's happening –' She stopped, her words as insubstantial as a mist.

And Harry gently covered her mouth with his hand. Slowly, slowly he pulled her deeper into the room. Dropping his hand from her he closed the door. The click of the lock was soft. She stood, shaking slightly with each beat of her heart. Turning back to her, he walked around her in a circle. Looking at her throat, the back of her neck, her elbows. The street sounds filtered through the window. But only they existed, he and she. In that limpid moment.

At last Harry laid his hand on the small of her back and then they were kissing, licking, biting. Coming home.

Later. Stevie opened her eyes. She was on the floor and Harry was asleep next to her. She pulled herself up very quietly and began to gather her clothes. Her bruised eye throbbed and her arm felt heavy and numb from where she had lain on it. As she bent to pick up one of her stockings, she glanced at him. And she was transfixed. The skin on his face was clear except for where the day's stubble was already pushing through. But instead of making a shadow the hair was so fair that it made him glow. He sighed a long sigh but did not wake. She let the stocking slip out of her hands. Dropping back to the floor, she sat cross-legged by him and holding her fingers a small distance from his face, she traced his features in the air.

Later again. The room was darkening. Harry opened his eyes with a start. Alarmed for a moment he sat up and looked around the room. Stevie was in the wicker armchair, asleep, her head at an awkward angle to her neck. He could see her pulse. She looked more fragile than he could bear. The shadow of guilt caught him unawares. What was he doing? For God's sake, he was not only breaking his marriage vows but he was sleeping with someone he was charged with watching. This was wrong every way one looked at it. Morally and professionally, he was compromised. There was nothing right with it. Except, as he looked at her, everything seemed right. This was a looking-glass world. He quietly pulled himself to standing, his legs reluctant with sleep. As he stretched, his eye was caught by her desk under the window. Stepping towards it, he idly glanced at the books and papers strewn across it. Slightly concealed by a list (biscuits, whisky, lemons, paper, eggs, fix Victor's lead) was an airline ticket. He picked it up – a flight to Shanghai this very weekend.

Her voice made him jump.

'Spying on me?'

Harry didn't turn to her. His eyes were fixed on the thin paper in his hand. His voice was low and unsteady. 'Stay. Don't go. Not now. Please.'

Night had fallen. Muted blue and red light sidled in through the slats of the blind. They had found their way on to the bed. He was deep inside her and had begun to pull away. She drew him back to her and, not reasoning, she whispered, 'Stay.'

Not long after that they lay silently, limbs laced round and over each other. The miracle of fitting had numbed their thoughts for a while longer. Neither wanted to move because the world would rush in and this would be lost. Maybe for ever. For now this was enough. Stevie sighed and Harry felt her hot breath on his shoulder and thought it might actually have burned him.

'Why wouldn't you speak to me, after you came to the office?'

Stevie rolled away from him, unpeeling her sticky limbs from his. He persisted.

'A polite "no, thank you" would've been enough, you know. You didn't have to leave me not knowing anything.'

Stevie levered her legs out of the bed and leaned down, picking up her underwear from the floor. She was afraid she was going to cry so she spoke fast, the words cramping each other, and without looking at him she put one leg and then the other into her knickers.

'I know you'll never leave her and I wouldn't want you to. If you must know, the reason I like you is that you're already married to someone else and can't try to get married to me. But I won't sneak around more than is dignified. Those are the rules.'

She picked up her dress and threw it over her head, struggling a little to get her arms into the right place.

'Rules?' Harry sat up.

'We can have some fun as long as nobody gets hurt and –'

'No.'

This was so vehement that Stevie turned to look at him. The force of her glare made him stutter.

'I mean, yes, we can have fun, of course, but that's not what this is about. I don't think it's going to be so easy to just – look, I'm trying to say.' He faltered, 'Damn.'

Stevie slipped on her shoes. 'It's all right. You don't have to suffer for this. I know you're a gentleman and all but please, spare me the agonies. We both knew what we were doing.'

She was so aware of the flimsiness of her argument that she didn't look back as she reached the door. Relenting for a moment she said, 'You can call me if you like. I can't guarantee I'll talk, though.'

Harry stopped her. 'Where are you going?'

She looked at him guardedly. 'Why, what's it to you?'

'This is your flat.'

Chapter Eight

It was unbelievably hot in the room and it was so crowded it seemed unlikely to her that there were any Europeans at all left in Europe – they must have all been there in that small low-ceilinged nightclub. Considering the onslaught of grim news from England it wouldn't have been surprising if they were. Stevie and Declan sat at a corner table and matched each other shot for shot, shouting over the music. The alcohol burned her throat and made her feel alive.

There was a gap in the swirling, tightly packed crowd. In that split second she saw him for the first time since the day of the first-aid incident – could it really only have been three days? This was the encounter she had been dreading since he had left her bed. Everything was suspended. Harry was at a large table, near the swaying, shuffling dance floor. His hand was on the back of Sylvia's chair, loosely playing with her hair. A gold strand was wrapped around one of his fingers. The gesture was intimate and like a knife through her.

Maybe she gasped because something made Declan follow her gaze. He caught sight of Harry just before the crowd closed round him again. He shook his head – surely this magnificent girl wasn't pining over a great, lanky Brit. But moments later Stevie was on her feet. She walked as close to Harry's table as she could, pointedly swaggering. Harry felt her rather than saw her. He picked up her scent just after she swung past his chair and, alert as any animal, he knew the back of her. Excusing himself, he stood up. Sylvia, equally alert, seemed to take note of the alacrity with which he pushed towards the exit before she turned back to the company.

Outside in the slightly cooler air, Stevie was waiting in the shadows. She saw Harry burst out of the narrow club door into the alley. He looked from right to left and she let the rush of adrenalin fill her at the sight of him. She relished for a moment the urgency with which he looked for her. His need was palpable. She stepped towards him and then her back was pressed hard against the wall, bricks indenting her flesh as they kissed. Each part of their bodies as close to the other as possible. An urge to be one.

Rowdy voices. A group tumbled from the club into the alley. In the half-light they were amorphous. One laugh was momentarily shrill and Harry gave Stevie a look of such yearning that she almost laughed too. The situation was simultaneously distressing and absurd. Then he stepped forward into the core of the group and was subsumed. Stevie, holding still in the deep shadow, watched them stagger along the alley, Harry's head above the others, his arm over Sylvia's shoulders. It was pain that she felt.

The British Army briefing hut was large and solid if lacking in any niceties. Military and fit for purpose. Every uncomfortable fold-up chair was in use, the world's press preferring to sit while at work. Stevie stood insolently against the back wall and listened to Harry whilst remembering the feel of him on her. She had her notebook open in her hand but made very few notes. Jishang was eager for any military information from Hong Kong. His last cable had reminded her in no uncertain terms that it was important to go to all the briefings. She had almost heard his familiar admonishing voice with its disconcerting cut-glass English accent as she read the last line. 'Do not under any circumstances attempt to write about the war preparations.'

She looked at Harry over the sea of heads. Jishang's words echoed in her ears and she felt a blush of confusion. There was guilt towards her unfinished business with Jishang and she promised herself that when she saw him the first thing she would do would be to confirm their status as friends and partners. She did not think he would be much surprised.

But overwhelmingly there was her shameless obsessive desire for Harry, she was helpless in its grip.

And there he was, upright and dapper in his uniform. His voice effortlessly carried the authority invested in it. She could see the tousled back of Declan's head in among the others.

'In conclusion, I'd like to stress that in the unlikely event of an invasion we have every confidence that the island and its territories would hold out long enough for the Chinese Army to mobilise and enter into the engagement alongside the British and Canadian forces. Every confidence.'

A balding man in a double-breasted suit stood up. His tone was harsh.

'Quite right to be confident, Major. I mean it's not as if the Japanese could possibly form an intelligent fighting force capable of threatening ours, is it? And what with the Russians now wading in against them too, well, they're doomed, aren't they.'

Some laughter. But Harry didn't smile.

'We are confident, sir, but it would be a grave mistake to underestimate the enemy threat. One might consider a force able to occupy China to be a formidable one by any standards.'

'Is that why the women and children are being evacuated?'

'We have clearly stated many times that this is a precaution. But one worth taking, I think we all agree.'

'Not a sign of loss of nerve, then?'

'Absolutely not, sir. Hong Kong is as safe as any other part of His Majesty's empire and will be vigorously defended as such should the need arise. Thank you.'

Harry stepped away from the microphone and the buzz of voices gradually rose. The reporters stretched and picked up their dropped pens and closed their notebooks and wondered where to go for lunch. Harry shook a few hands as he made his way to the door. Stevie was waiting.

'Do you have every confidence, personally, Major Field?' she asked as he brushed past her.

'Personally? I think Hong Kong is indefensible. And there's no reason on earth why the Chinese would rush to rescue us.'

'Can I quote you?'

'What do you think?'

He grinned at her and she was overwhelmed by him again before he was reclaimed by the world and swept on by.

Stevie was a whirlwind. She gathered armfuls of strewn clothes, the coloured fabrics slipping as she ran. Opening the closet door, she threw them in, slamming the door shut on the unkempt pile. In the bathroom she stared at her reflection. Her hair was beyond help but her cheeks were flushed and her dark eyes sharp. She turned the tap and patted some cool water on to her face. A happy shiver and a fast brush of her teeth. I'll have to do, she thought, though there were discernible bags under her eyes and the laugh-lines dug deeper than she liked.

Harry meanwhile ignored the ringing telephone and, dropping a file of papers on his desk, rushed out of the office. Ken Ramsay, at his typewriter, chose not to ask where he was going.

When the doorbell rang Stevie sprinted for the door, stopping for a second to shove a pair of knickers under a cushion of the sofa. Victor opened an eye from his corner but knew better than to get in her way. The door wasn't closed behind him before they were scrabbling with each other's clothes, Harry's uniform joining her dress on the floor.

Harry, naked and transfixed, sat on the edge of the bed. Stevie straddled him, her legs tight around his waist. They were very still. She could feel the pumping of his heart and smell the sour sweetness of their lovemaking.

'I love you.'

Stevie seemed not to have heard.

Again. 'I love you.'

She closed her eyes against him. Against the words. He took her face in his hands.

'I love you. And I want to be with you.'

'Well, don't.'

Harry tightened his grip on her waist and lifted her off him. He almost threw her on to the bed. She was still there, tightly guarding her heart, when he left a few minutes later.

Victor glanced up at the sound of the banging door.

Stevie didn't.

Chapter Nine

The meal had been a great success. Lily was glowing with the pride of it. Her family had been surprised when she had suggested she might bring her American room-mate for the day. Lily had been keeping her city life at a remove from her home life. Away from them, it was easy for her to enjoy and embrace her assimilation as a British citizen, wearing her European-style skirts and high-heeled Mary Janes. Even her cheongsams were a little tighter, the side splits a little higher. Her family didn't mind. Lily had a job and was giving them enough to feed everybody including the family next door, so what she chose to keep separate was her prerogative. All in all, the arrival home of Lily and this disappointingly dark American woman was cause for celebration. Lily didn't mention to them that Stevie was Jishang's lover. It didn't seem absolutely necessary and the omission was hardly a crime. It would have embarrassed Mrs Li, her mother, who would have worried about the etiquette. What was the traditional form for welcoming the mistress of a distant and illustrious cousin? It wouldn't have been immediately obvious; much hand-wringing and discussion would have ensued. Lily was shrewd for eighteen and understood where omission was preferable to disclosure. She had come a long way from the farm and took particular pleasure in her beautifully manicured hands. Her nails were long and perfectly maintained, usually bright red or, depending on the occasion, pearly pink. Today they were dark red, like the walls of the house.

The journey to Lily's village took about an hour from Hong Kong island. It might as well have taken a century, judging from the difference in the pace of life. Leaving behind the paved streets, the cars, the neon signs, the advertising hoardings and the twentieth-century speed, Stevie was enthralled by the slowing down. Oxen drew wooden carts along the paths between fields. The sound of a million insects vibrated through the air. Her cotton hat was futile against the strength of the sun and she envied the wide straw hats that cast a shadow over the villagers' entire bodies.

This was rural mainland China. Vast, stubborn and quietly surprising.

The family compound was a whisper to the shout of Madame Kung's country retreat. The dust had won the battle on the open veranda and the single-storey building looked in on itself like a mountain valley. Life was lived in the shade lent by a tortured-looking orchid tree to one side of the courtyard. The table had been drawn right up to the peeling trunk and every chair and box in the house had been put into service. The family were having a big day.

Stevie, however, felt she was being given a rare insight into the everyday life of a traditional village compound. Lily did nothing to disabuse her. She was happy to see her despised backward home through the eyes of a foreign stranger. She relished every word of Stevie's appreciation for the feast they were served. Nothing seemed too small or insignificant to pique Stevie's interest. Lily could no more have understood Stevie's fascination than she could have read a Russian novel in the original – but she did understand that Stevie saw value in this place. And that, for the time being, was enough for her.

The plates were cleared away and jasmine tea was being poured when a young man appeared on the veranda. His loose trousers were stained red from the dust of his journey. Lily saw him first. She raised an arm as if to wave him away. Stevie followed her alarmed gaze. She instantly recognised him as Chen, the young man from the battle of Kun Lung Wai, as she and Declan had taken to calling it, the angry young man with whom Harry had been in conversation.

Lily spoke to him tersely in Cantonese.

'You picked your moment.'

'Nice welcome. A feast and just for me! You shouldn't have.'

The rest of the family seemed almost paralysed with confusion. Stevie, not understanding all the words but alert to the atmosphere, rescued them by standing up and introducing herself. She held out her hand. 'I'm Stevie Steiber, Lily's friend from Hong Kong.'

He approached the table, throwing a sibling glance of triumph in Lily's direction before he shook Stevie's hand. 'Chen. Lily is my sister.'

'I think I saw you before. You were in Kun Lung Wai a few weeks ago.'

Wariness replaced amusement in his eyes.

'No. I don't think so.'

'Yes. I'm sure it was you. There was some trouble. You talked to my – my friend Major Field.'

'No.' Chen smiled again. 'An easy mistake to make. We are all similar to your eyes.' He sat down, his wiry body still coiled. 'As you are to ours.'

Chen picked up a teacup and drained it. 'Are you the American woman who writes for that Shanghai magazine?'

'Why?' Her tone was neutral, guarded by habit, expecting the familiar criticism. What does a foreigner know about Chinese business? What is it to her? Why should she have a voice in the politics of the nation?

Lily, assuming offence, came to the rescue in rapid English. 'Please forgive him, he's a thug. We haven't seen him for months and to be honest we'd prefer it if he never came.'

'No, it's all right. I don't mind the occasional thug.'

Chen leaned towards her, his voice low and level but his delivery gruff with passion.

'You consider yourselves radical but this is just debate and talk. Where are the facts about what's happening with Mao? Why don't you publish them?'

'The magazine is debate. That's its job and its title.'

'You have a duty to tell what's happening. The Communists are being demonised when all we are doing is fighting for better working conditions, for decent hours in return for decent wages, for an end to child labour, a voice in the running of our country. These are basic human rights. You have them in your country, why shouldn't we?'

'The magazine is a forum for discussion not a podium for making speeches.'

Lily, exasperated and ashamed of her brother's rudeness, said, 'You don't need to fight the government, you need to join it.'

Chen snorted. 'Go back to your fashion magazines, little sister.'

'What's wrong with the government, anyway? They freed us from those traditions you're so against, they're all for the new way of thinking and they're all scholars and poets and well-educated people so they should know what's best for us. They're not just a bunch of ignorant peasants and boys like you.'

Chen ignored her and turned back to Stevie. 'You see, while dumb people think like this we have to watch the Kuomintang steal all of China's resources and hide them in banks in America and Switzerland. There's no time for this kind of bourgeois talk. Maybe later. But not now. Now we need people to know what is actually going on.'

'Write it and we'll publish it.'

He turned away in contempt. 'Tell your playboy boyfriend that Shanghai isn't the centre of the universe.'

The insult was clear and it landed. Stevie laughed, an insult in return.

Lily, pink with embarrassment under her stiffly rolled film-star hair, hissed at her brother. 'Leave her alone, Chen.'

Stevie put out her hand. 'It's fine. He's right. The Communists should be heard too, otherwise they'll be marginalised from the mainstream argument.'

Chen nodded and stood up, stretching. 'I need a wash.' And, in the familiar slouch of young men everywhere, he swaggered across the courtyard towards the house, kicking up dust as he went.

Mrs Li followed him and Lily started a torrent of excuses: he's only young, he needs to learn, he's always been undisciplined but really, no manners at all, this Communist thing was getting out of hand . . .

Stevie reassured her that she was not offended and leaned back in her chair. The pale leaves on the tree were almost translucent in the sunshine. She could see their skeletons.

* * *

Two days later Stevie had finished a draft of her first interviews with Madame Kung. She had had enough of the stifling heat in the apartment and decided to take the package to the post office herself. She was sending the pages to Jishang for his comments before she redrafted and then finally she would show them to Madame Kung herself. She enjoyed the bustle and crush of the streets after the solitude of her room and had decided that she'd go straight to the market and buy noodles and pak choi and maybe some water chestnuts on her way home and surprise Lily with a meal. She turned the corner out of the alley into the wider street and there right ahead of her she saw Harry. She ran to catch up with him but in the moment before she reached him, Sylvia stepped out of a shop and took his arm.

Stevie stopped in her tracks. A sudden mist in front of her eyes, such heaviness in her bones. She watched them as they got lost in the crowd, their intimacy burning into her.

Harry threw off the sheet but still the night air lay heavy on his body. His wife was an ocean of linen away from him. He knew she was awake too.

'While I'm in Australia you can decide what you want, Harry.' Her voice was small but clear.

He waited a moment before he answered, the darkness soaking him. 'What do *you* want?'

Another small pause. 'A man who loves me.'

'Yes.' And the weight of it was crushing. 'I'm sorry.'

He could see Sylvia, the young girl of a few years ago, as distinctly as if she were standing at the end of the bed. There was always something unclear about her, smudged somehow around the edges. That was part of her charm, a wispy transparent effect that made him feel that he would never fully understand the shape of her. Pale, small and fair, she was in his mind permanently out of focus and this fragility seemed to him alien and female and quite how it should be.

The romance of their meeting had sealed their fate. He was the new young, promoted officer joining her father's regiment in Hampshire. She was nineteen, recently released from boarding school and discovering her power in a world of men. She was much sought after. There was even the occasional tussle among the men. And this in itself fired Harry's resolve.

He won the day and their wedding photographs were a cliché even as they were taken. He, straight-backed and handsome, his hair slicked so tight to his head he looked like a seal, she delicate in cream lace and a veil the length of the aisle. But even as they ran under the arch of honour what Harry felt most keenly was not passion but victory. As for Sylvia, she did not seem able to dispel a veil of disappointment that her moment of glory was over so fast. Neither had any idea of how to live.

They instantly established separate spheres and crossed the lines only on occasion and with fair warning. The delicacy of intimacy was marked by resignation on her part and damaged by fear on his. Her skin seemed so thin he felt he might tear her.

And now he had.

Chapter Ten

Harry was already frustrated. The transcript of the week's communications between the Japanese occupying forces on the mainland and the collaborating Chinese government in Nanching was not being taken seriously enough by anybody. Even Ken Ramsay was shrugging at it.

It seemed so clear to him that the long-standing policy of the official Kuomintang government, led by Chiang Kai-shek, of fighting the encroaching Communist Red Army, 'first internal pacification, before external resistance', was allowing the Japanese to push further and further into China. Chiang Kai-shek's personal stance that 'the Japanese are a disease of the skin, the Communists a disease of the heart' wasn't working. The Chinese army was ill equipped and under-trained and had been facing one of the most efficient, aggressive and brutal armies in history for the last eight years. The losses had been catastrophic. The Japanese had shown themselves to be merciless in victory. Poison gas, air raids, massacres and rape – they used whatever weapon served them best. They had even resorted to the bizarre but effective tactic of dropping plague-carrying fleas from their planes, causing mass deaths from outbreaks of bubonic plague.

Harry knew only too well from his familiarity with the country that the Japanese would be as stubborn in their pursuit of victory as they were in their pursuit of pleasure and culture. China was effectively split, and weakened by years of both civil and defensive war. The Communists had just renewed their offensive by blowing up a coal mine in the north and there were open conflicts between the Nationalists and the Communists in government territory.

In addition, it seemed equally obvious to Harry that Japanese aggression would only be increased by the proposed boycott on oil sales recently suggested by the Americans. As the war in Europe accelerated, with Britain suffering terrible nightly assaults from the air, the Allies' eyes were turned away from the East. Nobody was paying enough attention.

He turned his anxiety on the stocky figure at the next desk.

'It may be innocuous to you, but has it occurred to you that there might be a reason why I'm the senior officer, Ramsay?' Ken blushed scarlet instantly. Harry knew he was being heavy-handed but pressed on, his general sense of frustration growing. 'Any mention of Hong Kong by the Japanese on the airwaves is relevant, regardless of whether it actually says "we are planning to bomb it until the whities burn".'

The door burst open and Harry wheeled around, blazing. But it was Stevie who got the first words in, propelled by her own fury that had brought her running through town to his door.

'They've arrested Chen. You've arrested Chen. He's just a boy. What the hell's that about?'

The two men looked at each other, dumbfounded. Ken's face could only have been more red if it were actually on fire. His powers of discretion had been severely tested during the weeks of Harry's dalliance with this cavalier American woman with the fierce eyes. But he had no idea what the etiquette was for this situation. The rule book had utterly let him down.

'You're taking children away now, are you? The glorious British Empire scared of a little boy? Call yourselves men? Hah!' This last, an expression of contempt in any language.

Harry mustered every remaining scrap of patience and turned to Ken. 'Excuse me, Sergeant Ramsay.'

He stood up, cold and firm. 'I'll give you two minutes, Miss Steiber.'

It was with enormous relief that Ken realised he was being invited to leave the room.

The minute the door was safely closed behind Ken's broad shoulders, Harry tore into Stevie.

'Don't ever, ever do this again.'

'You stop taking children from their homes at gunpoint and I'll stop complaining.'

'This isn't a game, Stevie.' She could feel the sharpness of him and recognised the sting of fear. 'The world's your playground, I know, but there's serious business in it. Stick to your idealistic debates and let the grown-ups get on with keeping you safe.' Harry walked towards the door. 'I'll see you out.'

Stevie knew she'd overstepped the mark and her courage was receding with every moment.

'No need.'

'Yes, there is.' His hand was on the door handle. 'I want to be absolutely sure you've gone.'

Stevie, glittering with passion, gestured to the huge map of the world pinned to the wall.

'You're entitled to your soldier's high ground, Harry, and I know you think I'm some kind of dilettante fool and you can dismiss me all you like, but what do you know about how people live? It's all papers and theories and reports for you, but have you seen the men and women of mainland China struggling to keep their families alive against the odds? Have you? I have, and it's a depressing sight. But it's also a real sight. People, Harry, people. In the end that's who it's about and if you don't respect that and if you just fling your force around to pick on young boys just because you can –' she paused '– you'll lose.'

Harry, loving her more in this moment than ever before, was determined not to show it. 'All right, you're travelled and open-minded and the lucky people who get the benefit of your wit and wisdom are quite right to worship you. This isn't a popularity contest, it's a war. Now, if you don't mind I've got a territory to help protect.' He turned the door handle.

Stevie stood her ground. 'What about Chen?'

'As if you don't know. He's part of a Communist destabilising cell, that's why he was arrested. He's busy spending his time spreading the word to the good people of Hong Kong that supporting Britain is supporting their own oppression.'

Stevie reeled for a moment. The article Chen had written for *Direct Debate* had been didactic and somewhat adolescent but he hadn't expressed anything too inflammatory and she and Jishang had both agreed that it was valuable to have a contribution from a fresh voice. His admiration for the leaders of the so-called war of liberation was clear but he hadn't expressed any antipathy to the British. She squared her shoulders.

'Yeah? Well, good for him.'

Harry closed the door again. He tried to keep his voice calm but didn't do a very good job of it. 'You won't think that when those real people of yours, your Chinese neighbours, hold a knife to your throat in the mistaken belief that the Japanese will be kinder masters and give them their freedom.'

'Maybe they're right. You should question some of your own loyalties. Do you know what the British did to the Indians in the revolution?'

'Mutiny.'

'Whatever. They made them lick up the blood on the roads.'

He took a step towards her. Incensed. 'You're only pretending to be so stupid, aren't you? You know, all that travel, what's it done for you? I'll tell you what – it's been an excuse for you not to make a personal commitment to anything. But neutrality is a luxury you may not always be able to afford.' He turned away from her. 'Congratulations, you've found a way to escape from real life and avoid loyalty to anything.'

His words sliced into her. Somewhere deep down she knew he was right.

Harry glanced back over his shoulder as he opened the door wide. 'I can't do anything to get the boy out of jail, but I'll make sure he's all right.'

Stevie held on to the pain inside as she walked past him. 'Pompous suits you.'

She didn't look back as she walked along the corridor but she knew he was watching.

They both knew it hadn't been about the state of the nation.

The day had started badly. The boat trip was usually a great pleasure. Madame Kung's boat was a plaything. A yacht with a polished wooden hull and more luxurious white canvas chairs than the Metropolitan Hotel. Normally, Stevie was delighted when the entourage packed up and drove down the Peak to the waterfront. This time she had felt sick at the very sight of the waves – green and sparkling like tiny mountain ranges. By the time they were settled on the cushions and had cast off into the harbour Stevie was the same colour as the water, but most definitely not as sparkling. She was unusually quiet as Madame Kung and her coterie of lucky ladies chattered under the swaying awning.

They had disembarked on the mainland and made their way to the estate and still Stevie had barely joined the conversation, let alone entertained Madame Kung as she was supposed to. She was, frankly, being a bit of a bore. They were assembled in the long, low-ceilinged drawing room that ran the length of the innermost courtyard. Outside, the yard was bleached by the fierce sun. Inside, an elderly woman was on her knees in front of Madame Kung, begging for her help. Her voice was shrill with despair. She didn't raise her eyes to Madame Kung's as her plea came to an end. The empress raised her languid hand and the woman shuffled forward, still on her knees, to kiss it. She thanked her over and over and pulling herself awkwardly to her feet, she backed out of the room, her eyes still on the floor.

Madame Kung turned to Stevie, who sat with the other women on small formal chairs along the edge of the room. The high collar of her elegant black lace dress framed her impassive face and the huge pearls in her ears were translucent in the afternoon light. Her words were incongruous, from another age.

'Her son is to be executed tomorrow. I can do nothing for her.'

Stevie had been concentrating on her fight against the haze in her brain.

'Executed – what for?'

'He's an opium addict. It's hopeless.' Stevie instantly had a flash of the comforting black stuff and felt a pang of desire. Madame Kung looked keenly at her and took in her untended hair, her unmade-up face. Worst of all, the girl didn't seem to be wearing any lipstick. She raised a thinly arched eyebrow. 'You must smarten up. Keep polished. Just because other people are getting into this ridiculous war panic you must not let yourself go.' She stood up and there was much scraping of chair legs on wooden floorboards as the other ladies followed suit. Beckoning to Stevie to catch up, Madame Kung sailed towards the door. 'I hear you have a new admirer.'

Stevie was startled into a stutter 'I don't know what – I mean, no. Who says so?'

Madame Kung's small mouth was close to her ear. 'Be careful, that's all. Where there's talk there's trouble.' She set off again, raising her voice, her French-heeled slippers clicking as she walked.

'My husband wants me to leave Hong Kong, he says it's too dangerous here.'

Everybody present understood the warning. Things must be getting very bad.

'Where will you go?'

'Who knows – back to America, maybe.' She reached the door and it swung open, pulled by the ever-vigilant but amazingly invisible servants behind it. Madame Kung's voice lowered for another intimacy. 'If you ever need me, Wu Jishang will know where I am.' Her butterfly hand hovered for a brief moment on Stevie's wrist. 'You know, you could really be quite pretty if you made the effort.'

Stevie was suddenly overcome with dizziness. She tried to speak but her legs buckled under her and she fell to the floor. All was nausea and darkness.

She saw the intricate pattern and felt the fabric of the day bed. The light hurt her eyes and the taste in her mouth was bitter. But even as she struggled out of the haze she knew this was no hangover. For a blissful moment she was home. It was her mother's sturdy figure that stood stiffly by the window. The word 'Mother' may even have escaped her lips. Relief and surrender held her captive and she never wanted to move again. It was shattering when she heard Madame Kung clear her throat to deal with this altogether nasty business and not her mother after all.

'Some delicacy will be necessary.' Stevie closed her eyes against the words. 'I suppose the father must be informed. It is usually advisable.' She paused. Stevie was acutely aware of the pulse in her neck. 'You'll have to go away for a while. You won't be judged too harshly, one understands that accidents happen. Unfortunate, of course, but it's not the end of the world. You know, I'll never forget the birth of my first child.' A small laugh. 'I thought I was going to die.'

Stevie was finally, terrifyingly, out of her depth.

Part Two

Chapter Eleven

As August came to an end and the sweltering summer enveloped everything, Stevie found herself mercifully able to forget the crisis that was upon her. The magnitude of it allowed her a kind of paralysis and whole hours could go by without her thinking about it. Then something, a veil of nausea or a child's cry in the night, would jolt her into herself and she would feel heavy with dread. The fact that Harry was away on some kind of mainland reconnaissance trip (she gleaned enough to guess he was liaising with both Chinese factions in Free China beyond the New Territories) was a huge relief and for the first time since he had taken root in her she barely noticed the days passing. His absence was a respite from reality.

Madame Kung's words echoed in her head only to be joined by others.

Lily worked it out almost straight away but said nothing. She might have been young but her watchful, wily admiration made her zealously alert to Stevie's moods. She noticed how Stevie seemed to be finding it harder to get out of bed in the morning. She saw how she didn't leave the typewriter for lunch and that when she did eat, it was only plain rice and the occasional bowl of soup. But the biggest clue was that Stevie had somehow turned in on herself. She was quiet. She was quiet when Victor peed on her silk skirt. She was quiet when the war news got louder. She was quiet when Harry told her he was going to the mainland and might be gone for weeks. And most tellingly she was even quiet when, in a brief telephone call, Jishang told her that he'd taken it upon himself to send the as yet unfinished manuscript of her book to a selection of American publishers.

Stevie struggled with the physical changes in her body. Every time the clammy film of nausea claimed her she resented it. Every ache in her swollen breasts, each light-headed episode gave more fuel to her sense of betrayal. It was her own body that was betraying her. It was engaged on an adventure that didn't concern her and which bypassed her own needs without consultation. She felt utterly alienated from it. Occasionally, she looked at herself in the distorting mirror that leaned against the bedroom wall. It was as if she was assessing someone else's body. Her detachment served her well.

One day, not long after the conversation with Madame Kung, she was shifting the metal filing cabinet across the living room. It was preventing her from opening the window fully and had been irritating her all morning. She had been trying to read the corrected proofs that Jishang had sent back. It was her own article on the British government's unfair and unreasonably jumpy treatment of the Chinese population of Hong Kong with particular reference to the arrest of Chen, as she put it, 'a possibly misguided but essentially innocent seventeen-year-old boy accused of being a Communist agitator and held, pending a trial in the notorious Stanley prison'. She had read the same sentence about fifteen times, unable to concentrate, and had finally thrown the pages down in frustration.

Putting her back into moving the filing cabinet instead, she was in the process of inching it out of the way when Lily rushed in, dropping her shopping basket as she came. 'What are you doing? Are you crazy? You could lose the baby.'

As the words left her mouth Lily tried to grab them back. It was too late. They stared at each other over the dented grey cabinet, both equally stunned by the acknowledgement.

Stevie stepped backwards. 'How did you know?'

'I just knew.'

'When? When did you realise?'

'I don't know. A few weeks ago.'

'Have you told anyone?'

Lily was indignant. 'Of course not. Have you?'

Stevie sighed a long sigh and sat down. 'No.'

'Nobody?'

'Nobody.'

Lily went back to the door and picked up the shopping basket. 'I suppose you'll have to sooner or later.'

'You're not shocked?'

'No. It's your business.' She shrugged. 'And his.'

Stevie looked at the floor. There were track marks dug into the wood by the filing cabinet. Lily's voice sang, glad to talk about it at last.

'My mother had eight of us and my sister had her first last year, a little girl. She called her Lily after me, isn't that sweet? I was there with her, it was very exciting. The doctor said he'd never pull her through, but it wasn't so bad really.' Lily laid the brown-paper packets of food on to the table one by one. 'I do remember her saying to the nurse "Kill me, kill me I want to die . . ." '

Stevie almost laughed as she put her head in her hands.

As the days passed Stevie was alternately either muted and listless or bursting with manic energy. The only event that penetrated her daze was Lily's despair at discovering that she wasn't in fact British.

When the government had announced on the radio that all British women and children were obliged to register for the evacuation, Lily had been ferocious in her denouncement of this measure. Why should she leave her home town when the war wasn't even upon them? Since the British government had made it quite clear Hong Kong was in no real danger, surely it was unnecessary? But in the end, being an upstanding citizen, she had done as instructed.

When she came home from the government building it was the first time Stevie had seen Lily cry. Apparently, she had been British enough to be a taxpayer but she wasn't British enough to be evacuated. This was exactly the kind of political hypocrisy that would normally have roused Stevie into a storming rage but there was no energy to spare. Lily's upset did penetrate a little, though. She sat her down at the dining table and made her tea, watching while she sipped it between sobs.

Later she held her hand as another bout of furious crying took hold of her. She stroked her damp hair, the strands falling like wild brushstrokes over Lily's temples, and ran a silk scarf under the cold tap before tying it round her head.

When she had recovered enough to talk, Lily looked at Stevie, very grave in her unlikely silk turban.

'From now on my name is Lei-Ling.'

Stevie stroked her hand again.

'It's very pretty,' she said.

'It's the name my mother gave me. It means I will make a big noise in the world.'

'I don't doubt it for a minute. Your mother is a very wise woman.'

Lily nodded, then tilted her chin defiantly even higher and took another sip of the cold tea.

There was a wild wind and she was neck-deep in the turbulent water. She fought for breath. Her eyes sprang open. A glass of water had spilled from the side table. It dripped on to her naked arm. Harry was sprawled asleep beside her. She got up and made her way to the window. It had thick iron bars on it. Panicking, she pulled on them, she had to get out. There was the unearthly sound of screaming.

Stevie sat bolt upright, shaking with fear. Daylight streamed into the room through the part-open window, on which there were no iron bars. Victor was leaping up and down at the end of the bed, in which there was no Harry. She must have fallen asleep fully clothed. Her hands rested on the neat swell of her stomach. How the hell could this be happening to her?

After waking from the dream she ran into Lily's room and insisted that they go immediately to the market. When Lily wondered what it was they were going for, Stevie explained that she absolutely must have some lychees as a matter of great urgency. Lily didn't bother to argue.

The market was a screaming collision of languages and conflicting selling techniques, both Chinese and Western, and the jumble of overloaded wicker stalls didn't acknowledge the shadow of an invasion. A man squatted behind his rickety stall, which displayed a precariously piled abundance of sweets in jars. Next to him there was a hoarding which exhorted the passer-by to 'Drink Johnnie Walker Red Label Whisky'. A handwritten poster outside a narrow shop proudly declared a

'Fresh Shipment of American Honeydew Melons and Manila Watermelons'. Hanging from the awning of another shop were twisted ribbons of dried meat in layer upon layer. Stevie and Lily passed the shoemaker, the stamp-maker and the tea stall with its ornately decorated urn. They were accosted by shrill shouts for their custom, which they ignored.

They were in Li-Yuen alley, walking on the shady side, when Stevie noticed that something had shifted in the air, as if an invisible mist had unfurled. The market was still crowded and busy but the atmosphere was muted. As they reached the end of the alley they passed a woman she recognised, the wife of a British embassy man, and the extraordinary thing was that she was crying. In public. Right there on the street. Her two small children clung to her legs. There were suitcases by their side, a battlement. The world swirled past them, eddying, but they stood firm. The evacuation became a sharp reality and with a jolt Stevie felt the shadow of the war fall and darken the street.

Lily tugged at Stevie's sleeve, urging her on. Stevie glanced back at the evacuees.

'Bet you're happy not to be British now.'

'You may laugh but it's confusing. I've always thought of myself as British.'

'Take my advice – thank the good Lord for this stroke of luck and get on with your shiny new Chinese life.'

Lily neatly sidestepped a pile of sand being shovelled into sandbags by a team of sunburned, bare-chested Chinese men, and drew Stevie on into the next market alley and towards the fruit stalls. Stevie caught sight of an opium pipe set out on a stall and her gaze rested longingly on it. She felt the frightening and sudden prick of desire. She tore her eyes away from the pipe and a now familiar wave of clammy nausea rose in her.

She stopped walking and held herself still, concentrating on not actually throwing up. Lily put her hand gently on Stevie's arm, frowning with concern.

'When does he get back?'

Stevie shrugged. She didn't know.

'Are you going to tell him?'

Stevie turned away from her, towards the stall where they were standing. She picked up a small jade figure, not really seeing it. She was fighting her own tears. This was ridiculous. She was a grown woman and there had been quite enough crying already for one day. But the mention of him, unexpected, had ambushed her. She shook her head.

'I can't. How can I? I don't even know what I'm going to do about it.'

The jade was cool and smooth in her hand. Lily took it out of her hand and scratched at it absent-mindedly, leaving a thin scar of even paler green across it.

'Do you know who that is? Kuan Ti. He's the god of literature and warfare.'

The stallholder shrieked indignantly and gestured to Lily to put the god down. Stevie felt the wave of nausea recede. She raised her eyebrows, examining the figure closer, seeing it now.

'Really?'

'Yes. And pawnshops.' Lily passed the pale-green ornament back to her. 'It's not jade, though. Soapstone.'

Stevie laughed and as she did so a voice cut through the hubbub of the market like a machete. It came from right behind her.

'That's very pretty.'

Stevie knew who it was before she turned round. The pale-blue eyes were too close to escape and gave nothing away. Stevie stiffened in a combination of guilt and fear. Sylvia went on without missing a beat.

'Your dress is rather lovely too. European, it must be?' Smart in her little cream suit, Sylvia gestured to the immaculate skirt. 'Local tailor, I'm afraid,' she said self-deprecatingly.

Stevie could feel Lily's disapproving frown and she took a step away as if to excuse herself, but Sylvia was still talking.

'I'm looking for a memento to take to Melbourne with me. Something small.'

Stevie's voice seemed unnaturally bright.

'Yes, I heard you were leaving,' she said.

A tight smile. 'I'm sure you did.'

'It must be very difficult for you. Going away.'

'Not really. To be honest I haven't been well since my marriage. The air here doesn't suit me. The humidity.'

'I'm sorry.'

'It's not your fault.' She swivelled away, hesitated and turned back to face Stevie again. She was so close Stevie could feel the slightly sweet warmth of her breath on her face.

'Look after him, Miss Steiber.'

She stepped neatly away, melting into the crowd of jostling shoppers. Stevie couldn't bear the ferocity of Lily's glare. She felt immensely alert and her bones ached. Chastened, she put the small god back on to the stall.

Chapter Twelve

September 1940

He came back unannounced. Stevie only knew he was there when she woke up, her heart sparked with adrenalin, a noise having penetrated her dreams. He was standing, already naked, in a shaft of neon-tinged moonlight, and she had the briefest feeling that he was a visitor from another time, another place. She called out his name and he came to her. Kneeling by the bed he took her hand and kissed it, holding it as if he'd never seen it before. Feeling her fingers one by one, each one a revelation. Everything else was darkness but his touch was a fine wakening. She pulled him on to the bed. They lay for a moment, their two bodies still, held at full length, skin to skin.

The sound of the doorbell finally stung Stevie awake. As she opened her eyes and saw Harry flung wide across the bed on his stomach next to her, she assumed it was another of those vivid dreams. Singularly vivid in fact, since she thought she could actually feel the soft skin of his forearm. The bell was ringing again but she basked for another moment in the idea of him being there. He stirred. He really was there. She remembered the night. Her hands flew to her slightly rounded belly. Still the bell rang.

Pulling her faded cotton dressing gown from the floor, she wrapped it tight around her. As she got near to the front door she could hear Declan's voice calling from the other side.

'Coffee. I need coffee.'

His tall, bulky body had been leaning against the door so, as she opened it, he almost fell on to her. He obviously hadn't slept.

'Just don't talk too loudly and be very very nice to me and I'll be all right.'

She walked into the living room and he followed, his loping walk exaggerated by the lack of sleep. Victor looked up from his corner and in one or two leaps was hanging from the central light fitting. He swung there, keeping a wary eye on Declan. Stevie noticed that Lily had left the teapot on the table. She checked to see if it was still warm. Her voice was creaky with sleep.

'You can't stay long, I'm busy.'

Declan stretched his long body out on the chaise, making himself comfortable.

'Maybe if I swung from the chandelier you'd be more pleased to see me.'

Stevie poured the lukewarm tea into Lily's already used cup.

'Don't count on it.' She handed the cup to Declan. 'So, what's up?'

'I've been thinking for days and I've got something to say so don't stop me. Sit down.'

Stevie sat on the edge of the table. Declan always cheered her up. He was funny, unpredictable and earnest in equal measure. He had a huge capacity for partying but somehow never lost sight of his ambition for a moment. He was, she thought, alert even when semi-conscious from over-indulgence. Best of all he was never boring. She waited, and he didn't disappoint.

'Harry is clearly completely immoral and not good enough for you. So here's what I think. You should marry me.'

Stevie opened her mouth to laugh but Declan swung himself forward. He held his hand up to stop her, and leaning towards her and holding her gaze with absolute sincerity, he went on.

'I've thought it through. You need somebody who's free to love you, i.e. not married, and I need somebody to take care of me and my work, i.e. you. Perfect match, you see? And I don't mind a bit that you're older. I quite like it actually.'

Stevie sighed. 'Oh, Declan.'

'Is that a "yes"?'

'Is it?' Harry's voice came from the bedroom door behind them. They both turned to see him standing there. He looked from one to the other. His voice was polite. 'Well, is it?'

Stevie turned back to Declan.

'I can't just look after your work. What about mine? And that nice girlfriend of yours, what would she think?'

Crushed, Declan mustered his courage.

'Damn. You're turning me down. I can't believe it. I had it all worked out.' He shook his head, recovering himself. Then he stood up, brushed his trousers down, pointlessly, as they were beyond repair, and threw his shoulders back. 'Right.' He gave a mock salute to Harry. 'I'm off to get myself a uniform, maybe that'll do the trick.' Letting his shoulders sag into their usual slight stoop, he turned to Stevie. 'Can I still call for you tonight? The hacks meeting needs you.'

Stevie smiled, she couldn't help it. 'Sure.'

'Awful coffee, by the way. You need a new supplier.'

As the door closed behind Declan, Harry's casual tone, as usual, belied his feelings.

'Well, that's good. I'm glad you're not going to marry him.'

Stevie looked at the floor.

He continued, his voice lower. 'It means you can marry me. Before she left, I asked Sylvia to give me a divorce.'

Stevie shivered. Now what? She walked to the window. Outside, the ideograph banner fluttered. A bird swooped along the street and away.

'That's meant to be a good thing, by the way.' His voice was nervous now.

In return Stevie could hear herself, brittle with false brightness. 'I'm not going to marry you. You're not my type.'

'What are you talking about? You think you're my type?'

'You're a soldier.'

Harry took a step towards her. 'Not for ever. I'm going to be a charismatic university professor whose students are all the more in love with him because of how besotted he is with his wife.'

Stevie turned back into the room. 'I can't marry you. I'm married already.'

Harry was shocked into silence. He blinked a few times. This was the first he'd heard of it. Finally he shrugged.

'So, get a divorce.' Stevie felt the nausea rise. Harry went on, as casually as he could. 'By the way, is it anyone I know?'

Stevie sat down. The chaise was still warm from Declan's prone body. She took a moment to compose herself.

'Jishang. We got married last year in Shanghai to keep the Japanese from shutting down *Direct Debate.* They were closing all the printing presses owned by Chinese people. By being married to a foreigner Jishang could continue to run the magazine. And anyway I don't believe in marriage and all that stupid pointless public anointing, so it made sense to do it. Pragmatic. Public. And his real wife didn't mind. She knew it was for legal reasons only. I don't think it even threatened her once. She's always been perfectly charming to me.'

Sensing his eyes on her she glanced at him. 'Exactly what type am I, anyway?'

'You're the exasperating, drug-taking, sharp-tongued, difficult type who thinks love will limit her freedom.'

Stevie spoke more passionately than she intended. Protesting too much. 'Love *is* limiting. If I loved you I'd have to stay with you through thick and thin and feel guilty if I ever liked anyone else and be nice to you all the time. Or not. Which would be worse.'

There was a silence. Harry shook his head. 'If you push people away often enough, they go.'

Stevie looked at him, long and searching. Then she stood up, walked over to him, took his hand and put it on her belly.

'This is why I can't marry you, if you must know. It would be just too much of a cliché apart from anything else.'

Harry steadied himself as he began to understand.

She spoke fast, the words had been waiting to be spoken for weeks. 'I haven't decided what to do about it yet but don't think I'm going to be all noble and deny myself the baby just because it would be proper and would avoid the scandal and it might destroy your army career.'

Harry's voice cracked, his hand still on her. 'My God, Stevie –'

Her voice was calm and gentle. 'It's all right. Don't panic. Whatever happens I won't make any demands on you.'

Harry, equally gentle, covered her mouth with his hand. He was shaken but clear. Happiness focussed him utterly. It seemed to him that they shone with it, the two of them standing there. 'Shut up. Shut up, you impossible bloody person. Of course you don't have to marry me if you don't want to. But I want this baby.'

Stevie had no words as the tears came.

'We were made for each other, you for me, I for you. And I don't care about anything else. We can do this however you like, married, not married, living on different bloody continents but you can't stop me loving you.'

He dropped his hand, which was wet with her tears. She saw his eyes, wide with amazement, and something collapsed inside her. A sea wall of defence wearing out under the onslaught of the ocean.

Chapter Thirteen

January 1941

The jail was on the far side of the island. They had been made to wait outside the gates and an hour had passed. Though it was fairly cool when they first arrived at seven, and despite the fact that it was midwinter, the morning was getting more oppressive by the minute. Stevie had found a mound of gravel waiting to be spread on the perimeter path of the compound and was perched on it in the shade of the wall. The weight of her belly was now a burden.

Lily was too agitated to sit. She paced the minutes in a neat circle, never too far from the gate itself. A few military vehicles had come and gone. The soldiers who got out or in were focussed and, unusually, not distracted by the sight of the two women. There was a sense of controlled urgency.

When the gate finally opened and Lily saw him she cried his name out loud. Stevie drew herself to her feet while Lily threw herself on her brother with tears of relief and exclamations of happiness. Chen was even thinner than before, his adolescent awkwardness exaggerated by the scrappy state of his hair and his clothes. Where before he had the standard veneer of youthful rebellion, Stevie could see when he turned to look at her a new set of conviction in his eyes. For a moment the sharpness chilled her.

'You have to thank Stevie. She wrote about you and spoke to people. It's because of her you're out.' Lily pulled Chen towards Stevie. He held out his hand.

'Thank you. We appreciate your support.' His tone didn't say thank you, his tone said I don't need you or anyone else. She shook his hand.

'I did nothing. Really.'

'Well, thank you for nothing then.' A small smile.

'All I can do is write about what's happening. That's all.'

The gate opened again. Sergeant Ken Ramsay hesitated before taking a tentative step towards the huddle of figures. Frankly, he was nervous of Stevie at the best of times. He cleared his throat and they turned towards him. His eyes were still adjusting to the glare of the light.

'Look, Miss Steiber, sorry to bother you but there's a couple of things –' He came to a stop, at a loss as to how to explain.

'Yes?' She always seemed awfully nice but Ken wasn't equipped to interpret her smile and he felt quite out of his depth already. He literally got on to his back foot.

'No. It doesn't matter. No hurry or anything. Another time maybe.'

Lily, one arm still around her brother, smiled her pretty, languid smile at Ken. He blushed instantly.

'It's all right, Sergeant, now's as good a time as any.' Stevie turned to Lily. 'Why don't you make a start. If a bus comes, take it and I'll see you back there.'

'Are you sure?'

'Yes, Lily, I'm sure. It may surprise you but I can still catch a bus on my own, you know, and you need time with your brother.'

'All right. Thanks.' She lowered her voice. 'And it's Lie-Ling.'

'Yes, sorry.'

Lily, her arm still on her brother's shoulder, walked away. Ken's gaze followed her. His appreciation of her neat backside was interrupted by Stevie.

'You've been sent to warn me off.'

Wrong-footed again, Ken stammered. 'Yes. How did you know?' The surprise in his voice almost made her laugh.

'I've been expecting a quiet word in my ear. I knew this would happen. Ever since we decided to keep the baby. Well, you've done the nasty job and you can go back and write a little report saying that Miss Steiber was pleasant but non-cooperative. Her exact words were that she would appreciate it if the British government would stay out of her private business and that she has no intention of causing Major Field any public embarrassment.' She picked up her handbag, dusty with gravel. 'There, it wasn't so bad after all, was it?'

Ken coughed. 'I'm sorry but that's not what – I needed a word about something else, actually.'

Stevie was taken by surprise. 'Oh, yes?'

'You're a known contact of a certain Wu Jishang.'

Stevie frowned, she was much less secure on this territory. 'Of course I am, that's no secret, you know.'

Ken dropped his voice to a professionally discreet whisper. 'The thing is, we know he came to Hong Kong to raise money and buy arms for the Communists.' He hesitated. 'Look, I'm to advise you to be more careful. You know how hysterical the entire Colony is at the moment. Nobody really buys our reassurances and anyway the population is much more afraid of the commies than they are of the Japs.' Another pause. 'Just be careful, that's all.'

Stevie was struggling – she knew that Jishang had interests and sympathies, of course, despite the fact that their work was all about maintaining an objective voice in the swirling vortex of aggressive political factions – but she had no inkling that he was perceived to be an actual supplier to the Red Army. If that was true, well, she was having difficulty deciding what it would mean. She herself had a natural leaning towards the liberating Chinese and a natural antipathy to the entrenched Nationalists who had turned their backs on the vicious Japanese agression. The Japanese, the Napoleons of the Far East. Jealous for centuries of China, their huge neighbour and cousin who seemed to have everything: culture, language, riches, historical precedence. They had set their sights on conquering her and having seized her relatively by surprise, they had taken advantage of the heavy-lidded assumption of the Chinese that nothing could overwhelm them, let alone the tiny, troublesome island of Japan. Arrogant China may have been, but nothing could validate the degree of cruelty that Japan was visiting on her. Stevie had seen the crippled, the mutilated, the broken victims of their warmongering. Somebody had to fight back and frankly she didn't care who it was. Jishang an active Communist? It seemed unlikely but she knew better than to second-guess him.

Smiling blandly, she gave nothing away. 'I see. Thank you for the warning.'

Ken, hugely relieved that his duty was done, nodded. He turned to leave.

'Does Harry know?' Her voice was quiet and she seemed suddenly vulnerable. Ken nodded again.

'I see.' A pause. 'Is he in terrible trouble – because of this?' She gestured to the swell in her dark red dress.

He shook his head. 'Don't worry, everyone knows we couldn't do without him.'

'Thank you.'

Her hand rested for a moment on his sleeve, then she turned and set off, incongruous in her pregnancy, away from the unhappy military man and his unhappy military duty.

She inhaled the salty air and dug her fingers into the warm sand. From where she lay the leaves of the palm trees looked like propellors and she smiled at the surreal thought of them taking off into the unusually cloudless sky.

'What's so funny?'

She turned her head and squinted up at Harry's silhouette. He had taken his shirt off, his trousers hung dangerously low on his hips and were rolled up almost as far as his knees. He looked like one of those henpecked men on the saucy seaside postcards that they sold in the stationers' shop to homesick Brits.

'Why are Englishmen so keen to see themselves as fools?'

'I don't know that we are.' He sat down next to her and without thinking, his hand came to rest on her belly. He called over to Takeda, who sat on a fold-up canvas chair under the trees a little distance away. 'What do you think? Englishmen – are we fools?'

'Not all of you.'

Harry's laugh warmed her as much as the sun but still Stevie was not entirely at ease in Takeda's company. She was immensely proprietorial of Harry and their increasingly rare days together. He was working harder than ever and she told herself it was the intrusion of another person, no matter who, that she resented. In general, Stevie was relishing their peculiar isolation, being in the city but somehow not of it. Their social exile was not a painful thing but she was loath to admit that occasionally it was hard work being an outcast. When Harry had proposed that they invite Takeda on their outing to the beach she could hardly say no. Takeda had no family in Hong Kong and Harry had made it clear that their friendship was more than just professional. There was nothing in particular about him she disliked. He had been extremely kind to her despite the circumstances and was, in fact, one of the very few people that she and Harry could safely socialise with.

'At least you English can laugh at yourselves. I think that disqualifies you from being genuine fools.' Stevie's words were delivered lighty but there was sting in them and the two men were both adept enough to feel it.

'It's true,' said Takeda, from his seat in the shade. 'We Japanese take ourselves far too seriously. It's a flaw.'

'Maybe you merit being taken seriously,' said Harry.

'At all times? I don't think so.' Takeda snorted with laughter. 'You made a good job of puncturing the self-importance of old Morioka-san.'

'Maybe. But it didn't do me any favours in the long run.' Harry turned to Stevie to explain. 'He was our riding instructor. He got a little more than he reckoned on when he wanted me to change my seat.'

'The horse took a chunk out of his hair.'

'It was nothing to do with me, old chap.'

Stevie particularly hated it when the two of them reminisced about their time in Japan before the war. She felt excluded and simply could not relate to Harry's admiration for Takeda's compatriots.

She pulled herself up to sit. It really was too hot to lie out for long but oh, the glory of the sand and the sea. Here on the beach she felt very far from the anxieties of the city and this was a rare and welcome respite.

Takeda was still laughing, puffing out his cheeks in glee. 'I blame the horse – must have been European. It clearly had no sense of communal duty. Far too individualistic.'

'Yes.' Harry's hand lifted from her belly and brushed through his hair. Grains of sand fell in a small storm. 'A Japanese horse would have felt too much shame to disrespect a senior officer in such a way.'

Stevie yawned. 'Pass me the water, would you?'

Harry delved into the canvas rucksack they had brought with them and pulled out the thermos flask. He shook it. 'Ice has all melted.' He nodded his head in the direction of the small restaurant further up the beach. 'Shall we?'

Stevie held out her hand and he helped her on to her feet. Takeda stood too and folded his little chair. Soon the three of them, an unlikely trio, were making their way along the edge of the sand. The rangy Englishman, a rucksack over one shoulder and his sandals slung over the other, reining in his long strides so as to walk shoulder to shoulder with the large-bellied, short-haired woman, also barefoot. Trailing behind them the over-heated, round Japanese man struggling to keep hold of his folded chair. Stevie imagined them as a comic sight, one of those post-cards again, but she held back from commenting on it. She was too content just watching Harry's and her feet making tracks in the damp dark rim of sand.

Chen turned his intelligent gaze to the perfectly rendered hem of the jacket he was holding.

'It's amazing how they do this. Look, perfect. And the light in here is terrible.'

Harry leaned towards the tweed and nodded. 'Marvellous, yes.' He looked up at Chen. 'Isn't this rather a bourgeois concern?'

Chen laughed, showing his small, tidy teeth. 'You could say that politics and vanity are different sides of the same thing.'

'That may very well be so but don't let that great leader of yours hear you.'

'Mao is not as hardline as you might think.' Chen folded the scratchy tweed over his arm and lowered his voice. 'But I won't tell him if you don't.'

Harry held up both of his hands as reassurance as he said, 'That jacket will keep you warm in the mountains. If, that is, you were ever planning to be in the mountains.'

Chen threw him a glance and spoke deliberately. 'Yes, you're right. I like to be prepared for any eventuality and a walk in the mountains is possible.'

Harry, stooping slightly in the low-ceilinged tailor's shop, patted Chen on the back as he turned to go. 'Jolly good. I hope you have a good trip.' He stepped out into the bright light of the day, leaving Chen to settle up with the sharp-eared and -eyed tailor.

When, a few minutes later, Chen left the small shop carrying his brown paper wrapped parcel under his arm he was not alone. Harry stayed at a discreet distance behind him, unseen, all the way.

In truth Chen's release from prison had not only been due to Stevie's efforts. As usual where Harry was concerned there was more to it than met the eye and it served him much better for Chen to be active than for him to languish behind bars. Their rendezvous in the tailor's shop was just one of what had become regular meetings. However, Harry thought it might be more revealing to keep a more surreptitious eye on him as well.

Outside a lushly perfumed barber's shop, Chen met up with Ping Wei, a brush-haired, smiling boy. The two young men chatted easily; teasing, pushing and shoving each other all the way through Central. On the edge of town they parted ways and Harry, lurking incongruously in the doorway of a lingerie shop, made a snap decision to follow Ping Wei instead of Chen. Almost immediately he regretted it as the boy loped along mile after mile, deeper and deeper into the countryside. Harry flagged slightly when he realised that this was not going to be a short stroll. In fact, it was further than he had ever been into the almost unpopulated hinterland. They walked beyond the village of Tai Long, where Hakka fishermen honed their traditional and ancient skills. The sight of Harry, five minutes behind the oblivious Ping Wei, caused a momentary pause from the quick-fingered unravelling of the nets, but his nodded greeting reassured them and the fishermen turned back to their labours.

The steep footpath wound along miles of spectacular coastline, mountains on one side and erratic inlets and bays on the other. The surf was far below, a rolling carpet that would defeat any but the most skilled of sailors. It could not have been further in atmosphere from the urban, modern city port of Hong Kong Central.

It was the devil of a job to remain unnoticed once they were away from the village and Harry was sure that if he had been following Chen he would have been spotted before they had even left the town of Sai Kung. As it was, drenched to the skin with sweat and desperate for some water, Harry paused on the narrow track and watched carefree Ping Wei whistling as he threaded his way sure-footed down to the narrow beach. The boy turned a couple of handstands on the sand as he made his way to a fisherman's hut nestling under an overhang of rocks on the remote beach.

Harry heard the welcome sound of a small waterfall and found a trickle of cool water crossing the path. He stooped down to it and cupped his hands. After taking a long drink he splashed his face and neck and could feel his skin alive with the sting of it. He calculated that they were on the Eastern edge of the rugged Sai Kung peninsula and carefully took the time to store the details of the fragile timber lean-to under the overhanging cliff before wending his way back to civilisation.

Two months later it was spring and the weather was cool and clear. Stevie, lying in bed, waiting for Harry to finish work, could not get comfortable. She lay first on one side and then on the other but it was no good. She turned on to her back and listened to the muted sounds from the street. The occasional car growling, the clatter of wooden rickshaw wheels on tarmac, the soft footfall of drunks in the sultry night. She thought about Jishang. She had heard very little from him since the day they had said goodbye at the airport. For six months they had been communicating by cable on urgent magazine matters and sending corrected proofs back and forth in the post but their intimacy had leaked away without her even noticing. He asked no questions and she asked none in return. Her life in Shanghai had become so distant it felt as if it belonged to somebody else.

With relief she heard the key turn in the door and Harry's voice call through the apartment.

'I know you're not asleep.'

'Well, you're wrong. I am.'

'Excellent. You won't want any of this ice cream, then.'

He appeared in the doorway holding aloft a cardboard box from their favourite Italian ice-cream maker.

A little later the lights of the city spread out below them in the night as Stevie and Harry lay close, naked and on their backs on her balcony. His hand rested on her swollen belly. They spoke quietly, intimately. Almost murmuring.

'When the alarm sounds you'll need to get as fast as you can to Yang's boat.'

'Yang?'

'Yes. The very same. Let's just say he has uses other than purveying narcotic drugs and leave it at that.'

He glanced at her. She wrinkled her brow, gently teasing.

'I'm not sure I'll remember which one it is, it's been so long since I was there.'

Harry shifted his weight on to his elbow so he could see the neon light in her dark eyes. 'This is important, Stevie. It's all arranged. He'll be waiting. When you get to Macau, Yang will pass you on to somebody who'll see you out into Free China. You're to wait there for any messages. But no more than a week. If you don't hear anything somebody will help you move on.'

'Why so serious?'

'Look, the Japanese haven't exactly gone away like they were supposed to. The embargo is infuriating them much more than anyone anticipated. Frankly, they're seeing it as a provocation. Everything points to them taking the gloves off.'

'I see.'

'Bloody politicians. If they had any idea of what we're up against.' The image of a photograph that he'd seen that afternoon came to him in all its horror. The child, maybe six years old, sitting on the dirt ground, holding his mother's loose hand and staring at her insides, which were coiled around her, pulled out through the split where she had been cut open from throat to groin. The Japanese soldier, bloody bayonet in one hand, nonchalantly lighting a cigarette.

Stevie mistook his urgency for anger but in fact it was fear. 'We've underestimated them for too long. First we dismissed them as our little copycat allies and now we dismiss them as weak. Well, I know better, Stevie, and I don't see a way out. Plumed hats and marching bands won't save us now. Do you understand?'

'What does your friend Mr Takeda have to say?'

Harry would not normally have risen to her teasing. She had no understanding of his relationship with Takeda and indeed, why should she. He himself was far from clear about it. He found it so difficult to unweave his complex feelings that he seldom chose to delve into them. When he did think about it, it was only ever in brief snapshots, well framed and glowing: a narrow street lit up by the colourful kimonos of the women like so many hummingbirds, a quiet courtyard covered in layers of pale-pink blossom as if there were snowdrifts in the sunshine, a steaming bowl of clear broth in a small overheated dining room, Takeda's young smile splitting his flushed face as he accepted victory in the boxing ring. But there was a kind of heat that rose in him when he thought too hard about it. The memory of his time in Japan was relegated to the furthest unswept corner of his mind. He had a sense of it lurking and murky. But at the same time he held it close and could hardly bear any shadow being brought to bear on the happiness of his youthful Japanese adventure.

'I know he's perfectly charming and extremely useful to you.'

'He's one of the best men I've ever known.' Harry couldn't look at her but he didn't have to, he knew her eyes were wide with astonishment. She didn't say anything.

'You're not crass enough to dismiss an entire nation because of the actions of a few individuals, are you? I don't suppose you feel personally responsible for the wholesale slayings of the Red Indians? Or do you perhaps secretly hold against me the atrocities of the Boer War?'

'Of course not. That's not the point.' Stevie struggled to explain her discomfort around Takeda, who had always been kind and considerate to her. Not being able to articulate her unease she settled on another tease.

'Go on, admit it, you're just trying to get rid of me. Well, guess what, it's too late, buster.'

But he didn't reflect her lightness. He was firm and intense. 'Listen to me. This is an island, Stevie. You need to know. We won't be able to hold them off and there's no reason to suppose that they'll behave any differently here. You saw them in Shanghai.'

She had seen them. But the pitiful swagger of those soldiers who strode through the International Settlement had been no indication of the unique kind of hell that they were wreaking elsewhere in China. She had read the eyewitness reports and would never forget them.

Stevie took a deep breath. 'It doesn't scare me, whatever you say.'

She held her arms up to the sky. Through her fingers the stars were slipping.

'You've been practising running away all your life. Well, here's your chance to put it to some use.' He reached up and took one of her hands. 'Promise me that when I say it's time, you'll go.' She looked at him. 'It's not just your life you're playing with.'

That was below the belt in every sense, and he knew it. She pushed his hand away and clumsily drew herself up to sit. She had to lean back against the brick wall of the balcony to make room for her unfamiliar bulk. The sound of traffic hummed in the heavy air. The bricks still held the warmth of the day and were soothing on her aching back. There was a kick from inside.

Harry sounded equable. 'We'll never be alone again, you know. What with little Winston or Mabel or whoever.'

'Will you resent it?'

'I don't know. Maybe.'

She shifted again, uncomfortable. 'When we met you were spying on me, weren't you?'

Harry said nothing, which was eloquent in itself.

'You can't tell me what to do.'

He sighed. 'And don't I know it.'

There was another small silence between them. And then her hand sought his again. 'All right.'

'All right what?'

'All right, if the time comes I'll go to Yang's boat.' She glanced at him. 'Happy now?'

He grinned. She could see his teeth pale in the gloom.

She shook her head. 'God, what's happened to us. We used to have such a good time.'

Chapter Fourteen

April 1941

She could hear a scream but it took her time to realise it was her own.

It was the inevitability of it that had frightened her as the massive muscular contractions filled her torso and she realised she had no dominion over them. And once the fear had taken control she lost herself. She had changed her mind, she said, bent double as she clung to Lily's skirt, she didn't want the baby after all. It was all a terrible mistake. Then the darkness and absoluteness of her body and the primitive battle for life was her universe. There was nothing beyond.

Harry wasn't there. It was Lily who paced the room and dampened the cool cloths and massaged the small of her back as she moaned. And it was Lily who called the ambulance. Lily who was pacing the corridor. Lily who had to endure the screams, the urgent swishing of the door. Open. Closed. Open. Closed. The running of the doctor. The shine of metal instruments. The piercing red on white linen bundled in a nurse's arms.

'Get away from me. I'll kill you,' she shouted, but Lily in that corridor was relieved. One thing was for sure, Stevie was alive.

Opening her eyes after another eternity abandoned to the shadow world behind her eyelids, Stevie was astonished to see, distorted by the reflection in the chrome of the overhead light, what looked like a raw, red animal being peeled out of her. A living blood clot.

'Look! He's perfect. Your baby son.'

The slimy, slippery thing was brought to her for a moment and then taken away. Her whole body was shaking now, a quake of shock waves.

And then surrender again. More invasive meddling. More mopping. More, different pain.

Later she forgot the world beyond this one. She forgot the visceral urgency of the pains. But she never forgot the dislocation of self. It tore something out of her and remade itself. Like internal scar tissue, hardening and reinventing. A new and, it would prove, invaluable survival tool.

Meanwhile Harry was in a jeep somewhere on the mainland. The primitive suspension throbbed in his aching bones. Every rut was an ordeal. The binoculars pounded on his chest at every jolt. His feet were too hot in the heavy boots. They had worked hard to make contact with this man, a renegade Communist agitator prepared to give details of their campaign against the Japanese in so-called Free China beyond the border of the British New Territories. Harry hoped he might get some new insight into the state of affairs in the Japanese army.

In the glimmer of the headlights he could make out a shack on the edge of the paddy field. He was amused momentarily to recognise a version of medieval fortification in its slit windows. He was a ten-year-old boy again at Cardiff Castle. It was raining, of course, but he was enthralled by the grassy mound that led directly to the sheer, windowless and featureless walls of the castle keep. Somewhere else Roger, his brother, was shouting for him. But he was alone under the vast wall, his fingers touching a brick that had been laid centuries before. He was touching history. He was happy.

'Bugger!' Suddenly blinded by a bright light aimed directly at him, he felt Ken lunge at the brakes. The tyres spun. Glancing at Ken, he saw the sweat shining on his face.

'Is he our man?'

'Can't tell.'

'Here goes.' Harry checked for his revolver as the crude metal door of the jeep closed behind him. The ground was heavy with mud. He could feel Ken's solid presence a few steps away. He muttered for both of their benefits, 'Every piece of information counts.'

It was a fundamental tenet of faith. Their lives were at stake for it.

It was hard to relate the peachy creature peering out of its tight cotton wrapping to the slippery, nightmare thing of hours before. Stevie was aware that she was enjoying the effects of a medical shot of morphine. The sun shone lazily through the white net curtains and the entire ward was bucolic and sunnyside-up. There was a dull throbbing through her body and every muscle ached as if she'd sprinted up a mountain. But nothing mattered.

The baby was right now in Harry's awkward hands. The mud from the paddy field swathed the soles of his boots and his skin was rough from lack of sleep. He had a bemused and softened look that she had never seen before. She gazed at him while he peered at the tiny boy.

'He's awfully small.'

'He's perfect.'

Harry nodded. 'Yes.' And he gave her a glance of such extreme amazement that she laughed out loud.

'He looks just like you.' She stroked his face. 'Only not so well read.'

'Hmm. I think he looks exactly like an angry toad.' He looked back at the boy. 'What about Richard, for my father?'

'No. I've been thinking and I've got it.' A smile. 'Paris. Short for parasite.'

He snorted before offering, 'Benjamin, for your father.'

'No. Henry. For his father.'

He looked at her properly now and they smiled hugely at each other. He decided against mentioning to her the hard time he had been given by the Matron. She had stood, self-appointed guardian to the new mothers in her care, at the door to the ward and refused him entry. In no uncertain terms she had made clear that as his wife was not one of her patients he had no right to go in. He had been forced to pull rank and mention the name of the colony's chief medical officer, Dr Clarke-Russell, as his close personal friend. Reluctantly, she had stepped aside. He glanced towards the nurses' station at the end of the long room. The Matron was glaring at them, even now. It seemed that her own moral standing was being challenged more deeply with every tenderness that passed between him and Stevie. Her very bearing shouted, 'What's the world coming to?'

From the nurses' station the tinny sound of piped mellow jazz, an instrumental version of 'Fools Rush In', was interrupted by a radio announcer.

'President Roosevelt has communicated to Emperor Hirohito of Japan a strong warning in an attempt to avert war in the Far East.'

His son stirred in his swaddling. The cartoon-length eyelashes fluttered and he opened his eyes. It was the life in them that delivered to Harry the jolt of revelation. This was a person. A small one but a person nonetheless. It was a miracle. He turned back to Stevie, overwhelmed with a new respect for her. Just then, even the stampeding hooves of the four horsemen wouldn't have budged him. The whole world and everything that mattered was contained between them. The rest could go hang.

It had been decided that they would set up home in Stevie's apartment. There were obvious reasons why Harry's place wouldn't do, although it was more comfortable with its brand new kitchen, fitted with every convenient appliance money could buy. Sylvia had been bored and unhappy enough to apply the full force of her energies to the renovation of her home. It showed. But Harry had never felt relaxed there and Stevie didn't want to live in the glare of Sylvia's interior decorating. The formality of the apartment seemed to reflect the fact that the whole thing had been an exercise in sublimation for Sylvia. And anyway there was something disrespectful in bringing another family into the shell of a failed one.

In contrast, Stevie's apartment couldn't have been less ideal as a place to bring a new baby home. There was limited and unpredictable hot water in the building. The walls were thin and the domestic arrangements and disarrangements of her neighbours were all too audible. The neon of the street signs meant that absolute darkness never fell. And then there were Lily and Victor, each in their own way displaced by the new arrival.

Lily surprised herself by not being drawn into the role of mother's help. She thought the baby was fine and she appreciated his dark eyes and vulnerable bald head. But she was not his mother – she was his mother's friend. Besides, she was busier than ever. The secretarial job she had taken at her uncle's furniture emporium was occupying more and more of her time. Aware that the war and the Japanese occupation had compromised all business on the mainland, he was doing what all conscientious entrepreneurs would do in the same position – he was taking advantage. By importing goods from the carpenters and upholsterers of the mainland on to the island for next to nothing he was then re-exporting the same chairs, tables and wardrobes back into Free China with an astronomical mark-up for his trouble. They might have been Communists but they still needed chairs for their backsides and tables for their dishes, he argued. Consequently, Lily left the apartment early and often didn't come back until very late.

Victor was another matter altogether. He had come with the flat. The previous tenant, a Russian girl, had left him behind when she went back to Shanghai. The relationship she had made with a prominent Chinese government adviser had turned sour over her allowance and she had decamped overnight. The government adviser had given her the baby monkey as a gift on her arrival and she clearly felt no obligation to take him back with her. She had also left behind a short, swingy ocelot jacket which Stevie was sure she must have regretted as soon as she was on the plane and which Stevie had enjoyed inheriting.

When Jishang had first opened the door, having collected the keys from the rental agency, Victor had been so hungry that he hadn't even had the energy to attack him as well. Stevie, standing behind Jishang, had pushed him aside and run to where Victor was curled up on the tatty sofa. She had fallen in love with him instantly. He had survived by drinking water from the kitchen tap which conveniently dripped, but he was thin and lethargic and depressed. The flat smelt rank and bitter. The rental agent hadn't even checked the inventory when the Russian girl had left a fortnight previously, so he had languished forgotten and alone. Stevie took it upon herself to nurse Victor back to health. She had lavished attention and exotic foodstuffs on him. And he had returned the favour by focusing all his simian passion on her.

The new baby had to be kept away from Victor. A wary eye was necessary at all times to ensure Victor didn't repeat his initial welcome of sitting on the baby's face.

Those first few days were a blur of fear and awe in equal measure. Harry was hardly ever there. He didn't talk about what he was doing when he was at work but he carried a sense of urgency with him. He was almost always in uniform. The amount of information on the wires and coming from their contacts was increasing every hour. It was all he and Ken could do to read all the reports. Everything pointed to military movements on the mainland. The Japanese army was on alert but it was far from clear what the activity might mean for the island of Hong Kong.

A fortnight after they had brought the baby home, Harry, aware that his uniform shirt was badly in need of a wash, answered the phone. It was in the hallway on a side table which was missing a leg. It swayed dangerously as he lifted the receiver.

'Yes?'

He heard Ken's anxious voice. 'The department of public health wants to know what the routine should be when –' he stopped himself '– if the Japanese make a move on us.'

'It's all in the manual.'

'Yes, but now they're worried that the game might have changed. Somebody's spreading rumours that the manual is out of date.'

'Of course it's out of date. It was written last year.' Harry shifted his weight to his other foot. 'Look, just tell them that their first and most important job remains containing any panic.'

There was a yell from the bathroom, followed by the appropriately panicked voice of Stevie.

'Help! Help! Quick!'

Harry excused himself. 'Sorry old chap, got to go,' and failing to contain his own panic, he abandoned the phone and ran to the bathroom.

Stevie was on her knees by the side of the bath. Tears ran down her face as she sobbed. The tiny naked boy was cradled in her hands, which were hovering over the water.

She shouted, 'Take him. Please take him.'

Harry leaned down and carefully picked him up. Stevie sat back on her heels.

'I can't do this. What if he falls in the water? What if my hands are too slippery to hold him? What if he doesn't like it?'

Harry glanced at the oblivious smile on his son's face. 'He's fine. Look.'

'You don't understand. I mean, I really can't do this. Any of it.' She felt the tightness in her throat like a garotte. 'I'm not the mother type. It's not fair on him.' She was almost wailing now. 'You should have stayed with Sylvia, she'd know what to do with a baby.'

The phone was ringing again, echoing along the hallway, shaking the table with every ring. Harry transferred the baby on to his shoulder and, holding him with one hand, he offered the other to Stevie.

'Come on, come with me.'

Stevie, blurry with unaccustomed tears, let him pull her to her feet.

In the living room, Harry laid the baby in his basket. Stevie blew her nose.

'I'm sorry. It was all a terrible mistake. I thought I could do everything and now I see that right here there's something everybody else can do but I can't. He's so small, Harry. I look at him and can hardly believe it's possible for him to breathe through that tiny nose. How can I keep him alive?' She was crying again, exhaustion freeing her. 'I'm useless. I'm sorry. And my mother had four of us.'

The phone was ringing again, bringing with it a fresh sense of doom. Ignoring the beckoning of his other life, Harry put his arms around Stevie's sobbing body.

'Four? No time to lose then.'

And Stevie found she was laughing and that he was kissing her. And that she felt safe again.

Chapter Fifteen

December 1941

It was a Sunday night and the hotel ballroom was full. It felt as though they were dancing on the *Titanic*. There was an air of defiance and anticipation everywhere in the colony these days, and nowhere more so than in this glittering jewel-box. The closer the Japanese army came, the more defiant people grew. It was as if they had already been serving a sentence for too long and the long-awaited execution might actually bring some relief. At least they would know what their fate was to be. Waiting for the inevitable was torture in itself. The only thing that was still a matter of opinion was whether the defence would last long enough for help to come from elsewhere.

The official line was that Hong Kong would hold out for weeks. The plan in the event of an invasion was for an evacuation from Kowloon on the mainland to the island, which would then defend itself as a fortress until ships arrived from Singapore to see the Japanese off once and for all. The optimists among them held that Hong Kong would not only be successfully defended but would also become an offensive base for attacks on the Japanese in China. Great faith was put in the line of redoubts which ran east to west across the New Territories about twelve miles south of the border. Minefields had been laid as protection from an aggressive approach by sea and seventy-two pillboxes had been built in a string across the centre of the island. The plate-glass windows of the department stores were criss-crossed with shiny adhesive strips like spiders' webs to prevent them shattering. The optimists also pointed to the recent arrival of two battalions of Canadian soldiers. Raw and young and untried they might have been, but surely they represented a real intent on the part of Churchill to defend the island and not abandon it to its fate? Yes, they were French-speaking and yes, they had arrived without any extra motor transport but only a very few, Harry among them, knew that these troops had officially not been recommended for operational consideration owing to their extreme youth and lack of experience. The people of Hong Kong were encouraged to believe that the reinforcements constituted a warning from Britain to her enemies.

A small orchestra on a platform at the end of the room played 'The Best Things in Life are Free'. Swathes of red curtain were draped behind them and potted palms perched on either side. The dance floor was packed with couples and the atmosphere was frenetic and loud. Men, mostly British, stood at the bar, their voices raised over the music. Many of the women at the tables and out on the floor were Chinese.

Stevie's head spun as she let Harry lead her around and around in the dance. The skirt of her dress slipped between her legs, the cool of the silk was soothing to her hot skin. It had been eight months since the baby had been born and this was the first night she had agreed to leave Hal, as he had quickly become known. She had drunk several gin-slings in order to relax enough not to fret about him. Lily was looking after Hal and was under instructions to sit on the sofa in such a way that she could see him in his basket through the open bedroom door. She was only supposed to leave the sofa if she was in urgent need of the bathroom. Stevie's breasts had returned to normal, to her great relief, and her stomach though softly rounded didn't perturb her. She saw it as a badge of honour. The agony of her milk coming in and having nowhere to go had been resigned to the general memory of discomfort from those first few weeks. The regime of bottles and powdered milk and porridge and rice was fully operational.

In the first few weeks after Hal's birth Stevie had only been brought out of her daze by the generous cable of congratulation from Jishang, which had differed so far in tone from the communications she had received from her mother and sisters that she had cried in gratitude. It said: BOY OH BOY A BOY STOP SINCERE CONGRATULATIONS FROM OLD BOY. She knew it represented a kind of truce. A few months earlier she had broken the news of her pregnancy in a carefully worded cable over which she had agonised for days. The nonchalance of his reply had stung more than she could have predicted. He really did not seem to mind, there was no hint of emotion in it. 'So you will stay in Hong Kong. Shall I return your apartment here to the rental agency?'

The communications that followed had been entirely work-related and he had not once asked her how she was feeling. A part of her had been grateful but a larger part longed for him to rage at her so that she could yell back and assuage some of her guilt. The only time Jishang had sounded aggrieved was when it became clear that she was not going to finish the manuscript of the book before the birth of the baby. It occurred to her that the book had been their shared project, their baby, and now another was taking precedence.

In contrast her mother had not made any attempt to control her outrage. Every word she wrote – and over the months there were many – was dipped in indignation and self-righteous resentment. Her grandchild a bastard! Her daughter a harlot! Her own reputation in tatters! The local church praying for her! Her sisters, in turn, offered a disapproving chorus of concern for the situation rather than for her and none of them was able to understand that Stevie might actually be happy. Soon she stopped opening the letters and they lay pristine in the back of a drawer, mumbling from their offended moral high ground into the dusty dark wood.

Her concerns were more immediate. Both she and Harry were desperate to reclaim the island that had been their affair. Harry was disconcerted by the amount of stuff that the baby had brought into their lives. He couldn't go into the bathroom without newly washed damp nappies attacking him from the washing line that now hung permanently between the bath and the door. There was constant washing, folding, attending to these squares of cotton. The apartment smelled of linen and baby pee and milk. He didn't mind but he was bemused by it all. Stevie had been living it for every hour of the day and night whilst Harry felt like a visitor to this new land. His colleagues saw more of him than she did.

This night, though, was theirs.

Stevie caught the glare of Phyllis Clarke-Russell as she swirled past with her husband, the Director of Public Health. She was one of the few British women to have avoided the evacuation. She had taken advantage of the last-minute decision to make it voluntary and not mandatory, and had opted to stay in her domain. Phyllis quickly looked away. Her disapproval of the scandalous situation was palpable. Stevie felt relieved that she had escaped the full brunt of Hong Kong gossip about her by being so caught up in the exhaustion of her new Hal-centred world.

'Really. Parading themselves like this, it's disgraceful.' She had heard the rustle of predictable outrage from the smug cocktail drinkers in the lobby as she and Harry had walked in. Stevie was immune to it. She had never cared much for the opinions of others and she actually felt a pang of victory in stirring things up. After all, Hal was their private business – how serious could the public consequences possibly be?

She surrendered to the music and the heat of Harry's hand on the small of her back. She didn't see the hotel manager skirt the dance floor unusually fast and approach the platform, attracting the bandleader's attention. Without compromising his rhythm the bandleader leaned down and listened to the whispering manager. He furrowed his brow and let his baton fall to his side. The orchestra faltered, then stopped playing. A scratchy double bass note was the last to linger.

The dancers came to a standstill too, confused by the sudden silence. Harry dropped his hand from Stevie's back and looked at her before the manager's announcement cut through the quiet. He talked too loudly into the microphone, unused to it.

'Ladies and gentlemen, your attention please.' There was a nervous giggle from a table at the side. 'I'm sorry to interrupt but I have an urgent announcement.' He cleared his throat. 'All military personnel are advised to report to their posts immediately. Thank you.'

The silence lay heavy. Gradually a low rumble of frightened conversation rose and almost all the men in the room started picking up jackets, kissing their partners, making their way out.

Harry turned to Stevie, his voice low and calm. 'There's money in my accounts both here at the Bank of Hong Kong and in England.'

Stevie shook her head. 'I don't understand.'

'Yes, you do. You know what to do.' And she did understand. She shivered and fear blurred her vision. Harry was already on his way to the door, his jacket in his hand. There was no time to take it in. In seconds the room was emptied of men. It was a ballroom of women, each silent and alone.

Stevie had got as far as the street when the unearthly scream of a siren punctured the city, letting the air out of it and deflating it beyond all recognition.

Chapter Sixteen

Fear smelt like overblown lilies.

Stevie crouched by Hal's cot. He slept on and off. She rocked herself back and forth. The sirens cut into her mind, paralysing her. Should she pick him up and run through the streets? What if the bombs fell? She had lived with bombs before when she had taken a detour to Chungking, the seat of the Kuomintang Nationalist Chinese government. She had not been afraid then. What had happened to her?

There was an explosion so loud that the room shook. The central light swung, casting terrible shadows, like a ghost train she had once been on as a child.

Across town, Lily curled into herself under a teak table destined for the Communists of Free China. She had tried to reach her family as soon as Stevie, alone and tear-stained with the news, had run back into the apartment the night before. But she had only got as far as her uncle's furniture warehouse. Hours passed as death rained down.

In the village of Kun Lung Wai an elderly Chinese man ran through the street. The tremors from the shelling sent up clouds of dust. In his arms was a shiny new first-aid box. Stumbling, he came to the small girl who lay bleeding where she had fallen. He dropped to his knees and struggled to open the box with trembling hands. He did not see the black boots striding towards him. There was a shot. The old man keeled over, the first-aid box slipping on to the dusty road.

The shells came one after another across the harbour from Kowloon and dive bombers screamed over Central as the air assault continued. It was relentless. The air in the streets was thick with acrid smoke but all Stevie's awareness was here where Hal was refusing to take the bottle. His shrill screams bore into her. She hadn't moved from his side for twelve hours. Her dancing dress was stained already with sweat and tears. It was hours later that the door opened and Lily was there. Having failed to get across the harbour she had decided to go back to Stevie and Hal. They fell into each other's arms.

It takes time to calibrate a new existence and to navigate a new world.

Harry could smell the fear too. But from where he was, it smelt of stale sweat and heavy cotton twill. He was in the shelter under Government House with a few of his men and the recently appointed Governor, who was so new he barely had a grip on the geography of the island. He had arrived less than two months ago from his previous posting in Barbados; a position that had probably prepared him to mix a perfect cocktail but certainly not to wage war with a battle-hardened and implacable enemy. His staff were not much better equipped – his second in command had in fact arrived the day before. Harry understood this to be quite in keeping with London's dismissive and conflicted attitude towards Hong Kong. An attitude that meant they had not been able to grasp, even now, that Great

Britain was in real danger from those funny little men from the Far East.

'Where the hell are our planes?'

'They were all put out of action in the first offensive yesterday, sir.'

'All of them?'

'Yes, sir. There weren't very many in the first place and they were all at Kai Tak.'

'The air force is effectively out of action?'

Harry nodded. This was an agony – watching the faces of the men who were supposed to be in charge finally realising quite how bad things were and knowing that he and his colleagues had been trying to communicate this more and more desperately for months. It was not as if the Japanese hadn't announced their intentions loudly from every international podium and at every opportunity for years. Before the two-month-old embargo the Japanese air force had been flying planes with American engines running on American fuel and loaded with shells marked 'Made In England'. He remembered the recent *Reader's Digest* article which had stated categorically that the Japanese air force was a joke and that the Japanese were incapable of efficient flying because they had an inferior sense of balance.

There was a shout from across the room from a radio operator.

'Smugglers Ridge. There's nothing coming back, sir.'

Harry could picture the bunker. He had been there only last week. It looked north through wooded country towards the border and south to the coast and the harbour. Steep steps led down underground. The only light came through the gun-slits in the concrete and the air shafts above the narrow corridors with cheery names like Shaftesbury Avenue and Regent Street. Wind blew over the ridge and whistled in the electric cables overhead. It was the key position in the defence plan. And already there was silence on the radio, just the white noise of broken communication. Here was the harvest of years of indecision.

Defend to the last? Defend until support could arrive? Don't bother to defend? Abandon the mainland and defend the island? Make a token defence to save face? If only Churchill's personal conviction that the Colony was, in fact, indefensible had been known more widely. 'If Japan goes to war with us,' he had said, 'there is not the slightest chance of holding Hong Kong or relieving it. I wish we had fewer troops there but to move any would be noticeable and dangerous.' An even smaller garrison would have announced to the world that Churchill was essentially prepared to abandon Hong Kong to its fate. It consisted of two British infantry battalions, two Indian Army battalions, a few bits of artillery both mobile and fixed, the Local Volunteer Force made up of bankers, dentists, accountants and boys, a few small warships, two flying boats and three torpedo bombers without any torpedoes. Fifteen thousand men at most. Courageous residents, both military and civilian, who had already been betrayed by their government and by their own prejudices. The Japanese army was twenty-six miles away, fifty thousand experienced and brutalised soldiers.

The year before, Harry had written a report on the fact that the Japanese combat boots were far superior to those of the British soldiers. They were light, supple, rubber-soled, while the British boots were heavy, hob-nailed leather, unchanged in design since the Boer War. He was fairly sure the report had gone unread. There had been too much talk in white ties over whisky sodas and not enough trench-digging or preparation of food, water and electricity supplies. The island would not survive on cocktails alone. There had been a last-minute change of mind, hence the arrival of the Canadian boys, but it was, in his opinion, far too little far too late.

'We're evacuating Kowloon, sir.'

'Jolly good men, jolly good.'

'Got a message for the troops, sir?'

There was a short silence while the Governor gathered his thoughts. He was pale under his Caribbean suntan. 'Fight on. Hold fast for King and Empire. God bless you all in this your finest hour.'

Harry caught Ken's eye and saw a shared flicker of mutiny there.

The journey through the streets of a terrified and paralysed city was surreal. Familiar and yet not so. Some shops were open, defiant in the face of the chaos that raged around them. Some were sealed and shuttered as if they would never open again.

Stevie had explained to Lily that they had to get to the harbour, that there was a boat waiting for them and Lily had shown Stevie how to tie Hal into a cotton scarf, wrapping it around her body so he was tight against her chest, his head to one side. They had tried with a silk scarf first with a print of the Eiffel Tower on it, but the knot kept slipping. Lily carried Stevie's rucksack, into which they put a few nappies, the tin of powdered milk, the bottle and a small blanket. Stevie had slipped a lipstick that had been lying on the three-legged telephone table into her cardigan pocket. They had been halfway down the stairs before Stevie shouted 'Oh my God, Victor!' and to Lily's regret they had gone back up to find him. He lay, shivering with inexpressible monkey fear, in a huddle under the sofa. Stevie had to coax him out with the last of their supplies of chocolate, but it was Lily who had to carry him wrapped round her front as she crept through the night streets like a beetle with an all enveloping carapace.

People gathered on corners, whispering. Rumours of pillaging spread as quickly as they were invented. The Japanese were already on the island. No, they were miles away and this bombardment was just a smokescreen, and their goal was elsewhere. The British army was on the mainland repelling the Japanese with great success. Or they had already been defeated and were at that very moment being massacred en masse. The Japanese were planning to use the island as an enormous jail. They were planning to enslave the entire population. They were going to liberate the Chinese and set them on the British. They were going to do a deal with the British and kill all the Chinese. The British were finished but the Communists were attacking the Japanese army from the rear and would decimate it within hours. This had been the plan all along.

The information void attracted more and more bizarre speculation. Nothing was certain except that the island was being bombed from the sky and shelled from the mainland.

Then came the news of Pearl Harbor. The Americans were entering the war. It would be over in days. No, they had a secret treaty with Japan in which Hong Kong was sacrificed in return for Singapore. No, it was the other way round.

Stevie and Lily had gone a long way towards the harbour before they had to take shelter. A plane flew low over the island, low enough for those on the Peak to see into its windows. They crouched behind a shuttered market stall, Stevie's pulse making a bass line to Hal's timpani. The bomb fell far enough away for them to take comfort in survival, but near enough for them to feel the aftershock. Not much later they stumbled towards the sea. The boats heaved and scraped against each other in confusion. Stevie ran ahead, crossing the bridge of boats with sure feet. Suddenly she stopped. She twisted around, trying to get her bearings. Where was Yang's junk? Surely it had been here, between the peeling yellow hull and the old river boat. Lily saw the panic in her eyes.

'What is it?'

'It's gone.'

'These boats never go anywhere. Look again. Maybe over there?'

'No.' Stevie repositioned her feet for balance. 'It's gone.'

And they stood for a moment, silent but for the lapping of the waves and the distant emergency sirens carrying across the water. A warehouse further along the harbour's edge was on fire, the flames reflected in the water, a beautiful cocktail of orange and blue. Stevie felt only relief. She had done as Harry had asked and now, by a miracle of convenience, she could stay near him with a clear conscience. Lily, seeing her smile, sighed in irritation. She would never in a thousand lifetimes understand her. But she sure as hell was not going to let her or the baby die on her watch.

Harry waited in the hut on a small jetty on the far side of the island. The swarm of mosquitoes distracted him from worrying too much about what was going to happen. At dawn, a lean, modern motor launch slipped across the harbour from a fishing inlet on the mainland, unseen by most of the lookouts and expected only by very few.

Harry looked up – a streak of bloodied mosquito smeared on his shin where he had just slapped it. Yes, the sound of a boat. He checked his watch – absolutely spot on time.

'Smarten up, chaps.'

Caps were slung on, jackets adjusted, shoulders straightened. Harry nodded almost to himself and stepped out of the hut. The wooden jetty creaked, protesting the weight of the four men. The sliver of ultra-modern marine engineering slowed as it approached the jetty. Its engine, impressively quiet, became silent as it pulled up expertly, barely brushing against the old boards. Harry waited. He was coiled and still. If this was an ambush and a trick, he was a clear target. He stood facing the boat, his hands by his side, the other officers in a phalanx behind him.

A uniformed sailor leaped off the boat and secured it. Harry's eyes were on the men standing, also in silence, on the shiny deck. Their uniforms were immaculate, their dark eyes betraying as little as his own. The Japanese army officers disembarked, taking their first unofficial steps on to what was officially British territory.

Harry stepped forward and bowed slightly.

'Sir.' The senior Japanese officer bowed and responded. He held out his hand, in which there was a letter. Harry reached and took it. The transfer was efficient and precise.

'Thank you.' Two more small bows and the Japanese turned back to their boat. They were gone as smoothly and silently as they had come. Harry and his colleagues stayed exactly where they were until even the wake had disappeared. Water lapped against the struts of the jetty. Mosquitoes took advantage and fell upon their prey. Not one of the men moved to brush them away.

'Well done, men. Thank you.' Harry's voice split the buzzing of the orgiastic insects. The boat was out of sight. The whole encounter had lasted three minutes. The men fell into a frenzy of mosquito killing. There was laughter and relief. But only Harry knew that the letter was a formality: the demands in it were never going to be acceptable and this exchange would not hold off the invasion by even a minute. It had been a necessary rendezvous, but would only ever be an easily forgotten footnote in the endgame of Japanese military ambitions in the Far East. He knew too well the subtle weave of etiquette that served as an excuse for barbaric behaviour. His time in Japan as a military exchange student had been revelatory as well as personally thrilling. And of course he understood the importance of his experience to a British military command with little or no knowledge of the East. But he also understood how little weight should be placed on the Japanese need to have been seen to follow the diplomatic line of engagement before continuing with its imperialistic expansion. It was only a matter of time.

In the aftermath of her dismay at Yang's disappearance Lily had persuaded Stevie that the safest place for all of them would be at her uncle's house, and she and Hal were drawn without question into the embrace of Lily's family. They opened their door, offered their food, set out a mattress on the floor among their own and expanded their hearts enough to allow them in.

That second night, in the half-dark, there were sleeping bodies everywhere on the floor. The noise of the shelling had increased, unbroken now for hours. Stevie lay awake under a window. Hal was asleep, tucked tight next to her. Her hand lay gently on his little chest, rising and falling with the life in him. There were occasional flashes as explosions lit the night sky. Then a terrifyingly loud blast and the window above them shattered. Stevie instinctively covered Hal with her own body. As the shocks receded, Stevie lay for a moment among the glittering glass splinters. The fear was terrible.

Smoke, shouting, chaos. The night was dark but for the white lights of explosions. They were high on the Peak among the sweet-scented shrubs. Soldiers ran in and out of the billowing smoke. Harry had lost sight of Ken almost immediately. They had been fighting for hours and it was no longer clear how many Allied soldiers were left on their feet. He could hear his own breathing magnified under the noise of the bombardment. The smoke cleared for a moment. Harry's face was distorted by a yell and then he fell.

The sky was alive with stars. It was beautiful.

It was the fourteenth day of the battle and in the courtyard of the family compound, Lily sat cross-legged on the ground in the shade of the gnarled tree. Hal was lying on a blanket in front of her and she was dangling a twig with a leaf on the end of it just out of his reach. He was enthralled. There was a stillness and quiet in the courtyard. The only movement came from where Stevie was working. Hunched over a sheaf of paper, she was furiously writing in longhand with a pencil. Her wrist ached. If they hadn't been carrying Hal, she thought, they could have brought her typewriter. Shamelessly, she determined that as soon as the bombing was over she would get back to the apartment and reclaim her typewriter. And her shampoo. She hunched over further to reread what she had written.

She felt consumed by a raw and urgent need to bear witness.

The gate was flung open. Everybody looked up. The exhausted and filthy figure of Chen almost fell into the courtyard. His mother, Mrs Li, who had braved the bombardment to cross the harbour from her Kowloon home as the Japanese approached, rushed to him. Lily instinctively picked up Hal. Chen pushed his mother aside and came to Stevie, who had abandoned her writing and stood up. Papers fell to the ground.

'I'm so sorry,' he said. His voice was hoarse.

Chapter Seventeen

When Stevie stepped out of the compound the streets were eerily quiet. There was a communal holding of breath. Those few who dared to go out scuttled through the rubble, barely taking the time to notice which buildings had taken the hardest hits and which stood bizarrely unscathed. The city was a mouth with broken and missing teeth. It even reeked of a new putrid scent. An ominous aeroplane buzzed low over the harbour, its engines half-drowning out the message that came through a loudspeaker from Kowloon and drifted on the wind across the harbour. 'Home Sweet Home' was being played over and over again and was interrupted by the occasional announcement delivered in perfect standard English:

'English soldiers, think about your wives and children. Surrender and you can go home. Give up and the Japanese will protect you. Trust in the kindness of the Japanese army.'

Stevie stumbled as she half-ran, half-walked through Central Hong Kong. She noticed details as if she were watching a film – a gutted building, a table ready for a meal, open to the elements on the first floor as if on a stage set; a bottle of Rose's lime cordial lying unbroken in the middle of the pavement; a stocking tangled around the wheels of a shattered car, a flimsy warning flag in the harsh daylight.

She could think of nothing except the mantra she was repeating over and over under her breath: 'Please let him be all right. Please let him be all right. Please let him be all right.' Her mind was numb but for that hope.

She had not fainted when Chen brought the news. But her legs had folded under her and she had slipped to the ground of the compound. Unable to speak, she felt as though she were in a nightmare in which she would never find her voice again no matter how loud she shouted. She mouthed 'No' over and over again. It was Lily who, having thrust Hal into the arms of Mrs Li, had grabbed Chen by the shoulders and assaulted him with questions, not waiting for an answer.

'Where is he? Is it bad? What's happened? How do you know?'

Chen shook himself free of his sister and knelt down in the dust near Stevie. He took her hands in his and spoke quietly. He spoke as a man of authority and not as the sulky youth of previous meetings.

'There was a disastrous battle on the Peak above Repulse Bay. Many men died, we have no numbers yet, and we don't know how many were taken prisoner. Major Field was very bad when we found him. He was handed to the Red Cross.'

'How bad?' She felt she was screaming but he heard a hoarse whisper.

'Bad.'

'Did you see him?'

'No. I heard his name and spoke to the comrade who brought him in.'

'How do you know it was him?'

'Major Field is well known to us. He is one of the few my comrades would recognise.'

'You're sure?'

Chen nodded. 'I'm sorry.'

Stevie had slipped into another dimension. One in which time flowed quite differently. She felt as if she were forcing herself through deep mud; every inhalation and exhalation required an enormous effort and appeared to be taken in slow motion. Simultaneously her mind was moving so fast she could hear the wind it created as it sprinted through the possibilities.

Chen went on. 'They didn't listen to us. We told them there was no point in defending the mainland and they should concentrate on the island. We knew the Japanese had maps of everything. We knew they planned to split the island east to west. We had clear information. They wouldn't listen. They think they know everything and that we're just another useless band of native troublemakers. They don't understand. To dismiss us is to make a very big mistake.' He tightened his grip on Stevie's hands. 'They should have listened.'

Stevie struggled to her feet. Chen helped her.

'The Red Cross?' she asked.

Chen nodded again. Stevie turned away and started for the gate of the compound. Lily grabbed her by the arm.

'Where are you going?'

'To find Harry.'

'You can't go out there. It's madness. What are you thinking?'

Stevie gently freed herself. 'I'm going to find him.' Her voice was so firm and clear that Lily stepped back. They all watched her go.

It was only after she had closed the gate behind her that Hal started to cry.

'Please let him be all right. Please let him be all right.' Stevie had not stopped since she had left the compound. She was wet with sweat and a raw blister had opened up on her heel where her shoe was rubbing. Her limbs were heavier than seemed possible and even when the ear-splitting shrill of the air-raid siren knifed through the streets she didn't falter. 'Please let him be all right. Please let him be all right.' When she finally registered the siren she ducked inside the first door she saw. She spun in the revolving doors and in the sudden gloom half-recognised the Hong Kong and Shanghai Bank.

A round, flushed face loomed towards her. Mr Evans, Senior Bank Manager, was holding the fort single-handedly. An imperious voice on the telephone from London had insisted that someone from senior management should man the building. It seemed he was fully expecting large-scale looting by the savage Chinese population at the very least.

'What are you doing? The bank's not open.'

'I heard the siren.'

He could hardly deny her a haven but if he could have, he would. The last thing he wanted was responsibility for some random person, and a woman at that.

'Why are you out in the streets? For God's sake, madam, it's not safe.'

'I'm going to medical headquarters.'

'On official business?'

'To see Dr Clarke-Russell.'

He glowered at her suspiciously. It occurred to him that he had seen her somewhere before. Of course here on the island that was extremely likely but – suddenly his tone changed to indignation.

'Wait a minute. I know you. You're that – that woman.'

'Probably,' she conceded.

The fat man moved to bar her way into the building. A shell hit nearby. Windows shattered around them. Mr Evans was not having his finest hour. He was intent on showing his disapproval of the scandalous woman in front of him, one who had dared to bring a British officer and therefore the entire British Empire into disrepute. It was a stand-off. The revolving doors spun again.

'Miss Steiber. What are you doing out and about?' Stevie saw the lofty figure of Dr Clarke-Russell and at the time it didn't seem at all strange. It was absolutely as it should be. Later she learned that this apparent miracle wasn't so very amazing. The administration office of the medical services had been established in the bank building for its central location and sturdiness. She leaned into him. Her voice was the whisper of despair.

'It's Harry. You have to tell me.'

Evans spluttered with rage. It was bad enough that she was here in his bank on his watch but now she was shamelessly – utterly shamelessly – mentioning her lover's name! He turned to Dr Clarke-Russell for support.

'I've already told her to go home. It's ridiculous. Running around town as if nothing were happening.'

Clarke-Russell interrupted. 'It's all right, Mr Evans. She's with me.'

The bank manager's eyes widened in surprise as the Chief Medical Officer of His Majesty's Colony of Hong Kong put his arm around 'that woman's' shoulders and led her towards one of the bank's precious leather armchairs.

The building was set apart in its own grounds. Again there was that strange calm. Again the held breath. Trees and grass. Serenity and silence, broken when the ambulance skidded to a halt outside the building. The passenger door opened and Stevie climbed out. She ran across the gravel and up the steps to the imposing entrance. Once inside, she felt the sudden cool of the wide lobby. She stopped – there was nobody to ask. She hesitated for a moment before running up the big marble staircase, taking two steps at a time. At the top she ran into a nurse carrying a pile of laundry in her arms. Stevie, panting and impatient, asked her a question and then she turned and ran back down the stairs, slipping on the smooth steps. She had to catch on to the ornate balustrade to keep her balance.

She turned to the right and sped along a corridor. Her shoes squeaked on the linoleum. At the end there was another staircase. She ran up this one, turned left at the top and stopped. She put her hand on to her heaving chest as she fought to regain her breath. There was blood on her ankle from the blister which had now burst. She kicked off her shoes and left them there as she walked, more soberly and not limping any more, along the corridor. She glanced into each room as she passed.

'Please let him be all right. Please let him be all right.'

Every bed was occupied. Men and boys lay in various degrees of brokenness but she hardly took any of it in. She was intent. In the fourth room she came to, she saw through a sliver of open door the familiar sandy head of Sergeant Ramsay. She stepped back to recover herself a little, through the treacle of slow motion. She smoothed down her wild hair. She pushed the door open and stepped inside.

There were only two army cots in the small, light room. Ken Ramsay lay in one. He shouted out, tossing and turning, unconscious but delirious. He threw off the thin sheet and Stevie's eye was drawn to where his left leg should have been.

Unable to register any shock at the sight, her eyes bored intensely into Harry. He was covered by a sheet. His face had lost all colour. His skin was polished and shiny like wax. His eyes were shut and he was absolutely still. Stevie stood right by him. She leaned over until she was so close to his skin she could feel the very slight, shallow breath of him. In one movement she pulled the sheet off. Someone had clumsily put him into hospital pyjama bottoms but his torso was white with bandages. One of his arms was bound in tightly across his chest. There was a time-line of blood seepages – the older ones already rusty, the new vivid. But his limbs were all there.

'For goodness' sake, what's going on?' The young doctor stood at the door, stunned at the sight of this dishevelled, bare-footed woman holding the sheet off the body of one of his patients. Stevie dropped the sheet and flung herself into his arms. She clung to him as if she were drowning.

'What's wrong with him? Will he be all right?'

The doctor awkwardly shuffled Stevie towards the door. They might have been dancing. He lowered his voice.

'You're his wife?'

Stevie was still clinging on. 'You must tell me.'

'The paralysis is due to the bullet shaving the nerve.'

'Paralysis?'

'There's hope that when the shock subsides the left arm might regain some movement. There is also a slight infection in the wound but we'll see.'

'He'll live?'

'I'd hope so. It's too early to call.'

The doctor stepped away and Stevie swayed. He steadied her. 'Look here, I think you'd better sit down.'

'You can't make me leave him.'

'I'm not sure anybody's supposed to be here just now.' But even as he said it he brought a chair in from the corridor and put it beside Harry's bed. Stevie sat. She had barely taken her eyes off Harry's waxen face. He looked strangely unlike himself – inhabiting a limbo in which she could not reach him. Dr Roger Holroyd, twenty-five years old and dealing with his first casualties of war, was dumbstruck by the expression of anguish on her face. It was his first intimation of the pain that would rain down on them all.

He left her, not that she noticed his departure. When he returned an hour later she was asleep where she sat, her head against the wall.

There was hellish chaos all around. Everywhere people were running and screaming, their clothes on fire, their flesh peeling from their bones. Stevie was trying to run but she was carrying Hal and an enormous tin of porridge oats. Both were slipping out of her grasp.

She woke up shouting. At the first sight of Harry in the narrow bed she thought she was still dreaming. In that moment she felt all the fear fall away and the relief was a thing of wonder. She half-stood, a smile coming. Then she smelt the sharp tang of bleach and medicine. Sinking to her knees, she clutched a handful of hospital linen and felt the iron bar of the bed cutting into her chest. Harry stirred but was still again. Her throat was more constricted than she could bear. Refusing the tears, her whisper was intense.

'I damn well hope you can hear me, you bastard. This is why I didn't want to love you. You made me love you and now look. Now look. I love two of you and what can I do for either of you? Nothing. Nothing. I'm all used up by useless love.'

She flung the handful of sheet back on to the bed and pulled herself to standing. Nothing had changed. He was there and she was there and this is how things were. She walked to the window. In the formal gardens the rose bushes were ludicrous and lush. Irritated, she turned back into the room. Harry's eyes flickered open. He caught sight of her.

'Hal all right?

Stevie dressed her face in a smile. 'Oh, yes.' She hadn't thought about him since she had left the compound decades ago. 'Yes, he's having a fine time.'

By the time she had reached the bed, his eyes were closed against her again. Stevie dropped into the chair and dared to take his hand. No response. Her head sank into his broad, familiar palm.

Later, Harry opened his eyes. Stevie felt his grip tighten on her hand and she sat up. He was staring at her, wild with fury.

'What the hell is wrong with you?'

She blinked, trying to grasp the meaning of his question and struggled for an answer. Nothing seemed immediately appropriate.

'Nothing that a long hot bath wouldn't fix.'

He pulled his good hand away from her and for a moment his face was contorted in pain as the sudden movement vibrated through his damaged body.

'You make me sick, you know that? This isn't a fucking game. You may as well put a pillow over Hal's face right now and be done with it.'

Stevie recoiled. The mention of Hal frightened her. He was far away in another universe and she couldn't let herself think about him. Her teeth ached.

'What are you saying?'

'You should have gone when you had the chance. You promised. But no, you knew best. You just couldn't resist, could you?

Well, congratulations you've signed a death warrant for both of you. This is a war, you stupid woman. Not a stinking parlour game.'

The rant was causing him too much effort. He was hyperventilating and spots of colour spread like a rash over his face and neck.

Stevie felt each word like a blow. Harry sank back on his pillow. She spoke without looking at him, her voice low so as not to betray the hurt.

'We went to the harbour but Yang had gone. His boat wasn't there.'

'Those boats never go anywhere.'

'Well, his has.'

She glanced at him. His eyelids were shuttered again. Her eyes burned with the acid of tears. Thank God, he was all right.

The December afternoon light was gentle. The trees shivered slightly, small patches of silver shining like sequins on the thinly veined leaves. Stevie's forehead was going numb with the cold where she was leaning against the window glass. Harry's voice startled her upright.

'Where's Hal?'

She turned to look at him, still pale as tissue paper. 'He's with Lily. We're staying with her family. It didn't seem safe in the apartment and they've been very kind.'

'How long have I been here?'

'Two days.'

'What's the damage?'

Stevie took a step towards the bed. Before she could answer he said, 'Just tell me what it is.'

'Your arm. They think it'll be fine.'

'But they don't know?'

'No. They don't know.'

Harry nodded. 'Thank you.'

She held herself very still, afraid of her own collapse.

'Ramsay?'

Stevie glanced across at the other bed. Harry's eyes followed hers.

His voice was full of admiration. 'Tough little bugger.'

Stevie chose not to answer.

'I'll find out what's going on.' Harry's voice was surprisingly firm. 'There should be a network in place to get people off the island. Yang wasn't the only one.' A pause. 'What a bastard.'

'I hope you don't mind my saying, but one might have guessed an opium dealer just might not be the most trustworthy of chaps.'

They caught each other's eyes and he smiled. She thought for a moment that the joy of that small smile might choke her.

'We made plans for a line of escape with the Communists. Do you remember that young man you rescued so heroically from prison?'

She cleared her throat. 'Of course. Chen, Lily's brother. He brought the news about you being hurt. If it wasn't for him I might not have found you.' Her voice faltered.

'He will know. Ask him. They'll be aiming for Macau in the first instance.'

'Maybe I should send Hal with him. He might –'

Harry's interruption was freighted with fear. 'Are you mad? You think he'd survive without you?'

She shocked herself with the realisation of what she was saying. 'I don't know. I wasn't really thinking.'

'Promise me you'll never do anything like that.'

Stevie came to him, wanting to soothe. 'Is that what you think of me? That I'd do that?'

'Promise me.'

'All right. All right. Promise. I promise.'

Stevie knew that somewhere not too far away from this new life was the shadow life that she'd been living before she met Harry; a shadow life in which she might well have been able to send her baby boy away in the belief it was better for him, and in the conviction that it was better for her. With a degree of shame she took Harry's hand again.

'Are you hungry?'

Harry shook his head. Gripping her hand hard enough to hurt, he searched for words. 'Bloody hell, old girl, bloody hell.'

Night had fallen. It was silent in the huge old building but for the occasional moan rolling along the corridor like a gust of wind. Ken lay still on the other side of the room, his breathing shallow in spite of the morphine a harried nurse had re-administered just before dusk. Stevie was lying next to Harry on his bed. It was not comfortable. She was clinging on to the metal side bar under the mattress so as not to fall off. But she wouldn't have moved for the world. There was a pale glow as the restless clouds drew veils back and forth over the moon.

Her own voice, like ripples of water, ebbed and flowed. 'What about Madame Kung's house on the Peak? It's empty now and the air is better there and Hal can roll around in the dirt as much as he wants to. And I'll cook –'

Harry snorted an interruption. 'Now that really is going too far.'

Stevie frowned in the darkness. 'Yeah, you're right. I won't cook. But I might sweep occasionally.'

'Are you sure?'

'Don't be so surprised. The war's having a big effect on all of us, you know. For instance –.' This time she interrupted herself.

'For instance?'

She spoke slowly, unsure how he would take it. 'For instance I can be officially Chinese which might protect Hal and me. As Jishang's wife they can't argue with the paperwork. The papers have even got a nice red wax seal on them. The Japanese like things like that, don't they? And they'll be busy with the Brits and the Yanks. It'll be ages before they get round to the Chinese.' Her tone changed, losing its forced, bantering note and becoming solemn. 'I thought I'd never see you again.' She turned to him, her face a reflection of moonlight. 'Don't ever, ever do that again. Just be with me. Always. Please.'

'Won't that inhibit your freedom?'

Stevie leaned into him, holding him tight. He cried out in pain. Pulling back, she apologised, alarm like an electric shock running through her. 'Sorry. Sorry. Are you all right?'

He grimaced. 'What's love without a little pain?'

Later still. They were lying next to each other again. Dawn unfolding. Stevie kept the murmured conversation going.

'So the house is big, right? Huge, even. And you're cooking a pasta dish in the lovely kitchen.'

'Fish pie. I'm cooking fish pie. With fresh salmon and the vegetables are . . .'

'. . . .the vegetables are still in the ground because I'm on my way through the garden to pick them, no, Hal's going to pick them.'

'You're not in the garden, silly. I know where you are. You're in your God-awful messy study, writing. Writing about how dull country life is and how you wish you were in New York.'

'Ah, yes. New York. I'm on my way to my desk at the paper and I'm just stopping at the deli to pick up a couple of bagels and coffee.'

'Yes, a coffee.' They both were silent for a moment, relishing that coffee, smelling the lush dark beans. 'And I'm in our apartment with Hal trying to teach him to speak with a proper English accent.'

Stevie reached out and touched Harry's lips with her fingertips. 'I love you.' And this time there was a different silence between them.

They must have slept at last because Stevie opened her eyes into full daylight. She turned on her side towards Harry, aching all over. He opened his eyes. 'You all right?'

'I think so.' She yawned. 'Though I've scared myself sick by writing poetry. Things can't get much worse than that.'

'As long as it's not about me.'

'Just get fit and quit fretting over my writing.'

'I am fit.'

Stevie raised her eyebrows.

Harry widened his eyes in mock protest. 'Want me to prove it?'

Their kiss, raw and inappropriate, fell victim to a commotion in the corridor. Separated by raised voices and running feet, Stevie murmured 'Next time' close to his ear and their complicit smiles warmed the space between them.

The door burst open. A young nurse, not yet twenty, stood there. Fear brought her straight to the point, sheer disbelief in her voice. 'We've surrendered. There's a white flag on the police station. What are we going to do? It's Christmas.'

Stevie shook her head, the clammy blast of terror gripping her again. It was Harry who spoke.

'No more jokes about the Italians, then.'

A huge muffled explosion shook the glass in the windows. The nurse screamed and held on to the door handle for support.

Harry was serious now. 'They're blowing up our big guns.' The nurse began to sob, her hands to her face. Five or so of the walking wounded and a couple more nurses jostled into the doorway. One of the men, leaning on crutches, shouted louder than necessary in a voice stiff with fear. 'Major Field, is it true? Do you think it's true?'

Over him, she could hear the shrill, angry tones of an older nurse. 'I don't understand. It's impossible. How can we have surrendered?'

The small group had made its way into the room. In the other bed Ken shouted out, unconscious but disturbed. The angry nurse was at the window. Her scream cut through the rest of the noise like a razor. 'Oh my God.'

There was a rush for the window. Stevie stayed right where she was, sitting on the edge of Harry's bed, her legs somehow useless, her mind back in the slow motion place of those hours before she found him. The bundle of nurses and soldiers at the window murmured among themselves, holding on to each other. Stevie felt Harry's hand on her back. He was encouraging her to stand up. At first this seemed impossible but soon she found she was on her feet and had taken the three steps to the window. Over and around the heads of the others she saw nothing out of the ordinary. But then down the hillside, as if in a children's game, she spied the tiny, distant figures slowly making their way up the road. Infinitely slowly. And behind them the military trucks. It took a moment for her to register that they were Japanese. From a distance all soldiers look the same.

Hollow with disbelief, she turned back to Harry. He knew what she had seen without her saying a word. Leaving the huddle at the window, she went to him.

His voice was clear over the throbbing in her head. 'You must find Li Chen. He'll know what to do.' Then he frowned. 'By the way, how exactly did you know where I was?'

'Doctor Clarke-Russell knew where you were. The Red Cross lists.'

He nodded. They didn't touch.

Later, in another time and place, when she thought about those twenty-four hours they seemed to exist in a quite different dimension. They were suspended hanging in the white space between what had been and what was to come. Heavy with poignancy and longing, they were visible through a smoky veil of hope and delusion, which in this case was almost the same thing. The tumult of a broken world brought them crashing back into reality but even then she clung on to their shared refuge in that hospital room until the very last moment.

It was the arrival of Clarke-Russell that blew away the last wisp of curtain and everything became horribly hyper-real and crisply in focus. The huddle of nurses and patients had moved on, looking for comfort elsewhere, and maybe an hour had passed since Stevie had seen the reality of the invasion. They heard Clarke-Russell's voice, oh so reasonable and measured from the corridor.

'The food supplies are adequate for the time being.'

And in a flurry of activity he pushed open the door and was in the room followed by three Japanese officers and the familiar rotund figure of Takeda. Stevie had time to stand. Harry tried but failed to sit up.

Clarke-Russell held his hands up in dismay, his bedside manner immaculate. 'No, no, my dear chap, stay quite still. No sense in undoing all our good work, is there.'

He indicated Stevie, sweating through her already days-old shirt. 'This is my colleague Miss Steiber.' Not allowing room for any awkward questions from his military escort, he turned back to Harry. 'These gentlemen asked most particularly to meet you.'

Stevie had to swallow a spasm of laughter. It was as if they were in a drawing room in Suffolk or Mayfair. It was only later that she understood that Dr Clarke-Russell's manners were saving their lives, that it was for just such a situation that those manners had been invented and refined over the conquering centuries.

The Japanese men bowed. One set of manners meeting another. Which was more powerful? Who could say, but it was the bowing men who had the upper hand in that room on that day. Takeda said something in Japanese to his military colleagues in which Stevie recognised the words 'Major' and 'Field'. They bowed again. Harry replied in grave tones. There was more bowing and Clarke-Russell began to usher them out of the room.

'There are sixty-four men here in the hospital at the moment and twenty-five medical staff. Shall we?' He went to the door and held it open for them. The officers followed. As Clarke-Russell led them away, Stevie could hear him, efficient and dignified. 'The main thing, as I see it, is that it's imperative to keep the island free of epidemics such as cholera.'

Takeda had hung back. He took a step towards them and looked from one to the other.

'I'll do anything I can,' he said, fast and low He was gone in a shuffle of grey suit.

Stevie shifted the weight on her feet, her muscles taut as high wires.

'What did they say?'

'They said they were bowing in respect of my injuries.'

'And you, what did you say?'

'I accepted their respect.'

'What the hell does it mean? What does it mean?' Stevie could feel her voice rising as hysteria began to overcome her. 'And that bastard Clarke-Russell, collaborating before the surrender is even recognised. At the first sign of danger there he is cosying up to the enemy, all pals, and giving them a fucking tour of their new territory. What happened to putting up a fight? It's unbelievable.' She was shaking with indignation.

Harry had closed his eyes but his voice was firm. 'He is the Chief Medical Officer. His duty is to the entire population regardless of their ethnic origins – and that duty is to keep them as healthy as possible. He will continue to do his duty as long as it's permitted.' He opened his eyes. 'And so shall I.'

As the scale of the catastrophe that was befalling them rolled out before her like a landscape of grey ash, she heard Clarke-Russell's voice from the door.

'There's an ambulance going back into town now. You'd better get in.'

Stevie didn't move, frozen in the present and unable to take a step into the future.

Clarke-Russell's voice was sharp, the tones of crisis management. 'Now.'

Harry nodded at her, an encouraging brightness in his expression as if she were a little girl hanging back, being coaxed reluctantly to go through the door into a party. She went to him and, leaning over his body, she brushed her lips against the pin-sharp stubble of his face. The sickening smell of antiseptic and decay lingered in her hair for days. She was quite distraught when she could no longer smell it, pulling strands to her nose and inhaling over and over to no avail. But there in their sacred white room she breathed his stale breath and he said, 'Don't forget, I'm on a promise.'

It was with a soon-to-be familiar heavy feeling of dread that she followed Clarke-Russell's urgently beckoning hand into the new world order.

Chapter Eighteen

Nobody had thought to cut his body down. He hung from the twisted tree as if delivered there by a gust of wind. But it was not by natural means that his neck had been bound by the pale rope knotted around the branch, nor was it the wind that caused him to swing. It was the invisible ripples of air that came with each explosion no matter how far away.

The ambulance had brought her to the gate and she would not have recognised the courtyard but for Victor hanging there. The compound had been ransacked. The remains of furniture littered the yard and roaming sheets of newspapers skittered around them like demented farmyard animals. She stood for minutes; it took a very long time for her mind to compute what she was seeing: the poor little creature, grotesque, his tongue swollen and blue, lolling out of his whiskery mouth.

She didn't have time in that moment to register any grief. Lily was rushing towards her and she could hear the small noises of Hal buried deep in the cotton scarf in her arms. She felt the skin of him and the warm wash of tears on her own face. Lily was talking very fast. Stevie couldn't understand what she was saying, just the rush of words in her ears. The surreality of it all became even more absurd when she saw Phyllis Clarke-Russell, tall and gaunt, walk out of the house followed by her daughter Margaret.

Phyllis' dress was ripped right across the front. Her slip was also torn and Stevie noticed her underwear and automatically assessed it as expensive. Possibly French. Now Phyllis was talking.

'They took our house. I didn't know where to go. They were so rude, shouting, shouting and they threw my things down the staircase. Just took them and threw them – you can't imagine. Some people, the Evans and others, wanted to stay on the Peak, but I didn't want Margaret anywhere near those –' she struggled for an appropriate term but her education defeated her '– those terrible men. Thank God the boys are away at school. I don't know how I'm going to send them their tuck parcels, though, the post offices are all closed. I just don't understand what happened. We were supposed to hold out against a siege for three months. My husband told me everything, it was all planned down to the smallest detail, you know.'

Stevie clutched Hal to her and laughed out loud. It was all so ridiculous. All of it. All the stupid plans and the secrecy and the plotting. All the talking, all the fighting, all the killing. Ridiculous.

'What's wrong with that? Why are you laughing, are you mad?'

'There's nothing wrong with that. Except that it didn't work.'

Margaret was looking up at her from under long, pale lashes. She was whispering so quietly it was just sounds carried on a breeze. Stevie stepped closer to the little girl. 'What's that, Margaret?' But she wasn't talking, she was singing. It was the same thing over and over in a tuneless wheeze. 'One two three four five, once I caught a fish alive.'

Stevie glanced at Phyllis, who pulled Margaret closer to her and said, 'She's been singing it since we left. When the soldiers stopped us she just kept singing. I think that was why they let us go. I thought at first they were going to – that the worst was going to happen.' Phyllis pulled the torn dress across herself in a vain attempt to cover the damage. 'They held me so hard and they were shouting and they tried to pull Margaret away from me but she held on and was singing. It was her favourite nursery rhyme, you know. When she was a baby.'

And then Phyllis' body just contorted in on itself. She was in the grip of terrible spasms but no sound came.

There was only the whisper of 'One two three four five' from Margaret's pale lips.

Stevie reached out and, with one arm tight around Hal, held Phyllis with the other and felt her convulsions vibrate through her. She stood her ground, containing them, while Phyllis' stoic, brittle self was drowning.

And inches above their heads Victor's long, skinny arms waved gently in the tree – a nightmare flag of surrender.

The floor of the main room was littered with dreaming bodies. Phyllis and Margaret had been given the best spot, by the niche where the house god squatted, unblinking and useless. In the moonlight Stevie sat with her back against the wall and looked closely at her battered, American passport, at the photo of a younger, less knowing and less weary self. Stevie considered her as distantly as one might an old school friend with whom one had lost touch.

She remembered going to the photographer's studio in Utica to have the picture taken. It had been a cold day and when she'd taken her hat off her hair had stuck to her head in the shape of its crown. The photographer had flirted with her and she had blushed and shivered under the sudden hot lights. The smile in the photograph was wholesome, yes, but also alert and shadowed by a wilfullness. She knew she wasn't much to look at, her mother had told her enough times, but she wasn't going to let that mar the picture. She was going places after all. That was what the photo was for. And that passport had been a kind of totem to her. As long as she had it she knew who she was and everybody else knew too and she would be safe, protected by the invisible shield of being an American.

Taking her dark blue gabardine coat out from under the other clothes that made up her pillow, she found the hem and began unpicking the stitches. The thread wouldn't come at first, but as she tugged, it eventually gave. She pulled out just enough to allow her to tuck the passport in between the lining and the coat. As she slipped it into the gap she knew she was peeling away a part of herself. For all her vaunted independence this small book had been part of her courage. She was letting it go. So who was she now?

She woke to a piercing scream. She was clutching her coat in her arms. In the gloom before dawn she strained to identify the shadowy figures shuffling in the room. The movements were urgent but oddly quiet. There was another scream and Stevie understood it was Margaret, her young voice incoherent with fear. Stevie scrambled to her feet in time to see Phyllis, with Margaret clinging to her skirts, being manhandled through the door by several Japanese soldiers.

'No. Stop. What are you doing?' she yelled.

Phyllis turned her head towards her as she was pushed through the doorway. 'It's all right, I knew they'd come for us. We'll be fine.' She was amazingly calm, almost serene. 'And by the way, I thought you should know, I never liked Sylvia.'

It took Stevie nearly all day to cross the city – a journey which before, in her other life, would have taken half an hour. *Before* haunted her; when there had been food and drink and cocktails and music. When there were tailors to make you copies of dresses and there was a piano bar and olives. When there were markets and movies and orchid corsages. *Before* lay over everything she saw like a double exposure.

She had left at dawn. The tyre tracks of the truck that had taken Phyllis and Margaret away were still warm as she ran out of the gates of the compound. The smell of hot rubber mixed with jasmine made her feel slightly nauseous. Or maybe that was simply the lack of food.

It had been only a few hours since her journey back to Lily's compound from the hospital, but the fresh damage to the streets made negotiating them complicated. It was a dreamscape in which familiar roads ended in a pile of rubble and well-trodden alleys no longer existed. Apartment buildings had sunk into the ground, and everywhere there were fires. A haze of dust hung and swirled, obscuring things, melting their edges like a snowstorm. At one point Stevie stumbled over something that gave as her heel dug into it. She looked down. An arm, perfect but for the mangled stump where a shoulder once was, lay as if carelessly dropped. The palm of the hand faced upwards, the fingers curled over on themselves.

She saw several military vehicles cruise along the devastated streets but nobody stopped her. The blister swelled again on the ledge of her heel. She ran and when she couldn't breathe she walked, until she was heading up the steep slope of the hill.

She imagined that maybe Harry was standing by his window, miraculously better, his bad arm in a sling but better, and that he could see her as she came back to him. She tried to walk with a positive swagger and lifted her head so he could read how much better things were and how he shouldn't worry for Hal and her.

When she reached the hospital she raced across the gravel past the ambulances and made straight for Clarke-Russell's office, surprised when nobody challenged her. He was at his desk as she knew he would be, exhaustion etched in the lines on his face. He looked up, wearily, as she came in. And again she was sideswiped by the sensation that everything familiar was altered. He was and was not himself. His features had slipped into a new alignment.

'There was nothing I could do. I'm sorry,' she said.

As he stood up he was shaking his head. 'No, I'm sorry. We think he's been taken to Argyle, to the officers' camp.'

Stevie wondered what he was talking about. 'They're not going to take Margaret to a military camp, she's only eight.'

'Margaret?' His daughter's name seemed to puzzle him.

'There was no time. They just came and took them. It was over so fast. They didn't even have time to take any clothes. But Phyllis was calm, she said something about knowing they'd come. They'd been stopped at a checkpoint in the afternoon, you see, and she had actually told them her name and given the address of where they were headed and everything.'

As Clarke-Russell understood what she was telling him, he swayed and had to support himself with his palms on the desk in front of him. 'I see.' He stared at the pile of orderly papers, the lowlands of a defeated bureaucracy.

His voice was changed and halting. 'I was afraid that might – I'm so tired.' The glimmer of weakness in him frightened Stevie almost more than anything else.

He looked over to her and, remembering, he pulled himself upright again. 'Stevie, it's Harry, there was a nasty moment last night. They asked all of us, everybody here to sign a pledge not to attempt an escape. He wouldn't sign. I tried to convince him but it was point-blank refusal. You know Harry, stubborn as a mule.'

Clarke-Russell was still talking as Stevie turned and ran. The corridor stretched out, endless, she couldn't move fast enough.

His bed was empty. The bedclothes were coiled like a skin, shed on the floor. The dent of his head was in the pillow. Her hands flew to her mouth, an instinctive suppression of a scream. There was a movement in the periphery of her vision. She spun around and in the other bed where Ken should have been, a bald middle-aged man writhed, his face completely covered in bandages. Then she saw she had been mistaken: he was not bald – the whole top of his scalp was missing.

Stevie backed out of the room and Clarke-Russell caught her as she fell.

The cup was hot in her hands. The steam warmed her face and she was glad of it. The tea itself was dark and bitter. But she understood it wasn't the drinking that mattered. It was about the ritual of it. The making and the receiving and the time it allowed for both parties to somewhat recover themselves. Clarke-Russell sat opposite her. They were in the nurses' social room. There were several scratchy armchairs and in the corner was a shiny wooden phonograph on spindly metal legs.

His voice was soothing, practised from years of telling people bad news. 'It was always only a matter of time for him, you must have known that. If those gendarmes or Kempeitei or whatever get half a chance they'll have us all.'

'Who are they?'

'They're supposed to be the new civilian police force. But they answer to the military. It's a sham, naturally, to make the population feel they're under Japanese governance, not just army law. They're known for their ruthlessness. Brutal chaps to put the fear of God in you. You don't want to get on the wrong side of them.'

'What about you? Did you sign?'

'Yes, I signed. I'm not a soldier.'

'What will they do to him?'

Clarke-Russell sighed and coughed before he spoke. 'Listen, my dear, we are led to believe that people are being held according to international law as prisoners of war. They say the rest of us are free to go about our business.' He leaned forward, frowning. 'Harry's friend, the plump chap – who is he?'

'Mr Takeda? I don't really know. He's something to do with business development here. He works for a company that make lenses for glasses. They've known each other a long time. They knew each other in Japan.'

'Yes.' Another audible exhalation. 'It's not clear whether Harry will be helped or compromised by his connections. Be very careful.'

'He's been kind.'

'Nobody will like the idea that Mr Takeda might offer some protection to his friends. The gendarmes would take badly any perceived threat to their authority. As for us – well, knowing the enemy isn't always read as straightforwardly as it might be. Just watch out. People might think he's trying to put one over on them.'

'Harry?'

'Not him, his Japanese friend. And they might be right.'

Stevie bowed her head over her tea. There was a cloud of scum riding on its surface. Suddenly disgusted, she put the cup down on the table beside her.

Clarke-Russell's hand was hot and dry on hers. 'When they come for me you must not under any circumstances attempt to do anything.' The palm of his hand radiated heat. 'Don't try to communicate with me. Don't send food and hide what you have.'

She surprised herself with how long it took for the reality of what was happening to sink in. She really could not comprehend it. There must be a way to get to Harry. There must be a way to find Phyllis and Margaret. There must be a way to stop this ludicrous situation. How could it be that life as they knew it had just stopped? Like a clock or a heart, halted. She remembered something.

'Sergeant Ramsay, did they take him with Harry?'

He shook his head. 'The infection was overwhelming. It might even have been for the best.'

She was a long way into town before she came to a standstill, so stricken that she could hardly see. Everything was blurred by the haze of fear. She did not notice the slim Japanese man, suave in his well-cut suit, who had followed her since she left the hospital. He stopped too, at a discreet distance, and examined his fingernails. Across the street a Japanese soldier walked past, dragging an elderly Chinese woman behind him on a string. Like a dog.

Chapter Nineteen

The days passed in a kind of trance. It seemed marvellous that normal activities were still undertaken. They went to whichever market was rumoured to have food for sale. They bought it and they cooked it and they ate it. They washed themselves and their clothes with care, using as little soap and powder as possible. They adapted to the new world order and didn't indulge too much in the luxury of analysis or prognosis. Stevie became obsessed with anxiety about running out of powdered milk for Hal. Lily was irritated by it.

'If you had breast-fed him like a normal person you wouldn't be having to worry about it.'

And, unusually, Stevie felt she had nothing to say. The hospital had assumed and she had assumed and before there had been a chance to think otherwise Hal had been taken away and given a bottle and she had been left to soothe her milk-swollen breasts with cold flannels. Oh for that milk now. She was condemned instead to scour the devastated city in search of it, climbing over the impromptu barricades of fallen buildings, and bartering her watch without a second thought when the price quadrupled overnight.

Every time she ventured forth it was into a different landscape. As in a nightmare where a place is familiar but altered, she could never depend on a certain building or turn in the road to be quite how she last left it. And everywhere the flag of the Rising Sun insulted her. It flew from every conceivable place, tattooing the island. The first time she had seen the harbour after the surrender she had taken a route through what was left of Victoria Square and had paused for a moment to get her bearings in the rubble. Glancing out at the water she had seen the masts of sunken and scuttled ships lying at tipsy angles, reaching up to the sky like so many gravestones. No less moving were the carcasses of cars lying in the road like prehistoric animals, useless and mysterious. And the burned-out and looted shops, naked and open to the elements.

Fires still burned and there was danger not just from the Japanese soldiers but from the mobs of ruthless Chinese looters armed with axes and staves. The second time she went out of the compound in search of milk, the sudden thump of an explosion shook her, the ground beneath her feet shifting with the vibrations. Walking into the odd silence that followed, she turned the corner of the Central market on Queen's Road. There was a huge crater where the shell had just exploded. Outside a restaurant a table set for dinner was covered in what at first glance looked like linen. It was a snowdrift of plaster.

She waded through a shimmering sea of shattered glass and then she heard the screaming. Glancing up, she saw a small crowd of people trying to rescue a man who hung by his hands from the balcony of a house. He was making a terrible noise although his mouth had gone, and his leg was attached to his body by the thinnest thread of flesh. He was silhouetted against a spectacularly beautiful scarlet sunset. Everywhere there was living flesh reduced to messy smears. Mangled, twisted, torn, blackened and contorted bodies lay in a jigsaw puzzle on the shards of glass.

Stevie's unwavering focus on her mission insulated her from the worst of what she had seen. Finding a tin of milk was a victory and she watched over those tins as closely as she watched over Hal and would have fought over them as fiercely. They represented her ability to keep him alive.

She lost the energy to write anything down. There were moments of intense wondering – where was Jishang? Did he know what was happening in Hong Kong? Did he ever think of her and worry? And Declan? Was he filing great stories while she was chasing tins of food? Her instinct to bear witness was as sharp as ever and the noise and destruction all around took root in her. She told herself she would remember enough when the time came. For now, each day was about survival not testimony.

One evening Mr Li, Lily's father, talked about his fighting days in Manchuria at the beginning of the Japanese invasion in 1931. He spoke in a low voice and Lily translated. Their voices were a murmur in the cold night.

'As each wave of Japanese soldiers came we shot them down and then the next wave came, climbing over the dead bodies, and we shot them down, and then the next and the next until the river was full to ground level with bodies. Then they walked over them to the other side where we were. And then we ran. They've been fighting like this for years. We knew, so why didn't the British?'

The next night he packed up and went to sleep at his brother's furniture shop. It wasn't open for business and there was nothing much left to pillage but it was his duty to safeguard the family's concerns come what may. There was no conversation or speculation between the women left behind in the compound. It was enough that they lived through the day.

One night, a cool evening, Stevie settled Hal in his basket. She borrowed a cardigan of Lily's which only a few weeks ago she would have sneered at for its being pale pink, but for which now she was unreservedly grateful. She began to help Mrs Li bring the rice to the table. As soon as she heard the voices, she knew. The men were hurling words at each other with a heavy incoherent ostentation. The tone was transparent. They were drunk and out of control. They kicked open the gate and stood, wide-legged and swaying for a moment before the man at the back pushed them forward and they were in the compound.

The women froze – a tableau of domesticity. The steam from the rice bowl warmed Stevie's face. A small table was set in the courtyard. Lily and her mother were already seated. Stevie was poised to serve the food. It could have been anywhere at any time. The shouting started up again and one of the men stepped towards the women, his gun in one hand waving erratically around the yard. He glanced several times over his shoulder at his baying companions. They were pack animals, primitive and pumped up with the renegade spoils of war. There was no doubting their intentions. No need to share a language. The communication was clear – as predators they circled their prey.

Mrs Li began rocking back and forth, chanting an age-old song for mercy, her voice scaling heights as she begged. Lily clutched the edge of the tablecloth as if it could save her. It slipped softly over the varnished table, bringing utensils clattering to the ground. Stevie understood that they were all playing out an ancient ritual.

The ringleader, still shouting, stepped up to the table and swiped at it with his gun. The jug of water tipped over, spilling on to Mrs Li. She fell to her knees, still rocking back and forth, now knocking her forehead against the table in a rhythmic percussion to her prayer. The soldier brought his gun down on her head. The crack on her skull echoed through the yard but she did not falter in her song. Stevie wondered why he had to shout like that. On and on. Maybe it was the only thing he had to keep himself on course?Maybe if he stopped shouting he would stop in his tracks, look about him and withdraw, puzzled at his own behaviour and apologise for having disturbed them. Maybe this was the same reason Mrs Li kept on singing – it sustained her survival. As long as he was shouting he existed, as long as she sang so did she.

The shouting man circled the table. Lily kept her eyes down and was quite still. He paused briefly behind her before catching Stevie's eye. This seemed to invigorate him. He lunged at her and his grasp on her neck was painful. His fingers were dry and rough. She felt the edge of his sleeve rubbing against her collarbone. There was an overwhelmingly rancid smell of stale clothes and fermentation, sharp at the back of her throat. With the gun he knocked the bowl out of her hands. Soft white grains rained on to the table like cherry blossom. The bowl rolled on the ground. Stevie noted with bizarre satisfaction that it did not break. Then she was being propelled across the yard, the pressure on her neck making it hard for her to swallow. She could see the other men approaching the table. One of them kicked the old lady so that she fell on to her side. Her chanting continued, quieter now, a background noise. Stevie felt the fingers on her neck tighten. The man was pushing her through the open door into the sleeping quarters.

An alarming and urgent thought gripped her. 'Ssshhh,' she said and put her finger to her lips. The man grunted, disconcerted but not diverted from his goal. She was insistent. This was a vital command. 'Don't wake the baby.'

Understanding the gist of this, he looked around and saw Hal's basket. Stevie's voice was low.

'You mustn't wake him up. He's sleeping.'

She really meant it. Not disturbing Hal had become the only imperative. The foul breath of this man must not in any way come close to the fresh newness of her son. The man muttered and looked her in the eye for a moment. She saw something that shocked her beyond anything else. He didn't care. Like an animal there was nothing he could understand except satisfying his aroused appetite. In that moment she understood – the rules of life were changed.

The soldier suddenly let go of her neck and grabbed her wrist instead. He had seen the glimmer of something shiny. Inserting his clumsy fingers inside her sleeve he pulled at the silver chain of her charm bracelet. Stevie put her hand over his and helped him – trying to undo the clasp.

'Yes, look it's lovely. Wait, don't break it. Let me.' She managed to catch the tiny silver trigger with a nail and the chain was released. It slipped off her wrist, dropping and coiling on the floor. The man squatted to examine his prize. The charms were delicate in his filthy palm: the kitten playing with a tiny red ball in memory of the Siamese cat who had slept on her pillow all through her childhood, the leprechaun cross-legged and clutching his knees, a wicked smile between the saucer ears. It had been given to her on her first day of high school for good luck. The galloping horse that she had bought for herself the first time she won at the races, a motor scooter from the boy who'd thoughtlessly taken her virginity, an alarm clock with its arms set at five past six, a wake-up call from her best friend at college who had spent years trying to get her out of bed in time for class, a swan with an s-shaped neck, a vain attempt on her mother's part to encourage Stevie to feel more like a swan than the ugly duckling she knew her to be, and the silver coffee pot from her father in tribute to her inability to master rudimentary cooking skills. Shiny little markers of her progress through life.

Another grunt and the chain was in his pocket. Just as his eyes rested on her again there was an angry yell from the yard and the dry crack of a gunshot.

The man dropped to his knees and crawled quickly to the door. From where she stood in the room Stevie could see a scuffle in the yard. The shouting of the soldiers took on a different tone. It was purposeful and aggressive and there were Chinese voices now. One of the Japanese soldiers was lying in the dust and another was being held from behind, a gun hard at his temples.

With a lurch of hope, Stevie recognised the familiar figure of Chen together with another young man. In their loose peasant clothes they had the double advantage of surprise and of not being blind drunk.

'Come out and let me see you. Come out.' Chen's order, though in Cantonese, brought Stevie's assailant out into the yard, his hands up, his feet dragging. Stevie could hear Chen and his comrade shouting but she ran over to Hal's basket and stood guard over him, his sleep determined and amazingly uninterrupted. She was more alert to his quiet snuffling than to the yelling and fighting outside. Soon she was aware the skirmish had abated and there was only Lily's sobbing to be heard, underscored by the haunting, fragmented sound of the old lady's song.

The night was still upon them. Stevie, sitting on the step of the sleeping room, listened to Chen as he talked. His companion,

Ping Wei, a thick-haired boy with a goofy smile, sat quietly on his haunches nearby. She took a drag of the raspy throat-burning cigarette he'd lit for her. It was a Pirate, the cheapest brand, and in former days she would never have dreamed of smoking one. It was for rickshaw men and street vendors. Now it was all that was available and she smiled as she thought of how war brought a certain democracy to bad habits as well as to everything else. They whispered though nobody could hear them. The remaining Japanese soldiers had melted into the night. Chen and Ping Wei had dragged the dead man's body out into the alley beyond the compound gates. Lily and Mrs Li lay inside the house, curled up against each other, recovering through the balm of sleep.

'The streets are dangerous, even for us. Men like those, they are hungry and have been too long fighting. They've forgotten.'

Stevie glanced into the yard where the marks left by the soldier Chen had shot were clear – a gash in the earth from where he fell led to the gate where he was heaved out.

'Who is us?'

Chen nodded towards the gently smiling Ping Wei. 'We work with others. We have ways of passing information and also supplies. We have plans and we won't let Hong Kong be forgotten in the bigger story.'

'Ah, the communistic society beckons and will take over the world.'

Chen smiled, the gap in his front teeth made him look even younger than he was.

'I hope so. The rest of the world can make up its own mind but it is the future for China.'

'You're very sure.'

'I am. And I can assure you I am far from alone.'

'I'm kind of envious of your conviction but I'm too damn adolescent and contrary to ever quite follow the thinking when the thinking is proscribed, do you know what I mean?'

'Believe me I do know, but there's something going on that is maybe hard for you to understand. Let me put it like this, there are times when independent thought is a luxury and for the sake of all the great mass of people it's necessary to follow a line.'

Stevie frowned. 'I guess so. That's the nature of revolution.'

'Exactly.'

'But what I don't understand is why you comrades are risking your lives to help us defeated capitalists?'

'Perhaps this will help explain.' Chen took a deep breath. 'Yu Bao was twelve years old. Japanese soldiers came to her house and cut her face with their knives so that her daddy would do what they said. She remembered all sorts of details: how the soldier who held her smelt very bad. How they made her father touch her little sister in her private place and then made him put a bottle inside her and how she was crying and how her mother tried to stop them so one of the other men split her mother's head open with a sword.'

'Oh, God.'

'There's more.' He took another pull on his cigarette, the light burned brightly. 'If you have the stomach for it.'

Stevie gave a small nod, her instinct to bear witness overcoming her feelings of repugnance.

Chen's voice was harsh as he whispered the litany of horror to her in the semi-darkness. 'She told us there were five of them, five of these animals. Her father was made to lie on top of her little sister but he chose to suffocate his own daughter rather than hurt her. The soldiers were so incensed by this that they stabbed Yu Bao with their bamboo sticks and then they cut her father all over with their swords, at which point she passed out. When she woke up again the house was an inferno. They had set fire to it.'

Stevie was shaking her head.

'We found her in the burned-out remains of her family house, half-dead from the injury caused by the bamboo stick that had been forced into her vagina.'

He inhaled the last of his cigarette and flicked the butt across the courtyard. 'She died in hospital.' He glanced at Stevie but she had covered her eyes with her hands. 'So maybe you can see that your idea of whose side we comrades might be on is a disappointingly simple point of view. Sorry to be so blunt, but it is.'

Stevie uncovered her eyes, liking him now more than ever. 'Yes, I do see.' They were silent for a moment before she nudged him gently. 'By the way, what happened? You seem so reasonable. You're supposed to be a wild revolutionary. You ought to look out, in a minute I won't trust your credentials.'

'Wu Jishang told me that you were surprisingly reasonable too.'

Stevie felt a physical lurch somewhere near her heart. 'Jishang.'

'My cousin.'

'Where is he? How is he?'

'Alive.'

'That's all?'

Chen shrugged. There was a moment of silence. Ping Wei had picked up a twig and was drawing patterns in the ground with it. He looked like the young boy he was and not the man capable of so recently killing another. She could hear the creak of the twisted tree's branches in the courtyard as she struggled with the realisation that she couldn't know how Jishang was, that she couldn't know how anybody was. Declan, Harry, Phyllis – hell, even the manager of the Peninsula Hotel ballroom whose announcement had stopped the music; everybody was lost in the darkness.

Chen picked up a small stone from the ground and tossed it from one hand to the other. Without looking at her he said, 'There's something you could do for us.' She waited. The stone traced its arc a few more times before he went on. 'They're putting the officers in a camp at the Argyle Street barracks. Some things need to be delivered there. We would show you how.'

She felt suddenly cold. Argyle Street. That's where they had taken Harry.

Chen's voice was level, casual even.

'Soldiers imprisoned in Argyle are allowed to receive food parcels. The object would be hidden in the food. I have to be honest, it's a risk. If you were to be found out, nobody could do anything for you. You must understand this.'

Found out? This was insane. What exactly was he asking of her? What about Hal? What would happen to him? What might happen to her? She flinched with the remembered smell of that disgusting man so recently upon her. She knew that the romance of Chen's request, the possibility of adventure, would have been irresistible to her before. And she was tugged back by the memory of Harry shouting that it was not just about her any more. But in the very act of being careful she rebelled. What did it matter that it was crazy? Who was she if not the fearless woman of her own making? The girl who flung convention on its quivering back with the force of her will? Was the fact of being a mother a life-sentence of caution and petty-minded fear? This would be her chance, finally, to do something for Harry. She remembered something that Harry had told her and, as she turned to Chen, Hal cried out from inside – a small dreamy wail.

'Have you heard of a group, a sort of network, who are helping people escape?'

'Why do you ask?'

'I thought maybe you – it doesn't matter.'

She dropped the end of her cigarette to the ground and got up to soothe her child, her great love and at the same time her great burden.

Chen smiled his young boy smile again. 'I'll tell you one thing, you'll never make a career in espionage.' He stepped close, eyes level with hers. 'When Major Field and the others first talked about setting up a network in case of an occupation I thought they were crazy. How could white men come and go without being seen? Impossible. But they weren't crazy. We come and go as their eyes and ears. There are more of us than you might think.'

'Yes,' she said. It was agreement enough.

After Chen and Ping Wei had gone Stevie, satisfied that Hal was lost in sleep, slipped under her blanket. She lay her head on the blue raincoat that deep inside contained her previous identity.

Chapter Twenty

January 1942

During the first few weeks of the Japanese Occupation there was an eerie veneer of normal life. Stevie had been amazed to see copies of an English language newspaper called the *Hong Kong News* being sold on street corners. Published daily, it gave a sickening impression of a distorted normality. Along with advertisements for familiar venues, a daily Japanese language lesson and an overall jaunty tone, it contained laughably blatant propaganda.

That morning, as she stood at the table, impatient to be alone for a few minutes, a headline had caught her eye. She looked up from the paper, shaking her head. 'You saw the mess they made of Lane Crawford the other day?'

Lily squinted at the needle she was trying to thread. 'I couldn't believe it. There wasn't a shelf with anything on it.'

'Right. Well, apparently the pillaging is an invention of the British propaganda machine. Oh and Lane Crawford isn't Lane Crawford any more. It's the Matsuzakaya.'

Lily rolled her eyes. 'It'll never stick. They're trying to call the Peninsula something else too.'

Lily leaned over her shoulder and pointed at an advertisement. 'The snack bar at the Hong Kong Hotel is serving tempura.' She went back to her skirmish with the needle and thread. 'Are you going to wrap the tins as well as the fruit?'

'I thought I would, yes.'

'Don't use the whole lot, save some sheets for lavatory paper.'

'Best thing for it.'

They exchanged a smile. Stevie tore off a sheet and began to wrap one of the tins arrayed in front of her.

'At last.' Lily held up the needle, finally threaded. 'The light's terrible in here.' She stood up and headed for the door.

As soon as she was out of the room Stevie fumbled in her pocket for the sharp piece of metal that Chen had given her and, putting it carefully on the table next to the tub of lard, she checked over her shoulder to make sure she was unobserved. The tub was deep enough for her hand to sink in up to her wrist. The white sticky fat oozed between her fingers. She ducked her head further under the washing line that was strung across the kitchen. A nappy kept edging into her line of vision and she was irritated. The lard smelt sour. Her stomach churned. An odd side-effect of being constantly hungry was that all sorts of smells made her nauseous. This was not a good thing in a city that no longer had refuse collection and in which everywhere there were putrefying corpses becoming compost, trapped under the ruins of their homes.

She leaned over the table and dug the small radio part deep into the blubber. Then pulling her fingers out, she spread the fat over the top, smoothing it as best she could.

The pram had arrived that morning. It had been left just inside the gate and been greeted with amazement by Lily and Mrs Li. There had been much debate as to the provenance of such a fine gift. It had in truth seen better days, designed for a uniformed nanny to trot around the Serpentine in Hyde Park, high-handled and very springy. It was most decidedly not a rough terrain vehicle but Stevie, knowing that it had come from Chen, had acted both delighted and surprised. Then she had announced that she had a great idea: she would take the pram with a food parcel for Harry to Argyle. Neither Lily nor Mrs Li could understand why she would take such a risk but Stevie had worn down their objections in the end. It was just as well they had no idea of the true nature of the expedition. A food parcel was one thing, smuggling radio parts into the camp was quite another.

At the last minute Lily was reluctant to let Stevie and Hal go alone but Stevie, thinking fast, had passed on the quickly invented rumour that there might be potatoes coming in that day and Lily was persuaded to head for the market instead. Stevie didn't like the subterfuge but knew that if anything went wrong, the less Lily knew the better.

Hal was wrapped in her grey sweater and surrounded on both sides by the baskets of food. She had put everything she could find in them: a packet of tea, a loaf of not-quite-stale white bread, two tins of sardines, a fat tomato and some peaches she had harvested in the night from a neighbour's tree. While Lily and Mrs Li had practised pushing the pram across the yard, Stevie, in the kitchen, had hidden the tub of lard under the sardine tins in one of the baskets.

The journey started badly. Stevie had just about got used to pushing the pram, though one of its wheels didn't turn properly. All the shops on Queen's Road – now Nakameiji-dori, a brand-new sign announced its Japanese name – were shuttered but the pavements were lined with hawkers selling piles of food at extortionate prices along with candlesticks, pots and pans, plumbing pipes, electric lights, bedding and porcelain trinkets, all clearly freshly looted from the abandoned flats on the Peak. She wove past them, half-expecting to recognise something of her own on a stall. There were the usual long queues of Chinese families waiting to receive cooked rice from the newly established congee kitchens.

In a narrow street she had to step back against the walls of a building when a convoy of Japanese military lorries rolled by. She knew well enough to keep her eyes down and not catch the eye of any of the soldiers and she mentally checked the pocket in which she had put her identity card. Woe betide anyone who was stopped without one. She wasn't the only non-Chinese person in the streets but she was one of the very few. The British and Americans had been interned at the former military base at Stanley but German, Swiss, Portuguese, Spanish and Scandinavian nationals were still at liberty. Her card identified her as Wu Stevie, the wife of a Chinese citizen.

As the last of the lorries passed she glimpsed the pale faces of European men and women, small moons in the dark interior of the trucks. When one of the lorries slowed a thin voice called out.

'They're taking us to Stanley. We were in the Peninsula Hotel. Name of Taylor. Please get news to my mother in Manchester.'

It was thrown out with the same hope as a message in a bottle.

She pushed on and from a vantage point at Wyndham Street she caught sight of an implausible scene. The cricket green had been transformed into a giant car park; it shimmered in the sunshine. There were hundreds of cars in neat lines, their bodywork sparkling. Every car on the island that hadn't been destroyed in the invasion must have been there. Big American limousines and tiny British Austins, a democracy of stolen vehicles. And as she watched she saw other cars being loaded on to the deck of a cargo ship. Further out in the harbour there were crates of what looked like canned food being transferred from small boats on to another large ship. The Japanese were taking everything. She stared for a moment too long. A Japanese soldier turned the corner and she glanced up. Two Indian policemen in ill-fitting uniforms were at his side. She had seen quite a few former Indian Army soldiers. They were cynically being encouraged, as fellow exploited Asians, to join the Japanese civilian police force rather than accept imprisonment among their oppressors. The soldier stooped and picked up a broad piece of wood, the size of a baseball bat, from the rubble. He threw it directly at her. It caught the top of her head and she staggered from the force of the blow. She did not cry out and, disappointed, the soldier moved on. Tears of humiliation and pain burned the back of her eyes as she steered the pram past the lump of wood.

She whispered, 'It's all right, baby, it's all right,' but since Hal hadn't woken up the words of comfort were more for herself.

The Star Ferry trip across the harbour was an ordeal of tense vigilance and by the time she got to Argyle Street she was exhausted. There was a queue of hollow-eyed, mostly Chinese women and their oddly subdued children waiting to deliver food parcels. Everybody seemed to have a layer of dust on their skin – a matt greyness had settled around their despair. The ground was uneven, pebbles and lumps of earth kept getting stuck in the pram wheels. Luckily, Hal didn't seem to mind. Lying on his back was a new adventure and he wasn't missing being tied tight in his sling. The sky was blue, the day pleasantly cool. Stevie concentrated on not falling too far behind the woman in front of her. They walked in a kind of parade along the outside perimeter fence of the camp. They were mostly silent. Progress was slow but Stevie was aware of a young Chinese woman behind her.

She had a small child hanging on to each hand and they were dragging tired feet and seemed unnaturally quiet. An incongruous birdsong rose above the sound of tramping feet and the squeaking of the pram wheels.

At a little distance behind the wire fence the prisoners also walked. This was their daily ritual. On both sides of the fence Japanese soldiers patrolled. The women and the prisoners scanned the lines, looking for each other. Stevie studied each gaunt face in turn. Would she see Harry? Suddenly there was a shrill shout. The Chinese girl directly behind Stevie had rushed to the wire.

'Jamie – they've cut off our water. Jamie!'

One of the men, emaciated and exhausted, made a rush out of line towards the fence. Before he could get close a soldier on the women's side of the fence ran forward and pushed the crying girl with the butt of his gun in the small of her back. She moved on, sobbing. In front of her, Stevie speeded up and forced herself not to stare at the spot in the pram under which lay the doctored tub.

As they approached the gatehouse they slowed again and came to a standstill. Women and children waited, some squatting, some shifting from foot to foot, but all silenced by a combination of resignation and anxiety. Stevie was aware of the occasional soldier strolling past the line but she averted her gaze so as not to call attention to herself. Curiously, what she felt wasn't fear but a kind of anticipation. A low-level hum of adrenalin. A few steps forward. A few more. And she was at the gate. A guard peered into the pram. Hal, playing with his newly discovered hands, smiled at him. The guard poked around in the shopping baskets. Stevie kept herself very still. He picked up one of the baskets. The one with the tub in it.

She felt panic rise in her throat like bile. Her fingers tightened on the pram handle to stop her reflex desire to tear it out of his hands and run through the gates with it to find Harry. To rescue him. To see his long-limbed body and be comforted. To bring back their life.

A slim man in the high-booted uniform of the sinister gendarmes stepped out of the shadows beside the gatehouse and smoothly took the basket from the guard. There was a short exchange between them and the guard moved on to the girl behind, who was still quietly crying for her Jamie. Dapper and all the more menacing for the pleasant tone of his voice, the gendarme smiled at Stevie as if they were old friends. He leaned into the pram and stroked Hal's face.

'That's a great kid you've got there.' His English had an American tinge to it. Stevie restrained her urge to slap him away from her baby. Her jaw was set tight against making a mistake. He straightened up and indicated the basket he was holding gingerly in his fingers. 'And this is for?'

'Major Harry Field.' The tremor in her voice almost derailed her.

He weighed the basket in his hand. Then he picked out the tub of lard. For a moment it seemed as though he might open it. He examined the label. A second later he dropped it back among the other groceries. He gestured to the guard and handed him the basket with a small nod, saying, 'Major Field.' The guard picked up the other two baskets as well and took them in the direction of the camp gates.

Stevie tore her eyes away from the baskets as they continued their journey into Harry's hands. A journey she herself longed for. Stiff with the effort of behaving normally, she managed what she hoped was a smile to the gendarme. 'Thank you.'

Then she pressed on the handles in an attempt to manoeuvre the pram around the other way. All she could think was that maybe she had just signed Harry's death warrant. Maybe Chen had conned her into this delivery, which, in a moment of awful clarity, she saw was certainly an act of stupidity and madness. She might as well have primed a bomb and addressed it with Harry's name. What proof did she have that Chen was what he said he was? Yes, he was Jishang's cousin – at some complicated remove – but what did that really mean in the scheme of things? And for that matter, it was not exactly clear where Jishang's true loyalties lay. She wanted to turn back and grab the baskets out of the guard's hands. She was so consumed with doom-laden thoughts that she didn't notice the gendarme keeping pace alongside her.

'May I walk with you?'

She glanced at him, startled.

He laughed, a tight grim staccato sound. Mirthless. 'I don't want to say goodbye to my little friend.' And he put his hand on the side of the pram.

Stevie concentrated – one foot in front of the other and again and again.

'I do hope they are treating Major Field well.' His voice was smooth and insinuating. 'I met him a few times, you know, and I always found him to be most candid.'

Stevie nodded. 'Yes. He is.'

'You are American.' Not a question, a statement.

She glanced at him. His hand still rested on the edge of the pram. 'I have Chinese papers.'

He nodded as if she was just confirming to him something with which he was already quite familiar. 'There is an agreement, you may have heard, to repatriate all American citizens.

A mutually beneficial exchange. There will be a ship, not ideal of course should you suffer from seasickness but a way back nonetheless.'

Stevie was a fly in a perfect web. She shook her head. 'Like I said. I have Chinese papers.'

He stopped suddenly, his voice formal. 'I am inviting you to an appointment at the gendarmerie tomorrow at three. It's in the Supreme Court building. My name is Nakamura.'

Leaning into the pram he squeezed Hal's cheeks. 'You are quite something, kid, quite something.' Then, turning sharply on his heel, he walked back towards the gatehouse.

Stevie barely lifted her head on the journey home. She was passing a small park when, alerted by the shouts, she glanced up. The first thing that caught her eye were the white armbands of the gendarmes. The men were laughing. One of them waved his bayonet in the air in a kind of celebration. The limp body of a baby was impaled on the end of it, its limbs loose, its head lolling like a doll. Oddly there didn't seem to be any blood.

The next day at two in the afternoon, Stevie and Lily stood together in the house. Stevie held tight to the squirming solidity of Hal and her voice sounded firmer than she felt.

'If anything happens to me – if I don't come back, please get a message to Harry. And to my mother.'

Stevie inhaled the sour-sweet smell of Hal and then plunged him into Lily's arms. They were standing in the sleeping room. She had taken great care to dress well. Lily had resewn the loose buttons on her shirt and her straight grey skirt was freshly ironed. She had not slept except for maybe a few fitful minutes towards dawn and she felt strung out like a thin rubber band.

She reached down and picked up the gabardine coat. Fumbling with the lining, she retrieved her totem and held it out to Lily, its cover tired but still there.

Lily seeing what it was, took a step backwards. 'No, you keep that. You never know, it might make all the difference in the end.'

Chapter Twenty-One

The pseudo-classic façade of the Supreme Court building was supposed to convey the idea of power and justice marching shoulder to shoulder through the empire, ensuring the security of all those lucky enough to be ruled by the British. Now that it had fallen so fast and so comprehensively into the hands of another empire-building nation, it offered Stevie little reassurance as she walked up its steps, past the towering wall of sandbags, to the veranda. What protection was there now from the mighty scales of justice?

Among the uniformed soldiers Nakamura lounged conspicuously against one of the pillars, sallow and sinister. He smiled as he watched her climb the steps. As she approached he waved away the guard who stood ready to ask her to identify herself.

'Miss Steiber, how marvellous. So punctual.' He glanced at his watch, a heavy gold affair, and flicking open a silver cigarette case offered her one of his gold-tipped Turkish cigarettes. As he held out the case she caught a glimpse of the revolver in its strap under his right arm. She took one of the cigarettes, slim and silky in her fingers as she turned it. When he leaned towards her again with the flickering flame of the lighter she inhaled deeply, savouring the smooth, strong tobacco. The sharp burn at the back of her throat was a pleasure, a taste from a recent past that might as well have been centuries ago. He indicated a row of simple wooden chairs that were lined up in the shade of the veranda.

'I'm so sorry my colleagues are running late.' He shrugged apologetically. 'There is much to do.'

'I can imagine. It must be awful for you.' If he understood her tone he didn't acknowledge it. She cursed herself silently and smiled a small smile at him.

He slipped the silver case back into his breast pocket. 'I hope not to keep you waiting too long. After all you must get back to your baby. A baby should not be separated from its mother unless it absolutely can't be helped.' And with that, the threat almost explicit, he wandered, louche and unhurried back to his pillar.

Stevie sat. She was acutely aware of the wooden bars of the chair pressing against her back, the sound of the soldiers pacing across the front of the building, the slight soreness of the blister on her heel – waiting. Maybe half an hour passed, maybe longer. It was time enough for her to have slumped in the chair and closed her eyes, pressing her fingers to her temples. A shout from the oversized entrance door made her flinch. She sat up straight and saw the guards stand to attention in a flurry. A stocky, bushy-haired gendarme officer marched officiously along the veranda. When it became clear he was approaching her she stood up. He looked at her with no interest and barked, 'Papers.'

She picked up her handbag and, clicking open the clasp, rifled inside so clumsily that she tore the silk lining. 'Sorry, yes. Just a minute.' She pulled out the pass she had carried since her careless and light-hearted wedding to Jishang in Shanghai. The pass which identified her as a Chinese citizen.

The gendarme studied it for a while. 'You are American?' His eyes were still on the paper, with its spidery ideographs.

'My husband is Chinese.' She hoped her voice did not sound as thin as it felt to her.

The officer raised his eyes and stared at her, brow furrowed. 'You have Chinese husband?' He shook his head, contemptuous. 'Why?'

The question flummoxed her. She said the first thing that came into her head. 'Because he's handsome.'

He looked at her with derision. Then he spun on his heel and headed back the way he had come. Stevie guessed that he wanted her to follow him. Clutching her bag to her chest like a shield, she walked towards the imposing door. The full weight of the stone edifice was crushing. She felt herself disappearing, her edges blurring with every step she took.

Nakamura was behind her at his practised discreet distance. The muted sound of their footsteps tap-tapped on the polished parquet floor. Then came the sharp knock on a thick dark door and the moment of suspension before the gendarme turned the brass knob and pushed the door open.

The room was long and large. Three windows looked out on to an inner courtyard and light from them fell in heavy girders, striping the space with shadows. At the far end was a wide desk, the shine of its red leather surface visible even from where she was standing. With a jolt she recognised the man who sat behind it, barely looking up to register her presence. It was Shigeo, the man who had punched her during the fracas at Kun Lung Wai. He was wearing the uniform of a gendarme this time and his demeanour was quite different. He was a man at home in his fiefdom, secure in his unassailable position of power. Stevie briefly wondered what kind of man had sat at this desk a few weeks ago and whether he had borne the weight of responsibility with the same degree of entitlement.

Next to her she noticed that Nakamura and the officer were bowing deeply from the waist, their heads as low as they could feasibly get them without falling over. She copied them. Shigeo glanced up and waved a dismissive hand. The officer left the room, bowing and walking backwards. Shigeo addressed Nakamura in Japanese, who then indicated a chair which was set at an angle in front of the desk.

'Sit.'

It seemed to take a long time to get to the chair. As she walked, Shigeo watched. There was something about his watching that made her uncomfortable about her threadbare stockings and the button on her sleeve that didn't quite match the others. Something was wrong in the room and it didn't yet occur to her that it might not be her. She sat. A small distance behind her, just beyond her peripheral vision, there was another chair, into which Nakamura settled.

Shigeo clasped his hands in front of him and gazed at his own fingers. Stevie swallowed, trying to clear the constriction in her throat. After the longest time, Shigeo's voice, soft and bored, filled the vacuum. Nakamura translated, the words coming like an echo behind her.

'Why are you here?'

'I was told to come.' She turned round to look at Nakamura. 'Yesterday, you told me.'

The thud of Shigeo's hands hitting the leather-top desk vibrated through the room. Stevie jolted back to look at him. Later, she realised he had obviously understood her and that the translation was just for show, part of the game. He shook his head, impatient. His voice was harsh. Again there were the implacable tones of Nakamura as he bowled the English words at her.

'When did you come to China?'

'Nineteen thirty-six.'

'What year did you marry?'

'Three years later. Nineteen thirty-nine.'

'Where did you live?'

'In Shanghai. I lived there for four years. Then I came to Hong Kong.'

The questions came fast and she was still struggling with the tightness in her throat. As Shigeo threw out the next round of Japanese she felt an actual pain in her chest. Harry's name, he had said Harry's name.

A stab again as Nakamura repeated it. 'Do you know Major Harry Field?'

'Of course I know Major Field. I'm his girlfriend. We have a baby.'

Shigeo unclasped his hands and laid them flat on the desk in front of him, wrong-footed by her frankness. This time he spoke in English, dispensing with the farce of translation. He leaned forward, directing his sharp focus at her, in which lay the first real intimation of his capacity for cruelty.

'You love Field?'

Stevie could not answer. She almost couldn't understand the line of questioning. She had anticipated many versions of this encounter during the previous sleepless night but she was not prepared for this.

Now the question came from behind her, Nakmura's voice this time. 'Do you love Major Field?'

Stevie's internal struggle was compounded by fear. What was she supposed to say? What did they know? What had happened to the tub of lard, to the radio part? How incriminated would Harry be by her attempt to get it to him? Why were they asking her this absurd question? And with such urgency? Why the hell should she tell these men her private feelings?

'Do you love Field?' Nakamura again, insistent. 'Do you love that man?'

Her voice emerged loudly and clearly. She looked Shigeo directly in the eye for the first time, sitting forward and returning his intensity.

'Yes, of course I love him. I love Harry Field.'

Shigeo received this incongruous confession of love with equanimity. He glanced at Nakamura. Stevie sat back a little in her chair, the chill of the metal frame seeping through her shirt. She felt feverish and weak.

Shigeo's voice was quiet and lisping again, almost weary. 'Ask her about him.'

Nakamura flicked open a notebook that he took from his breast pocket. For a hysterical moment Stevie imagined he had pulled out the pistol. She glanced over her shoulder wanting to see the bullet before it hit her. But a series of questions flew at her instead.

'Why was Field in Chungking?'

'I don't know.'

'When did he go to Singapore?'

'As far as I know he hasn't been there.'

'What is his relationship with Takeda-san?'

She shook her head, thinking fast, not wanting to implicate Takeda in this situation but aware that she must say something. 'They know each other from Harry's time in Japan.'

'When was he in Shanghai?'

'I'm not sure exactly. Many times.'

'What was he doing there?'

'I don't know.'

'Who are his contacts among the Communists?'

'Communists? Why would he contact them?'

Acutely aware of Shigeo's eagle stare, Stevie felt sweat spread across her body, clammy and cold. And still Nakamura's voice came at her, an onslaught of question marks.

'How do you find food? What money do you have? Who is helping you?'

Stevie, her hands clasped in her lap, dug her thumbnails into the back of her hands. The sharp pain was preferable to the dull ache of her head as she fought a kind of numbness brought on by the increasing hopelessness of her situation.

'How much money did Major Field pay you?'

She gasped, affronted. 'He doesn't pay me. I make my own money. I'm a writer.' And then for good measure, 'I'm famous in America.'

She regretted it instantly. A new awareness flickered across Shigeo's face.

The afternoon light had faded and in the dim room the three figures waited, suspended for the next move. A chess game with no clock. Shigeo broke the tension by making a dismissive gesture to Nakamura, waving his hand in the direction of the door. Galvanised, Nakamura instantly stood up. Bowing to his senior officer, he walked the length of the room, his heels clicking on the polished wood floor.

Shigeo waited until the door was shut before he pushed back his chair, almost wearily, and moved out from behind the desk. He went to the nearest window and stood there, looking out into the bare courtyard below.

Stevie counted the pounding beats in her chest. There was something different in the room now, a creeping presence that she thought might choke her. When he spoke he did so in English without turning from the window, as if she were an afterthought.

'Now let's see. You came to China in 1935.'

Was this a trick? 'Actually in 1936.'

'You came to Shanghai and married Mr Wu Jishang in 1940.'

'Nineteen thirty-nine.'

It was the suddenness that frightened her the most. Before she knew it, he was standing right above her, his knees almost touching hers.

'So you are famous. You think Japan afraid of America? Do you? You are fool.'

He waved his sheaf of papers at her. The flapping of the paper got louder and louder. It was the unbearable sound of bird's wings. She had had enough.

Standing up, she said, 'Don't call me a fool.'

She saw it happen. She saw the glimmer of light in the back of his eyes burn brighter. She saw the moment in which he gave himself licence. There was an infinitesimal moment of suspension and then he put his hands on her shoulders and pushed her back down into the chair. Standing two inches away from her he put his hand to his trousers and began undoing the buttons at the fly.

The heat of him was on her face. The smell of him was all around, sour from a long day, the carbolic of soap mixed with something sweet and vain, some kind of cologne. She stopped breathing. She was nothing. There was only a rushing of blood, a firing of muscles, a tension of ligaments and nerve endings. Everything was opaque and at the same time sharp in its detail.

His hand reached inside his trousers. His other hand gripped the back of her head. He moved another step closer. The weight of his hand was forceful, insisting. Her mouth was on his flesh. She gagged. She was suffocating. Her eyes were so tightly shut that only other sensations continued the narration.

Soon he pulled away. Still holding her by the hair with one hand, he dragged her to her feet. The sting of the slap was a shock. She opened her eyes and she saw hunger for power. She saw evil. As real as the floor beneath her feet and the darkening sky beyond the windows. In that moment she knew her fate and she knew her choice. Later she tortured herself – why didn't she just run for the window and jump through it? She could have flown out in a shower of glittering glass and ended it all right there.

The business was dispensed with fast. He was practised. The mechanics were vile and banal. He threw her against the desk, bent her over so her face was twisted hard on the red leather. One hand stayed fast on her head, fingers twined tight into her hair. With the other he tore at her clothes. She was silent. She was nothing.

He was done. She heard him walk away and opened her eyes on to the scratched blood-red leather of the desktop, a pen rolling back and forth back and forth in an echo of movement. She didn't move a muscle. Instinct kept her still, playing dead. She heard his footsteps falter. He must be at the door. The ceiling fan whirred. The silence weighed heavy.

His voice came as if from another planet, making its way through the treacle air.

'You are fool, see.'

She heard the sound of the door opening. The click of the lock. Then silence again.

She might never have moved again but she heard more footsteps. Drawing herself up and leaning against the table she sensed the presence of someone else. She turned around, aware that her underwear was ripped and hanging around one ankle. From the door Nakamura, not surprised at the state of her, made a surreal bow. She stepped out of her underwear and, unsure what to do with it, picked it up and bundled it tightly in her hand. She walked towards the chair and collected her handbag. The clasp was stiff and she struggled for a moment before opening it. She pushed the torn testament to her shame into its depths.

'You are free to go back to your beautiful boy, Miss Steiber. Who, by the way, is not of course Chinese; British, maybe? American? We shall see.'

And what she said was 'Thank you.'

Chapter Twenty-Two

Afterwards she walked blindly under the burning sun, knowing only that she must get clean. Stumbling over a kerbstone, she glimpsed an open tap in the shadow of a narrow alley. She crept into the shade and, cupping the water in her hands, she tried to remove all trace of her assailant from her body. She scrubbed her skin raw and she knew, somewhere ancient, that she would never be the same again. As the cold water soaked through her skirt and down her legs she registered the murder of her old self. And what she thought was – who am I now?

Walking again, like a ghost through places where once there had been walls, she felt a shameful gratitude that he hadn't killed her. And then like a blow, she understood that he had not shown her mercy, he had let her live because she was insignificant. He was not afraid – she was nothing in his universe. There was no need for him to expend more thought or energy on her. He had extracted what he required – his dominance and her submission.

After some time she registered a familiar doorway. Jishang had taken her there a couple of times before they had established the habit of going to Yang's boat. The building was undamaged, the entrance low-slung, sharing a doorstep with a Shanghai restaurant. She did not question why her tortuous route had delivered her here and she did not hesitate. Stepping inside the smoke-filled, claustrophobic room, she almost cried out with relief. Not waiting for her eyes to acclimatise, she stumbled towards an empty day bed. There were no discreet curtains here, and she felt no need to hide herself, just a compulsion to forget. It wasn't defeat she felt but despair. Self-annihilation was the only thing she craved. There they were, the same men. The same closed shutters. The same opium equipment on the same low tables. She reached out her hand for the pipe.

A knife tore through the hanging nappies. The gendarmes were on a mission to destroy. They pulled every drawer out of every cabinet and emptied the contents over the floor. There were snowdrifts of documents. They plunged their knives into cushions, adding a greyish sludge of feathers to the drifts of paper. They ripped a deep, clean wound through the mattress in Hal's pram. Lily held the crying baby tightly in her arms, crooning words of comfort as much to herself as to him. Her mother, the old lady, lay huddled in a corner of the sleeping room. She had barely moved from there since the night of their ordeal at the hands of the drunken soldiers. Her face was turned to the wall as she braced herself against the blow she dreaded. It didn't come. The men left without threatening the women and took nothing with them. As an exercise in terror it was perfectly effective.

Standing in the shambles left by the gendarmes, strips of nappies hanging from the washing line like bandages, Lily could not calm Hal. She was angry with Stevie. What business of hers was it to go running around after the English in the first place? Maybe if she hadn't gone to the hospital she wouldn't have known where to go looking for Harry. Maybe they could have just waited with their heads down until the storm had passed. Then there would never have been the summons to the Supreme Court. Where was she? She did not dare to turn her mind to the possibilities. Her fear was making her angry. She had been left with a mute mother and a screaming baby who didn't belong to her. Stevie had a job to do right here and Lily was bloody well doing it for her. Or rather, failing to do it well enough. Hal had been howling for hours, which was not like him. Usually he accepted distraction or consolation quickly and easily. But nothing would satisfy him today. He had cried so hard she had thought he would be sick. What the hell was she supposed to do?

Harry could feel the damp of the earth seeping through his pyjama bottoms. The sounds of voices came and went. The bar of light crept across the dirt floor as the hours passed. His shoulder ached and he had stopped trying to slap away the mosquitoes. Occasionally he changed position. His mind was numb but he had faith that because he could talk to his captors, he would be able to communicate to them, letting them know that there was no need to treat their prisoners in such a brutal way. Soon, he was sure, they would be given some basic comforts. Food. Washing facilities. This apparent brutality would turn out to be just a result of the chaos of the early days. He knew there were other men in other huts on the military base and he did not doubt that he would soon be able to secure a more comfortable existence for them all. His admiration for the Japanese was profound as was his belief that they were innately decent human beings working to a different but equally honourable set of principles. Yes, they could be heavy-handed at times. There was nothing to be said in defence of the massacres or the disgraceful acts of terror in China, but he was convinced these were individual breakdowns in order and not the manifestation of a policy. As men they were all soldiers and mutually respectful of each other. He felt certain they would be fair-minded in victory. It was only a matter of time.

He was really very thirsty.

When the door was thrown open Harry was blinded momentarily by the intensity of the light. It had been nearly two days and his throat was too dry for him to speak. He bowed. The soldier held out a tin cup towards him. Harry reached for it and as his fingers touched the cool tin, the soldier pulled it away, emptying the water out on to the ground. Harry watched the water fizz momentarily as it drained into the earth. Believing it to have been an accident, Harry looked back up at the soldier – he was laughing at him. In that moment a new understanding overwhelmed him and his legs buckled. From the ground Harry felt the door swing closed again and he thought for the first time in his adult life that maybe the weight of the darkness would kill him.

He closed his eyes.

He was in his bedroom at home and his brother was holding the eiderdown over him and lying on top of it with all of his ten-year-old weight. He was suffocating. He couldn't call out, the dense fabric was in his mouth. Roger bounced up and down, holding the cover tighter and tighter. There was no light. There was no air. There was nobody to hear him anyway. Nanny was in the kitchen and his parents were elsewhere, going about their urgent and mysterious lives. It was just him and Roger. And Roger was killing him. With superhuman effort eight-year-old Harry twisted out of his brother's grasp and slid off the bed, gasping for breath. Cheated, Roger yelled a war cry.

Harry ran out of the door, sliding on the linoleum, along the corridor and down the stairs. He was almost flying. The telephone was in the hallway. He picked it up.

The operator's voice, a distant echo, said, 'Hello? Hello?'

Harry rasped into the receiver, 'Help. Police.'

'Police?'

'Yes. Police. They have to arrest my brother. He's trying to kill me.'

Roger had now reached him and Harry dropped the receiver and ran again. Out into the garden across the drive and on to the pale-green grass. Through the hydrangea beds, huge purple blooms swiping at his face, and finally out into the orchard. Panting and nauseous, Harry stopped. He waited, braced for the next attack, but oddly Roger didn't come. Harry gradually calmed down. His pulse stopped racing. He could see the bare branches of the apple trees and he felt the sting of his twig-whipped shins.

Later, it was impossible to tell how much later, Harry was hungry. He ventured back through the bushes. As he stepped on to the lawn he saw the car, black and shining in the weak autumn sunshine. This was confusing enough but he noticed that the passenger door was open and as he began to run he saw his father hunched over the steering wheel. When he was close enough to touch the door he stopped. Roger was lying on his father's lap, his face buried, and he was howling a strange animal cry. His father glanced up with unseeing eyes. There were tears all over his face and running down his neck. Harry, terrified, turned and ran right back to the end of the orchard. He squeezed his small body as tight into the boundary wall as he could and, holding his knees to his chest, he willed his fear away. After a while he was distracted by a spider devouring a fly and he stayed there quite lost until he heard the heavy stamp of his father's approach. The strangeness was confirmed when he saw that his father was walking through the mud between the trees in his city shoes. Harry stood up.

He could never remember exactly what words were used but his father broke the news of his mother's death with characteristic bluntness. And Harry did not know how to find a reaction to it. Empty and afraid, the little boy nodded. And the man, bereft and inadequate, turned on his city heels and walked back through the trees.

Harry was brought back to reality by the blinding light from the door of the hut. When it closed again, there was a basket lying on its side where it had been thrown.

He crawled towards it, his bad arm useless. A ball had rolled out of it, and picking it up, he identified it as a peach. It wasn't until he had bitten into it and felt the juice assuage the dryness of his throat that he was persuaded he wasn't hallucinating. Despite knowing better he swallowed the velvet-skinned fruit almost whole. Then, still on his knees, he explored the basket, animated by a kind of desperation.

There was a tub. Of what? Lard? Groping at the lid, his fingers were too weak to get purchase and twist it open. With one last effort he gritted his teeth. He levered the lid off. It spun out of his grasp and skidded over the dirt floor into a corner of the hut. He was about to discard the tub when he noticed that the label was peeling slightly. He held the unlikely tin close to his face. The label was definitely not secure. He lifted the edge and slowly peeled it back. There was a piece of skinny, pale-blue airmail paper hidden under the label. Harry carefully pulled out the delicate whisper from elsewhere and, holding it towards the ray of light that came from under the door, he read words that were as nourishing as food, in handwriting as familiar as his own.

Darling, we're fine. Plenty of milk supplies. Hal is bonny as hell and I'm fashionably slim. Be safe. We're waiting for you.

The door burst open. He put the note in his mouth and swallowed. Now the words would really be part of him. The flimsy paper dissolved almost without effort, as if designed to be disposed of in this way. He had time to half-rise from his knees before the open-handed blow from one of the soldiers threw him back on to his hands and knees. Looming above him, another of the men casually kicked him in the small of the back. Harry fell forward. The pain burned through him. He was on fire. Those swallowed words couldn't protect his body from the onslaught. He thought maybe it would never end.

Hal had cried himself to sleep but Lily couldn't stop pacing. She walked up and down, up and down. She walked to keep herself calm, to prevent the fear from taking hold; its clammy hand hovered over her with every step she took across the yard. Across and back. When Chen sidled in through the gate and closed it tightly behind him she barely broke pace. She glanced at him long enough to ascertain that he was in one piece, then kept on walking.

'Mama?'

Lily indicated the door of the sleeping room with her head but didn't say anything.

'Everything all right?'

Lily snorted. 'All right? You ask if we're all right? Mother doesn't move or speak, I don't dare leave the compound, I'm looking after someone else's baby and I've got no idea when I'll eat again but apart from that, yes, we're all right.'

'Where's Stevie?'

Chen only asked as an afterthought. He was intent on having a quick shave and getting back out into the slippery world. Lily's answer brought him to a standstill.

'She went to the Supreme Court yesterday and hasn't come back.'

'Yesterday?'

Lily nodded. There was a huge sense of relief at sharing this information but at the same time the fear crept closer.

His voice was low. 'Why?'

Lily's voice rose in panic. 'She took food to Argyle and a gendarme followed her back. I don't know why she had to go there anyway. It was stupid to go right there and be seen and have her papers checked. Stupid.'

Chen moved very fast. He was at the gate before Lily understood he was leaving. 'Where are you going?' she asked, but her plaintive voice followed him out and she was alone again but for the baby and her fear.

Chen ran, always staying close to the buildings or what was left of them; he negotiated the new cityscape without hesitation. Like a whisper he insinuated himself through alleys and along wide avenues until far beyond the city he reached a wooden fishing shack, hunched against a rock in a small bay. His knock was sharp on the weather-beaten door.

'It's me, Chen,' he rasped.

He pushed the door open. Two men in loose fishermen's clothes were squatting in the candlelight. They looked up, alarmed. One of them was the gentle-faced Ping Wei, the other had intelligent eyes glittering above his fine, high cheekbones. Jishang was hardly recognisable, but that was the point.

'I wasn't expecting you back so soon,' Jishang said, rising to his feet. 'How was she?' He smiled. 'I hope she didn't mind my not coming in person. What did she say, will she meet me?'

Chen didn't take the time to close the door. He said, 'Stevie was called to the gendarmes yesterday.'

Ping Wei stood up. Jishang's eyes darkened with concern and he took an urgent step towards Chen.

'And?'

'And she hasn't been seen since.'

Jishang paused, his normal composure unseated. He thought fast. 'She's too well connected to disappear. Even the gendarmes wouldn't take that chance.'

Ping Wei spoke quietly. 'Do you think they found the radio part?'

'We'll know soon enough. If Major Field is still alive we can assume they didn't.'

Jishang brushed past Chen and stepped out through the open door. Chen's voice was young and insecure.

'Where are we going?'

'I have a fair idea of where she might be.'

Chen scurried after Jishang, who was melting into the darkness. Ping Wei made as if to follow too but Chen stopped him. 'Wait here for news.' The young man's eyes lowered in acquiescence and he waited until the other two had vanished before withdrawing into the hut.

Stevie lay on the day bed. Her eyes were half-closed. The opium smoke formed a haze around her. She stirred and reached out again for the pipe. But another hand got there first, moving it away. She tried to focus through her daze. There was somebody, a coolie, who looked like Jishang. She smiled and muttered something quite impossible to decipher. Then she slid back on to the cushions. Her eyes closed against the world.

* * *

A little later, Lily, too tired to be afraid, looked up from where she was sitting on the veranda steps. She kept one hand lightly on Hal's chest as he lay across her lap, splayed out in sleep. She immediately recognised the skinny outline of her brother silhouetted in the gateway, but who was that with him? As they approached, to her amazement, she made out the broader, taller man to be Jishang and she saw that between them they were half-supporting, half-dragging the limp body of Stevie.

Her first thought was that Stevie was dead. But her relief on discovering that her friend was alive was quickly followed by fury when she learned that she had been found in an opium den. It was all she could do to restrain herself from lashing out at Stevie. An opium den! She couldn't differentiate between her anger and her disgust. Chen had to lead her out of the room, stiff with resentment and worry. Jishang stayed with Stevie and waited, patient as time itself.

In the pale dawn light Jishang lay on his side, watching her sleep. A slight breeze from the open window whispered across her face and she opened her eyes. Her first feeling was one of disappointment. She was alive. She was also numb, so deadened that it didn't surprise her to hear Jishang's voice.

'You must be thirsty.'

She shook her head, feeling the clean cotton of the pillow against her cheeks.

'Why did they let you go?' he asked, his voice even but urgent.

Her eyes closed against him.

'What did they want to know?' He pressed her, not without sympathy but clearly in need of an answer. Other people's lives were at stake.

There was no response.

He lowered his voice to an almost inaudible whisper. 'What did they do to you?' But he already knew the answer.

Tears ran from under her eyelashes. She turned away from him, huddling as close to the wall as she could, holding herself tight – her entire body a fist.

Hours later, Stevie uncoiled herself, aching from the tension. Jishang, her sentinel, handed her the waiting glass of water. She took it and awkwardly pulled her reluctant limbs into a sitting position. Her body felt different, alien. For a wild moment she thought that maybe it was actually someone else's. Then quickly the horrible truth returned and she understood that this was the way she would always feel. The scar tissue was hardening and she was remade. She would never be the girl she had been before.

Jishang spoke so quietly that even though he was close enough for her to see the pores of his familiar smooth skin she had to strain to catch the words.

'I'm sorry. Chen should never have asked you to help. It was reckless and dangerous but he is young and therefore stupid. He wanted to be a hero and of course getting a radio into Argyle is one of our aims but –' He sighed. 'I'm sorry.'

Stevie kept her head down. Her eyes focussed on the weave of the dark-red blanket.

'You know, your friend Madame Kung is helping us. She sends money. Even-handed of her, don't you think.'

Stevie blinked. That name seemed to belong to an ancient time. It was an echo of another life.

'She's in America,' he continued, 'but she keeps a very close eye on all of us. I wasn't much use in Shanghai so I came to see what I could do here. There are many people, Stevie, many people. Resistance to the Japanese is not confined to the political factions, whatever the Communists may claim.'

Jishang stopped and suddenly he was talking in what seemed almost to be a different language. He was speaking to her from his rare, raw centre. 'Stevie, you're difficult and stubborn and you're also brave and clever and you must look after yourself and your baby now. How far do you have to go before you can admit this? How hurt do you have to be? Maybe only death would be enough for you. But you can help more by staying alive. You can tell the world what's happening here. Stevie, do you hear me?'

Stevie raised her eyes and found comfort in the familiar darkness of Jishang's insistent gaze. He went on, 'And although you have many of the characteristics of a good wife, I accept that fidelity isn't one of them.'

He glanced towards the door. On the other side of it real life went on. Hal gurgled, tied tight in a bundle on Lily's back. The fruit on the trees ripened. Mrs Li pulled her shawl over her face as she stayed resolutely turned to the wall.

'Luckily, as you know, I make it a habit not to care too much about anybody and in that we've been well-matched.' He added this for old times' sake but they both knew the depth of the lie. He turned back to her. 'I know you're not mine, any more. And this isn't your war. You're a fighter but this isn't your battle.'

Stevie drew herself tighter, the foreign body that was hers braced against further pain.

'Why have you come back?' Her voice, though familiar to her, also seemed to belong to someone else.

He shrugged. 'Let's say I'm keeping an eye on my interests.'

Stevie shook her head. 'God, I'd forgotten how irritating you are.'

She thought that maybe he smiled, but in the half-light his fine profile gave nothing away. Through the window, across the soft, pink light of dusk, a flock of geese flew in perfect formation.

Jishang unreeled himself and stood up, stretching to ease the aching of his muscles.

'We need food,' he shouted as he took long strides towards the door.

'Make it yourself,' Lily yelled back from the courtyard, bad-tempered from anxiety. But she was already on her way to the kitchen.

It took Stevie some while to move. By the time she dragged herself outside Jishang had gone, like a pantomime character, almost in a puff of smoke. She pulled herself along the wall, learning how to use this new body of hers. When she appeared in the courtyard Lily was halfway across it, a bowl of warm soup in her hands, Hal in a papoose on her back. She stopped mid-stride. Steam from the bowl made a film on her face. They looked at each other across a divide far deeper than the few yards of bare earth that separated them.

Stevie spoke first. 'I'm sorry.'

Lily stood as implacable as stone.

Stevie struggled. 'What can I say?'

The stone Madonna held her ground. There was a grim silence. Stevie leaned her head against the wall. Hal made a small, sweet gurgle.

Lily could not help herself. 'He's fine. Though you don't deserve to have him.'

At those stinging words, tears came flooding down Stevie's cheeks. Hot like blood. She wailed, a terrible primitive sound.

'I'm sorry. I'm sorry. I'm sorry.' She was sorry for everything. For the war, for the brutality of it, for bringing Hal into this world of fear.

She grieved as she stood against that wall in the quiet courtyard in Hong Kong. And Lily, unable to grasp the meaning of her grief but recognising it as profound, softened. She let go of her resentment and at the same time let go of the bowl. It dropped on to the hard dirt and shattered loudly. The noise startled Stevie into silence.

Lily laughed nervously. And as Stevie tried to draw breath she found laughter replacing the keening. Lily pulled her into her arms. Stevie, taller by a head, leaned into her friend and opening her eyes she saw the curious face of her baby peering at her. She laughed again, and still there were tears, but the three of them stood for a moment supporting each other. Then holding on to each other and gasping for breath they went to the kitchen in search of more soup.

The rain came and later, while Stevie held Hal until he slept, Lily went to fetch Stevie's bag from near the gate. Jishang and Chen had dropped it there when they had brought Stevie back. As she picked it up the clasp flicked open and Lily saw the torn, scrunched-up underwear. She quickly closed the bag and glanced over at Stevie, who was rocking Hal and humming to him. She blanched with pity. She never asked Stevie what had happened. And Stevie never said.

But here, now, in her friend's kitchen with the dying light obscuring their features and her baby safe and asleep beside her, Stevie allowed herself to take comfort. She turned her face towards the door and to the darkening sky. A bird swooped through the fat raindrops from the shelter of one tree to the next.

Chapter Twenty-Three

Harry heard the rain. There wasn't a part of his body that wasn't in pain. It was possible that bones were broken but between the bruises and the sharp edges inside him he could not decipher what was what. He had lain where they had left him for a long time. Squinting through the one eye that wasn't completely sealed by dried blood and swelling, he could see the gap under the door. Occasionally the shadows of feet passed by but clenched though he was in anticipation, nobody stopped. After a while he stopped expecting another invasion of his hut. He stopped expecting anything at all. In his mind he groped for the technical terms of medieval fortifications and grappled with the frustration of not remembering. Yes, of course it was a crenellation but what the hell was it in Portuguese? God damn it. The noise of the rain on the corrugated iron was a welcome distraction. And at first so were the drips that fell more and more insistently on him. Realising that finally he would not be made better by being wet as well as broken, he tried to haul himself out of the way. The enormous effort that this entailed winded him. Well, he thought as he lay, shaking and exhausted under another leak from the roof, at least I'm alive. And if he'd had the energy he would have laughed.

There was the sound of Japanese voices passing outside – and he was no longer lying broken on the floor of a hut in Hong Kong. He was lying on the thin mattress roll in the dormitory at the Military Academy in Kyoto, trying to contain the hysterical laughter that Takeda's imitation of their colonel had brought on. It had been pitch-perfect, right down to the slight lisp. It was a year of laughter. His pleasure at discovering the delicate beauty of the landscape and the fragile beauty of the social etiquette had been intense. Every day since the ship had brought him to this new land Harry had thanked his lucky stars and soaked up every new challenge, mopping his plate with relish. He was twenty-two and glad to be alive.

He had fenced and ridden and run. He had shot guns and arrows. He had listened to incomprehensibly unfamiliar music and eaten food that had brought tears to his eyes. He had drunk the colourless alcohol and admired the fierce autumn leaves. But the first time he had been in the boxing ring he had nearly come a cropper. The shouts of the other young men had echoed through the wooden hall. The stomping of their feet raised his blood and he launched into an attack on the much smaller, slender boy who was in the ring with him. But the boy had slipped out of his reach and in a series of light-footed moves he had made a fool out of Harry, who was left swinging wildly and spinning, dizzy, sweat stinging his eyes and unable to locate his opponent. The fight ended badly for him when a left hook to his lower jaw dropped him to the canvas floor. He opened his eyes to see the blurry face of Takeda leaning over him, anguished at his victory. Harry had loved him from that moment on.

They were an odd pair, the leggy, golden English boy and the slight, vivacious Japanese one. Odd but inseparable. Harry had nothing but admiration for Takeda's sweet nature, vast curiosity and obstinate loyalty and it opened something within him that had been closed for as long as he could remember. He surrendered his guarded cynicism, allowing himself a new softness for which he was grateful.

One evening at the end of a long day hiking in the mountains they had found themselves in a small village, where the arrival of an Englishman caused a stir. Before too long a small crowd of young men had gathered in the guest house and the atmosphere began to sour. The Washington Naval Treaty had just been signed and Japan had been prevailed upon not only to stop building warships but to return newly conquered Shandong to the Chinese.

A pock-marked young man with fashionably slicked-back hair spat on the floor near Harry's feet.

'Go back where you came from, white boy. What business is it of yours to tell us what we can do.'

Takeda did not bother to translate. He put his head down and without warning ran at the ringleader. He winded him but that was not enough of an advantage to avoid the brawl that ensued. Half an hour later they were in their room tending to their wounds. As he dipped the end of the thin towel into a bowl of warm water, Harry watched his blood swirling, entwining with Takeda's.

Takeda followed his gaze. 'This makes us brothers.'

'What, you mean we have nothing in common and will punch the daylights out of each other given the slightest opportunity?'

Takeda grinned. He had heard all about Harry's tribulations with Roger. 'No. Not like that. We will be different brothers. We have chosen it.'

'Jolly good.' Harry winced as Takeda dabbed at a cut over his eye. 'I agree.'

And so that night their friendship was sealed. As the years passed and they gradually stopped writing amusing letters to each other and life became a more serious undertaking, Harry had often thought of his time with Takeda as the best of his youth. The world of politics had conspired to drive a wedge between the young men but neither of them had ever forgotten. Then came that moment two years ago in which Harry had caught sight of Takeda coming out of the Japanese barber shop in the Hong Kong Hotel. It had been six years since they had shaken hands and said goodbye. Takeda had filled out and was no longer the willowy young man of before, but the cheerfulness in his wide-set eyes was the same. They had embraced one another, delighted that life had swept them on to the same shore again.

Harry had put his hand on Takeda's elbow and pretended to whisper, 'You know your friend the barber is sending information back to Japan.'

'I'll remember not to tell him my holiday plans in that case.'

'You do that.'

And they had both beamed, delighted that they could pick up their friendship again, and without needing to acknowledge the great information game their countries were asking them to play.

It took the guards some time to bring Harry round. The soldiers had assumed that he was dead and one of them kicked his body to make sure. There was no response. But they were under orders to bring him to the senior officer, so they did. He hung between them, limp and pathetic. His legs trailed behind him as they dragged him across the compound. The officer was not impressed. He shouted at them and they left Harry on the ground as they went in search of the medical officer. The senior officer walked around the Englishman's inert body, and then, picking up a carafe of water from his desk, he casually tipped it over him. Harry had the good grace to splutter. As the medical officer came in he contributed to the arousal of the prisoner with a firm, efficient slap across the face. This time Harry opened his eyes as best he could.

'You are Major Field?'

He couldn't see who was asking this question but he nodded, relieved to hear a cultured Japanese voice.

'You know what this is?'

The officer leaned down and held a small coil of metal in front of Harry's good eye.

He shook his head, trying to speak. 'I can't see very well.'

The officer pulled him up so that he was sitting. More pain. He cried out.

The officer offered him the piece of metal to look at again.

Harry peered at it, making a supreme effort to be helpful. 'Maybe a mechanical part?'

The officer spoke low and clearly. 'This is a variable capacitor, a crucial item for building a radio transmitter, and it was smuggled into the camp for you in a tin of lard. Who sent it?'

Harry was genuinely perplexed. 'For me? I don't know. I mean, I've never seen it before.'

The officer sat back on his heels. 'Where did you learn Japanese?'

'Kyoto.'

'I thought so. I can hear the accent.'

'And you are from Tokyo?'

'From the suburbs, yes.' He regarded Harry for a moment. 'You can help us, Major. It will be good for everybody.'

Soon Harry was lying on a mattress on a truckle bed. He was wearing a clean cotton shirt and trousers. His wounds had been cleaned and bandaged. His broken bones were bound into splints. He still could not see very well. One eye had closed up completely and the other gave him only a blurred window on to the room. He felt like a human being again. So when the officer came to see him and afforded him respectful greetings before he sat close by his bed, Harry was filled with hope. His faith in the essential decency of the Japanese was reignited.

'So, Major Field, maybe you can tell me something more about the radio part.'

'I really have no idea, sir.'

The officer leaned towards him and, laying his hand on Harry's broken fingers, he squeezed. Harry yelled, caught by surprise.

'I think you understand, Major, that some information would be most welcome.'

'I don't have any information.' The officer released his fingers and Harry composed himself. 'Look here, it can't have been unexpected that there would be some form of resistance to your occupation. I suspect there are many people who will do everything they can to try and subvert your control. It's only natural. But I am an officer in the British Army and I am here under your jurisdiction. I have no knowledge of the details of any such resistance.'

The officer waited a moment before going on. 'Why would such a thing be sent to you?'

'I don't know. I suppose I am a senior officer. People would know that.'

The officer stood up brusquely, scraping his chair across the dirt floor. He nodded a curt farewell.

Harry raised his voice after him. 'Thank you.'

Moments later two guards stomped in and seized Harry, pulling him roughly to his feet. They dragged him to the door of the hut, from where he had a clear view of the parade ground.

A line of young British and Canadian officers knelt on the parched grass, their hands tied behind their backs. The officer walked towards them and, raising his sword, he sliced the head off one of the boys. The young body stayed upright where it was for a second before keeling slowly to the right. Another boy, red-haired and skinny, screamed as the head rolled across the bumpy ground. A stream of blood spread across the arid earth. The others, brutalised, knew better than to draw attention to themselves and kept their eyes down. None of them looked up at the severed head. One man swayed and fell forward in a faint.

The officer glanced over his shoulder at Harry and then raised his sword again. Harry yelled 'No,' and began to run towards the kneeling men. The row of eyes watched him with surprise and hope as he propelled himself towards them. But his bruised and weakened legs buckled and he stumbled and fell. The officer lowered his sword and walked back towards him.

He spoke in Japanese. 'You have something to tell me?'

'Yes, yes, yes. Just please stop.'

Pale under his freckles, the red-haired boy heard Harry reply in Japanese and, rigid with fear, he watched as the British major was raised to his feet by the Japanese officer and, with a Japanese arm around his shoulders, was helped back to the hut. The young soldier could not control his shaking even though the crisis seemed to be over. Orders came from one of the Japs. They were to pick up his mate's body. His mate's head.

He yelled without thinking, 'Fuck off, you fucking animals.' Alarmed, one of the other men, older, more weary, put his hand on his shoulder.

'It's all right, Hopkins, leave it to us.'

Nothing in Frank Hopkins' nineteen years had allowed for the possibility of this experience.

For Harry in the stifling hut the insistent voice of the Japanese interrogator was drowned out by the other voices in his head. Stevie comforted him with whispers from their lovemaking and then moments later she was challenging, afraid. 'It's all bullshit, you're all the same. What's the difference between you and them? Between us and them? Nothing – except that they have better boots.'

'We're defending a civilian population not killing them.' Harry's words were loud in his head but came out only as a murmur. The Japanese officer leaned towards him.

'What was that? You must speak Japanese.'

The man's face came briefly into focus. Harry shook his head. 'It's not just the boots.'

He was rewarded with another slap across the face.

'I am a reasonable man, Major Field, and I don't understand why you are insisting on the death of more of your colleagues.'

Harry saw the blurry figure of his interrogator walk towards the door. The voices in his head became a cacophony: Hal's screams, Stevie's whispers, Takeda's soft Japanese, and he felt his sense of self slip out of reach, and over it all he heard his own voice, acrid with resignation. 'All right.'

'You have something to say?'

Harry, bent over on himself, began to talk.

Chapter Twenty-Four

It was Jishang who saw the first glimmer of lights on the coastal path. He and Chen were trying to collate their lists of the killed, wounded and missing.

'Chun Lei-ming?'

Chen shook his head. 'No sign since she went to see the silk merchant in Shek-O.'

'He was a new recruit?'

'I haven't met him. He came to us through reliable channels, though. Lei-ming is very canny.'

Jishang raised his eyebrows. 'She is also very young.'

Chen was defensive. 'Are you questioning our methods?'

'No. But would you say she was missing? It's been a week.'

Chen reluctantly put her name in the missing column. It was a long one. The piece of paper was covered with spidery characters. Jishang had stood up from where he was squatting on the sandy floor and had moved to the door. Beyond the dark sand the moon lit a path over the waves. And then he had caught the glint of light somewhere far above them in the dense overgrowth of the cliff.

His voice was low. 'Why would Ping Wei come overland?'

'He wouldn't.'

Chen joined Jishang at the door. There was another glimmer of light, moving along the path high above. It took them moments to extinguish the oil lamp and, slipping out of the hut, move soundlessly under the overhanging rock towards the small waterfall that gushed down the rock face. Stealthy and fast, first Chen and then Jishang disappeared behind the flowing water, pulling themselves up the sheer cliff with practised speed.

They were far out of view and hidden in the curves of the neighbouring bay by the time the Japanese squadron swarmed into the hut. They did not see Ping Wei's little boat chug to shore. They did not hear his screams. But the flames from the burning hut cast a glow into the sky which could be seen for some miles.

Ping Wei's torture and death were not officially recorded anywhere.

Harry's horizons shrank to wrap him in a befuddled, slow-motion series of actions – breathe, eat, shuffle to and from the latrines. His injuries had healed enough to allow him to queue for food with the other men. He habitually kept his eyes on the ground so he could not see who was talking. But he could hear the loathing in the words.

'If that fucking traitor Limey thinks he can come in here and lord it over us he has another think coming.' Frank Hopkins' freckles blazed in his sunburned face as he muttered to the Toronto man next to him.

'He's been kept separate since he got here, what's that about? Special treatment doesn't come for nothing.'

The two young men considered this fact in silence. Frank eyed Harry's stooped form as he waited in line a few paces ahead.

'I saw him that day. The Jap bastard was giving him water. Looking after him, all fucking smirking and friendly. What do you think about that?' A shrug from the other boy. 'I'll kill him if they don't. I've twisted the necks of any number of creatures on the farm.'

'Yeah.'

'What happened to watching each other's backs?' He gave the ground a particularly vicious kick. 'Well, from now on he'd better watch his.'

Harry didn't see Frank gather himself, he only saw the gobbet of spit as it landed in the thin stew in his bowl. He glanced up and caught the young Canadian man's eyes and saw the fierce, unadulterated contempt. He looked away again instantly. What he saw in Frank's eyes confirmed exactly what he felt for himself. He had no argument with it.

Harry took his tainted bowl and sat on the ground, his back against the whitewashed barracks building. Those men closest to him made a point of shuffling further away. Harry ate the stew. He considered Frank's saliva to be no more than he was due.

The same thoughts played out in his clouded mind in a loop he could not escape. He grasped only at the faint hope that the fisherman's hut had been found empty, though the fact that he had been allowed out among the other men implied that the Japanese had been satisfied with what, and whom, his betrayal had led them to. He welcomed his ostracism. He was not the man he had thought himself to be. For him there was no escape.

Chapter Twenty-Five

March 1942

Stevie did not have time to dwell on the assault in the Supreme Court. The news of Ping Wei's death dismayed them all, as did the clear fact that they must have been betrayed. Amid much fevered and inconclusive speculation as to the source of the betrayal, the group had disbanded and Chen only very rarely slipped into, and quickly out of, the compound. Jishang had not reappeared; Chen claimed not to know where he was. There was no sign of Declan and she chose to take this as good news.

Pressing concerns of day-to-day survival occupied Stevie's waking hours. Even during a war and under a hostile occupation one still needed money and Stevie and Lily's family had come to the end of their resources. Her overriding obsession was still finding powdered milk for Hal; she could not rest unless she had two reserve tins in her possession. There was, however, enough of her reporter's instinct intact to ensure that she made notes of everything she heard and saw. The Chinese population was dying of starvation. The food supplies the British authorities had stockpiled for use during the expected months of siege were shipped to Japan. As were one thousand cows belonging to the Hong Kong Dairy Farm – leaving only five hundred on the island. Most of the Chinese members of the British Legislative Council were prevailed upon to join the Japanese 'Rehabilitation Committee', a committee that had no actual voice and was unable to do anything to prevent the systematic bleeding of the island's resources. Supplies of all kinds diminished. Stevie had smiled when she saw a woman dressed in a perfectly cut cotton frock made out of mattress ticking. And Lily reported seeing two old school friends of hers in chic shorts made from Australian flour bags.

One day she was in Cat Street, a steep, stepped alley lined with booths selling books. There were first editions, gold-embossed leather-bound books from the finest libraries of Hong Kong; medical and engineering encyclopaedias, rare, precious, beautiful and in every language known to man. They were being sold by the weight to be used as fuel. For a few yuen she bought a nineteenth-century copy of Milton, inscribed to a Chinese man from a fellow student at Cambridge University. As she carried it home, *Paradise Lost* weighed heavy in her hands.

There were occasions in the night when an image or two would slip back into her mind: the scratched red leather on the desk, the highly polished wooden floor, his hand smoothing his hair, and she would choke on her panic and disgust. A shout from across a street in Japanese could render her paralysed and drowning in shame.

Lily developed a fever. Stevie stayed in the compound, providing cold compresses for her forehead and changing her damp sheets. She didn't resent it as such but she wasn't exactly a born nurse. She bore it stoically but the added strain of not being able to go and get more supplies of milk while at the same time watching the current tin dwindle, drove her half-mad. On levering open the final tin she found that the powder in it had been replaced with flour by some unscrupulous market trader. She picked up her wallet and discovered to her dismay that she only had a few coins left. Something had to be done.

The next day Lily was well enough to swallow a little soup and Stevie had formulated a plan.

It was early evening by the time she got there. She stood for a few minutes on the road a little way from the main gate to calm herself after the exertion of climbing the hill. Her chest ached and her legs felt heavy. She knew she looked awful. When she was getting ready she had brushed her hair and been quietly distraught at the handfuls that had come out on to the brush. Applying the stub of her carefully rationed Revlon lipstick, she had stood back and, narrowing her eyes, thought that maybe despite everything she might pass muster, as long as he didn't look too closely. She had put on her navy-blue dress with the white polka dots and puffed sleeves, tucked her thinning hair into a French plait and bound some of the sweetest-smelling jasmine she could find in the courtyard into a small posy tied with the last of her ribbons.

The posy had wilted slightly during the journey, as had she, but she held it firmly as she approached the gate. Previously, she had only ever been here in a car and had not thought about how one might actually get in if arriving on foot. She searched for a moment or two before she saw a door bell half-hidden by wisteria. She watched the white-uniformed servant walk along the gravel drive towards her as if she were watching a scene from a movie, something familiar but imagined. It did not seem possible that this groomed and quiet existence was real whilst in the alleys and streets of the city far below people were scrabbling to survive on their wits against all the odds. She announced herself and was admitted.

She followed the man through the lush, tropical simulation of an English country garden. It felt like a holiday to smell the delicate, fresh scents of grass and lavender. She had grown used to the reek of the destroyed city and she barely noticed it any more, except occasionally when a particularly foul stench, a mixture of decomposing bodies and human excrement, wound through the streets. She slowed her pace and inhaled the memory of happier times.

Takeda was standing at the edge of the perfect grass carpet surrounded by blooming roses. He aimed a bow and arrow at the archery target at the far end of the lawn. The string vibrated with tension. Then the arrow was released and with a thud it hit the target.

Stevie walked a few steps behind the manservant. She was transfixed by the whiteness of his gloves against the green, green grass. As they approached, Takeda squinted at them before he recognised her. Then he dropped the bow and held out his arms as if to a long-lost relative.

'Miss Steiber!' He seemed genuinely delighted, moved, even. 'My goodness, what a pleasure.' He came forward, stepping over the abandoned archery equipment.

Stevie held out her hand and discovered that she too felt moved by the sight of him. Her voice was not as firm as she would have liked it to be.

'Mr Takeda. I hope you don't mind.' She glanced over her shoulder at the impassive servant and lowered her voice further. 'I don't know if you remember but you said that if I ever needed help.'

Takeda kept his voice level and his smile warm as he shook her hand vigorously,

'Of course. Of course. May I offer you a drink of some kind?' And he lay a solicitous hand on the small of her back as he led the way towards the open French windows. He felt her flinch at his touch and let his hand fall.

She relished the comfort of the soft sofa as she waited for the tea to be poured. The Japanese ceremony was almost as convoluted as the English. There were cakes and pastries laid out on a tray and almost before she realised it she was eating one. And then another. The buttery sweetness was overwhelming and while she ate she surreptitiously felt the smooth cotton chintz of the sofa with her other hand and enjoyed the miraculous cool of the lovely room. The curtains hung in an elegant sweep and the parquet floor gleamed with polish. For a moment the image of Madame Kung gliding over that very floor flashed into her mind. It was two and a half years since that first decisive encounter. Two and a half years and a lifetime ago. She glanced up and looked around the room again. There wasn't a hint of dust on the gilt frame of the old-fashioned hunting painting hanging above the fireplace. Silver-framed photographs on the closed lid of the baby grand piano were reflected in the glossy black wood. Madame Kung would have approved. But the photos were of other people. Other smiles in other places.

As soon as the servant was dismissed, Takeda leaned towards her. His expression was grim as she explained something of what had happened.

'Harry is in the camp at Argyle and a few weeks ago I tried to take him food but I was stopped and told to go to the Supreme Court.' She faltered but Takeda had already interrupted.

'The gendarmes? Why?'

'My papers, I think. I don't know.' And the sharp sting was behind her eyes, the dry closing of her throat. 'We haven't any money left, Mr Takeda. I can't feed the baby. Lily's ill and I don't know what I'm going to do. I don't know how to keep us going. I'm Chinese for now but who knows how long they will accept that and then what? Half the men I know are dead and the girls are standing in line with cup in hand waiting for a hand-out of thin rice stew.'

Takeda had stood up, he had gone very pale and was almost wringing his hands as he spoke. 'I understand.' He looked at her. 'When was this, the interview with the gendarmes?'

'Like I said, a few weeks ago. Six, maybe? Seven?'

'They came to see me too.'

'You? Why?'

Takeda was pacing. 'This is bad, Miss Steiber. Very bad. This is the trouble I feared.'

'But I don't understand, what's it got to do with you? It was all about Harry.'

He sounded angry but in fact he was aggrieved. 'I've always felt a certain – a certain loyalty to Major Field. They know this.' He fixed her with a stare 'And I am an honourable man.'

'I know.'

He was agitated and forceful, quite unlike himself. 'So I too have been questioned by the gendarmes. About you. I'm only glad I know nothing of what you may have been doing.'

A blush spread across her face. She had been more stupid than even she had realised; stomping like a fool into a terrible game whose rules she did not understand, implicating and endangering others. Many others. The voices of recrimination were loud in her own head but Takeda was speaking with such urgency that she heard him above them.

'Listen to me. There's a plan to repatriate all American civilians. There's to be an exchange, Japanese citizens in America for Americans under Japanese occupation.' He frowned. 'But, as you say, you are carrying Chinese papers. There would be questions raised about your nationality.'

'Repatriated? You mean – sent home?' The words seemed hard to grasp, slippery and unlikely.

'Yes – home.'

She heard an echo of Nakamura's voice and then she saw the shadow of her mother and caught the faint scent of leather and freesias that clung to the hallway of their house. Home.

Takeda was thinking hard. 'You'd have to refute your Chinese marriage and volunteer to go into the internment camp at Stanley. I don't know how long it will take for the exchange to happen. There's so much negotiation and nobody knows what or who they can trust. And of course there's always the chance it may not happen at all.'

She shook her head. 'I can't. I'm sorry. I can't. What about Harry? And Lily?'

Takeda's voice shook as he grasped her hands too tightly. She was surprised by the anguish on his face. 'You must. It's your only chance. You think the war is going to end well? You think it's going to end at all? You want your little boy to grow up in the shadow of fear as a third-class citizen on an occupied island? For what? For the romantic idea of being somehow close to Harry? You think he would want this? If you give up this opportunity at the very least it would be misplaced loyalty. And God knows I know about that. But at the worst it would be murder. You have no choice.'

He stood up again. 'The fact is I can't protect you any longer. I'm being sent back to Tokyo.'

She understood instantly. His war was over and he would be returning home very far from a hero. 'Oh, I'm so sorry.'

'We are all prisoners of the war one way or another.' He shrugged and gave a small bow. Then he walked across the room to a delicate little desk that stood under an ornate mirror. She could hear the incongruously comforting hum of a lawnmower and the quiet ticking of a clock. He opened a drawer and pulled out a large brown envelope which he proffered to her in a quick movement. She had the impression he would withdraw it if she didn't accept it equally fast.

She stood up and took it. Then she clasped his hand, standing close enough to smell his lemony eau de Cologne. His fingers were dry and cool.

'May I see him? Please may I see him? Fix it for me, Takeda-san. I'm begging you.'

He was momentarily taken aback by the physical contact but recovering nimbly he shook his head, a smile breaking out on his pale face.

'You overestimate my influence, Miss Steiber. Greatly, may I say.'

'But is it possible?'

'I am flattered.'

She let go of his hand and stepped back, feeling extremely foolish. 'I'm sorry.'

'Is there anything else I can do?'

Stevie thought for a second and was only half-joking when she said, 'I'd kill for a bath.'

The pleasure was intense, almost as engulfing as any other she had known. The water, hot enough to sting and blush her skin a broiled pink, contained and comforted her. Beyond the open Tudor-style window a tangle of jasmine blew, tap-tapping on the small glass panes.

She lay marooned with her hands on her belly and looked at the sunken seascape of her distorted legs, her toes protruding at the far end like stones flung beyond the edge of a landmass. She had hardly been able to bear the fact of her body since that terrible day, let alone look at it. Now, in this stranger's bathroom in a stolen moment of calm she allowed herself the beginnings of an appraisal. It was disturbing to her that there was no visible scar, not even bruising to announce the damage. There should have been purple and blue contusions, raw blood vessels mapping the surface, swellings and bones at sickening angles. But, no, it was an invisible wound. Nobody would avert their eyes from her disfigured face and whisper to their children not to point. Nobody would offer to help her mutilated limbs negotiate the street. Nobody would know. It was a secret and the weight of it was hard to bear.

She closed her eyes and let the tall sides of the bath contain her until the water cooled and her fingertips wrinkled like used tissue paper. Then, sitting up in a tsunami of lukewarm water, she scrubbed herself with the bar of lavender soap and stepped out on to the mat.

As she caught sight of herself in the mirror, she saw that her hair was thinning and shiny grey hairs caught the afternoon light. Her dress hung off her bones, her skin was flaky dry and curdled in colour. She averted her eyes and tried to concentrate on the marvellous scent of lavender that still clung to her as she opened the door back into the house.

Stevie still smelt faintly of lavender as she bent over a sleeping Hal that night. The scent might have lingered longer had she not thrown up as soon as she got home. Her poor shrunken stomach had been too shocked by the richness of the cakes and pastries to contain them. Now she peered down at Hal and wondered how he would like fresh milk every day. And grandparents. And no soldiers with guns. She stroked his face and allowed herself for the first time to remember the sidewalks of Utica, the shopfronts of her youth. And like a slap she felt a spasm of longing for all those everyday assumptions like food and work and a cup of coffee. Maybe life didn't have to be like this. Maybe Hal could grow up in a different world. Maybe.

She was suddenly afraid of her own thoughts – could she go? Could she really give up her freedom on the chance that there might be an exchange and that she and Hal might really get back to the States? Could she leave Harry, and Lily, and the old lady and Declan? Declan! Where was he? She thought suddenly of Phyllis and little Margaret and wondered how they were surviving in the camp. How could she even think of joining them there? It was impossible. She shook her head and delved into her bag for a rare cigarette. As she did so, she found the envelope that Takeda had given her earlier that afternoon.

Inside it there was enough money to keep them all for a month and a photograph. Harry and Takeda standing arm in arm, young and fit, wearing white fencing uniforms, their faces radiating with enormous smiles, their foils raised high in a salute.

She stared at it for many minutes, hoping it would provide an answer. By the time she put it back in the envelope their faces had blurred. She had not registered that she was crying.

She went into the kitchen to wash her face. Every detail of their compromised way of life struck her anew. She couldn't even look at the useless tin of powdered milk. But all at once she knew what she was going to do. She glanced into the tiny shard of mirror that hung over the sink and grimaced. She snorted to herself. 'Mother's going to be very disappointed by my lack of grooming. I sure have let myself go.'

Chapter Twenty-Six

April 1942

The rackety old pram barely made it over the ruts of dried mud. The ritual walk along the perimeter fence at Argyle was as silent and as tense as the first time. But Stevie was spurred on by a feeling of defiance that had driven her across the harbour and over the obstacles that threatened to de-wheel the pram and disrupt her own private act of rebellion. Despite Lily's tearful and furious pleading she was determined to take the supplies for Harry to the gatehouse herself. This was the last time she would be able to do so, and Lily had sworn on her life that she would continue to take them when Stevie had gone. Stevie had offered to give her all her remaining clothes in return. Lily hadn't said no. Her old passion for clothes had not faded. A few weeks earlier Stevie had found her poring over the pages of an old copy of *Vogue* she had pulled from the smoking ruins of a building.

Stevie's armour of obstinacy did not protect her entirely, however, and the underlying fear was hard to ignore. During the whole journey she had been convinced that Nakamura was watching her and, although she hadn't seen him, she felt sure that he was slipping out of sight down alleyways just beyond her vision. But she pressed on, girded by a new sense of fatality. The worst had already happened.

She lined up with the other women outside the gatehouse, shuffling slowly forward. She did not raise her eyes to those of the guard when he held out his hand for the basket of food and her identity card. From behind her eyelashes she watched as he passed her card on to a second guard while he himself searched through the basket. There was hardly anything in it. Supplies were more precious than ever and though there were cocktails to be had in all the big hotels, there were almost no basic groceries on the streets. She stopped herself from protesting when the guard took a bite out of the one good pear then spat it out before dropping it back into the basket.

The second guard said something in Japanese. Stevie kept her head down. He spoke again, louder this time. She glanced up. He seemed to be beckoning her into the gatehouse. She looked over her shoulder, expecting to see someone else to whom he was gesturing. The young, frightened woman behind her shook her head. Stevie looked back, panic rising. The guard raised his voice again.

She pointed at herself. 'Me?'

He nodded impatiently. She felt again the sickening sensation of her face against the cold, hard desk. The weave of the uniform fabric. The fetid, hot smell of Shigeo as he stood too close. Concentrating on not shaking, she willed the images away and with the help of the first guard who with incongruous good manners lifted the other end, she manoeuvred the pram into the gatehouse.

Here there was a different kind of quiet. Flies threw themselves against the windows. There was a metal field desk, a typewriter, a fan. The second guard closed the door and pointed to a chair. Hal began to make disgruntled noises. Maybe the stifling, airless room was disturbing him. Stevie picked him up and took him on her lap as she sat down.

'You are Miss Steiber?'

'Yes.' A deep breath. 'I am.'

'Wait here.'

The guard left the room and locked the door after him. Her mind reeled. Obviously it was all over for her. But what about Hal? How could she get him to Lily before they did their worst? She had taken one gamble too many and in her stubbornness had killed them both. Holding him so close he was almost a part of her again; she relished the smell of him and whispered as he protested, 'Oh, my lovely boy. I'm so sorry.'

Hours passed. The light dimmed. The room was silent but for the death rattle of trapped flies. Outside the dusty window the endless parade of women and children slowed and then stopped. Hal settled in her lap and slept again. She rested her head on his.

The light snapped on. Stevie jerked her head up, blinking in the bare bulb's brightness, adrenalin spiking. She saw two men. Recognising one as the guard who had locked her in she glanced at the other. He was standing to attention just behind the guard. He was not in uniform. He was Harry.

Stevie shouted his name and half-stood up. All was confusion. Hal woke and wailed as she half-dropped him to the floor. Harry seemed to be smiling. Yes, he was smiling, his thin face stretched to its limits. The guard stepped aside, stiffly indicating the desk and the two chairs on either side of it. Harry walked to one of them, supporting his paralysed left arm with his right hand. Stevie, clutching Hal tight, stumbled to the other. With her free hand she reached for him across the desk. At the same moment he reached for her. Palm to palm at last. It was only then that it came to her that she wasn't dreaming. The only imperative was to touch him and the intensity of his presence froze her mind. She could not think, only feel. They both spoke at the same time, searching for reassurance, Stevie's 'Why are they letting us?' counterpointed by Harry's 'You're leaving. I'm so glad.'

'Leaving? How do you know?'

He shook his head because of course he couldn't say Takeda's name. But she understood. And so it was decided. Until that moment she hadn't realised that she was actually going to give herself up. To give herself and her son and her freedom up to fate. She was accepting that there were currents and tides beyond her control. She was accepting and it was necessary but also a relief.

They laughed. And they spoke fast, very fast, to say as much as they could. But neither of them spoke of the fundamental changes that they had experienced. The way that they were both new-minted by compromise and survival. It wasn't possible. And it never would be. They would have to make do with this new version of each other, the same only different.

Harry reached out towards Hal, who was leaning into Stevie's chest, a comma. 'He's grown so much.'

'Yes.'

'Have you been all right?'

'Yes.'

'Not too hungry?'

She shook her head. 'No.'

He shifted as far towards her as he could, the chair legs tipping him. 'You're still a terrible liar.'

'No. We're fine.' Her smile was a necessary thing, empty but necessary. 'You know us. Charmed lives.'

He lowered his voice. 'Our old friend, the one who has been kind to us, don't worry about him. He's masterful, don't underestimate his diplomatic talents.'

'That's all right, then. But I've underestimated his compatriots in lots of ways.' That was too close. She struggled for a joke. 'Their capacity for alcohol is pretty impressive for a start.'

'And you should know.'

The humour was mirthless but she respected him for it as he did her. How else to talk in this surreal situation?

'Are you all right? Are they treating you all right? How's your arm? Have you seen a doctor? You're very thin.'

'I'm fine,' he lied in return.

There was a loud rapping on the door. They both leaned further towards each other and Hal woke up, squashed between his mother and the desk. He protested. Stevie clutched Harry's hand.

'No. No, this is impossible.'

The guard who had brought Harry in and had then withdrawn while they talked, opened the door and had a brief conversation with the officer who had knocked.

Stevie and Harry's eyes were locked on each other. He gripped Stevie's hand and pulled himself across the desk to her. At last, there were his lips, dry and sore, on hers. This was the kiss that had to say it all.

Hal yelled louder.

The guard turned to them, very anxious. 'Stop immediately. This is a military camp.'

Stevie began to pull away but Harry pulled her close again. 'Don't stop.'

'It is finished.' The guard grabbed Harry's shoulder and pulled him to his feet. His chair fell, the noise of metal on concrete like the end of the world. As Stevie struggled to her feet Harry was already being dragged through the open door.

She stumbled across the room, Hal's wails bitter in her ears, and she saw Harry being taken deeper into the darkness of the camp. His head was turned back to her over his shoulder as he walked. The lights from the perimeter fence cast shadows across him as he moved in and out of their rays. Faster and faster, further and further away. A ghost already.

Part Three

Chapter Twenty-Seven

New York – August 1945

'I have here in the studio with me a woman who will certainly be familiar to many of you –' the smug-voiced radio presenter was young. An air of entitlement clung to him. Stevie glanced towards the producer's box and there, through the glass, she could see Hal, his three-and-a-half-year-old busyness causing havoc. He waved at her, pressing his hands against the window. She waved back.

'She scooped veteran correspondents with her acclaimed book about the Chinese Soong sisters and now she has written the most, well, shall we say the most uninhibited book of the year – *Inside Hong Kong*.'

Stevie gave her full attention back to the interviewer. The euphoria and surprise that had flushed through her on discovering that the draft manuscript of her book about the Soong sisters had been published while she was incarcerated at Stanley had long ago diminished. She had finished it in the frenzied days before her voluntary admission to the camp. She had left it with Lily in the hopes that she could keep it safe, and Lily had taken it upon herself to pass it to Chen. In this roundabout way the manuscript had reached Jishang, who had masterminded its delivery to the States. The pleasure Stevie had felt in being taken seriously had not been enough to overcome the sinking realisation that the book had not made any real difference. Not in the world and not to her.

This second book, *Inside Hong Kong*, had been intended as a pressing analysis of political life in Hong Kong during the China crisis, but her inclusion of the birth of Hal had placed her in the harsh spotlight of gossip-mongering, prurient pundits. Once the supposedly shameful story had found its way into the national debate, she and Hal had taken refuge at her parents' home in Utica. The scandal had broken around her like a tidal wave and when it became clear that the undertow was too strong to resist, she had come out of hiding fired up with a new anger. Who were these people to judge her? How dare they rain contempt on her? What gave them the right to the moral high ground? And the fact that she had not even hinted at her own true suffering gave her the confidence to answer all the finger-pointers. Uninhibited? If only they knew the half of it.

'So, Stevie Steiber, first of all may I congratulate you on being free.'

'You may, of course. Thank you.' She smiled, charm itself. 'But let's not forget freedom is a relative concept.'

The presenter, having been warned that Stevie could be a tricky interviewee, steeled himself. Without missing a beat, his silky purr of a voice rolled on. 'Yes, I suppose so. But secondly I'd like to congratulate you on your splendid book. It is of course rather, how shall I put this? Uh – racy. . . .' His pauses were purposeful, his implication clear. Stevie looked at him without answering. Sensing that silence, that most feared taboo of radio, was threatening to fill the studio he rapidly picked up again.

'I'm sure our listeners would be interested to hear about your experience of being taken into the very bosom of Chinese life. For instance, strange to relate, you were even married to a Chinese man?'

Raising her eyebrows and ignoring his explicit contempt, Stevie shot back. 'I suppose you mean you're curious about sex?'

Caught out by her bluntness – sex, she had used the word sex, oh my God, and it was only mid-afternoon! – the presenter stuttered live on air for the first time since he had misread a weather report when he was a rookie announcer at a station in Colorado. 'Well, no, no, I –'

But Stevie, her eyes glinting with mischief, was not to be stopped. 'It's a funny thing, mankind's fascination with the sexual behaviour of another race. You know, the first thing the Belgians do when they get to the Congo is sprint to the nearest brothel to find out if it's true what they say about African women.'

The interviewer made desperate signals to his producer, aware that his glittering career on this flagship New York station was utterly dependent on the good will of the housewives who tuned in, and for whom this conversation was spinning in quite the wrong direction.

'And the first thing you American men do on arrival in Shanghai is ask if what you've heard about Chinese girls is true. . . .'

Now the producer was on his feet behind the glass, gesticulating wildly to shut her up.

'And you know something else? I heard exactly the same stories about the African girls and their sexual prowess as I did about the Chinese girls.'

The interviewer signalled back at the box, a neck-slitting motion. Hal waved happily at the grimacing man, who had just registered that Miss Steiber had said that word again and that he was surely on his way back to the late-night slot.

'And the funny thing is the Chinese men told me the same stories. Only this time it was about the white people. You'd be pretty pleased to hear how prodigious the Chinese imagine you white men to be.'

The smile had not left her face. This was the most fun she had had in a long time. A sheen of sweat lay on the interviewer's fine features as he tried to regain his vocal composure.

'So, Miss Steiber, as we were saying, it was against all the odds that you survived the Japanese occupation of Hong Kong.'

'It was. But there are thousands of other people, Chinese people, British, Russians, Americans still trying to survive. And do you know what? The most important thing I have to share with you and your listeners today is that I'm more convinced than ever that there are no victors in war. We can hardly stand on moral high ground, having just unleashed the atom bomb on a civilian population.'

Alarmed at the mention of news that was still so fresh and contentious, he tried to interrupt, but she was still talking. 'Do you know what I've learned? I've learned that courage is an ordinary thing. It belongs to the most surprising people. I've seen it. To many listeners here in the States it's possible that the war seems distant. When we hear the numbers of those murdered in the conflict it sounds like mathematics and not like human beings. Human flesh. Human hearts. Those with loved ones abroad will know what I'm talking about. And now – now there are hundreds of thousands more victims. Just nine days ago women were preparing their children's meals or clearing up their breakfasts and children were in the first few minutes of their lessons in school, getting out their exercise books and settling down to the day.' Her voice was low and brimming with passion. Even the interviewer was leaning in closer to her, drawn like a herring on the line. 'In not one but two terrible blasts their – and our – worst nightmare has come to pass. I've witnessed the immorality of warfare and even I would not wish such a fate on the families of the men who caused me such pain.' The bitter smell of Shigeo constricted her throat and she paused.

Taking advantage of the moment and unable to bury his natural vindictiveness, the radio man interrupted her. 'Noble sentiments. But isn't it a bit rich, Miss Steiber, if I may say so, for you to be making moral judgements? After all, some of our listeners may feel that your own personal morals leave something to be desired.'

She leaned forward, the fire of battle in her eyes. 'What exactly do you mean by that?'

He felt certain he had regained the upper hand. 'You have a son.'

'Yes.'

'And you are not married.'

'That's right. Do you have a point?'

The woman was shameless, and feeling the ground shifting under him once again, the interviewer glanced in desperation at his producer, who pointed at the large clock on the back wall and held up two fingers. Two minutes. He turned back to his loathsome guest.

'Did you – uh – did you bring back many interesting recipes for Chinese dishes?'

But Stevie was not to be thwarted. 'My private life is none of anybody's goddamn business and if what you are implying is true, if the people of New York, of this great nation, have even the slightest interest in or opinion about my personal morals I would be very surprised. It is the moral hypocrisy of this country that is disturbing and frankly hard to believe.'

His voice, when he had recovered, was firm and authoritative, the kind of voice he did best, the one that had guaranteed him his career and the attention of star-struck younger men in the darkened corners of bars. 'Thank you, Miss Steiber. It's been most fascinating but regretfully that's all we have time for today.'

Stevie pulled off her headphones and made her escape, pulling on the heavy soundproofed door with both hands. It swooshed shut behind her. The interviewer's voice, smooth as cream, poured through his microphone.

'Next week we'll be talking to Priscilla James about her cat sanctuary on Long Island.'

Hal's small, hot hand was curled in hers. She slowed her pace to match his. Now they were a block clear of the radio station her anger had faded to a familiar background hum. She took some deeper breaths and, though the air caught in her chest, she felt better. What was the rush after all? They had the whole afternoon.

New York still thrilled her. Two years of it had not dulled her appetite for its energy. At first she had loathed the childish enthusiasm and persistently positive outlook of her compatriots. They seemed like an insult to the life she had lived, the life that was real and vile and stinking and brutal. The American determination to see the sunny side, to believe the best, to assume a bright future, had sickened her. Hiding in her parents' home, sleeping in the bedroom she had shared with her sisters as a child and waking every day to the smell of coffee and the sound of birdsong, was so surreal that she had drifted through the formless days as if hallucinating.

Her family had circled her warily. She may have been the prodigal daughter, but it took much longer than anyone might have anticipated for them all to come to a working understanding of each other's needs. Her mother's intolerable piety towards her and Hal filled her with resentment. Stevie could not bear the way her mother wore her new-found open-mindedness so stoically. She would have found it much easier to deal with indignation rather than this self-conscious kindness. In the end they had come to an accommodation. Her mother behaved as if her daughter were a tragic widow not a sinful single mother, and Hal – the 'poor little mite' – was a kind of orphan, not a bastard. Stevie kept her irritation out of sight, but she could not bring herself to be grateful, which was what she knew her mother wanted above all else.

In those first strange months Stevie would sit in the garden under the canopy of the elm tree while the weather was warm. Hours would pass in a daze while Hal was fussed over by his grandmother. Then one day she had started writing again and she had not been able to stop. She was compelled to it. She wrote longhand, unable to bear the sight of the typewriter that had accompanied her through her previous life. And it was only when, nearly a year later, she had come to the end of her story that she was able to emerge blinking into the balmy spring air, a new version of herself.

The thought that this spasm of writing might become a book had not been the point. When a small, local publishing company had asked to see what she was working on she had given it to them without overly considering the possible outcome. They quietly published *Inside Hong Kong* and copies were displayed in the bookstore in Utica for a few weeks before being retired to the bookshelves at the back. Nothing could have prepared any of them for the impact it would have. A regional politician somehow got hold of a copy and wrote about it in his column in an upstate New York paper. He cited it as an example of the loss of moral backbone of the American people due to the wastefulness of the war and evidence of the erosion of American principles and so on. This in turn had spiked some interest in the city and, in a sudden explosion of argument, the book was used to draw battle lines between the old and the new, the acceptable and the beyond the pale, the upright and the immoral. In other words, all hell broke loose and Stevie was at the very centre of it.

Her instinct to hide was rapidly replaced by her determination to stand up and fight and she found that she was already armed and girded. Nothing frightened her now, not even the literary critics of New York. And nothing incensed her more than narrow-minded armchair moralists. She was primed, ready to be engaged in the present and saved from the past.

Yet she had forgotten none of it. Far from it. There were many phantoms that visited her dreams. The day of her surrender to the prison camp would return regularly; Lily weeping, her thin arms wound around both Stevie and Hal. The pile of cotton and wool garments on the floor where, in her torrent of tears, Lily had thrown the clothes Stevie was leaving her.

Stevie could hear Lilly's wail, 'What about me? What am I supposed to do?' She had actually stamped her foot.

'You'll be fine, I know you will be. Just think, no more irritating arguments with me and no more stupid nappies.'

Lily's crumpled face was more than she could bear. Stevie hugged her but her voice cracked.

'If I get to America I promise I'll send a ticket for you.'

Lily sobbed louder.

'Chen will look after you. And anyway this whole thing has got to be over soon, you'll see.' Lily nodded, trying to get a grip on her tears.

Stevie, lightening her voice, gestured towards the carpet of clothes, arms of cardigans lying at broken angles like so many tangled limbs, the colours spilled. 'It would be a terrible waste if they ended up in Japan along with everything else.'

Lily had sniffed in agreement and bent down to pick up a particularly coveted grey shot-silk skirt. Stevie had noticed that Lily's immaculately tended nails were dry and cracking.

Then there had been the surprisingly polite form-filling in the barracks at Stanley internment camp, almost as if she were checking into a hotel. Albeit an exceptionally bureaucratic one. The acrid smell of the primitive latrines overwhelming the odour of sickness and sharp carbolic. The thin mattress through which she could feel every tired spring of her narrow cot in the long dormitory shed. The faces, knife-edged with hunger and anxiety. And then the almost unrecognisable woman who had fallen to her knees at the sight of Stevie.

Phyllis had lost almost all of her hair and what was left of it was grey. The strands were pulled back into a scrappy rat's tail tied with a piece of string. It was the string that stayed most vivid in Stevie's mind. The contrast with the soignée woman who had leaned so enthusiastically into conversation with Jishang in her perfectly appointed living room, was so stark as to be absurd. Stevie had slipped on to her knees also and held out her hands to her.

'Help me. She's gone. She's gone.' The lament blew through her like the wind. Phyllis was bent over, her forehead scraping the dirt ground. Stevie heard her grief and looked at the piece of string containing those few strands of feeble hair. Margaret had died of malaria in the third week of their internment and Phyllis had lost her grip on her mind. Stevie held her hands, the bones so fragile, like bamboo shoots, and felt that she was touching paper, while Phyllis' fragmented keening broke over her in waves. It was the echo of Phyllis' voice, thin and harsh, that woke her in those fresh American nights.

And then, at last, there was the exchange of prisoners, Americans from the camp for Japanese citizens from the States. The entire event had felt like a dream and none of them had believed it would happen or could have imagined it would go so smoothly. Her fellow Americans were a motley collection, part adventurers and chancers and part members of the establishment. There were shop girls and plumbing engineers as well as bankers and several men and women whose pre-war resources would not have stood up to too much scrutiny.

Even when they were on the ship, the *Asama Maru*, and it was leaving Victoria Harbour for the last time, steaming past the islands and the mouth of the Pearl River, Stevie had not been able to take it in. She had held Hal close, a shield against the guilt of abandoning Phyllis and the others. Then there was the strangeness of that first month at sea, when they were free but not yet free, and she walked through the days almost without reflection in a kind of limbo. The wife of the American consul died on board, and a baby was born to one of the women from Stanley before they touched the coast of Africa at Lourenço Marques, the main port and capital of Portuguese Mozambique.

In the middle of the day, on 22 July 1942, they berthed alongside another ship, the *Gripsholm*, which was carrying the Japanese internees from America. There were blasts of welcome from the ships as flags were waved and the American sailors cheered. Hal waved back and laughed out loud and Stevie felt numb with relief.

The next day Stevie, with Hal wrapped firmly against her chest, had stepped on to African soil. The burning concrete of the dock warmed the soles of her feet through the worn leather of her shoes, as they walked away from the rusting hulk of the *Asama Maru* towards the *Gripsholm*. They passed a line of smartly dressed Japanese civilian families coming along the dock in the opposite direction. The Americans each had two small suitcases whilst their Japanese counterparts strained under their piles of luggage – including a number of Singer sewing machines and some small refrigerators. They were two human trails of victims of history.

On board the liner, a feast had been prepared. The Americans fell upon it like vultures, tearing at chicken legs and lamb chops with their fingers. Confronted with such abundance, the constraints of manners proved too burdensome and were jettisoned instantly. There were foods Hal had never seen before, such as olives and celery, and a hysterical cheer went up when the stewards brought in trays laden with turkeys. The sailors watched their new charges with a mixture of awe and pity. Stevie herself ate until she was sick. She had to stop herself cramming more and more food into her mouth. It took days to remember that it wasn't necessary to eat everything that was on the table, that there would be more again later.

And then they had reached America.

Her parents had seemed smaller, reduced by the passage of time, but also by something else. A veil of alienation from them and from her sisters obscured the homecoming. She wanted to run from their embrace. She was no longer their daughter, no longer their sibling. She was something new and ugly and knowing. This chasm of misunderstanding was the Grand Canyon between them and though they shouted valiantly across it, only whispers and shadows of meaning made it from one side to the other.

Hal tugged at Stevie, pulling her towards a pretzel stand and away from her thoughts. He was always hungry. Licking the fat grains of salt from the knot of bread as they walked, he hummed a private tune and Stevie tightened her grip on his hand. She could feel his pulse and it made her happy.

A little while later they made their way through the chaos of stalls. The streets were slick with waste, dense with people. Here in Chinatown the shouting had a different, shriller quality and the smell of noodles and peppery sauce burned her throat. For a moment she was transported to the corner of that restaurant by Victoria Harbour, memorising the angles of Harry's face. She yanked Hal's arm a little too hard and he dropped what was left of the pretzel. She braced herself for his wail but unnervingly he just turned and looked up at her, infinitely patient.

'It's all right, Mommy.'

'It was nearly finished anyway.'

'I know.' And he squeezed her hand.

Being comforted by him was too much and she turned away, pretending to look for the familiar doorway.

'It's somewhere here, right, Hal?'

And Hal confidently led the way between the parchment scrolls and the birdcages to the dark painted door of a decaying building. They climbed the sunless, damp tenement stairway to the third floor. Stevie waited for Hal, who refused her hand and pulled himself up by the banisters. She let him knock on the apartment door. A pause and then the door opened into a narrow hallway, light coming from a room at the end. The stocky Chinese man nodded at her and Hal ran towards the light.

The room was small and overburdened with Chinese antiques. Madame Kung, poised and refined, incongruous in this cave, sat just so on the brocade day bed. Hal jumped into her arms and was engulfed in a ladylike embrace. Her two bodyguards loomed large next to the inlaid cabinets. Stevie waited for Madame Kung to indicate a black chair, decorated with mother-of-pearl, before she sat.

'He is too skinny. You are not feeding him.'

'He eats all the time, Madame, if he ate any more he would actually become a cake.'

The older woman turned to the child in her arms. 'Is this true?'

Hal, torn between politeness and truth, whispered, 'I had a pretzel but I dropped it.'

She smiled and put him back on his feet. 'So go find the sweeties.'

Hal glanced at Stevie and then ran out of the room, followed by one of the huge men. This was a familiar ritual. The two women looked at each other, history heavy between them.

Stevie's voice was low with trepidation. 'They announced his death again.'

'Yes. I heard.' Madame Kung's long earrings glittered as she shook her head.

'It's not true?'

'It's not true.'

'He's still in the camp?'

'That's what I hear, yes.'

Stevie exhaled her relief. But Madame Kung's low voice stopped her.

'The Communist boy you helped –'

'Chen?'

'He was killed.'

Stevie clutched at the slippery pillow beside her on the chaise. 'You're sure?'

'You can't help the stupid.'

Stevie thought about the last time she saw him. She remembered his insolent expression and his unruly hair but also the way he seemed to be carrying a new gravity. He had been unshakeably convinced of the righteousness of his cause. It was a marked and potent passion in him. Now he had died for it. She whispered, 'Where? When?'

The earrings caught the light again as Madame Kung shrugged. 'Some time ago. I noticed his name in a report the other day. He was mentioned as having been particularly fearless during a failed assault on a town in the south-west a few months ago.'

'Anything from Lily?'

Again the earrings glittered as Madame Kung shook her head.

Stevie had been trying to reach Lily since she had arrived back in the States. She had written to every address she knew in Hong Kong and on the mainland. It was part of her weekly routine: letter to Lily, letter to Harry, letter to Jishang. There had been nothing in return. Nothing from Lily. Nothing from Jishang. And, most painfully, nothing from Harry. It was if they had all disappeared off the face of the earth. Sitting here with the street cries of Chinatown floating through the heavily curtained window, Stevie felt the familiar remorse. 'I should never have left her there.'

'You did what you had to do.' A pause. 'We all did.'

'Did we, though? Did we really? I can't get away from the thought that maybe there was something more I could have done. Something else.'

'And you don't think that is the human condition? Always knowing there might be something else? Don't waste time with such thoughts, it's the path of madness. We can only be responsible for our personal actions, after all.' Stevie was surprised by the forceful tone.

'Well, that's not always the case. Surely we all share some responsibility for the world we live in. I mean it's all cause and effect. If the context had not made it possible for the war to happen things might be very different.'

This was the most political conversation they had ever had and immediately Stevie regretted it. Madame Kung drew herself up.

'That is too naive, Stevie, even for an American.' There was a pause and when Madame Kung spoke again her voice was thick with emotion. 'Do you really think that a human being can bear the weight of guilt that the necessary betrayals and compromises of life bring with them? Do you? I do not. A life lived in a village, maybe, with no thought beyond the seasons passing. But even in such a small life, the little shifts of fate require compromise. Every decision carries with it the shadow of the choice not made. It's unbearable. No – I am not responsible.'

Stevie looked at the fierce figure on the chaise and understood that the dark corners of her conscience, where her husband's rapacious regime had laid waste huge tracts of her homeland, would not survive scrutiny in even the faintest light.

Madame Kung brushed an invisible crumb from her lap.

'Li Chen was a politician. You can be sure that your Lily was under his protection and will remain so. There is, I gather, honour among some of those thieves.'

'There was a boy, Ping Wei – Chen couldn't protect him.'

'That boy was betrayed. We none of us have weapons against betrayal by friends.'

Stevie frowned. 'What are you saying? You know who betrayed them?'

Madame Kung was silent for a moment. Then she spoke slowly, choosing her words with even more care than usual. 'I know about the incident. That is all.'

She signalled to one of her men to bring hot water for the teapot.

Stevie struggled with her impatience. 'Madame, what are you saying to me?'

'I'm saying we none of us are safe from those who know us best.'

Stevie let out a strangled groan of frustration as she leaned back against the chair.

'More tea, perhaps? And by the way, my dear, did you notice in the market today there's an absolute glut of tomatoes?'

Later, Stevie and Hal tumbled out into the broiling day. At Hal's insistence they stood a couple of blocks away from the Empire State Building and watched the men at work, already rebuilding the damage to the seventy-ninth floor. At this distance the three-week-old hole in the side of the tower looked like a gash in a painted backdrop. It was hard to imagine the reality of an aeroplane flying directly into the building. Stevie saw it as a metaphor for the fragility of the state. It had been a fog-bound mistake made by a confused pilot, and she chose not to think about the office workers burning.

They were weaving through the crush of people on the concourse of Grand Central Station when an announcement over the public address system snared Stevie's attention. There was an abrupt change in the announcer's tone of voice and she had broken off in the middle of the departure of the three fifty-four to Georgia from platform seven to clear her throat. Something about her tone slowed the entire crowd until it came to a standstill. The only movement came from a flock of pigeons, swooping and fluttering above their heads.

'An hour ago, today the 15th of August 1945, in a radio broadcast the Emperor of Japan ceded victory to the Allied Forces in the Pacific –'

There was a stunned moment of absolute stillness before the shrieks and whoops and tears of relief filled the enormous concourse. Stevie picked up Hal and held him tight. The young woman next to them wept as she hugged them both, then, looking into Stevie's face, she gasped.

'You're Stevie Steiber – I don't believe it. I can't tell you how much I admire you.'

But Stevie didn't hear her. She didn't hear anything. All she could think was that now Harry would come home. He would come home. She stayed there, absolutely still, while the world moved on and Hal held tight to her neck.

Chapter Twenty-Eight

September 1945

The announcements and lists and rhetoric washed over her for weeks. Rumours sprang fresh every few minutes but it was all so much background noise to Stevie. Her vision was as pure and unchanging as it had been for the years before the peace. Harry was alive and he would find her.

In her book-infested living room Stevie hunched low over the unwieldy keys of her typewriter. The clutter had multiplied while she wasn't looking and it now threatened the small space that was left on the desk for her elbows. Frustrated, she brushed a pile of newspaper clippings away. They fluttered to the bare floorboards in the breeze created by the slow-whirling fan. They seemed suspended longer than was naturally possible before they skipped over the dusty boards. She leaned back in her chair, her hands on her head. Let them lie, she thought. She noticed the faint sweat stains under her arms and dropped them. There was no one to see them but she had hoped to wear that blouse for at least another day.

Through the open window the distant sounds of traffic drifted in. A siren cut through the dense heavy air. Stevie shivered now and, sighing again, she set herself back into the hunched work position.

Her fingers poised. Nothing came.

She glanced again at the ghetto of papers and photographs, at one photograph in particular: a Shanghai party before the war, an international mix of people with drinks in their hands, much fun being had by all. Or nearly all. Squinting suspiciously at the camera out of the corner of his eye, Jishang, slim and immaculately tailored, scowled at the invisible photographer. Stevie covered the picture with an open notebook. Now only his long fingers could be seen encircling the stubby glass. Suddenly irritated, she slammed her hands on the keys. She muttered to herself as she pushed her chair back and stood up. The rusty metal legs dug more scars into the wooden floor.

She walked across the room. She didn't look at the pile of unopened cellophane-wrapped bouquets of flowers that lay where they had been left by the several delivery boys who had had to make the long, hot journey up the narrow stairs to her door, only to be met by ungracious snarls.

Stevie reached up to the small electric fan on top of the filing cabinet and switched it on to the highest setting. She stood for a moment letting the sluggish warm air blow across her face. She closed her eyes and leaned into the breeze.

Hal's voice came through the apartment door letterbox.

'Monkeys have willies, you know. They do. I saw.'

Stevie laughed as she walked to the door, lighter now in herself. The frenzy of little-boy limbs and hot breath on her face made her weak, as it always did. She had never grown used to the beauty of it and she had to fight for a second the feelings of fear and wonder. What could this miracle of vitality possibly have to do with her?

Her son climbed over her, obscuring her view, and Declan's light, Irish voice had to work at being heard. It didn't help that he was leaning against the door-jamb half out of breath from the stairs and laughing.

'Tell Mummy about having an ice cream.'

Hal, forthright, warmed to his theme. 'They're pink. I saw one.'

Stevie lost herself for a moment in the feel of her lips on Hal's lovely cheek. She didn't answer until Hal slipped out of her grasp and marched on chubby legs deeper into the room.

'They are too.'

Declan laughed and, catching his eye, Stevie remembered how much his lightness meant to her.

'Thanks for taking him.'

'I take all my hot dates to the zoo. Get any work done?'

'Not much, no.'

Declan leaned his broad shoulders away from the door and handed Stevie the small pile of letters he was carrying. They were warm from his touch.

'Can I have a rabbit?' Hal said. 'It could live under my bed.' He picked up a particularly fat and interesting-looking package from among the cellophaned bouquets. 'What's this?'

'Let's see.' Stevie was still on her knees; she could feel the gap between the floorboards cut into her skin. 'It says Hal Field. Now, who on earth could that be?'

'It's me. It's me!' It was impossible not to be infected by Hal's delight.

He sat down, his legs splayed out, and began to prise the package open with great care. Declan took a step closer to Stevie. His voice was quite different, low and anxious.

'You saw the paper?'

Stevie avoided his sympathetic eyes. She pointed at the pile of drooping bouquets.

Declan's voice dropped even further. 'I'm so sorry.'

'Don't be. It's no more true this time than it was before.' She said it with fierce conviction and knew she sounded as though she was protesting too much.

'Stevie – you're going to have to face it, you know, sooner or later. I'm sorry but you are.'

Her laugh was so inappropriate that even Declan, long-practised in Stevie's unpredictable responses, was taken aback.

He went on. 'The lists of all surviving prisoners of war have been published and ratified by both sides. He's not on it.'

'It's not just me. Madame Kung's intelligence people say he's still alive.'

'That old goat. Why is her word God?'

Stevie tried to ignore his tone. 'Her information is always good. You know it is.'

'What's she doing holed up in Chinatown anyway? Pretending she's down on her luck; it's laughable when everybody knows her husband stole the entire wealth of China.'

'I'm not asking you to like her.'

There was a shout of triumph from Hal. Stevie bent down to him but not before Declan had seen the shadow of doubt cross her face like a flinch. Hal leaned into the cardboard box, the discarded peel of wrapping pushed aside.

He pulled a face. 'Look, it's smelly.'

The turd lay, ugly, in a corner of the box. Dark patches stained the sides where it had moved around on its journey from the anonymous bigot right into Hal's infant world.

Stevie let out a noise, somewhere between shock and fury, and pulled the box away. She thrust it into Declan's hands and bent down to Hal.

Declan turned his head away from the box in his hands. 'My God, who would do such a thing?'

Hal was crying now. He did not know why exactly but he knew something was wrong. Maybe he'd done something wrong.

Declan knelt down too, the box still in his hands. Hal was silenced by the unexpected oddness of it. Maybe Declan was being funny to make him forget the crying. But Declan's voice was strangely wavering and passionate.

'Stevie, marry me. Please.'

She was gentle with him. 'Don't, Declan. Not again.'

'Why not? We'd have a great life. You know we would. And I loved you before you even met Harry.'

Stevie shook her head but Declan couldn't stop.

'What's so wrong with having a husband? The moral people would bugger off and I wouldn't get in the way of your work. I'd support you whatever you wanted to do.'

Stevie got up. Hal clung with his legs around her waist like a monkey. 'That's enough. Stop.'

'All right, maybe you don't need a husband but what about Hal? He could do with a father.'

He knew he'd gone too far.

Stevie's voice cracked. 'He's got a father.'

And of course Declan wished he'd said nothing because by then the damage was done.

A week or so later she was standing among the small huddle of reporters outside the Japanese Consulate waiting for another announcement on the progress of negotiations. There was no sign of life from inside. Her lungs burned reassuringly as she inhaled her cigarette.

'Hey, Bette Davis.' Declan had pushed through and was next to her, leaning close. 'No story here. Not even a janitor to give the low-down on their last supper. I got a tip, Vivien Leigh's at the Hilton.' He borrowed her cigarette and took a deep drag.

'I think I'll stick around here a little longer.'

He shrugged, passing the cigarette back to her. 'Wanna give me the keys? I'll get dinner.'

'No.'

'But I might be done before you. It makes sense, one less thing for you to think about.' There was a plaintive note in his voice.

She tried to swallow her irritation. She shook her head. 'No.' She didn't have the patience for this, for taking into account how badly he wanted to please her. 'Listen, I need to talk to you.'

'Yeah?' His insecurity was unbearable, his face so naked and vulnerable.

She felt very old. In a flush of shame she tried to back-track. 'Vivien Leigh at the Hilton with who?'

'With whom. What's up? Spit it out.'

Declan had his hand on her arm and was pulling her away. They stood a little distance from the others.

'So?'

Playing for time, she leaped on to her high horse. 'I just don't think you should assume my apartment is yours.'

'I assume nothing. I'm a reporter.'

'Look, it feels like you're kind of moving in.' She took a breath. 'I'm grateful for everything you're doing. You've been a great friend to both of us and Hal loves you, obviously.'

'It's been years, Stevie. Years. And we make sense, you and I.'

Her voice broke. 'If I could I would. Believe me. It's not you. It's – listen, I'm only saying this because I can see it's not fair on you, I'm sorry. I just can't.'

A cloud of cold anger shook him. 'I know you can't. But what exactly are you thinking? You think Harry is going to come back from the dead, like Odysseus, shiny and undamaged and claim you for his own like in some cheap romance? That can't be it.'

'No, no, of course not.' She was close to tears. 'I don't know.'

Declan's voice was sharp with misery. 'Take it from me, it's the damn, fucking hope that kills you.'

He walked away so fast that he was a blur. Or maybe it was her tears that did it. She stood for a while, numb, before peeling away from the bantering group of newsmen and walking aimlessly until, with a jolt, she realised she was late to collect Hal.

The hall was steamy and echoed with the voices of over-excited children. The next class had started and Hal sat alone on a chair at the side of the room, his legs dangling, his head hanging, the very picture of abandonment.

'Darling, was it fun?' She knew her voice sounded tight and self-conscious. The gym teacher had already made comments about how difficult it must be bringing up a child on her own. Consequently, she had made a point of always being on time to collect him and was obsessively careful that his kit was clean. He was probably the cleanest kid in the class. He slipped down from the chair and, still avoiding eye contact, picked up his jacket from the floor. The healthily proportioned gym teacher ran over to them. She was always running, maybe that was part of her job description but it hadn't done much for the width of her behind. The woman was smiling her dealing-with-parents smile.

'Everything all right now?'

'Yes, thank you.'

'You must be very busy.'

'Yes.'

'Good. Good.' She tousled Hal's hair proprietorially. 'We don't like waiting after class, do we?'

Hal stood politely still.

Stevie managed her own perky smile in return. 'No, we don't.' And she took Hal's hand and drawing him towards the door, rescued him from the familiar barely concealed moral indignation.

As she opened the door to their apartment she thought of Declan, and the pang of regret propelled her into the living room. He hadn't deserved to be dismissed so harshly. It wasn't his fault that she couldn't let him in. It had been nearly two years since he had brought some light back into their lives. Declan had found his way to New York via Dublin – as soon as he could he had taken his chance and headed for the New World. His paper was very happy to have him file the occasional freelance, poorly paid piece and he had picked up other commissions fast.

He had called her from the port and through the early morning fog she had heard his voice and momentarily mistaken it for Harry's. The jolt of it had stayed with her for a long time.

'I knew that the smallest noise could mean the difference between life or death. I was walking a tightrope into the unknown with nothing to trust in but a complete stranger leading the way.'

It was weeks after that call, as the light had dimmed in her apartment and the buildings opposite had become silhouetted against a spectacular sky, that Declan had told her about his escape from Hong Kong. His voice was low and he lit one cigarette after another. Finally, the night descended and all she could see was the orange point of light, a firefly in the velvet dark, as he talked.

Declan's Irish passport had kept him out of the camp at Stanley. For three months he had dropped out of sight of the authorities, writing as much as he could about what he was witnessing and taking down accounts of other people's experiences.

'How did you send them out?'

'It was tricky.'

'I'll bet.'

'At first I just put copies in the post. But it became clear pretty quickly that it wasn't going to work. The Japanese censors were just as efficient as the British and much more aggressive. They knocked the door off its hinges when they came to tell me to stop.' He took a long drag of the cigarette. 'I got the message.'

'So they knew where you were.'

Declan nodded. 'I thought I'd better activate my exit strategy.'

'Which was?'

'To find Chen. He'd said that if I was ever in need I should place an advert in the *Hong Kong Times*. It was to read "Frau Steinschneider offers singing lessons Reply to PO Box 230." '

'A bit Scarlet Pimpernel.'

'Exactly. It seemed ridiculous but the day after I put the advert in I was approached by a young Chinese woman outside my apartment. After some initial confusion and once I'd established she wasn't generously offering to have sex with me, she whispered very precise instructions in my ear.'

That evening, carrying as little as he could manage – a rucksack with a notebook and pencil, a chunk of bread, some cheese and a spare pair of socks – he had gone to a bar on Hollywood Road. There a man he had never seen before, wearing a chauffeur's uniform, had indicated that he was to follow him. Throwing himself into the hands of fate, he had done so. They did not exchange a single word. Taut with tension, he had climbed on to a tram behind the man.

'And, you know, the strangest thing was how silent it was on that tram. The dearth of European faces was not too disconcerting but the lack of chat was. The defining characteristic of a Hong Kong tram ride has always been the deafening, animated shouting, right?' Stevie nodded in the gathering darkness, not wanting to get up and turn on a light. 'Well, nobody spoke or even caught each other's eye. We passed Japanese soldiers in the street and not even the foolhardy looked at them. Most hung their heads to avoid any eye contact because that was all it would take for the tram to be halted, boarded and emptied. You never knew whether it would be your body by the side of the road with your shopping bags spilled and your hard-won vegetables rolling under the wheels of the passing cars. I kept my eyes on the seat in front of me, I'll never forget that frayed tartan, and held the chauffeur's hat in my peripheral vision.'

They had got off at Shaukiwan beyond the yacht club.

'We were headed for the water's edge. I could hear the lapping of the waves and I saw a glimpse of a couple of sampans in the darkness.'

Stevie could imagine their low hulls pearly against the dark water.

'The chauffeur gestured to one of the boats and I lowered myself in. The chauffeur climbed down into the other. I had just enough time to notice that the sampan was being rowed by a woman before I was pushed down flat against the boards at the bottom of the boat and heavy blankets were thrown over me. God, it was damp and the stench of fish and unwashed bodies was bad enough, but it got worse. There was a sudden bright light sweeping over us. Searchlights from a Japanese warship. The sampan must have been illuminated as if it was day. But amazingly there was no break in the steady slapping of the oars.'

He couldn't say how long the journey had lasted but in the end he felt the hull bump against a stony beach and the smothering blankets were lifted off him. Again without a word, he was helped on to dry land. The man who was waiting for him was wearing the uniform of a Chinese Nationalist soldier.

'The big surprise was that the Communists and Nationalists were working together in common cause against the Japanese.'

'Not before time.'

'Damn right.'

He had followed the soldier across dense bush country, the stars providing hazy light as they waded through a river and finally, near dawn, stumbled into a small village. In a windowless room dimly lit by a candle, the leader of the local Communists welcomed him with words he could not understand but with a generosity he could.

'Picture this, on one end of the table was a pile of revolvers and on the other a feast of noodles. Not to mention the most welcome warm beer I ever drank. I was given a bed and slept right through the day. In the early evening a kid of about twelve woke me up and, though God knows I was aching all over, he took me to meet the most astonishing person I ever saw. There was this imposing dark-skinned bloke with long, tightly curled hair like twisted ropes falling over these broad shoulders. And he was done up in full military gear.'

'Are you sure you weren't hallucinating?'

'You'd think so, wouldn't you, but he was as solid as you or me. Actually, he was taller than me, stooping under the low roof, but the thing was he had these delicate facial features and a totally disconcerting sweetness about him. He said his name was Khan and he had a distinctively West Indian accent.'

'I see what you mean, astonishing. What was his story?'

'I wish I knew. Obviously I asked but he wasn't exactly forthcoming. I'm pretty sure he was a local warlord of some kind – he was conspicuously armed with a sten gun as well as a revolver. Anyway, he led me for the next part of the journey until we got to a village built on wooden piles because the land was so marshy, and Khan just melted into the darkness to be replaced by a Chinese man wearing a British uniform.'

'Curiouser and curiouser.'

Declan smiled but he wasn't going to be distracted from finishing his tale.

'From there the going was significantly more rough, the pathways barely marked. But by now nothing could surprise me. I was living moment to moment, expecting at any time to be ambushed or simply pushed into a creek and drowned. Hours later we came to a bay where, looming out of the water, there was a sailing junk manned by scarred and ragged sailors who evidently made their living as pirates. I worked that out when I saw the twelve machine guns they handled rather too casually. I was stowed in the stern and, five hours later, was set down on the coast of Free China.'

'God, Declan, that's some adventure.'

'You know what, the first thing I saw was a cheery Australian bloke and the first words I heard were "Fuck me, mate, you made it." '

Stevie roared with laughter and Declan joined her.

His voice was full of professional regret when he said, 'The biggest story of my life and I'll never be able to write about it.'

Declan, being Declan, had made irresistible inroads into her life immediately. And he had stayed there. Both she and Hal were quietly grateful for his good humour and energy and dedication to them. One evening maybe four or five months after he had appeared, he brought boxes of noodles in black bean sauce from the street stalls of Chinatown and they talked by candlelight in the tiny apartment kitchen. This was as close as she came to going out. She had never left Hal with a babysitter at night. It didn't seem right. This was only one of many small but potent effects of their trauma on their everyday lives. Declan had told her then, lulled by the flickering light, about how he had found his girlfriend's body in the rubble of her apartment building. He had helped to dig and the first thing they had seen was one of her hands, lovely and perfect and clutching the figurine of a small Chinese god. He knew it was hers because she was wearing the ring which he had refused to consider an engagement token but which she had shown around town as if it was.

Stevie had followed his bitter laugh with, 'Maybe it was. Maybe she was right.'

He had shaken his head and looking directly at her, his eyes glowing in the shadows of his face, had said, 'You know why I could never promise myself to anybody.' And before she could stop him he was declaring his love for her all over again and she wanted to believe it. Her hollow, sad heart answered his and for a moment she had thought, 'Yes, maybe. Maybe I can do this.' It only took another moment for her to understand the impossibility of it. He had stood up and drawn her to her feet and held her close, his heart beating next to her ear, the tremor of it through his body. For a brief moment she had felt the incredible, baffling relief of human contact. But it was quickly followed by a rising nausea. She had pushed him away and had pressed herself into the corner of the narrow kitchen.

All she could do was shake her head. Her voice was trapped inside her along with the words. There was nothing she could say.

Afterwards, she knew she would never have a physical relationship again. She was, quite simply, not able. She did not bewail and mourn this fate. She accepted it. It wasn't so bad after all. She was alive. She had Hal. She had her work. So what if a part of her had died? It seemed a small price to pay for survival. And she saw Phyllis' hair held in a string and heard her broken, mad voice and was grateful.

She didn't notice Hal picking up an envelope from the doormat. He lingered in the hallway, tearing the paper open as he'd seen her do so often. Unfortunately the opening did not go to plan and he followed his mother into the living room with the two torn halves of the telegram in his hands.

'I tore it.'

Stevie turned to look and in that moment saw what it was. A cable. Her pulse slowed. She moved towards him and held out her hand. He put the pieces of paper into it. Disconcerted by her silence and misinterpreting it as disapproval, he flung his arms around her legs. 'Sorry, Mommy.'

She shook him off gently and took the few steps to the couch. She held the twin slips of paper together, their ragged edges slotting almost perfectly into each other. She read.

Impossible to ask the things I want to know. Stop. I understand if there is someone else. Stop. Harry.

Hal's hands were on her knees, his face puzzled. 'Don't cry,' he said. 'We can fix it.'

Chapter Twenty-Nine

The cab drew up outside the low-lying arrivals terminal at New York Municipal Airport. The building hunched over on itself, a timeworn location for crisis and drama. Luckily, Hal's fidgeting during the journey had prevented Stevie from thinking too hard about what was happening. In the days since the cable she had been too feverish to take in the immensity of it. All she could do was try to keep her feelings of vindication at bay and concentrate on the details. Harry was coming back to her. He really was. Her every waking moment echoed to that refrain. Harry was coming back. But her sleep was disturbed by a nameless anxiety that woke her every hour or so and unsettled her. Everything had been about getting to this day, getting out of this cab and entering this building. She had no idea at all what would happen afterwards. No plan. No contingency. No imagined conversation. This was as far as she got.

Harry had sent the cable from Hong Kong on the first day of the surrender.

The mood in the camp had been uneasy for weeks. The guards, by turn jittery and lax, had escalated the paranoia of the prisoners into a kind of frenzy. Gossip had passed like electric currents through the whole camp, more extreme by the minute and at greater speed. They were all going to be shot. They would have to dig their own graves. No, they weren't going to be shot – in order to save bullets they would be locked in a hut and burned alive, or their rice rations would be poisoned.

It was in this fevered atmosphere that Harry noticed one day that the guards had disappeared. They had gone through the gate, in small, almost random, groups, taking their weapons with them. They had left the gate open. They had not come back.

Harry kept his eyes on the gate. His unexpected skill in getting vegetables to grow in the thin soil had earned him a certain quiet respect. In general he spoke only when it was absolutely necessary and avoided anything more than superficial contact with the other prisoners. He was on his knees, making sure that the runner beans were securely tied to their bamboo poles, when Frank Hopkins, who had developed a reputation as a troublemaker, ran past, shouting over his shoulder to another lad.

'Get a move on. I know where they keep the tobacco and there's nobody guarding it.'

Harry sat back on his heels and said, 'Be careful. The supply sheds are booby-trapped.'

Frank skidded to a halt. It was the first time Harry had addressed him since the terrible day of the beheading. 'Got something to say, have you?'

Harry shrugged and turned back towards the beans.

Frank's voice came again, tight with hatred and mistrust. 'Collaborator.' Harry didn't move. He had heard it whispered in the lunch queue over the years but it had never been spoken to his face before.

'Why would I listen to you? I know what you did and I know you're working for them.'

Harry spoke quietly without looking at Frank. 'Look out for the trip wires. They're just in front of the shed.'

Frank took a step backwards while he considered this. 'All right if you know so much, where have the bastards gone? Sid says they're waiting to shoot anyone who steps through the gate.'

'I don't know.'

'You would say that, wouldn't you. It would suit you just fine if they did shoot us all.' And he turned to his companion. 'Let's see what the others think.'

Harry waited until the sound of their footsteps had faded. Then he stood up. It had been at least half an hour since the last of the guards had left. In a daze of bewilderment, Harry walked the few yards to the gates. Without stopping, he walked on through them, expecting gunfire with every step. But it didn't come. There was a silence – the cicadas ear-splittingly loud, the dry leaves rustling like rain.

Harry walked with extreme caution, each step an exploration of a new reality. His emaciated legs struggled to bear his weight. He was barefoot and though the soles of his feet were as hardened as the sole of any shoe, the joints of his toes were stiff and swollen. He hadn't taken so many steps for years. The details of this escape were overwhelming. He was concentrating so fiercely on the mechanics of the undertaking that he was taken by surprise when he looked around him and realised that he had turned the corner in the road, the corner that for four years had defined his horizon.

The surreal nature of the day was compounded by the fact that the road led to a bus stop. And there were buses running from the stop. And the Chinese bus conductor made no attempt to stop him though he must have been entirely recognisable as a prisoner, white, ragged, skeletal. He was not asked for a ticket. It was only when he was sitting in a seat and could feel the harsh upholstery brushing against his shins that he cleared his dry throat and asked the woman opposite him, in English, if she knew whether there was any news.

She raised her eyes from her embroidery to take in his wretched appearance, then bent her head back down to her silk thread and said, 'People say the war is over.'

The woman's dignified caution expressed more of the horrors and the insecurities of war than any raucous celebration. Harry turned his eyes to the window but the tears were warm on his cheeks. He did not attempt to wipe them away.

The city of Hong Kong was in paroxysms of chaos. Harry walked through the streets and everybody looked exactly alike – stunned. They could not yet allow themselves to believe that the nightmare might be over. He found the post office still standing right where it had always been. Digging deep into his pocket he brought out the precious sheet of paper, a spider's web of foldings. It was the one letter he had and he had received it two years after it had been sent.

And he sent the cable in words quite other than those he had rehearsed.

Only then did he set about the lengthy process of finding his way home.

The terminal was busy. Stevie pulled Hal through the milling travellers, negotiating the usual obstacle course of luggage. She stopped in front of the national arrivals board. *Pan Am from Los Angeles. On time.* There was a strong smell of burned coffee and, as they were early, she drew Hal towards the cafeteria. To his surprise and delight she ordered him a milkshake, while she endured the bitter taste of the percolated coffee before relenting and adding the dusty-tasting cream and two spoonfuls of sugar from the bakelite bowl on the counter.

As Hal sucked the milky glass dry, Stevie's mind kept turning to the moment in which she would see Harry, and the moment was blank. She could see him. She could imagine his familiar long-strided walk across the hall, though of course he would be thin, but she could not imagine his face. There was a gap in her mind where his face should have been. She compulsively checked her watch. The second hand seemed to have slowed to an infuriating crawl. She patted her hair, the hair which had never recovered its former glory and sheen. It was short and she liked to think, gamine. Catching sight of herself in the distorting chrome of the coffee machine she quickly looked away. Who was this woman anyway? Her expression was taut with anxiety, lines cutting across her forehead, blue eyes dull, glints of silver gilding her boyish hair. Oh God, would this wait never end?

As soon as Hal had licked the glass clean, digging as far down the slippery sides as his tongue would allow, she helped him slide from the high stool and took him to the restroom. He was bound to need a pee at the crucial moment. Passing the mirror, she checked her reflection again. What would Harry make of her? Would he take one look and see the alteration in her, see that she was no longer the girl he had loved? Would he recognise her at all or would he pass his eyes over her face without halting? As usual she was surprised by the lack of visible scarring. To a casual glance she might be any woman who had endured the war years worrying about her loved ones. She dug the tube of lipstick out of her pocket and re-applied the red slash across her lips. She swivelled away from the glaring reflection and checked her watch again. Then, steeling herself, she took Hal's hand.

Something had changed in the hall. The atmosphere had shifted from waiting to high alert. It was all noise and action. Above them in the rotunda the mural seemed to spin with unlikely colours. She and Hal were part of a surge of forward movement towards the barrier. And now she saw that among the swollen crowd were men with cameras and recording equipment. There was even a large film camera being manoeuvred into place and focussed directly at the doors through which Harry would come. Still, Stevie did not understand that this might have something to do with her. It was an annoyance she had not envisaged, but then she had imagined this moment a million times, each time a little differently, so what did it matter that the reality was different again? Holding tight to Hal's slippery hand, Stevie strained to see between the slicked heads of the newsmen. Any minute now . . .

Then one of the men glanced at her. His eyes narrowed with recognition and the sour smell of him enveloped her.

'Hey, Stevie Steiber! How're you feeling? Nervous, I bet. How long's it been?'

And a microphone was thrust in her face and more questions were being shouted and the crowd changed its focus and was drawn to her so close that in the crush the faces and voices were a blur.

'I read in your book how you and the major met. Anything to add to that?'

'Did he get a divorce yet, doll?'

Then there was a sudden easing in the clamour and a surge forward towards the gate. And through a gap in the crowd Stevie caught a glimpse of a slightly stooped middle-aged man. Harry!

Or a new version of him. He was in his uniform and flanked by two American army officers. He looked much older. The skin of his face was burned dark and there were deep lines across it like furrows in sand.

In the instant that she caught sight of him she saw something of what survival had cost him. And she knew the reality of their meeting would be quite different from any of her fevered fantasies. Deeper. Darker. And she understood that he in turn would be able to see what survival had cost her.

She watched him blink in dismay as the camera flashes ripped through the hall and the yells of the newsmen echoed.

'Over here, Major Field, sir! Over here!'

All she wanted was to get away. It wasn't supposed to be like this. Panic gripped her. She turned away. Pushing. Pushing against the crush of the crowd. Hal's hand was slipping, her grip tight now on his wrist. Hal was crying. But the reporter with the bad breath had his hand on the small of her back and hustled her in the direction of the barrier. She struggled but could not dislodge his heavy, pressing hand.

And then there he was. His startled eyes were upon her as he was buffeted by the jostling crowd. But she could hear nothing. See nothing. Only Harry, his neck too thin for his collar. And all she could feel was the blood pulsing around her body.

Flash.

'You gonna marry her?'

Flash.

The reporter leered – his microphone thrust between them, breaking the silvery thread of connection.

'Time to make an honest woman of her, buddy, don't you think?'

Harry bowed his head in confusion as he said unhappily, 'What's going on?'

Stevie murmured, 'I don't know. I'm sorry. I think maybe the book –'

'Ah, yes, the book.'

'You've seen it?'

'I've seen it.'

'I'm sorry, I had no idea it would be read by anybody.'

Harry smiled and raised his eyebrows. It was a familiar look, half-teasing, half-cross, but he was being directed onwards by one of the army officers and as he walked away he raised his voice and addressed the reporters.

'I owe my life to her. That's all I can say.'

In a pincer movement the other army officer held out both arms to prevent the crowd following Harry. 'All right, folks, stand back, please. Major Field is here on official business, not as a private citizen. He is not yet discharged.'

And the circus dispersed as quickly as it had emerged, disappearing into the hall as if it had all been a dream. Stevie stood staring in the direction that Harry had gone. It took her a while to realise that she was not in fact nailed to the spot and that it was Hal's arms clinging round her legs that prevented her from moving.

Chapter Thirty

A dull, chalky taste was in her mouth. It didn't matter how many times or how ferociously she brushed her teeth, the taste remained. She thought she had suffered the worst of it. She thought the waiting and the hoping and the refusing to believe the reports of his death were as bad as it could get. But she had been wrong.

Declan had found her that night curled into a corner of the living room. She had managed somehow to walk across the airport arrivals hall and climb into a cab and open her apartment door and feed Hal and put him to bed. But then she was spent. For the first time since that terrible day in Hong Kong she had nothing left, no resources to cushion her from this new reality. Harry's face, so loved, so worn, so familiar and so pained, hovered in front of her eyes whether they were open or shut. There was disappointment and recrimination in it. There was resignation and recognition. But mostly what she saw was his utterly unfamiliar lack of certainty. And she was afraid.

From the moment the cable had arrived she had gone into a kind of trance, she could see now. A madness. The news of Harry's survival had filtered pretty fast into the media. It turned out that the appetite for this particular story with all its irresistible elements of scandal was not easily sated. Two days after the cable had come she had arrived home to the sound of the ringing phone and picked it up.

'Yes?'

'Is that Stevie Steiber?'

'Yes, speaking.'

'How are you planning on celebrating Major Field's liberty?'

'I'm sorry, who is this?'

'Are you expecting him to join you or will he return to his wife?'

She had the wherewithal to stutter, 'I have no comment at this time,' before dropping the telephone receiver violently enough to distract Hal from his car race across the rug.

Everything was concentrated on finding information about Harry. It was impossible to speak to him. He had been immersed in a lengthy British debrief. Then there was another cable. With the minimum of information it said he was heading for Los Angeles to help the American military collate their information about the war in the Pacific. After that he would come to New York. During this time Stevie formed a love–hate relationship with the telephone. It was an instrument of exquisite torture. She established a routine in which she would answer – in case, just in case it was Harry – but say nothing until the caller had announced themselves. Mostly it was the press in various guises. Sometimes it was Madame Kung or one of her people. Sometimes it was her family. Stevie would pick up the telephone, a rush of pointless adrenalin streaming through her, to hear her mother's anxious, ingratiating tones and she would sigh with the disappointment and tell her she was fine and could they talk tomorrow?

A month into the waiting, Stevie, Hal in tow, was heading back to the apartment from the post office. She had sent Lily another package – the most recent of many. She had absolutely no way of knowing whether any of them ever reached her but that didn't seem a good enough reason to stop sending them across the ocean like messages in bottles. She wrote letters full of Hal's latest mishaps or funny sayings. She kept the tone relentlessly cheerful and she asked for news in return. One time she had sent a box of Animal Cracker biscuits. Another time a cashmere sweater. This last package had contained the news of Harry's survival and a pair of navy-blue leather gloves with a rabbit-fur lining.

As Stevie approached her apartment building a man's shout rolled along the sidewalk from behind them. It came again – louder this time.

'Hey, Miss Steiber.'

Stevie glanced over her shoulder. An elderly man with thinning red hair was limping as fast as he could towards them. Stevie stopped walking and turned to face him.

'Yes, that's me,' she said brightly. After all, the sun was shining and she was full of good will to the world.

'I heard you on the radio at home a while back and as soon as I had the chance to come to New York I came. I've been waiting for you.' The man spoke in a Canadian accent.

'That's nice. Thank you.' Now the man was in front of her Stevie could see that she had been mistaken, he was not old at all. 'To whom am I speaking?'

She held out her hand. He looked at it for a moment before taking it and giving it a swift shake. 'Sergeant Hopkins. I was in Argyle.' His gaze was fierce.

'Oh, I'm so sorry.'

'I'm not here to talk about your morals and all that stuff.'

'Glad to hear it.'

'I don't blame you. You seem like a nice enough woman.' He put his hand on her arm and leaned close, lowering his voice. 'It's not the little bastard's fault, either.' He gestured with his eyes towards Hal.

Stevie, understanding with a sinking feeling the direction of the discourse, pulled her arm out of the man's grasp and tugged Hal to her with one hand while the other started digging in her bag for her door key.

'Your lover is no hero, Miss Steiber. He's a traitor.'

'How did you find me?'

'It wasn't hard.'

'If you don't leave us alone I shall call a policeman.' Stevie had retrieved the key and turned to the door.

The man's voice was insistent. 'I thought it was only fair you should hear the truth. You've fallen for his lies like everybody else. But I know. I was there. I know.' His pale-blue eyes were wide. 'One day the whole world will know what your Nip-loving Major Field did. I saw with my own eyes. Want to know why he was always talking to them? I'll tell you why, he was feathering his own nest. Saving his own skin while the rest of us were left to die.' His voice was shrill and crazy-sounding; there was spittle on his lips.

Next to her Hal was silent but Stevie could feel him trembling. The key turned in the lock and as the door swung shut behind them she could hear the man still ranting. 'Tell him Frank Hopkins is looking for him. The truth is on my side.'

The effect of the assault was far more profound than Stevie wanted to admit even to herself. Hal mentioned something to Declan and when he asked her about it she brushed the incident away breezily. But she found herself constantly on the lookout for Frank Hopkins and the shadow cast by his words pointed her in the direction of what Harry's survival might have cost. It was too dark to bear. She put it aside.

Meanwhile, bit by bit, other news came. Trawling over and again through the lists of those released from the Hong Kong camps she found many names she recognised. Young men whom she remembered playing cards with into the night, recklessly driving up the perilous Peak roads after way too many cocktails and after finally taking 'no' for an answer, showing her wallet-sized photographs of their girlfriends. It seemed that Mr Evans from the Bank had walked out alive too. But far more disturbing were the names she did not see. Phyllis was absent. And so was her husband Dr Clarke-Russell. The gap where their names should have been told of their grim fates. The nights brought them to her – Phyllis' desperate lost grief, her hands clutching at her. Stevie woke shouting, scrabbling, trying to prise Phyllis' bony fingers away from her body.

One day, a few weeks after the encounter with Hopkins, Madame Kung passed her a letter.

Shanghai, August 1945

Dear Stevie, As part owner of Direct Debate *you are entitled to half of what's left. Unfortunately that does not amount to much. The press itself was destroyed in '43 and the lease on the office fell into arrears not long after. The furniture was salvaged and donated to a school. Likewise the books that didn't burn in the bombing. My family is living in the mountains. I can be contacted through the usual channels and am pursuing various interests. I am well, Stevie, and hear that you are also. I am happy that is the case.*

Wu Jishang

P.S I thought you might be interested to see this picture of Comrade Li.

A newspaper clipping fell on to her lap out of the envelope. It was a black and white photograph of some kind of Communist rally. A young man was speaking with passion on a platform. Behind him was a young woman. Stevie looked hard – she couldn't see Chen anywhere. Then with a gasp she realised that the young woman in the plain peasant jacket and trousers was Lily. Her hair was hidden under a cap but there was no mistaking her fine features and the dimples in her cheeks. Stevie leaned closer – Lily's hands were in her lap and she was wearing a pair of leather gloves, the fur lining just visible at the wrist.

Stevie had held the paper close and cried as she sat in Madame Kung's crowded little apartment. For a moment she was in the beautiful bedroom in the dark night of the mountains, lying in silk sheets, surrounded and cosseted by Jishang's exquisite collection of lovely things. Of which she knew herself to be one.

Then finally one ordinary lunchtime Declan had called. Stevie picked up the telephone in her usual manner, waiting for the voice at the other end.

'Stevie. Maybe you've already heard this news.'

'What news?'

'Harry is back in New York. Apparantly, he's been here a week.'

Stevie let her silence speak for her.

Declan's voice faltered most unusually. 'I guess he hasn't been in touch with you.' A pause. 'I bumped into a guy who's covering a story on government plans for war crime trials. Harry is working with the prosecution team to get watertight cases on the senior Japanese officers.'

'Thank you for telling me.'

'Are you all right?'

She kept her voice steady. 'I'm fine.'

'Did you know anything about this?'

'No, I didn't.'

Stevie huddled as tightly into the corner as she could. Since the telephone call about Harry that afternoon she had withdrawn. Her breathing was so quiet and shallow that it barely registered. Harry was in New York. He was close. But he hadn't told her. A week! Why hadn't he contacted her? He knew she was waiting for him. Why didn't Harry want to see her? What the hell was going on? Was he working for the prosecution or was Frank Hopkins right and Harry was being prosecuted himself?

Declan's voice was faint as he called through the letterbox of the apartment door. Stevie flinched at the intrusion but kept her eyes closed against it.

When she didn't answer, Declan pushed the door open. It had been some long time since he'd been there. He looked around the room and was glad when he noticed it to be no more disordered than usual.

'Stevie?'

There were no lights on – but by the glow from the street lamps below, Declan could make her out tucked beside the iron radiator.

He was relieved. 'How many times do I have to tell you, lock the door at night. You never know what dreadful person might come in. Me, for instance.' His brittle lightness of tone did nothing to disguise his worry. 'Come on, Stevie, let's have a drink. How about it? For old times' sake?'

When there was still no answer he came close to her, squatting down.

'Did you take something, Stevie? Did you do something stupid?' He put a large hand gently on her knee. She flinched again but kept her head turned away and her eyes closed. Satisfied that she wasn't dying, Declan rose again and took a couple of steps back, then he settled himself into the armchair facing her.

'Know who you remind me of? Old Mrs Li, the old lady in Hong Kong with her face to the wall.' He waited for a moment. 'I know I'm the last person on earth you want to see but look at the state of you, girl. Someone's got to talk some sense into you. All right, so you didn't get the fairy-tale reunion at the airport and all right, Harry seems to be avoiding you. But for pity's sake, you're behaving like a little girl who hasn't been invited to the Prom. What is this? Where are you, Stevie? You're not giving up now, are you?'

He heard her try to control the sob but it escaped, muffled and hopeless. In an act of selflessness he stilled his own dreams.

'For all of our sakes, please, go find him, sweetheart.' He never called her 'sweetheart'.

She opened her eyes.

The next morning was cool and limpid. The window was open and the breeze brightened even the dustiest corners of the apartment. Stevie had been on the telephone all morning since dropping Hal at kindergarten. She gripped the receiver tightly – a lifeline.

'I don't understand. Are you saying I can't speak with him or that he can't speak with me?' Her voice was tight with restraint. 'I'm sorry but this is ridiculous.'

She slammed the phone down on to its cradle and in a sudden moment of decision she picked up her coat from the back of the chair and practically pulled the door off its hinges as she flung it open.

It wasn't until she was outside the imposing skyscraper that she paused to collect herself. She stood on the slippery reflections of the wet sidewalk and she listened to her own pulse as if to an engine ticking as it cooled down. She checked her watch – midday. Should she wait in a coffee shop until they all came out and grab Harry then? She glanced around for an appropriate place with a plate-glass window on to the street. Yes, there was one, right across from the building, its window comfortingly steamed up.

She had left the apartment without even looking in the mirror, compelled to action by the adrenalin of frustration. Now she was losing courage. She bent to catch her reflection in the side-mirror of a parked car. Her flushed cheeks, anxious eyes and unkempt hair irritated her. She straightened up and shrugged her vanity away. He wasn't going to refuse to talk to her because of a bad haircut.

Stevie negotiated the military-style doormen with her shoulders squared, a gaze directed into the building beyond and a flash of her press card. Not knowing where she was going, she followed the corridor and her instinct took her to the doors of the main conference room. She quietly opened the pale wood door and slipped into the back of the room with practised discretion. The slightly raked tiers of seats were half-full. Mostly men, but a few scattered women listened soberly as a man in a sharply cut suit spoke from the platform at the front of the room.

'It only remains for me to thank each of you for your valuable contributions to our better understanding of the process of this terrible conflict.'

Behind him, there was a row of men wearing various different military uniforms. Second from the right was Harry.

The speaker continued while a soft rustle of discreet seat-shifting and paper-gathering pre-empted the end of the session. He turned to the men behind him and gestured towards them, an acknowledgement both gentle and formal.

'You have experienced unimaginable sufferings. It is our duty and our intention to ensure that the world will never again have comparable dark hours to contend with. Thank you.'

Now the representatives removed their translation headsets and there was polite applause. Stevie slid against the tide down the wide shallow steps towards the platform. She was suddenly unbearably hot and if she could have turned around she would have. But it was impossible. She was being pulled towards him as if by a tightening thread.

As he stepped off the platform Harry was talking to one of his colleagues and it wasn't until he turned, mid-sentence, to find his bearings that he saw her.

They sat at a small formica table by the window of the coffee shop. There was steam and noise and life all around but between them was deep silence. The small space that separated them, the table with its orange plastic bird-of-paradise lolling in its vase and the salt and pepper and sugar, may as well have been the space between the sun and the moon. Two cups of burned coffee cooled. Harry had barely looked at her even as they walked across the street. They had not touched. She was acutely aware of his physical presence. He had stood at the counter to order and she had not been able to avert her eyes from him. Who was this bony, sunburned man in uniform? If she had not known, would she have noticed him if they had passed in the street? If they had found themselves by chance in the same coffee shop? Would her eyes have done more than brush over him?

Even now as he looked out of the window, seeing nothing, trying to still his own racing hope, she wanted him.

'I'm sorry about the ambush.' Her voice was low and he had to turn towards her to catch at the words. 'Thought you could avoid me, huh?'

Harry shook his head slightly and his tone when he spoke was both wary and angry. 'How could you write about us like that?'

The anger took her by surprise. She had thought that maybe he would be disconcerted, yes, or maybe he had changed his mind about her, but to have stayed away from both Hal and her because of the stupid book? She hadn't imagined that.

'It was about all the stuff before the war, the politics, I hardly mentioned us. I mean it's not about us, it's about the important things.'

'Complete strangers have asked me questions more private than even my own family would dare.'

'I'm sorry.' She was suddenly overwhelmed with exhaustion. She could easily have put her head down on the cold table and slept. The pale-blue surface was speckled with flecks of brown. 'I warned you, stay away from writers.'

Harry sat back in his chair. 'I will.'

Alert again, she looked at him. 'What are you saying?' The dread stopped her throat.

Harry hunched his shoulders even higher and she noticed how he supported his left arm with the other as he leaned across the table. 'Look, you're under no obligation to me. I appreciate everything you did to keep me alive while we were there. And I was never so happy as I was with you. But that was then.'

Stevie felt herself grow heavy and slow. 'Are you leaving me?'

Their hands were inches from each other.

'You and Hal have made a life for yourselves. Of course, you had to. I can't tie you to me, I don't want to.' His voice dropped even further. 'I'm tired and half-useless and I'm not the man you think I am.' He looked down at the table. 'I'm done in.'

'I don't care.'

'You don't understand.'

Her hand brushed against his. The skin felt rough but the bones were thin. 'I don't care what happened. I don't care what it took – you're here, you're alive.'

'It's no good.' He looked at her. 'You're free, Stevie. It's all right.'

The hysteria was rising. She thought she might throw up. 'It's not all right.'

And then he ambushed her. 'The thing is, I love you.'

'So then –?'

'So then, don't you see?' His fingers found hers and the electric shock of it nearly broke her. 'That's why I'm letting you go.'

The rage took her by surprise. 'Oh, yes, I see.' She pushed her chair back and the fierceness felt like a knife. 'I see clearly. It's flashing over your head in a damn neon sign. Coward is what it says. Coward.'

She took a few steps away but couldn't let it go like that. Despite the fury she did see clearly. And with the clarity came a kind of calm.

She went back to the table and looked at him and for the first time that day she really saw him, saw his strengths, saw his weaknesses, and knew that what she felt for him was love. But love in a new, unexplored form. Love as fresh as the love she felt for Hal when he was raw and alien. A whole continent of love, not desperate and needy and reliant on turmoil for its rationale but a place of lush, dark stillness.

'Want to know something? This is it. Life. Life is what's happening now, this instant. This moment.' She gestured around the coffee shop. 'This is all we've got, buster, so you'd better step up and take your chances while you can.'

She could see herself reflected in Harry's eyes. Twin shadows. And she knew she could walk away because it really was true that wherever she was so was he. Even if he wasn't ready to join her in the new world.

She was almost at the door when she heard him. He had called her name and was on his feet. She waited. The door opened and closed. A young woman swished past, her scent a wake behind her. Stevie stepped away from the door and found a pocket of quiet by the wall. Harry was close. He put both his hands on the wall on either side of her head and he looked at her.

'I'm afraid,' he said.

'So am I.'

The door opened and closed. Orders were shouted from the counter to the kitchen. At the table nearest to them a mother watched her teenage daughter light a cigarette and chose to hold her tongue. Outside the light breeze blew again; yesterday's newspapers wound themselves around traffic lights. A cab let three over-excited salesmen out on to the sidewalk.

And Harry heard her voice as if it was his own, 'What are you doing later?'

They arranged to meet in the park.

Stevie brought Hal to the playground and was pushing him on the swing when Harry arrived. The grey winter sky lifted and sharp rays of light pierced the clouds. Hal was instantly suspicious of this man and the way he shook his mother's hand. He started to cry and when Harry tried to lift him off the swing, he clung hard to the cold iron ropes and wouldn't let go until Stevie stepped in.

Stevie had explained on the way there that they were going to meet Hal's daddy. She could see that this was confusing to him. His daddy was a long way away and always had been, so how could he be here? From his scowl it was obvious that he was far from sure that he wanted one and when he saw Stevie smile at the man and heard her laugh in that special private way, he made it quite clear that he didn't. Later, when Harry had bought him an ice cream and Stevie had actually let him eat it, even though it was snacking, she hoped that Hal might be persuaded that maybe it wouldn't be so bad after all.

They walked slowly, their voices low while Hal ran ahead chasing pigeons.

'I'm sorry I didn't tell you I was here. When the debrief in California was over they asked me to help with the war crime prosecutions. I was very glad. I didn't care where they sent me.' He paused, dropped his voice even lower. 'Actually, I was more than glad. I was grateful.'

They watched Hal as he ran in circles, the pigeons always just out of reach.

'He's a tribute to you, Stevie.'

'I'm sorry he's been so difficult.'

'Hardly surprising, is it? I'm a complete stranger to him.'

'It's good he was so young. He doesn't remember anything from before New York.'

'Who'd have thought it, my son – a New Yorker.'

'Could have been worse. He could have been an Englishman.'

Harry glanced at her, a wry smile, the first today. 'God forbid.'

Stevie held his gaze. 'You're not a stranger to me, however much you may wish you were.'

Harry stopped. The leaves in the trees above them clattered in the wind. He struggled for the words. 'The problem is that I'm a stranger to myself.'

'That's why you need me. I'll remind you who you are.'

Harry tried to interrupt her but she put her hand on his arm to stop him.

'I knew you weren't dead. I knew it even when everybody had given up hope. And I wasn't just in denial; when I heard that Chen was dead I didn't doubt it was true. What I'm trying to say is that I don't care how tough it's going to be, it can't be worse than it's been already.'

Almost before she had finished talking, Harry pulled his arm away from her. He seemed to shrink before her eyes. He turned aside and then he took a few steps away. He didn't seem to know quite what he was doing, as if he was lost. Stevie held her breath, not wanting to deepen his obvious distress, but also not understanding it. His voice when it came was desolate. 'I had no choice. I had to do it. They were going to kill all of those boys. I had to give them something, tell them something to make them stop.'

Stevie suddenly remembered Frank Hopkins' vitriolic voice, spitting out those accusations, and as she looked at Harry, his troubled face worn into crags, she was clear that there were things she did not need to know.

'Don't. Please don't.' Stevie flung her arms around him. She wanted to contain him. Hold him together.

His voice cracked. 'Was anybody else there?'

'Where?'

'When they found Chen at the hut.'

'I don't know anything about a hut, my love. Chen died somewhere in the south-west, on the front line in a battle.'

Harry frowned as if trying to clear his head. 'In battle? Are you sure?'

'Yes. We can get more details if you want. Madame Kung's people are full of information.'

Harry didn't seem to hear her. He shook his head.

Misunderstanding him, Stevie said, 'If you don't trust the Chinese version, maybe your military people could find out.'

Still shaking his head, his voice was low. Stevie had to step right up to him to catch the words. 'I did a terrible thing, Stevie.'

For a moment the bare New York trees dissolved and she was in that stifling Hong Kong Supreme Court room and she felt again the pressure on her head from Shigeo's hand. A sharp wind cut into her and she leaned even closer into Harry. Her eyes were inches from his, their eyelashes almost touching. Her voice was firm. 'I don't care what happened. I don't care what it took. None of it matters.' She felt more intimate with him than ever. 'I love you and that's all there is to it.'

Harry could feel the warmth of her breath. He allowed himself to take comfort.

She felt a tug on her coat. Looking down she saw Hal holding up a bedraggled brown leaf. He was breathless and solemn though his gaze was triumphant. Stevie let go of Harry and bent down to Hal.

'That's great, Hal. Is it for me?'

He shook his head. 'It's for the man.'

Harry bent down now too. He accepted the offering with great ceremony. 'Thank you.' He slipped the stem through his buttonhole.

Hal was delighted. 'It's a medal.'

Harry saluted him and Hal laughed. Stevie took his hand and they all three walked slowly into their new world under the shadow of the trees, testing the ground, alert to the unexpected, making it up as they went along.

Much later

The night was a velvet curtain. His voice was soft. His touch, gentle.

'Is this all right?'

'Yes.'

'And this?'

'Yes.'

'This? No?'

'No.'

'All right. That's all right.'

A pause settled over them. Shared, the silence was as intimate as any passion. The whisper came from him.

'Can I look at you?'

'Yes.'

'Thank you. You're so beautiful.'

'I'm sorry.'

'It's fine. It's enough. Really, this is enough.'

'I'm so sorry.'

'There's time.'

'I just can't.'

'It's all right. It's more than all right.'

'Something terrible happened to me.'

'You don't have to say anything.'

'I do.'

'You don't. It doesn't matter. I mean, it doesn't make any difference.'

He had his own damage. His own scars. Some of which were visible and which she traced with the tip of a finger.

'I'd say the odds are three to four on.'

'Don't bet on it. Because what if I can't. Ever.'

'It doesn't matter. I can wait.'

'For ever? I don't think so.'

'Let's see. We have all the time in the world.'

He took her hand in his.

'Is this all right?'

'Yes.'

'Feel me. I'm here.'

In the photograph of the wedding they stand on the steps of City Hall in the spring sunshine. Hal hides behind Stevie's legs. Declan is on the step just behind them, his face half-obscured by Harry's hat. Madame Kung, immaculate and precise in her suit, stands next to Stevie.

Everybody is smiling.

Acknowledgements

There are many people with whom I have shared this adventure and to whom I owe great thanks. First among them are the amazing Amanda Boxer and Carola Vecchio, who have been kind enough to share their family's stories with me and let me take liberties with them. Caroline Wood, without whose encouragement and vision there simply would be no book, and everybody at Felicity Bryan Associates. I have been lucky enough to have Helen Garnons-Williams as my patient and clear-sighted editor, ably assisted by Erica Jarnes, Trâm-Anh Doan and everybody else at Bloomsbury. Thanks also to the inexhaustible energies of Rachel Holroyd and Sophie Dolan at Casarotto Ramsay who have kept many wolves from the door. My first reader Linda Fraser gave me the courage to keep going. Sandra Yarwood, Elizabeth Dench and Jenny Borgars had faith in this story long before it came together. My thanks also to Sue Brill, Marius Brill, Agatha Sadler, Sian, Kit, Caitlin, Molly and Helena Line, Claire Jephcott, Claire Scudder, Oliver Rose and Jane Haynes for unwavering and generous support of every kind. Also to Anne Stamper, the archivist of the Women's Institute, who helped me with some vital research and to

Phyllis Lusher for sharing her invaluable Hong Kong knowledge.

Finally, for their constant good humour and patience, sometimes against the odds, Bobby Allen, Rebecca Bowen and Romy Brill Allen, my undying gratitude.

Author's Note

I owe a huge debt of gratitude to the dazzling and brave men and, above all, women whose real life experiences inspired this novel. Most particularly I am grateful to the wonderful Emily Hahn whose own reporting is, as she hoped it would be, a spectacular 'social document'. Also to other adventurous newspapermen and women such as Tilman and Peggy Durdin from the *New York Times*, Corin Bernfelt, who was British *Vogue*'s knitting pattern editor before she travelled broken-hearted to China, Teddy White, the *Time* correspondent, Betty Graham, an independent journalist in Chungking, Dorothy Jenner, an Australian reporter, and the American writer Gwen Dew.

The characters in the book are figments of my imagination, apart from the Soong sisters whose real lives were more incredible than any fiction, as is often the case. I have taken great liberties with my imagined version of Madame Kung. The Peak was exclusively white in this period of Hong Kong's history and I've pushed the boundaries by locating Madame Kung's villa there, but Sir Robert Ho-tung was allowed to build on the Peak so there were exceptions. The historical Head of Medical Services was Selwyn Selwyn-Clarke, and he and his wife Hilda were definitively not like the fictional couple the Clarke-Russells. A fascinating fact is that Hilda Selwyn-Clarke was Madame Sun Yat-sen's secretary for years and a dedicated communist sympathiser. The character of Harry Field and his experiences as a prisoner of war and the resulting trauma bear no relation to those of the brilliant soldier and academic Charles Boxer, Emily Hahn's partner and later husband.

I quote directly from the governor of Hong Kong's rallying cry to the people of the island as the war was upon them.

I've used eye-witness reports where it seemed fatuous to invent: Stevie seeing the Japanese from the hospital window, the first set of questions in her interrogation and the Chinese woman being dragged on a rope come from Emily Hahn's experiences, as does the structural skeleton of the story. The war diaries of James O'Toole were invaluable in helping me understand the day-to-day workings of the Hong Kong prisoner-of-war camps. Gwen Dew's account of her treatment at the hands of the Japanese was extremely useful and the harrowing description of the young Chinese girl's death as related to Stevie by Chen is taken from an eye-witness account of the fall of Nanjing. The debriefing of Paul Tsui was an important source in relation to the heroic work of the BAAG (British Army Aid Group) and also for the description of Declan's escape route from Hong Kong.

I have made every effort to create an accurate historical context for my fictional characters to inhabit and any mistakes are entirely my own.

Bibliography

This list represents a few of the books that I found useful while writing the book.

Not the Slightest Chance: Defence of Hong Kong, 1941 by Tony Banham (Hong Kong University Press, 2005)

Escape Through China by David Bosanquet (Robert Hale, 1983)

Madam Sun Yat-sen by Jung Chang and Jon Halliday

Prisoner of the Japs by Gwen Dew (Knopf, 1943)

Stanley: Behind Barbed Wire by Jean Gittins (Hong Kong University Press, 1982)

China to Me by Emily Hahn (Doubleday, Doran & Co., Inc., 1944)

The Soong Sisters by Emily Hahn (Doubleday, Doran & Co., Inc., 1941)

All About Shanghai: A Standard Guidebook by H.J. Lethbridge (Oxford University Press, 1934)

I Escaped From Hong Kong by Jan Marsman (Reynal & Hitchcock, 1942)

Quiet Heroines: Nurses of the Second World War by Brenda McBryde (Chatto & Windus, 1985)

Hong Kong by Jan Morris (Vintage, 1997)

British Army Aid Group, Hong Kong Resistance 1942–1945 by Edwin Ride (Oxford University Press, 1981)
Shanghai by Harriet Sergeant (John Murray, 1991)
Hong Kong: Recollections of a British POW by Bill Wiseman (Veterans Publications, 2001)

A NOTE ON THE TYPE

The text of this book is set in Baskerville, named after John Baskerville of Birmingham (1706–1775). The original punches cut by him still survive. His widow sold them to Beaumarchais, from where they passed through several French foundries to Deberney & Peignot in Paris, before finding their way to Cambridge University Press.

Baskerville was the first of the 'transitional romans' between the softer and rounder calligraphic Old Face and the 'Modern' sharp-tooled Bodoni. It does not look very different to the Old Faces, but the thick and thin strokes are more crisply defined, and the serifs on lower-case letters are closer to the horizontal with the stress nearer the vertical. The R in some sizes has the eighteenth-century curled tail, the lower-case w has no middle serif, and the lower-case g has an open tail and a curled ear.